THE MUNICIPALITY OF LOST SOULS

THE HAUNTED DURSCOMBE NOVELS

JEANNIE WYCHERLEY

The Municipality of Lost Souls:
The Haunted Durscombe Novels
by
JEANNIE WYCHERLEY

Bark at the Moon Books

ISBN-13: 978-0-9957818-4-9

Sign up for Jeannie's newsletter:
eepurl.com/cN3Q6L

The Municipality of Lost Souls was edited by David Lyons
Cover design by Ravenborn Covers
Formatting by Tammy
Proofing by Johnny Bon Bon

Please note: This book is set in Victorian England in the United Kingdom. It uses British English spellings, colloquialisms and idioms.

This book is dedicated to my very own Phineas, Phil Tomlinson who shaped this story in numerous unseen ways.

A wonderful (and remarkably patient) friend xXx

CAST OF CHARACTERS

THE LORDS, LADIES, WITCHES, TOWNSFOLK AND VAGABONDS OF DURSCOMBE

Myrtle Lodge
Agatha Wick
Flora Wick, her ward
Hannah, her housekeeper
Tansy Wick, her grandmother, deceased
Lily Cuffhulme, nee Wick, Amelia's mother, deceased
Violet Wick, Agatha's mother, deceased

Hawkerne Hall
Lord Phineas Tolleson
Mrs Gwynne, his housekeeper
Matthew Salter, his butler
Arthur 'Wiggy' Wiggins, his old butler
Lucy Rose Poynton, Phineas's wife, deceased
Mr Ted Redman, head groom

Hollydene
Emily Fliss
Marmaduke Fliss
Mary
Joseph

Applecombe
Theo Bumble, Mayor of Durscombe
Norah Bumble, nee de Courcy, his wife

The Lanes
Sally Parrett, youngest cousin of Agatha Wick and Amelia Fliss
Thomas Parrett, her husband, a fisherman
Stanley Parrett, her son
Maisie Parrett, Thomas's sister-in-law
Meg Powell, Sally's young neighbour
William, a fisherman
Cornelius Minchin, the butcher's son

Municipal Hall
Alderman Edward Pyle
Jane Pyle, his wife
Alderman Croker
Mrs Croker, his wife
Mrs Ivy Croker, his dowager mother
Alderman Endicott
Alderman Goodwin
Colonel Haringey, Endicott's father-in-law
Alderman Gibbs
John Jeremy, clerk

The Blue Bell Inn
Giles, the landlord
Maddie, his daughter
Barnacle Betsy

Townsfolk
Edgar Ruddle, Durscombe's Harbour Master
Reverend Tidwell, curate St Thomas's Church
Dr Giddens, general practitioner
Pierre Songe, nefarious French sailor

Mrs Dainty, proprietress of Mrs Dainty's Tea Emporium
William, a bearded fisherman

Villains
Greeb
Henry Fitzroy
James Lammas
and a motley crew of ne-er do wells

1

DISASTER IN THE BAY

"Hold the horses steady, boy!"

"I'm sorry, Sir. It's all the commotion."

Agatha Wick shifted forward in the cramped confines of the carriage, curious to discover why they had been held up. The unsettled horses had the coach driver riled, but that wasn't all. A stable boy pointed his stubby finger in the direction of the bay and Agatha tilted her head to get a better view. Beneath black clouds, gathering ominously above, the ghostly spectre of a tall ship loomed before her, tilting at a 45-degree angle. It rolled heavily on the grey sea, the dark shapes of desperate sailors clinging to the rigging, rain lashing down on them. The light was failing.

Heaven help them.

The biting wind whipped at Agatha's hair, carefully coiffed beneath the dark shawl she had bundled around her. Cold fingers squeezed at her. She had fantasised about returning home to Durscombe on many occasions, had longed to watch her grandmother Tansy performing her magickal rituals on the shoreline, but she'd never imagined her eventual homecoming would be this extraordinary.

And so full of foreboding.

It had been seventeen years since Agatha had tasted the salty tang of spray from a rough sea. Seventeen years since she had stowed her trunk in the boot of a stagecoach and travelled away from Durscombe. Back then she'd been intent on a new life far from this insular Devon fishing town, and the incestuous community that inhabited it. But now she'd been forced home to attend to her grandmother's affairs.

Tansy Wick, renowned eccentric, local wise woman and herbalist, dead these past six months.

So, what black omen was this, that she should return as such tragedy unfolded not three hundred yards from the safety of the shore? Resisting the urge to ask the driver to crack the whip on the horses—to return to Exeter perhaps, or venture forwards to Plymouth—Agatha gave up waiting for assistance and instead stepped down from the coach of her own accord, although not without some difficulty. Her skirts and petticoats twisted and tangled as the wind lunged at her. There was no obsequious coachman to hand her down, for he'd disappeared to join the crowd. All eyes were trained on the stricken vessel, the spectators gathered in quiet watchful clumps, shielding their eyes against the stinging rain.

Agatha turned back to the carriage. "Quickly, Flora. Come with me."

A younger woman, a girl really—fifteen or sixteen years of age —reached forward to clutch at Agatha's strong hands and hauled herself out into the storm.

"What is it, Aunt? What's happening?" Flora's green eyes took in the hordes of people thronging on the quay and widened with alarm as she spotted the ship caught in a tempest of hell in the bay.

"It's nothing." Agatha replied sharply, her tone intending to encourage her ward to move more quickly. "Come! Let us seek refuge within, where it is sure to be warm and dry."

She half-dragged the girl to the inn, trusting that the coach driver would come to his senses soon enough and unload their belongings. Casting one final fearful glance at the ship rolling among the breakers, Agatha ushered Flora inside. The gale slammed the heavy wooden door closed behind them, providing a welcome barrier against the violence of the world outside. Agatha exhaled in weary relief, relaxing her shoulders in the warmth and sudden stillness of the ancient inn.

A huge fire burned in the grate of the main saloon to her left. It cast its cosy glow around the place, the cheerful orange flames reflected in the brasses that hung on the whitewashed walls and the coloured bottles of liquor on display behind the bar. Pewter tankards, hanging from hooks on the ceiling, swayed in place, disturbed by Agatha's abrupt entrance.

Agatha observed the roaring fire, sorely tempted to shelter beside it. However, mindful of the perception of others, she played the part of well-bred lady for a while longer and stood her ground by the main doorway. Shivering beside her, Flora cooed—the drama outside temporarily forgotten—as she attempted to engage the attention of a small curly-haired dog, a pretty silver colour, pacing in front of the fire. It sniffled at her and whined, its ears pulled back with anxiety. Agatha could only sympathise. The world was going to hell in a handcart in the bay beyond, and there didn't appear to be anything anyone could do about it.

Her patience was rewarded when a blonde woman, dressed as a washerwoman, a little younger than herself, and a few inches shorter, rushed out of the kitchen, drying rough red hands on her apron.

Agatha recognised her straight away. How could she not, with those intelligent pale green eyes so similar to Tansy's? But she held her tongue, waiting to see if the recollection was mutual.

"Good afternoon, Ma'am. Welcome to The Blue Bell Inn." The blonde woman, her accent broad Devonshire, bustled around Agatha and Flora, eager to be helpful. "Do you arrive with the mail coach? I do apologise that we had no-one available to assist you. The landlord is outside ..." She cast a nervous glance in the direction of the bay. "I'll round someone up to collect your trunks."

"Thank you. It is quite the drama out there." Agatha attempted to catch the woman's eye, but agitated, she had already turned to the small square window beside the door, recessed into the thick stone wall of the inn. She placed her hands on the sill and attempted to peer outside.

"My husband is out there," she explained. "He's a fisherman and was among those trying to row out to the ship, but I fear the waves are too high. I believe they will have turned about." Her breath hitched, a rush of anxiety. Agatha understood the dread she heard there, and the woman's resolve to remain busy while her husband's life balanced precariously in the hands of the fates.

"They have been trying to launch a rescue, then?"

"Yes Ma'am, but surely that poor ship is doomed?"

Agatha made a small noise in her throat. The younger woman turned from the window, and when Agatha cut her eyes at her ward, cast a swift glance at Flora before nodding her understanding.

Too late. "The ship is on the rocks, you mean? Oh!" Flora erupted, startling the little dog, who barked in response. "May I go and see, Aunt? Please?"

"Certainly not, child. Best we leave space on the quay for those who would assist rather than spectate. We would only be in the way."

"But—"

Agatha frowned at her ward but spoke gently. "Flora. For shame. Right-minded people do not gawp at the misfortunes of others."

The blonde woman tipped her head respectfully and indicated a door to their right. "I beg your pardon, Ma'am. Please come through to the parlour. I'll go in search of someone to offload your luggage afore the coach goes on its way."

Agatha turned the corners of her mouth up, relieved. "And if there is anyone who could offer us transport to—" Agatha raised her eyebrows in emphasis, "—Myrtle Lodge," before continuing, "I would be much obliged. It is not far to travel, but I am of a mind to complete my journey this day, despite the inclement nature of the weather."

"Myrtle Lodge?" The blonde woman scrutinised Agatha's face more carefully, her eyes fully meeting Agatha's for the first time. "Oh my!" She beamed in happy recognition, the skin around her eyes crinkling. "Why, surely not? Can it be?" She clapped her hands in delight. "Cousin Agatha? I sincerely beg your pardon. I failed to recognise you. Here you are all grown up! And dressed up! Quite the lady. It has been such a long time." She frowned, trying to recollect the length of time that had passed. "How long has it been?"

"Seventeen years, darling Sally." Agatha delighted by Sally's reaction held her arms out. The two women embraced until Sally pulled away and regarded Flora with excitement.

"And who do we have here?"

"This is my ward, Flora." Agatha took Flora's hand and pulled her forward. "Flora? I'd like you to meet my cousin, Sally Rundle."

"Sally Parrett now. Sally Rundle as was." Sally emphasised. "Your ward, you said?"

"Indeed." Agatha offered no further information, her voice oddly clipped. Sally regarded her with evident confusion, assuming Agatha had married in the intervening years, for she had no siblings of her own, and the girl had addressed her as aunt.

But now was not the time to pry. "I am pleased to make your acquaintance, Flora."

"How do you do?" Flora bobbed an elegant curtsey.

Agatha took a closer look at her cousin. Judging by the lines carved around her mouth and the faint grey in the hair around her temples, life had been a struggle. She'd aged more than Agatha in the seventeen years since they had last seen each other. Sally, at thirty-four years of age or so, appeared older. No doubt she had a few stories to tell.

Agatha would be happy to find time to hear them, but for now, she beamed and changed the subject. "Why, Sally. It is such a joy to see you looking so well. Of course, I fear we are both much changed by the passing of the years."

Sally shook her head in wonder. "Not you, cousin. You have grown into such a fine lady. Your hair even now burns like fire. Just as Tansy's did."

Sally's eyes flicked back to Flora, obviously still curious. She was a pretty girl with a clear complexion, dark eyes and hair, and a tidy figure. She did not much resemble Agatha.

"Poor, poor Tansy," Agatha pressed her lips together.

"Such a sad loss to us all," Sally agreed. "But her passing has finally brought you home? Myrtle Lodge has been standing empty these last few months since our Grandmother passed. I had heard she handed it to you as the eldest of us all, but I never thought to see you again in person. I assumed you would dispose of it."

Agatha shook her head. "It crossed my mind, but you see, I could not stand the thought of strangers in Myrtle Lodge." This was not the entire truth, but Agatha could not articulate her reasons and she knew Sally would approve of the white lie.

"I am grateful for that." Sally embraced Agatha again. "As Tansy would have been, I'm certain." She studied Flora once more. "Agatha and I were playmates when we were young girls," she confided. "Such good times. Happy times."

"They were." Agatha verified Sally's recollection but set her mouth in such a way that her cousin could not fail to notice her sudden discomfort.

"Where are my manners?" Sally exclaimed, alarmed at the thought she might have displeased Agatha somehow. "Please take a seat in the parlour, ladies, and I will fetch some refreshments. Oh, and why don't I investigate whether I can't find Lionel from the stables to take you to the Lodge? He might be available." With a slight bow, Sally scurried away in the direction of the kitchen. The battered door swung silently closed behind her.

Agatha gestured into the parlour and allowed Flora to lead the way. Another fire burned here, albeit a smaller one. It was a cheery room, in contrast to the rough sawdust and spittoons of the saloon, with several watercolours on the walls and rugs on the floor. Agatha plumped a cushion on an overstuffed armchair, curling her lip when it spat motes of dust into the air. "Divest yourself of your wet clothes my dear," Agatha instructed the girl. "Sit a while. I will return shortly."

"May I—?" Flora beseeched Agatha.

"You may not."

A look passed between the two of them. Agatha understood Flora's curiosity, of course she did. However she had always tried to shield her ward from the harsh realities of life. While economic considerations, among others, had forced a return to Durscombe, Agatha wished a different life for Flora than the one she had herself experienced while growing up in the town.

She rearranged her features, smiling gently as Flora obediently settled on the chair. "Very good, darling. I won't be long."

Drawing her shawl more tightly around her face, Agatha braced herself for an onslaught. She made her way quickly to the inn's main entrance, threw open the door, and stepped out into the storm once more.

The Blue Bell Inn stood almost at the far end of the quay, set twenty metres or so back from a natural harbour. To her left, a protective wall curved around the harbour, sheltering the customs and excise building and the harbour master's dwelling. A deep natural shipping channel headed out to sea, well known to the fishermen of the town and one that appeared on many charts. Beyond that, however, at the entrance to Lyme Bay proper, the rocks were treacherous.

A wide promenade began in front of the inn and curved away to the right. It led past the harbour, provided the southernmost boundary of the town, and edged around the beach, stretching for a quarter of a mile to the far cliffs. In better weather, women and children foraged for cockles and whelks among the rocks at the foot of the red cliffs while gulls hovered above their heads, loudly proclaiming their hunger, and awaiting an opportune moment to swoop. The fruits of such labour were sold to the merchants who frequented the harbour, often driving from miles around for fresh seafood.

Many a time, as a child, Agatha had walked along the promenade and watched the boats as they manoeuvred between the sharp-edged rocks, her heart in her mouth. She did not fear for the local fishermen, because knowledge of the layout of the coastline here had been drummed into them since childhood, handed down from man to boy. Their unspoken understanding of the tides and vagaries of the prevailing winds and currents was instinctive, running through the blood of Durscombe's natives. But for those outsiders who dared to navigate around Durscombe's shores? Time after time the rocks would bite back, greedy waters swallowing those interlopers—and their fishing boats—whole.

As a girl, Agatha had accompanied her grandmother to the foreshore on many occasions to assist in some rite or other. Tansy had a life-long fascination with the sea, and an uncanny ability to predict when one of the town's fisherfolk would be lost. At the dawning of a new morning, many a time you would find the pair—the wild-haired, bright-eyed grandmother and her skinny red-headed and bare-footed granddaughter—combing the shore for treasure, gathering seaweed and driftwood, shells and sea-creatures. Under Tansy's beady eye, Agatha would build a small fire, and together they would proffer their treasures to the gods and goddesses of the oceans, uttering prayers for the safekeeping of the town's residents, usually at the behest of a fearful sailor's wife.

Often clad in little more than a thin cotton shift, her long hair blowing free in the breeze, Tansy was the talk of the town, her name bandied about in scandalous whispers in parlours everywhere. Yet any fisherman's wife with even an ounce of superstitious dread, would seek her out. They would cross Tansy's palm with a token, a bribe, and beseech her to calm the seas and light a man's way home. Agatha had been her grandmother's able and willing assistant, but where Tansy had stood uncowed in the face of a violent storm, seeming to derive intense pleasure from the ferocity of crashing waves, the driving rain and howling winds, she had always instilled wariness in her granddaughter. "Remain humble," she had said, "for you are in the presence of immense power. The gods and goddesses will provide you with nature's diverse gifts but only when you demonstrate respect for the elements."

But now Tansy was dead, and Agatha had to face the might of this angry sea alone. She slipped gingerly over the greasy cobbles, feeling a familiar fizz of anxiety as the wind buffeted against her, the force of it trapping her breath in her chest. Keeping clear of the spray from the grey waves as they crashed against the quay, she stared aghast at the ship, closer now than before.

To Agatha's unschooled eye, the vessel appeared colossal. A transatlantic tall ship with numerous masts and ordered webs of rigging, it pitched and rolled in the angry sea, the sails stowed. Evidently the ship had been harbouring in the bay, but perhaps it had slipped its anchors at high tide. The gale had succeeded in driving the ship onto the rocks and all attempts to steer her back out to sea must clearly have been thwarted by the ferocity of the weather.

Agatha clenched her jaw painfully as she caught sight of small figures scurrying this way and that across the deck of the ship. Some stared overboard at the rocks, pointing with evident panic and shouting into the wind. Others hauled ropes, although for what purpose Agatha had no idea.

Surely, there was nothing to be done?

Clusters of locals huddled together in silence. Women, clenched fists covering their mouths, squinted into the wind or twisted their sopping aprons. Men stooped, shoulders slumped, yet stoic and stony faced. Young lads, paying the storm no mind, balanced on the harbour wall and shouted and gestured at the crew aboard the ship, but their words were whipped away by the wind. Round to the left, on the spit head, groups of hardened fishermen could be seen dragging their boats out of the water. There was no point to heroism if it meant leaving women without husbands, children without fathers, and no food on the table for anyone. The local men had made every attempt to launch a rescue, but they had failed. Aboard the tall ship it was now every man for himself.

Agatha snatched her breath as a deep rumbling boom echoed around the shoreline. The noise jarred her nerves further, and the shock of the vibration shot down her spine.

Close by, one or two younger women on the quay screamed in alarm and clutched at their neighbours. "The ship has hit the rocks!"

The sound of grinding timber rode inland on the wind, reverberating around the cauldron of the harbour, bouncing angrily from the cliffs, before flitting down the narrow lanes and into town, to be heard by anyone still sheltering behind closed doors.

Agatha twisted about to follow the direction of the noise, her shawl slipping from her head, her hair whipped loose. She shivered. Noisy, vengeful, angry spirits had taken flight — their shadows darting down slender alleys, seeking out the dark places. Agatha mentally repelled them, instinctively cocooning herself in a bubble of protective light and turned instead to listen to the raised voices on the quay behind her.

Men gestured at the struggling ship and, although reluctant to witness the horror unfolding in the bay, she looked with them. The tiny figures on the deck scurried around, frantically doing what they could. But all hope had faded. The ship *would* break up. Heedless of the sharpened fangs of unforgiving rocks that awaited them below the surface of the waves, those who favoured their chances of swimming away from the scene took a leap of faith, jumping into the churning water.

However, despite the obvious and imminent danger, most of the men chose to remain on the ship. And with good reason. Many sailors had never learned to swim, indeed many refused to learn. Tansy had told Agatha many times that death came easier to those who did not fight it. These sailors were doomed. Given their relative proximity to Durscombe's shore, this seemed doubly cruel to Agatha.

Distressed, incapable of breathing at the thought of the fate that awaited the sailors, Agatha veered away from the carnage. Clutching at her throat, gasping for air, she stumbled past the cursed mail coach that had brought her back to Durscombe. Her boots could find no purchase on the slippery cobbles, but fearing she would faint, she hastened onwards, rushing back to Flora, yearning desperately for the sanctity of the inn.

2

TANSY'S LEGACY

By word of mouth and correspondence, Agatha had engaged a housekeeper sight unseen. Her tiny circle of friends in the small village of Nettleham, not far from the city of Lincoln, had been comprised of women much like herself, respectable in the broadest sense of the term, but with limited means and even fewer worldly contacts. Agatha's persistent but low-key enquiries had ultimately paid off when someone eventually directed her to Hannah Marlow. Agatha, thus far, was pleased with what she had found.

Hannah, a plain and tidy woman of approximately fifty years of age, implicitly understood the delicate nature of Agatha's household and, as agreed, had arrived ahead of her mistress to ensure that Myrtle Lodge could be made habitable. With no prior knowledge of Durscombe or its inhabitants and no particular liking for the sea, Hannah would not have been compelled to join the congregation on the quay or on the cliffs even had she known about the stricken ship. Instead she had remained at the house, awaiting the arrival of her new employer.

In the week since Agatha had instructed Hannah to open Myrtle Lodge, Hannah had fully stocked the larder, beaten the rugs, carpets, curtains and wall coverings, dashed the dust and dirt from every nook, cranny and polished surface she could access, and scrubbed the stone flags in the kitchen and hallway. This had been no mean feat. Tansy had never been a particularly adept housekeeper herself and had struggled during her final illness to maintain the five-bedroom lodge to a decent standard. This meant a great deal of work for poor Hannah.

This afternoon Hannah had been busy making her final preparations; lighting fires in the rooms that were to be occupied, baking bread and concocting a hearty vegetable stew. Now she sat at the kitchen hearth, her knitting in her lap, patiently awaiting her new mistress.

Having endured a tense couple of hours at The Blue Bell Inn—while Sally searched to locate a man willing to tear himself away from the spectacle of the wreck and drive them and their luggage from the inn to the Lodge—Agatha and Flora were exhausted. Agatha stripped off her soaking outer garments, nauseous with the stress of all she had witnessed on the quay. She had little appetite, but forced herself to finish a small bowl of stew in order that Flora would follow her example.

"Would you care to move through to the sitting room, Ma'am?" Hannah asked, but Agatha, still silently appraising her housekeeper, shook her thudding head wearily. Despite her seat next to the fire, she was frozen to the bone and suffering with a strangely debilitating motion sickness thanks to endless hours travelling in the cramped coach.

"I think we shall retire shortly." She indicated Flora, dozing on the kitchen bench. Hannah nodded and Agatha lapsed back into silence and resumed staring into the flames of the roaring fire.

If she narrowed her eyes ... if she squinted ... or even if she simply allowed her brain to think a certain way ... she could see the faces ... actually *see* the shadows of whole beings. This was not her imagination. It never had been. This was her gift, supposedly — a lasting legacy from her grandmother. The flames took shape, flickering in front of her. People. Men. What Agatha could see, what she was witnessing here, were the final glimpses of the souls of men lost at sea. Twisting. Turning. Tormented. A dancing ocean of orange and red that robbed the men of oxygen and deprived them of the life each of them craved.

"No time for this. Not now," Agatha muttered, and turned her thoughts instead to the Lodge, but even this brought little relief. The ghosts of her grandmother, and indeed many of Agatha's forebears were everywhere here, difficult to silence, impossible not to see. Their spirits hissed and whispered and cackled in the shadows, not in a threatening way, only inquisitive and knowing. *Triumphant.* As well they might be, for after all, Agatha, their lost prodigy, had returned.

"I made up the bedrooms as you requested, ma'am." Hannah broke into Agatha's thoughts.

"I'm grateful. Thank you." Agatha had elected to sleep in the bedroom she had occupied as a child rather than take the largest room, on the grounds that she didn't want to disturb the space that had previously been so intimately acquainted with Tansy. She hadn't ventured into her grandmother's bedroom thus far. She trusted that Hannah would see to clearing it out when the moment came. She'd allocated Flora the bedroom Agatha's own mother had occupied thirty years' previously. No doubt the rest of the bedrooms would need refreshing. She'd see to it, in time.

Here in the kitchen she could picture Tansy standing over the fire and her big black cast-iron pot, meticulously stirring the contents therein with a huge wooden spoon. Dozens of tiny bottles would be precisely lined up on the kitchen table. Tansy would strain the contents of her pot through muslin and decant the liquid into the bottles without ever spilling a drop. Agatha and her cousins had often been called upon to cork the bottles and label them neatly in their best handwriting before stowing them safely away on narrow shelves in the pantry.

When the darkness fell, local women would call at Myrtle Lodge. Each would surreptitiously slip inside through the kitchen door, glancing around nervously and fumbling for pennies in their skirts. After a swift consultation, Tansy would proffer one of her bottles and a word or two of advice. Tansy was always generous with her remedies and her guidance. If the woman had no money, this did not pose a problem. Her granddaughters would almost certainly find a dead pheasant or a bucket of live crabs on the back step the next evening. It was all the same to Tansy. She had no need of money.

Agatha remembered the potions only as bottles of hope and illusion. Tansy, the gods rest her soul, had been a fool in many ways. She'd truly believed she could dispense spells and magick, but for the most part, as far as Agatha could tell, it had mainly been hocus pocus, a sleight of hand and an awful lot of luck. The downside to Tansy's 'conjuring' had been that the residents of the town and neighbouring villages spoke of them with trepidation and a certain amount of fear, and Agatha had hated that. As a child she had been pulled two ways, longing to be respectable and to be respected, while simultaneously eager to learn all of Tansy's tricks.

This was not to suggest that Tansy didn't have certain skills that defied definition. Her ability to scry and prophesy was renowned throughout East Devon and beyond. There could be no denying her eerie talents although she was circumspect about how and when and to whom she displayed those. This had comforted Agatha for she had no desire to be run out of town for witchcraft.

When Agatha had said as much to her grandmother, Tansy only cocked her head and smiled wryly, as though there was nothing that could be done with her granddaughter. Perhaps she understood that Agatha, a voracious reader, had half a head in the clouds and a longing for a civilized world of science and literature, somewhere far away from the sea and the close-knit, gossiping community of Durscombe.

Oh the irony, then, that Tansy had presented Agatha with a way to leave Durscombe, only for Agatha to belatedly realise she was the spit of her grandmother after all, with all that such a legacy entailed, and all the hidden gifts she'd claimed to despise.

A single piece of coal slipped from the fire and fell onto the hearthstone, interrupting Agatha's reverie. She stood and shuffled forwards, bending to quickly scoop it up with her bare fingers. She held it in the palm of her right hand without any discomfort, staring down at it as the colour shifted, red to black, black to red, red to black, burning from within and without. Only when she sensed Hannah's gaze, did she drop the coal into the fire and turn to look at the housekeeper. They locked eyes. Hannah smiled.

Agatha had chosen well.

"What do you see there?" Hannah asked.

Agatha glanced Flora's way, confirming she slept on. "Trouble," she intoned, her voice soft. "But that's no surprise. This is Durscombe after all."

Hannah frowned. "You went away from here, but you came back. Why?"

Agatha shrugged and considered her answer. Her limited finances had finally run dry. The terms of her grandmother's will provided for her and Flora, but only as long as Agatha resided at Myrtle Lodge. However, if the truth be told there had been more to it than that. For several months, perhaps years, she had heard the call of her foremothers. They had grown so rowdy she'd had to harken to them eventually. *Now* was the right time to return to Durscombe and bring Flora with her.

She didn't articulate her thoughts, shaking her head instead.

Hannah took this as a rebuke of her forwardness, although it hadn't been meant that way. "My apologies, ma'am."

"Not at all." Agatha held one hand in the air, right palm up. It was unmarked. "It is difficult to explain. I'm not entirely certain I had a free choice." She snorted. "Do any of us? No matter. What's done is done." She firmly closed off the avenue of conversation. "And please call me Agatha."

"Agatha," Hannah nodded, pleased.

Agatha indicated her ward. "Would you take Flora to her room, please? I'll lock up."

"Of course." Hannah took up a candle and gently shook Flora awake.

Agatha kissed the girl on her cheek and bade her good night, standing by the fire and watching as Hannah led Flora along the hall to the staircase. They disappeared from view. She listened as they progressed slowly to the stairs, ascended them and trod softly on the landing above. Agatha bided her time, senses keenly pricked, waiting for the house to become still.

Eventually all was quiet.

She made her own way along the hallway and pulled open the front door. It clattered a little, so warped and brittle had it become. No-one had used it in Tansy's day.

She loitered on the top step, sheltered in part from the worst of the blustering wind and the falling rain, inhaling the clean cold air, drawing the night deeply into her lungs. During the summer the heady scent of herbs and flowers had always filled the garden, but now in late October, with the garden so long neglected, Agatha could only smell the damp decay of leaves and rotting vegetables. Tansy had allowed her garden to grow wild over the past few years, but it wouldn't take much effort to tame it. Agatha had a good idea of how she'd like it to look. Between the three of them—Hannah, Flora and herself—they could cultivate a garden to be proud of, with herbs and vegetables galore. Perhaps this time next year the kitchen table would groan under the weight of Agatha's own bottles of coloured liquid and Flora would write the accompanying labels in her neat script.

But would the local women call on them?

Agatha could not divine the future. Not her *own* future anyway.

She descended the few steps to the drive and angled her head slightly, in the direction of the town. Durscombe lay down the hill at the mouth of the valley. Myrtle Lodge had no view of the sea, nestling as it did on the flat, with trees surrounding it on all sides, but Agatha knew from old in which direction it lay. Even if she had been a stranger to these parts, she would have turned her head and tasted the salt on the wind and gazed steadily seaward.

Tonight all of her senses throbbed and tingled, alive to the pain and loss of life so close by. Her throat clamped shut and her insides tightened when her thoughts turned to the men lost in the rough sea. Those who had chosen to jump into the water were certain to be long dead, while those who had remained on the ship, or who had clung to the wreckage, would have taken longer to die.

Some might yet live.

Agatha turned her face up to where the moon lay shrouded from sight and raised her arms reverently to the skies. The wind clawed at her clothes. It pulled her hair loose so that it billowed around her like the flames of the fire she had abandoned in the kitchen. Rain ran down her face, mingling with the tears she allowed to flow. She opened her mouth in a silent scream, a supplication to the gods and goddesses.

She remained that way for a long time, caught up in excruciating empathy, imagining the sailors as they fought for life, just yards from Durscombe's beach.

A very long time ...

Until agonised and breathless, she bent forwards and vomited.

Panting, her gut spasming, she straightened up, smoothing her wet hair, wrapping it around one fist. With her free hand she wiped at her streaming eyes and then her mouth.

All over now, for the sailors.

Every last one of them had perished.

3

THE HARVEST OF THE SEA

"Your heart is in the right place, but really—" Mayor Bumble drew himself up to his full height and glared at his shorter companion. "Do stop interfering Phineas, my dear fellow."

Standing in the taller man's shadow, Phineas's shoulders slumped. Phineas Benedict Tolleson was a diminutive man in many ways, standing at only five feet, but he had a good strong chest with a big heart residing in it, and a shock of bright auburn hair with matching whiskers that juxtaposed strangely with the misery of the day.

This truly was the calm after the storm. The world appeared to be holding its breath, for the wind had dropped and only the slightest of white-edged swells disturbed the sea. Under a sky the colour of spoiled milk, Phineas surveyed the beach with a deepening sense of gloom. How could the mayor be so cavalier about these circumstances?

The locals, dozens of them, congregated on the quay, nervy and solemn. The men were bareheaded and sorrowful, the women still and silent. Only the mayor and the aldermen of the municipality chose to walk on the beach this morning among the detritus the storm had cast forth onto the speckled golden sand. The wrecked hull of the *Eliza May* remained marooned on the rocks. High tide would probably finish her off once and for all.

Was this flotsam or jetsam? Phineas could never remember. It hardly mattered. Not when corpses stared at the sky with empty eyes and slack mouths.

He shuddered and surveyed the numerous bodies that had washed up overnight. Many more of them floated out among the waves. Phineas could see flashes of clothing and pale flesh. The tide would carry them out beyond the rocks where they would be caught in the prevailing currents of Lyme Bay and nevermore be seen.

It was this that had caused Bumble's impatience. Phineas had dared to suggest that the municipality might organise a rescue party to bring in the deceased, in order to affect the requisite Christian burials in a speedy and seemly manner. The mayor disagreed wholeheartedly, however, and had undertaken to make his displeasure known.

As was his general tendency.

Bumble could be an obstreperous character at the best of times.

"It is only proper that we consider the salvation of their souls," Phineas continued to argue.

The mayor remained adamant, and shook his head, his face stony. "Surely 'twas the sea that claimed their lives, Lord Tolleson? Is it not fitting therefore that it is the sea that provides their final place of rest? What think ye?"

Phineas rocked backward on his heels. *The sea is never restful,* he wanted to retort. *Just look at it even now!* Instead he rearranged his features, adopting a look of pious gravity. "Consider their relatives," he implored, but the mayor only shrugged and turned in the direction of the quay, scrambling along the sand with dogged determination. Phineas, not yet prepared to give way, valiantly scampered after him.

The mayor, realising Phineas still clung to his coattails, tutted loudly. "In God's name, Phineas. Surely you understand as well as I do that the municipality does not have the funds available to organise a funeral for every dead stranger that washes up on our shores." He pointed out to sea in irritation. "Not to mention those floaters that have to be physically brought ashore. Paupers' burials are all well and good, but somebody has to pay for them."

"The municipality—" Phineas attempted to interrupt, but Bumble was in full flow.

"Has very little put aside for such unfortunate eventualities. I'm of the opinion that Durscombe's coffers cannot stretch to so many funerals at this time. It is the thin end of the wedge, my good man. You *must* see that. Bury one and we set a precedent. Before you know it, the town's poor will be abandoning their dead all over the shoreline."

Phineas couldn't think of many occasions in his lifetime when a body had washed up in Durscombe, but he kept his peace. Bumble was mayor for a reason, and while Phineas was certainly Bumble's social superior, he only held his position amongst the aldermen of the town thanks to Bumble's continuing support.

It appeared Phineas could not press Bumble to launch a mission to bring in the floating corpses. "The men on the sand, however?" Phineas asked, his eyes wide, his face earnest. "They absolutely cannot be left there, Mayor."

Bumble scowled, swivelling on his heel to run his eye across the beach. There were probably two dozen men prostrate on the sand, as ungainly in death as they had been graceful and lithe in life. For one horrible moment Phineas feared Bumble would suggest nature take its course and allow the tides to drag the bodies back out to sea, or let the bodies rot where they lay, but fortuitously, Reverend Tidwell, curate of St Michael's parish church, chose that moment to appear at Bumble's elbow. The three men nodded at each other.

"A rum situation," Phineas intoned gravely and Reverend Tidwell, his bible clasped firmly to his chest, agreed.

"Indeed it is, Lord Tolleson, indeed it is." The curate fumbled in his pocket. "By your leave Mayor Bumble, I have instigated recovery of the unfortunate sailors. I have organised a party of men with strong physiques and stronger stomachs. They gather even now outside The Blue Bell Inn. They will load the wretched seamen onto a cart this very morning." He swiped at his brow with a large white handkerchief. "I have arranged a communal grave in the corner of the churchyard, and we will hold a joint service for them all at the earliest opportunity."

Bumble sniffed, wrinkling his nose as though he had encountered a bad smell. "I see." Phineas managed to conceal his sense of triumph as Bumble started to move away again. "Very good, Reverend Tidwell. Send the details to my office later."

"Most certainly." Reverend Tidwell gently restrained the mayor with a carefully placed hand upon his arm. "And if I may?" As Bumble turned back to him, Tidwell gazed into his face with open expectancy. "If the municipality could see its way clear to making a donation towards our not unsubstantial costs, I would be most obliged."

Bumble pursed his lips momentarily before offering a tight-lipped smile. "By all means. Of course, Reverend Tidwell. Whatever you require. I'm sure the municipality has the wherewithal."

"God bless you, Mayor Bumble."

"Indeed, indeed," muttered Bumble, before he nodded his goodbyes to Phineas and the vicar.

Phineas dropped his head and hid a smile as the mayor trotted away, chock full of his own self-importance. What an absurd character the man was. It had become traditional, over the course of numerous generations, that the highest office of Durscombe fell to a Bumble. Meanwhile Phineas, directly descended—according to family lore in any case—from Edward III, owed his position in the town thanks to his family's wealth and titles. Phineas, Lord Tolleson, would never be anything other than an alderman, but that suited him perfectly well because he had numerous other responsibilities to keep him occupied, as well as a seat in Westminster, if he chose to avail himself of it.

It was surely the case that every man in the town knew his place within society and was grateful for it.

Phineas, strolling up the sand toward the promenade, spotted several small groups of men gathered on the cobbles outside The Blue Bell Inn. Were these all Tidwell's men? The curate had described his party as strong of physique, and this they were, to a man. Tidwell broke off from Phineas to speak with the group on the right, who dutifully followed him to the edge of the promenade. The remaining group were a rough crowd; swarthy like fishermen, whiskered, yet dressed as landsmen.

Bumble stood among them, indicating the wreckage on the beach, and conversing particularly with the ringleader. This rough fellow, early thirties at a guess—dressed in a worn grey suit and heavy jacket and a battered top hat—had an impressive scar that ran the whole length of the left-hand side of his face from his eyebrow to his chin, apparently slicing through the eye too, for he wore an eyepatch to cover it.

As Phineas ambled closer, the scarred man leaned in towards the mayor with an impertinent level of intimacy that surprised him. The other men looked on, crossing their arms and leering, sprawling back against the cart parked behind them, or staring insolently at the mayor as Bumble and their spokesman chatted. Bumble held his ground, his confidence unwavering in spite of the scarred man's heated animation. Sharp words, unintelligible to Phineas at his distance, passed between the pair. Evidently they were having a difference of opinion, but the mayor must have said something that appeased them, for all at once the entire group of men guffawed. Phineas found this unseemly given the sombre setting. Perhaps Bumble sensed disapproval from a distance, for, conscious that others looked to him to set a good example, he held his hands up in surrender and smiled charmingly. The men nodded and the leader shook Bumble's hand.

A handshake with such a man? The familiarity of that simple action surprised Phineas most all. Bumble would have considered himself the man's social superior, well above fraternising with men from The Lanes. This behaviour seemed unusually out of character for him.

Reverend Tidwell had returned. He coughed politely, drawing Phineas's attention from the odd interaction in front of the inn. Phineas greeted him politely, pleased that the vicar had won his own small battle with the mayor. "Is there anything I can assist you with, Reverend? Would you allow me to help with the recovery?" Phineas indicated the bodies on the beach.

Reverend Tidwell shook his head in consternation. "No, no, no. That's no job for you, my dear Lord Tolleson. Leave it to the working men. But Heaven knows, there is always something a gentleman like yourself can do to help."

"Anything."

Reverend Tidwell beamed. "Then please do us the honour of speaking at the service on behalf of those lost last night."

"Of course, Reverend. It's the least I can do. And I will ensure you receive a donation for the memorial, too."

"You are the best of men, Lord Tolleson. God be with you, my son."

"And with you, Reverend."

Bumble had disappeared in the direction of Fore Street and Municipal Hall, presumably, but his men, having loitered a while, pushed past Phineas on their way to the beach, staring through him as though he didn't exist, oddly silent, faces set.

He found it disconcerting; it added a grim edge to an already wholly unpleasant day.

Loath to leave the quay, Phineas dawdled a while observing the activity on the beach from a safe distance, until he began to feel his presence was nothing if not mawkish. At least he wasn't alone. The whole town was out and about, watching the comings and goings on the seafront and in the harbour, and keeping up a running commentary on the state of the wreck.

Most obviously, the 'working men', as Reverend Tidwell had called them, along with their wives and children, were out in force on the quay, the youngsters shouting with excitement and jostling each other as they searched for a better vantage point. Meanwhile, the 'gentle' men moved among the wreckage on the beach, but for their part, their wives were more clandestine—staring down at the spectacle from atop the cliffs—and their youngest children were absent, hidden away in nurseries or swaddled by the hearth with an older female sibling.

"*Media vita in morte sumus,*" Phineas repeated sadly. In the midst of life we are in death.

It was a phrase that Phineas had brought to mind often since his young wife had died a dozen years before. At the time, despite the fact that they were perfect strangers in far too many ways, he had been horrified by her decline and illness and had felt responsible for her wellbeing, or lack of it. Afterwards, when the light had been drawn from her, he had gazed upon her stillness in their marital bed and noted his own heightened emotions. How was it possible to feel more alive in the presence of death than he ever had before?

A few years later when his father died, he'd experienced the same rush of emotion.

Now he lived alone. Alone, but with dozens of servants for company. He wasn't unhappy with this situation. In many ways it suited him well. He had no intention of marrying again, and he enjoyed the solitude. He had never loved his wife; indeed, he would never be capable of loving a woman, not in that way. His preference lay elsewhere. Nonetheless he found it pleasant to spend time with men and women of all classes. Phineas had always been a curious open-hearted individual and he basked in the company and conversation of people from all stations and walks of life.

Phineas realised he had come to rest outside The Blue Bell Inn. It was early in the day, not much past eleven, but no matter. The innkeeper would be serving. He pushed open the door. A throng had already assembled within, standing around and talking excitedly about the wreck and the events of the previous evening.

Barnacle Betsy, the landlord's little silver-blue dog moved among the men, avoiding their hard boots as she begged for titbits. She wagged her tail at Phineas, and he reached down to stroke her fluffy, curly head. "I've nothing to offer you," he told her, and she stared at him balefully before moving on to someone with more potential.

Phineas was thankful for the warmth of the inn—the fires were never extinguished here—and the familiarity of the scent of the place, of soot, stale sweat, herbs and hops. Phineas skirted the edge of the room and caught the eye of Maddie, the landlord's daughter. She winked and eventually made her way over to him.

"Ale, Lord Tolleson, sir? Or something stronger? You look a little grey around the gills if you don't mind me saying so." Maddie could only have been eighteen or so, and as pretty as a picture, but she was forthright and confident and could hold her own. She needed to. The inn could be rough at times.

Phineas, who had a tendency to be apple-cheeked whatever the time of year, and no matter how much alcohol he had or hadn't consumed, found it hard to believe that he looked pale, but he decided to humour the lass. "Brandy, if you please Maddie. Make it a large one to fortify my constitution."

"Turned your stomach has it, Sir? It is a sad day." Maddie winked and sashayed away, neither mournful nor sick. The wreck had ensured that business was booming, and her father would be pleased. When she returned with his brandy, Phineas took it to the small window, to watch the crowds milling around outside. Of the mayor there was no sign, but 'his' men were dragging a boat from its place and hauling it down the slipway. They would await the turning of the tide and be out in it, no doubt. These men could not be part of Reverend Tidwell's rescue party. But if they weren't recovering bodies, what would they be doing?

Phineas could clearly see in the distance that two carts had already been taken down to the beach, and the process of recovering the bodies had begun. Reverend Tidwell had been as good as his word, and he moved among the departed, kneeling in the sand

and praying beside each corpse. Once his prayer had been sent, a couple of men would join him and carefully lift the body onto the cart. The growing pile was then covered over with a large tarpaulin.

Most of the aldermen had followed Phineas's lead and deserted the beach and were now making their way in the direction of the inn. Phineas would have company. Meanwhile, many of the locals drifted the opposite way towards the beach, taking the place vacated by Durscombe's municipal officers. Phineas, watching from his vantage point in the window, witnessed someone stoop in the sand, and dig around a little. He recoiled.

Is this what would happen now?

As soon as the bodies had been removed, the locals would pick up any goods or items left behind, those that were salvageable, and make away with them. Phineas grimaced and hastily drained his brandy.

"Lord Tolleson? You look unusually ashen faced, my dear man." Alderman Edward Pyle had arrived ahead of the others. Pyle, a handsome well-built man in his mid-thirties, with bright blue eyes and neatly curled blonde hair, offered Phineas a gloved hand to shake.

"It's a terribly sad business," Phineas replied.

"It most certainly is," Pyle nodded, his face suitably grave, but his tone somewhat careless. That was Pyle all over. "Let me have that topped up for you, Sir." He indicated the empty glass in Phineas's hand. "And Fliss? What about you?"

Marmaduke Fliss joined them. Taller than Pyle but thinner, he gave the impression of being nothing but angles. Everything about him seemed to be pointed: a pointed nose, pointed knees, elbows and wrists and long thin feet. His dark hair, greying slightly at the temples made him appear older and more distinguished than his companions, but at least he looked as woebegone as Phineas felt. Fliss grimaced. "I really shouldn't, Pyle. Mrs Fliss will be wondering what has become of me."

Phineas experienced a pang of sympathy for Marmaduke.

From what he'd heard, he couldn't imagine for a moment that the elegant and fierce Emily Fliss would give two hoots about the whereabouts of her husband, although anything was possible behind closed doors, he supposed.

Phineas patted the man's arm. "Join us for one, Marmaduke. It will set you up for the day." Marmaduke pressed his lips together and grudgingly acquiesced. Phineas imagined the man might need a drink inside him to face up to Emily.

"Such a terrible night," stuttered Marmaduke. "I've heard of such incidents of course, in Cornwall and Dorset and the like, but never such a one as this on our own stretch of coast. Not to my knowledge at least." Marmaduke, Phineas and Pyle were of an age and they found themselves in agreement on this point.

Pyle had evidently been talking to the fishermen. "An accident is all it was. Word has it that the *Eliza May* was sheltering from the storm in the bay and slipped her anchors. She was driven inland by the high tide. The sailors couldn't get the sails up in those winds to turn her about."

"There was nothing they could do at all?" Phineas had never been a sailor, but the idea of being dependent on the weather, and so powerless in the face of such a storm, scared him witless.

Pyle shook his head, enjoying the fact that only he, among his colleagues, seemingly knew what had occurred the previous evening. "No. Apparently not."

Phineas shivered. His thoughts returned to the beach, mulling over the images he had stored in his head of the corpses there. "Any idea where the ship had come from and where it was going to?" he asked. This knowledge might give them a clue as to how to identify the sailors and notify their families.

"Not yet, but I'm sure once we get some boats out there, we'll find out more." Pyle nodded in the direction of the wreck in the distance, marooned as it was, shifting slightly on the rocks as the tide came in.

Phineas couldn't help but notice the swell that was building on the waves once more. Little crystal heads bubbled on their tips.

The light of the day had turned a peculiar shade too. Despite the lack of sunshine, the air itself seemed to glint too brightly. His temples ached in response.

"Perhaps we're due another storm," he commented. The other men stared out of the window alongside him. Marmaduke glowered. Phineas wondered what he was thinking, and might have asked, but they were startled by a roar from a group of men gathered around the fire. Giles, the landlord, had returned from the beach with a group of thirsty fishermen in tow, and they had dragged a barrel in with them. The landlord called for his son to open it, and the fishermen gathered around. Barnacle Betsy sniffed at their feet, curious as to the contents of the barrel. There was a whoop as the barrel was breached. A rich liquid gushed forth, spattering onto the sawdust on the floor. Several men rushed forwards to fill their tankards. Betsy lapped at the spillage.

"Waste not, want not!" crowed one fisherman and the others laughed, watching him drain his vessel.

The atmosphere in the tavern had moved from solemnity to jocularity in one shake of a rat's tail. "I surmise that's booty from the wreck," Pyle noted and Fliss nodded.

Phineas looked on, horrified by this uncouth display of behaviour. "No doubt. There'll be more of that in the days to come, I'll wager. May God forgive us."

Pyle grinned. "With any luck, he's not looking."

Several hours later, feeling slightly woozy, his cheeks red from the combination of proximity to the fire and the sheer amount of spirits he had consumed, Phineas unsteadily navigated the cobbles. The wind whipped at his coattails and ahead of him the sea had raised its voice to a roar. The tide had rolled further in and the breakers lashed against the wreck once more. The poor stricken *Eliza May*, completely devoid of masts and rigging now, looked a shadow of her former self as she ground her keel on the rocks. It wouldn't be long before she began to break up completely.

Phineas paused on the quay, blinking into the wind and swaying, regarding the sad spectacle of the once graceful ship. Seagulls hovered overhead, fighting against the squall, their cries sounding as mournful as Phineas felt. Over by the wreck he could see a flurry of activity, half-a-dozen small boats had ventured out there and men, far braver than Phineas, were navigating lines thrown to the ship and hastily secured onboard.

Would they recover any survivors?

Momentarily Phineas' spirits lifted. But the gashes on the wood at the ship's water line suggested there would be none. Any man remaining alive would have made himself known by now, surely? Besides, Phineas instinctively understood that the Durscombe men weren't looking for sailors, they were looking for goods. That knowledge, combined with the brandy he had consumed, turned his stomach sour once more.

The doleful sound of horses, slowly clip-clopping up the road towards him, caught his attention. The carts carrying the bodies of the drowned sailors had been brought up off the beach and were slowly being pulled along the quay towards Fore Street. Phineas assumed the drivers would then make the left turn up Church Street and carry their sombre load to St Michael's Church, where the bodies would be prepared for burial.

The covered carts drew level with him, the horses close enough to touch. Phineas removed his hat, bowing respectfully as the first and second carts rolled slowly past him. The tarpaulin on the third cart had worked its way loose, flapping in the wind, a flag at half-mast. As the horse pulling the cart came closer, Phineas had the sudden and bizarre impression that someone beneath the tarpaulin had come to and was now desperately fighting to extract himself from among the corpses.

The cart drew level. Phineas's curious glance into the rear revealed only a tangle of lifeless limbs. One exposed grey arm dangled carelessly over the gate. A blue mark had been tattooed onto the skin above the wrist; an octopus. Phineas stared it in morbid fascination. The cart bounced as the rear wheel hit a large rock, and the motion caused the loosely curled fingers to wobble. They beckoned obscenely to Phineas. He shuddered and averted his gaze.

But a perverse sense of wonder had ensnared him in its thrall. He followed the cart halfway up Church Street. He had witnessed death before, but not on this scale. Never this many corpses at one time. His mind played tricks on him, as a direct result of the brandy he'd consumed perhaps, and he found himself envisioning the jumble of limbs beneath the tarpaulin, the clouding of the eyes, the blue lips, the sallow skin. He forced his thoughts to turn elsewhere, but then tortured himself imagining these sailors so full of life a mere twenty-four hours previously. Strong and active, no knowledge of what was to come.

A dozen young boys ran screaming up the road, overtaking Phineas and chasing after the carts, daring each other to touch the exposed arm. They provided the catalyst that brought Phineas to his senses. He halted in his tracks and finally tore his gaze away, wishing he could simply return to Hawkerne Hall and put the whole sorry mess out of mind, but he'd agreed to speak at Reverend Tidwell's service, and he couldn't let the man down. The sooner the men were safely buried and out of sight, the better. The wrecking of the tall ship was a tragedy, and the loss of the sailors entirely regrettable, but it was rapidly becoming a tawdry and sordid affair the town could do without.

For now, Phineas needed to consume a hearty lunch and forget about the sailors. He donned his hat and turned sharply about, heading for Jerome's, the only gentleman's club in town.

"Media vita in morte sumus," he repeated to himself as he turned off Church Street and back into Fore Street. *"Media vita in morte sumus."*

4
ON A CLIFF EDGE

Emily Fliss breathed sharply and audibly through her nose in distress, but rapidly checked herself when she realised she would be overheard. Displaying emotion in public would do her reputation no good at all. Not that anyone important appeared to be within hearing distance, but there were plenty of people milling around, and talk of such a display of emotion would find its way back to those to whom it would matter.

Rapidly.

Reputation and status were two of the most important things in Emily's life, and she intended to guard them closely.

There were far more people in The Victoria Gardens, lining the edge of the cliffs, than she would have encountered on a normal day. Mostly they were women of a decent class and station, and children with their nurses. She acknowledged them as she walked, where appropriate, because in her role as an alderman's wife she considered it befitting to maintain societal niceties. Nonetheless, her shoulders knotted with unease. She didn't like crowds; the noise, the smell, the jostling. Her senses became overwhelmed. Today the sheer number of bystanders oppressed her and she feared she would faint.

It was the wreck of course. Everyone, who was anyone, had

arrived at The Victoria Gardens to promenade and gaze upon the unfortunate ship. From these cliffs, just forty to fifty feet above the beach, it was possible to view the *Eliza May* from a spectacularly good angle.

Come rain or shine Emily wandered through the cliff top gardens most days. Sometimes she walked with her husband Marmaduke, and on other days she strolled alone. Not entirely alone, of course because her maidservant would accompany her, but no-one could define Mary as 'company', so Emily was alone for all intents and purposes.

She chose to stroll here for a number of reasons. Durscombe's high society, as limited as it was, quite frankly demanded her presence. It was deemed a requirement for someone in her position to be seen out and about frequently. Emily did not consider this a hardship, for she loved to breathe the fresh sea air and watch the ever-changing view, the vista of sky and sea. She had always resided in Durscombe and the beach drew her like a bee to a flower. As a child she'd enjoyed a certain amount of freedom—at least while in her grandmother's care—down on the foreshore, and those memories warmed her heart.

But in any case, and most importantly for Emily, she knew she'd be bored to distraction at home.

Emily was a great society beauty, renowned in Durscombe for her looks, elegance and charm. With her thick lustrous hair—so dark it was almost black—her pale complexion and deep green eyes, she lit up ballrooms and church halls alike. On the arm of her husband Marmaduke, she dutifully graced every party and function in the town, attended every community event and fayre, gave generously of her time and money to philanthropic concerns, and was held up as an example of virtuous womanhood.

But Emily felt keenly that her very existence was a façade. She had not been born into her class, she had married into it, largely thanks to her mother Lily's efforts.

Now deceased, Lily had herself been a stunning looking woman, but with Tansy—Emily's grandmother—as Lily's sole parent, and unaware who her father was, she was effectively as poor as a church mouse. Lily therefore contrived to use her attractiveness to personal advantage. From the moment she'd begun to interact with the world at large, Lily had spun tales to anyone who would listen that her family were well-connected but had fallen on hard times and that her father had been a distant cousin of royalty.

Against Tansy's wishes, Lily had taken to attending church regularly. This proved to be the making of her. Her undeniable magnetism and allure eventually won her the hand of an up-and-coming local warehouse merchant. It was a great match. With Lily's looks and her husband's entrepreneurial skills, they had rapidly made a name for themselves within Durscombe's higher society and become acceptable company. After Emily's happy arrival, Lily poured all of her energy into her tiny daughter's social advancement, providing the best of everything—clothes, tutors, music lessons, parties—and plotting her ascent up the social ladder. Fortunately, Emily had inherited Lily's looks which gave her a distinct advantage. Then, when her father passed away prematurely during an outbreak of diphtheria while on business in London in 1845, as his only surviving child, she came into all of his money.

An attractive marital prospect, Emily had been rewarded with dozens of potential suitors. She had spurned each, only one more regretfully than the others, until Marmaduke Fliss had summoned up the courage to propose.

The Fliss family had lived in Durscombe for over seven hundred years and were well respected. In terms of wealth, they were second only to the Tollesons of Hawkerne Hall, owning acres and acres of glorious countryside in both Devon and Somerset. Residing at Hollydene Park, a medieval manor set in luscious woodland on the outskirts of the town, Marmaduke was the third Fliss child and second son. He had longed to study literature at university and travel far and wide, but when his older brother had been killed in a riding accident, Marmaduke had been forced to return from Oxford and take on the Fliss landowner mantle. He wasn't a handsome man, but undeniably he made for a good catch.

He adored his wife.

He would do absolutely anything for her.

Unfortunately, Emily couldn't bear to be in the same room as him.

She had imagined, once upon a time that she would grow to love Marmaduke, and perhaps she might have done, except that everything about her new-found wealth and privileged position exasperated her. She would never have articulated the notion as such, but Emily found her life tedious beyond redemption.

The wind fussed at Emily's carefully arranged hair and threatened to dislodge the fashionable black-feathered hat she was wearing, this despite Mary having carefully attached it using half a dozen jewelled hat pins. Emily had, as always, chosen her outfit with great care. Now in her mid-thirties she was proud to have retained the figure of a younger woman, helped in large part by the savage pinching in of her corset. Emily enjoyed turning heads wherever she went, and while she would not have called this vanity, others might construe it as such. For her part, Emily saw herself more as an ambassador of good taste and charm. At least attending to her wardrobe and picking out fabrics for her dressmaker provided a distraction from the monotony of running the Hollydene household.

"Mr Fliss is unforgivably delayed!" Emily hissed sotto-voiced. Mary, her maidservant and a dumpy young woman of just twenty-or-so, scrambled up the path to edge closer to her mistress. Mary didn't like heights and, without being too obvious about it, had been trying to steer clear of the cliff.

"Perhaps he has been held up on official municipality business, Ma'am?" Mary attempted to soothe Emily's anxiety, but her mistress only snorted in bad temper. *Damn the municipality.*

Mrs Goodwin, Alderman Goodwin's wife, and her daughter Gertrude chose that moment to stroll by. Emily nodded and murmured her greetings with a perfectly pleasant smile, which they returned equally sweetly.

Once they had passed, the smile quickly fell from Emily's face. "They despise me."

She glared after them and Mary followed her gaze. One or two of the older aldermen's wives had perfected the art of silent hostility that translated into polite put-downs and condescension. They chose to remember only where Emily had come *from* rather than where she had ended up. Many of them remained unimpressed by her distinguished record of good deeds and philanthropy. They regarded her as a jumped-up social climber and had long harboured the inclination to take her down a peg or two. Emily twisted her hands nervously, always sensitive to the machinations of others. "Mary. I'm tired. We'll return home."

Mary nodded and fell into step beside her mistress as they strolled towards the ornately curved iron gates that marked the park's exit. As they reached the road, a pair of horses—pulling a carefully laden cart, full of good-quality trunks, some furniture and a few household wares—laboured passed them, on their way up the hill and away from town.

"I wonder where that can be bound." Emily peered after it, raising her eyebrows, as it ambled away. She considered herself knowledgeable about all the ins-and-outs of Durscombe society, and had not heard a rumour of anyone moving in or out of the town.

Mary peered around her mistress, staring after the cart. "That's The Blue Bell Inn's dray, Ma'am, if I'm not mistaken. It's heading in the direction of Moor Lane. Mayhap it's going to one of the cottages there. Or the Lodge. I did hear a new housekeeper had been appointed to Myrtle Lodge, Ma'am."

"Myrtle Lodge?" Emily started, the pitch of her voice rising. *Her grandmother's house.* "Well, well. Who can be moving in there? I had not heard the property had been sold on." Not before time, perhaps. Tansy Wick had been dead and buried these past six months. She hadn't attended the funeral. As far as she knew, nobody had.

Emily regarded her maid, wondering whether the young woman would make some discreet enquiries. "You must find out who the new occupant is for me, Mary. Not that I'm one for gossip, you understand."

"No Ma'am. Of course I will, Ma'am. If I can, Ma'am." Mary liked to please Emily. "I'll talk to my mother. She hears all the g—," Mary bit back the word, "the latest."

Emily turned her face to hide her amusement. The wind had whipped up and the high-pitched shrieks of women were carried towards her. Craning her head, she stepped back through the gates. Something must have occurred at the wreck site. How else to explain the flurry of ladies who had rushed forwards to peer over the edge of the cliff. Her interest piqued, Emily gestured to Mary. "I'd like to see," she announced, navigating the path that wound its way between the manicured bushes and flower beds.

"Oh, mind how you go, Ma'am!"

Emily pushed on, ignoring the fear in Mary's voice.

"Don't worry, girl, I'll assist your mistress." The rich assured tones of a gentleman startled Mary and she spun in surprise, dropping a rapid curtsey.

"Mayor Bumble! I didn't see you there," she blurted. "My apologies. Thank you, Sir."

Bumble ignored the maid, stepping past her to lightly claim Emily's arm. He didn't ask permission.

She regarded him through cool green eyes, a small smile playing across her lips. "Mayor Bumble. Good afternoon."

"Mrs Fliss." She allowed him to lead her towards the cliff edge. "I trust you have been enjoying your constitutional, today?" Bumble indicated the wreck. "It is truly a spectacle to behold, is it not?"

Emily frowned. "It is a tragedy, Mayor Bumble," she returned, her face grave. "Surely it is incumbent upon us to remember that."

"And yet here we all are, ogling what is before us." He gestured extravagantly at the crowd with one gloved hand, the other held Emily's elbow in a firm grip.

Emily dropped her gaze from his handsome face, and directed it beyond the cliff, down at the sea. Small rowing boats darted in and out of the rocks, men with hooks leaned dangerously over the water, hauling items onboard. Several fishermen were clambering aboard the *Eliza May*, and slipping around on the broken deck. Perhaps it had been this that had caused the disquiet among the crowd of spectators?

"Those men?" Emily asked.

"Salvaging what they can." Bumble shrugged.

Emily turned to the mayor, searching his face. No hint that anything untoward had happened here, that men had lost their lives. And what did he mean by salvage? What would happen to the goods the fishermen rescued? Bumble's guileless eyes met hers. He smiled, giving nothing away.

"They will return all those goods to the rightful owners? The families of the lost sailors? Or the owner of the ship?" Emily couldn't help but ask.

"If he can be traced, I'm sure they will."

A flicker of sharp irritation crossed Emily's brow. "Let us hope every effort is made, then."

"Please don't worry yourself, my good Mrs Fliss." Mayor Bumble laughed. This attempt to soothe her served to irk Emily further. They went back a long way—once she'd imagined they would marry—and it seemed she was still a source of amusement for him.

In addition, the mayor and her husband had been good friends since boyhood. They worked well together at Municipal Hall. Over the years Bumble had become accustomed to Emily turning up at the municipal offices to visit Marmaduke, and at the same time she would wield her philanthropy against the mayor, like a weapon. She always had a new cause to fight, and she would confront him, demanding that he ensure the municipality increase their endeavours to feed and shelter and clothe

the poor. "Indeed. I'm sure every effort will be made," he told her.

Emily began to say more but Bumble cut her off. "And to that end I must return to my chambers." He gently squeezed her arm and bowed. "I will bid you good day, Mrs Fliss. I have urgent business to attend to."

"Mayor Bumble." Emily inclined her head, gracefully. She watched him stroll towards the exit of the gardens, her heart beating a little too quickly. Once upon a time she had badly desired their union, and when circumstances had dictated otherwise, she had snubbed him for several years. More recently relations had gown warmer between them. Secretly, she still found him desirable.

"Should we go, Ma'am?" Mary asked.

Emily shrugged, turning to observe the fishermen below once more. They slid about on the deck of the stricken ship, in the middle of water that was coloured an alarming red, the recent storms having churned up the sand and silt of the red clay undercliff. Seawater lapped at the fishermen's ankles in places, and little white breakers rolled across the deck. One more storm and another high tide, and there would be very little of the *Eliza May* left.

The rowing boats continued their mission to pick up anything floating in the water, and yet Emily from her vantage point could not fail to notice the items that were carefully avoided. The pale bodies of sailors that shifted and twisted in the water as nature bade them. Some appeared clothed, others did not.

"I fancy there are fewer corpses in the water than first thing," Emily murmured. Had they floated out to sea, she wondered, or sunk beneath the waves of the relentless incoming tide?

Just how long did it take before a body sank?

She stared at one of the bodies, face down in the choppy waves. She imagined him moving, wiggling his fingers, lifting his head, gasping for breath. The image took shape in her mind and she conjured the corpse alive. As he struggled for air, she saw his handsome face as clear as day, briefly submerged by a large silver crested wave. He fought to surface again. She allowed him, this dark-haired man, hair plastered across his head. He went under once more. She watched the bubbles ... bubbles of air expelled from his lungs ... and he sank like a stone before twisting in the water, rising, swimming up, reaching out to her ...

Emily's breath caught in her throat, a pulse in her head throbbing, her vision greying. Standing there, on the edge of the cliff, she swayed. The waves loomed large beneath her, the sea calling to her ... a rush of air—

—and she found herself tumbling forwards—

"No!" Mary cried, yanking at Emily in alarm. "Please come away from the edge, Ma'am! You're scaring me to death!"

Emily, suddenly and violently alive to her plight, shrieked. She sank into the girl's embrace, all of the strength ebbing from her knees. "Are you quite well, Ma'am?" Mary asked. "Come to the bench here. Let me call for the carriage!" Emily stumbled, allowing Mary—fortunately strong and physically able—to half-drag her toward the bench. She sank gratefully down, listening to the servant's footsteps as she raced away to seek the driver of their carriage.

Slumping forward over her hands, Emily concentrated on the pile of her skirt, willing her sparking vision to return to normal, and the constriction in her chest to ease. Gradually her breathing returned calmed and her peripheral vision expanded. Left alone, she became conscious of the sympathetic looks from other ladies in her vicinity. Straightening, she plucked a fan from her skirt and wafted herself, affecting a vague swoon.

"Oh, my dear," she heard the elderly Mrs Champion remark to her companion. "Poor Mrs Fliss is quite overcome. Such a sweet lady. So sensitive. This is all far too much for her."

"Whatever was Mr Fliss thinking?" The companion replied. "Allowing his wife out when—"

Their voices drifted away as they headed towards the gates at the exit.

Emily set the fan down and lay her hands in her lap. Beneath her voluminous skirts and petticoats, her knees continued to shake. She stared out into the bay, and beyond to the horizon. From this angle the *Eliza May* remained hidden from her view, but that didn't matter. She knew exactly where it was. How far it lay below the cliff edge. The distance from the cliff to the rocks.

The wind caught at her hat, tugging at the pins. Its cold voice whispering in her ear.

Her breath hitched.

There are sailors down there, floating in the water.

Dead.

When they don't want to be.

Their single dying desire had been to make land. And they would yearn for that for eternity. *Death magick is powerful magick.* Tansy had often told her so.

These sailors would achieve their avowed intention in any way they could. Not for them a permanent watery grave. No. The spirits of these sailors were already clawing their way, handhold by handhold, up the sides of the cliffs.

Emily shivered, waiting impatiently for Mary.

Any second now, she thought, *any second now.*

She remained frozen to the spot, eyes on the cliff edge, expecting white fingers to sprout among the tufts of grass now waving in the stiff breeze, to grimly clutch at the rocks, muscles straining, gripping anything that would hold their weight. She fully expected those dead sailors to drag themselves from the depths to collapse onto the earth before her. They would crawl with hostile determination towards the bench, opaque eyes entirely unseeing even as they gasped for air, then vomit red seawater from slack mouths.

The sailors come for me!

Instinctively she understood; nothing and nobody could save her.

5
THE NEW MAN

The morning after the sailors' memorial service, Phineas Tolleson took breakfast alone, reflecting with great solemnity on the passing of time and the relentless turning of the tides. By God's grace, he had all that he needed. So many others would never be as fortunate.

In his opinion, Hawkerne Hall could be considered one of the finest residences in East Devon, if not the whole county. He understood that his position as a peer and one of the wealthiest landowners in the region had occurred merely as an accident of birth, but nonetheless he took pride in his inheritance. Phineas would have been pleased to welcome an heir, but the chances of him spawning any offspring had died along with his wife. He could be lonely at times, and for that reason he took his opportunities for intimacy when they presented themselves—and only if there would be no chance of rumour and gossip—but for the most part he kept his personal life intensely private,.

His early marriage at the instigation of his domineering father had been a total sham, and he'd often felt extremely sorry for poor Elizabeth. None of it had been her fault. She'd tried to be a dutiful and good wife, and God knew Phineas had made every effort to do his duty by her, but he'd found the whole sorry situation distasteful. Now both his wife and his father were dead and buried and he would never force another woman to endure what Elizabeth had, merely to save face among his peers.

Nonetheless, Hawkerne Hall would certainly benefit from a woman's oversight. The huge estate cost an absolute fortune to run, a large chunk of his financial inheritance. It often seemed absurd to have so many servants running around the place, when the only person to benefit from their labour, was himself. Certainly, the multitude of servants kept the old place shining like a new sixpence—they were worth the expense—but he found attending to their various wants and needs draining at times. He therefore delegated most matters to his estate manager, and to his housekeeper, Mrs Gwynne. As long as his gardens were meticulously tended, and his horses beautifully turned out, Phineas was happy.

But that didn't stop him feeling lonely.

A cheerful fire burned in the grate beside him, but he ignored it and stared morosely through the French doors, out at the view beyond his cultivated grounds. Set high on the hill overlooking Durscombe, the rear of Hawkerne Hall had a splendid outlook across the stunning forested countryside and down to the coastline. From his seat he could take in both the sweep of the beach and harbour, as well as the town beyond. He couldn't see the *Eliza May*, hidden as she was in front of the cliffs, however when he squinted he was certain he could make out the specks of men and women combing the beach, searching for spoils.

Or perhaps that was his imagination. Needless to say, the thought of it alone was enough to put him off his breakfast.

Except there didn't appear to be any breakfast.

Perhaps the cook had forgotten about him. Phineas looked about in confusion and glanced at the clock on the mantle above the fireplace. Where were his servants? They knew he was partial to a pair of perfectly boiled eggs most mornings. Thus far they hadn't even provided him with tea. Should he ring for them?

His miserable reverie was finally interrupted when, at last, a manservant entered the room and hurried towards him. Phineas, not recognising the man at all, regarded him with some surprise. He'd been expecting his butler, and this was not he. Even more unsettling, the new man was not wearing the expected servant livery. Fortunately, he *was* carrying a tray laden with a teapot and milk jug, so the day was improving, albeit infinitesimally.

"I beg your pardon, Sir." The servant was younger than Phineas, mid-to-late twenties perhaps, with a shock of dark curly hair tied at the back of his head, and eyes as blue as a calm summer sea. He was tanned, and built well, more accustomed to outside work by the look of him. His frock coat, probably not his, was far too tight around the shoulders and upper arms, and his shirt grey from being washed too often.

Phineas stared at the younger man, perplexed by his presence, but not displeased by it. He felt himself more curious than anything. He had started to enquire as to the whereabouts of his butler, when Mrs Gwynne hurried in, her face flushed pink with anxiety, her eyes red-ringed.

"Good morning, Lord Tolleson, Sir."

"Mrs Gwynne." Phineas smiled with relief; some normality could resume. "Is there a problem?" He hoped not. His servants were interesting individuals, but he didn't wish to become intimately acquainted with their personal affairs or involved in any household drama if he could help it.

"Sir—" Mrs Gwynne looked at Phineas with beseeching eyes, as though she would rather not say what needed to be said.

"Mrs Gwynne, if there is any possibility you could appraise me of the situation this morning, I would be most obliged." Phineas' tone remained mild. It wouldn't do to upset his housekeeper. "Where has the rest of my breakfast disappeared to?"

Mrs Gwynne curtseyed once more, her words tumbling over each other. "Sir, I do apologise. Mr Wiggins was taken ill in the night and we didn't want to disturb you, but the doctor was called, and he thinks it is dear Mr Wiggins' heart, Sir." That would explain her watery eyes. Phineas feared Mrs Gwynne was about to burst into fresh tears. He hoped she would refrain from doing so as he was liable to join in.

He had long dreaded a day such as this. 'Wiggy' was an old man. A very old man. He'd been in service with the Tollesons for decades and promoted to butler in his father's time. Phineas looked on Wiggy as an old and dear friend, a trusted non-judgemental and discreet companion, an elderly uncle. He wasn't sure what life at Hawkerne Hall would be like without him.

"What can be done, Mrs Gwynne?"

"The doctor thinks very little can be done, Sir. He has instructed Mr Wiggins to remain in bed. He is in his room, Sir."

Phineas nodded, his heart sinking. "I will pay him a visit directly, Mrs Gwynne. No expense should be spared. Ensure he has everything he needs."

"I will, Sir. You are a good man, Sir."

Phineas brushed off the housekeeper's heartfelt approval, feeling more woebegone by the minute. "*Media vita in morte sumus*," he reminded himself aloud, a touchstone for life that kept him focussed on the present. The young man, still wielding the tea tray, temporarily forgot his place and openly scrutinised Phineas with fresh interest.

Phineas, sensing the young man's close examination, turned his head to regard him once more. Mrs Gwynne finally came to her senses. "Oh my apologies, Sir. This is Matthew Salter. I asked him to help me carry your breakfast through. He can assist you with anything you need this morning, if you wish it. This is simply temporary, Sir, until ... while we wait for Mr Wiggins ..." She didn't finish. Phineas didn't care to follow that particular train of thought anyhow.

Phineas wondered where the other household servants were. This fellow in his ill-fitting garb appeared barely house-trained. Not that it mattered really, Phineas supposed, he had rather lost his appetite. "Yes, yes, very well," he muttered.

"Go on then, lad." Mrs Gwynne addressed the young man more brusquely than she did her master. "Put the tea on the table and return to the kitchen to fetch his Lordship's breakfast. I do apologise, Sir. We are all chasing our tails this morning."

Phineas waved a hand. "Not to worry, Mrs Gwynne. I'm not hungry anyway."

"Now that won't do. You must have something. I'll see to it myself." With that, she bustled out of the breakfast room, closing the door softly after herself, leaving Phineas alone with Matthew in the now quiet room.

Phineas indicated Matthew should lay the tea out on the table and Matthew nodded, several long curls flopping around his face, beautifully framing his strong nose and full lips.

His pulse quickening, Phineas swallowed, and rushed to fill the sudden silence. "What are your normal duties, Matthew?"

"I'm in the stables with Mr Redman, Sir. Also the gardens with Mr Briggs."

"Indeed?" Phineas was surprised that Mrs Gwynne had chosen a stable lad to wait on him.

"I used to drive the carriages at Drake House, outside Abbotts Cromleigh, Sir. I did some inside work there too, as and when needed."

"Ah of course. Poor Lord Brigham." The elderly Lord Brigham had fallen on hard times. Now Phineas understood. "His cousin sold the house, I take it?"

"I believe so, Sir. I received a good reference. I am glad of the work here. I'm happy to turn my hand to anything."

"That's a commendable attitude, Matthew." Phineas studied the younger man with pleasure. "You couldn't turn your hand to some boiled eggs, I suppose? Then I'll pay a visit to Wiggy."

Matthew smiled. His teeth were surprisingly straight and fine, his face clear of pox scars. Phineas was struck by the young man's shining countenance, his air of vitality. "Of course, Sir." He bowed and quickly left the room, moving with an elegant grace, unusual in a person of his size.

Phineas watched him go, his heart beating slightly too quickly.

His emotions tumbled around in turmoil; concern for Wiggy, but ... something else.

He found himself looking forward to Matthew's return.

6
PLUNDER AND RECOVERY

For the next week, tides were high and winds fierce, but the *Eliza May* clung obstinately to the rocks.

Whenever there was a lull in the Autumn storms, the locals were out in their droves picking over whatever washed up on the beach. Each high tide brought a fresh influx of goods. Nothing was left for the sea to reclaim and in the end everything found a home. That which one man might pour scorn over, quickly became another man's treasure. At first light, children descended on to the west beach to pick through the night's leavings, while their fathers struggled to carry timber away. Each length of wood would be stripped free of nails and other furnishings. Women were happy with any lengths of linen, cloth or items of clothing that could be salvaged, and rumours abounded of one particularly fortunate lady and a casket of silk. No-one could be quite sure of the identity of the lucky beneficiary, although rumours spread like wildfire around the back streets of Durscombe that Mrs Croft, the baker's wife, had been sporting fancy undergarments in the days after the wrecking of the *Eliza May*.

Pewter plates, cutlery and tankards were shared out among numerous families, along with pots and pans from the galley.

Ropes, sails, empty barrels — everything found a new lease of life somewhere in Durscombe.

The fishermen who dared to board the *Eliza May* were well rewarded. Barrels of ales and rum were carted from the hold of the wreck and stored safely. Of course, there were a few in Durscombe who espoused and practiced temperance—so if the barrels fell into their hands they nipped over to see Giles at The Blue Bell Inn, who happily paid out money for a good product—but for everyone else, when darkness fell and the day's work had been completed, there could be much carousing.

Every day when the weather was fair, more small boats ventured out to the wreck, the fishermen picking through what they could find in the increasingly precarious hull. There were two or three confident divers in the town and they swam down to the seabed when the waves were low, hauling up further spoils to load onto the rowing boats. However—unlike the looting that occurred closer to the shore—even to the untrained eye, this plundering appeared to be more organised. The goods were brought ashore and stowed in a warehouse. People talked, but no-one was quite sure on whose authority they were stored or who the recipient might be.

For the most part nobody cared.

Except for Phineas.

He made it his business to be out and about either on the harbour or along the promenade most mornings, to his mind at least representing the municipality, keeping a general eye on what was happening. If a corpse was brought in on the tide, he organised for it to be taken to Reverend Tidwell. The bodies were cleaned, bound in cloth and buried rapidly, a necessity because as the days wore on, decomposition accelerated even in the cold water. In any event, corpses retrieved from the salt waters of Lyme Bay were not a pretty sight to behold.

And so it was that Phineas's attention was drawn to those who made repeated visits to the wreck of the *Eliza May*. He recognised the men crewing the salvage operation. Who could fail to note the man with the distinctive scar on his face, for example? These were the men on the quay, the ones Bumble had spoken with, the morning after the *Eliza May* had run onto the rocks. It therefore didn't seem too huge a leap of imagination for Phineas to conject that Bumble was the recipient of the warehouse goods.

Phineas pondered on this. He preferred to believe in the good of his fellow men, and it would not reflect well on the major's position to sanction such an operation for personal gain. It made more sense for Bumble to be involved in the recovery of the *Eliza May's* cargo only if he, as the mayor, was holding the goods temporarily to await the Receiver of Wreck. Surely Bumble's intention was to hand the goods over to that officer when he finally ventured down from London to Durscombe. Bumble wouldn't want to profit personally from such a terrible tragedy.

Would he?

Phineas wandered restlessly along the quay, day after day, spending hours studying the salvage operation, and quizzing the fishermen about what they had seen and the role they had played in the attempted rescue. To watch the rough crews of men as they stripped the wreck down to its skeleton saddened him. A once mighty ship reduced to a few beams. The young sons of those same fishermen observed their fathers and followed their instructions, picking up all that had been washed up on the beach, searching among the seaweed in the shallows or wading waist deep into the cold waters to haul items ashore.

It seemed abhorrent to be constantly on hand, inspecting all that was brought in, and yet Phineas took his obligation to the municipality—however misplaced in this case—seriously. On one notable occasion he witnessed a number of youngsters ripping items of clothing from a bloated corpse bobbing in the water. Phineas raced to the water's edge, the sea lapping over his riding boots, brandishing his crop and shouting admonishments at the lads. He sent a female bystander to search for the harbour master to help him bring the boys to task, but old Edgar Ruddle could not be found. It transpired later that he was asleep in the back room of

The Blue Bell Inn having consumed an unhealthy amount of illicitly-gained rum.

None of the other municipal officers were inclined to interfere in the recovery of the ship's goods. Phineas had a sense that with the exception of Reverend Tidwell—whose earnest disposal of the corpses with proper Christian courtesy was exemplary—nobody else cared what happened to the *Eliza May*, her goods, chattels or souls. It was a sad state of affairs, indeed.

It would be a relief to everyone when the ship had finally given up all of her secrets and disappeared into the murky depths of Lyme Bay once and for all.

7
HOLDING COURT

Mayor Bumble was holding court at Jerome's in Curzon Place. He frequented the establishment most evenings, entertaining the aldermen and other local dignitaries, minor nobles and members of the royal family down in Durscombe to take the air, alongside the wealthiest local merchants.

Tonight rain lashed against the Georgian windows and the wind rattled the old panes of glass. Outside, the air was cold enough that the driving rain might turn to snow on high ground, and those gathered inside the club were thankful for the welcoming fires, oil lamps and warm oak panelling. They huddled gratefully in the overstuffed armchairs and drank rich liquor from crystal decanters that sparkled softly in the glow from the lamps.

There was talk.

Some of the aldermen secretly chose to compare Bumble with his departed father somewhat unfavourably, but they would never have articulated these thoughts out loud or in his presence. The Bumbles, like the Tollesons, were a family of longstanding in the town, able to trace their roots back to the Norman conquest. The irony that many other families in the town—such as the Parretts, the Pyles, the Rundles and the Wilkins—were of even greater long-standing was totally lost on Bumble and his ilk. These old families from Saxon or Celtic stock didn't have a country mansion or a seat. In fact in many cases they were lucky to have a roof. For the most part they were paying rent or tithes on properties that belonged to Bumble and his aldermen friends, even in places where their forefathers had tilled the land for thousands of years.

Bumble had been elected mayor soon after his father, John, had passed away five years ago. He had inherited everything in one go: his seat, his wealth and the municipal mayoral role. He was not unhappy with his lot by any means, but he grasped every available opportunity to increase his fortune as and when circumstances allowed.

This is how it came to be that Bumble was sitting in Jerome's with a number of other like-minded gentlemen, boasting loudly about his recent fortune, thanks to the wrecking of the *Eliza May*.

Bumble grinned as Alderman Pyle lamented the loss of the ship. "Such a shame the ship is practically gone now. This weather has quickly laid waste to her. She was quite the welcome spectacle. Kept my wife amused for days. I don't believe Tilda has mentioned her requirement for a new bonnet on more than one occasion since the damned thing ran onto the rocks."

His companions roared with laughter.

"It is the same in my household!" Alderman Croker wheezed with merriment. "Mrs Croker has been camping out on the cliff in The Victoria Gardens for days now. She hasn't troubled me for anything except the carriage. It has been a blessed relief, quite honestly."

"I understand there was a cargo of silk aboard. Did your wife benefit in any other little ways, Croker?" Alderman Endicott, an older man with impressive sideburns from a mid-ranking Durscombe family, asked. Bumble narrowed his eyes at Endicott's catty attempt to wheedle information from the alderman.

"To what are you alluding? I'm sure I don't know what you mean, Sir." Croker's face was quick to flush.

Endicott waved off Croker's offence and leaned in conspiratorially. "Come, come now, Croker. We're all men of the world here," he whispered. "We know that everyone with the means, has gained a little something where they could. And some more than others." He tapped his nose and winked.

Pyle met Bumble's eye and subtly raised his eyebrows. Croker shrugged, uncomfortable at the turn of the conversation, but seated next to him, Alderman Gibbs, a merchant who lived close to the harbour and above his warehouses, nodded. "I had a chest full of cotton, but for the most part, sadly, it had been spoilt."

"I should think that's about the long and the short of it for most," Endicott sympathised.

Bumble leaned back in his chair, yawning. "Between you and me, Sirs, I have a warehouse full of saleable wares."

Pyle dropped his gaze. He'd heard such. *Crafty Bumble.* Pyle knew of Bumble's large warehouse down by the harbour, ostensibly dealing in fishing supplies, but he'd rarely seen much activity around it except for the last few days. That's where many of the goods from the *Eliza May* had evidently ended up. It all made sense now.

The other aldermen nodded in approval at Bumble's entrepreneurial spirit. They expected nothing less from the mayor.

"I decided not to leave the recovery of the goods to chance. All those barbarians from the back streets and peasants from the moor," he jerked his head, indicating the north. "I had some men collect my interests."

"For a price, no doubt," Gibbs chipped in. He wouldn't have paid for goods, even if he'd had the cash to spare. Rumours abounded of his growing debts, especially here at Jerome's.

"Oh indeed. A fair price. And no questions asked. There's plenty of profit in that warehouse." Bumble raised his glass, a self-satisfied glint in his eye.

"And what will you do with it?" asked Gibbs. He didn't possess much of an entrepreneurial spirit, truth to tell, and had little idea of how modern commerce worked. But then if the reverse had been true, he wouldn't have been facing financial ruin, after all.

"Ah fret not, my dear Gibbs. There are markets I can look to. Nothing will be wasted, and I'll turn a pretty penny."

Gibbs nodded, attempting to look knowledgeable. "Of course. One can only feel a little sorry for the owner of the vessel, I suppose, and the company that chartered it. Their losses must be heavy."

"Pish. That's what the Lloyds list is for," Endicott sneered. "Am I correct, mayor?"

"Indeed you are Endicott." Bumble met the eyes of the other men gathered around him, each in turn. He took the measure of them, before raising a finger, pretending to be struck by a sudden thought. "Why, 'tis a shame we can't organise a wreck a month. Just think of it." He directed his words to Pyle. "We'd all be rich, gentlemen. Exceedingly rich."

Pyle nodded in admiration. "Exceedingly," he repeated. He liked that idea very much.

8
AN UNEASY NIGHT

Emily, sitting at her dressing table, absently pulled a brush through her thick hair. She was tired this evening, and in spite of the fire burning in her bedroom, her hands were numb with the chill. Having accompanied Marmaduke to an engagement in Exeter, the return drive had been cold and arduous in the rain and wind.

Behind her, Mary sorted through the evening's clothes. Emily observed her through the mirror, admiring the young servant's efficiency. She was competent and no-nonsense, a quick learner, happy to do anything. This was exactly why Emily had chosen Mary as her lady's maid of course. She'd replaced a girl who had found herself in the family way and been summarily dismissed by the housekeeper.

Mary, sensing Emily's scrutiny, glanced shyly up and held out a cloak and a dress.

"I'll have these brushed clean for you, Ma'am. Do you need anything else this evening? A nightcap?"

"No, Mary. Thank you."

"Let me help you into bed then, Ma'am?"

Emily didn't want the girl to witness her reluctance to settle down for the night. "Yes."

Since the occasion on the cliff edge, nearly a week previously, Emily had suffered with night trauma. The kind she'd often experienced as a girl. Now, as then, she lay awake for hours, fearful that if she closed her eyes, bad dreams would startle her awake. The lack of sleep had begun to take its toll, so much so that she had been considering asking the doctor for a sleeping draught. She hated to do so.

Catching sight of her own ghostly reflection in the mirror, she dropped her brush on the dressing table with a slight clatter. The noise jarred her already frayed nerves and she sucked in a nervy breath. Sensing her mistress's jitters, Mary breezed over and tidied the brush away in a drawer, before turning down the bedcovers and helping Emily into bed.

Pulling the covers up to Emily's chest, Mary spoke softly. "Ma'am, I discovered something about the new inhabitant at Myrtle Lodge."

Emily perked up. "Oh yes?"

"Turns out she's not really new to Durscombe at all. Her name is Agatha Wick, Ma'am. Apparently, she is the granddaughter of Tansy Wick and used to live in the cottage years ago."

"Agatha has returned?" Emily blinked in surprise.

"Do you know the lady, Ma'am?"

Emily regarded her servant with slight exasperation. Did the girl know nothing of the history of the town? "Yes," she replied shortly, but hearing her own irritation she quickly recovered herself. Mary couldn't help being so young. She would not remember Agatha residing at Myrtle Lodge. *Was it such a long time ago?* Emily thought. *Am I that old?*

"Yes," she repeated calmly, striving for patience. "I knew Agatha. When we were girls."

Girls together. Agatha and Emily were of an age.

"She has her niece with her, apparently. A pretty young lady I hear."

"Is that so?" Emily's heart thumped in her chest.

"Of about sixteen summers they say." Mary chattered away happily, oblivious of her mistress's sudden consternation.

Dozens of questions ran through Emily's mind. *Why has Agatha returned now? Did she marry? Has she forgiven me?*

"You are certain it is Agatha Wick?" Emily needed this confirmed. *If it is, then—*

"Yes ma'am. I heard it from Mr Pyle's under-gardener, who had it from Lord Tolleson's housekeeper, I believe. Did you hear that Mr Wiggins, Lord Tolleson's butler, has been taken proper bad, Ma'am?"

"No, I hadn't heard that. I'm sad for them. Mr Wiggins is a splendid servant. Lord Tolleson will no doubt be—"

"Devastated I've heard, Ma'am."

"You've certainly heard a great deal," Emily chided. "Be careful what you repeat and to whom, Mary. It might bring you enormous embarrassment if you mentioned the wrong thing to the wrong person. And a servant who can keep their employer's confidence is worth their weight in gold. Remember that."

Mary blushed hot and red. "Oh yes, Ma'am! I would never—"

"I'm not insinuating for one moment that you would, Mary. Only it pays to remember."

"Yes Ma'am. Sorry Ma'am. I will remember."

"You may leave me now."

"Thank you Ma'am." Mary picked up the cloak and dress and tip-toed to the door, but turned when she reached it, her right-hand hovering uncertainly on the knob. "I promise you Madam, I would never ever betray your confidence."

"And that's all I can ask from you, isn't it? Goodnight Mary. Sleep well."

"You too, Ma'am." Mary dropped a curtsey, and still looking flushed and a little perturbed, sped from the room clutching Emily's soiled clothes.

Emily sank back onto her pillows. Many years had passed since she'd last seen Agatha. There had been minimal correspondence, all of it formal. She hadn't been aware of Agatha's intention to return to Myrtle Lodge.

Hadn't they agreed she would stay away?

What would her return mean for Emily? Her life, although dull, had settled into pattern and routine. Agatha would disturb the dust, she was certain of that.

Emily had warmed through at last. The memories of her girlhood, brought on by the news of Agatha's return, lulled her somewhat and she drifted softly into sleep. Deeper. Deeper still.

Dreaming...

Light as a feather, she floated under a warm sun in the bluest of skies, immersed in the sea, a sea sparkling and pure, a sea that truly reflected the brilliance of the sky. There was no swell to worry her, just a slight rhythmic ululation, and although she found herself alone, she experienced no sense of alarm. She was safe.

She allowed the waves to gently carry her where they willed. Here. There. Her body supported by the water. Every movement she made was light and effortless.

How wonderful to feel this free. Unencumbered. And so totally alone. To have no-one around demanding her time and attention, no-one bidding her to do this or that, or to attend here or visit there. It was a remarkable luxury to feel her body in this state of relaxion; there was no corsetry, there were no buttons, or ties or ribbons, nothing binding her. Had she ever been this free in her life?

Perhaps as a child. Out of Lily's sight.

Perhaps with Tansy.

And so she drifted, more relaxed than she'd felt in a week or more, and fell deeper yet into her dream, lulled by the solace and the soft rocking of her body in the waves.

Until she was no longer alone.

A figure swam towards her, skimming across the waves at first

... but the dream shifted and Emily watched in confusion. He—instinctively she knew him as a man, even before she could properly see him—travelled closer and closer, manoeuvring gracefully yet quickly. Surely it wasn't feasible, but rather than swim across the top of the water, it appeared to Emily as though he swam towards her, *up* from the seabed through the crystal clear saltwater. Given the ease of his movements, she might have mistaken him for some kind of mythical merman. In spite of his garb—for he must have been a sailor with his white blouson and dark trousers billowing around him—he propelled himself effortlessly to the surface. His arms and legs were strong, his skin tanned. Closer and closer he swam towards her, his dark eyes wide open, meeting her curious gaze. A long line of bubbles escaped behind him as he approached.

Oddly, she didn't feel threatened. In fact her heart skipped in happy anticipation. He burst through the water with a sizeable splash, rocketed into the air, spitting water like a seal, then breathing in a deep joyous lungful of air. Finally he faced her, laughing in melodic delight.

Emily smiled at him, shy in the face of his beauty. Handsome, with rugged even features and full lips, he had a slick of chestnut hair, worn shoulder length and tied at the nape of his neck with a limp blue ribbon.

And he was young. Younger than she. And so incredibly vital in every way.

He reached for her, his wet fingers tangling in hers. Emily jerked, gasping at his touch, as a powerful charge passed between them. When he didn't pull her close, only held her at arm's length, she had an urge to wrap herself around him and press the length of her body against his. She longed to feel his chest against hers, experience the heat of his loins, but instead they only floated together in the warm sea, with him holding her at arms' length. Emily stared into his dark brown eyes, flecked with gold. His were eyes she might drown in.

She could have remained there for an eternity. She wanted to.

But as suddenly as he'd appeared, he was gone again. He slipped below the waves and disappeared. Emily thrashed around, searching for him, plunging her head into the water, his loss a keening on her soul. The sea began to cool rapidly as the sun slipped west, the glorious pastel of the skies deepening and brightening.

She floated on her front, ducking under from time to time.

Where are you? Where have you gone?

The sea was the palest of sapphire blues, as clear as the stillest of freshwater lakes. As the sky lit up the dying day, flaming bright orange and red in a final defiance of the oncoming night, Emily gave her body permission to sink. She jack-knifed and cut through the water. Far below, she could discern the rainbow colours of the seabed, coral and seaweed, so beautiful and green and fresh, the perfect complement to the blue.

Has he abandoned me forever?

No. There!

There at the bottom of the sea ... someone moving.

He was waiting for her.

Come to me!

His eyes met hers, burning into her soul, but as he attempted to return to her, his foot somehow became entangled in a length of seaweed. He twisted and rolled in the water, thrashed about, valiantly trying to free himself. All to naught. The seaweed wrapped itself around his calf and yanked him deeper. He flailed, lashing out, and as he did so, his shirt changed in form and began to billow around him like a cloud.

No longer a shirt, but a long white dress ... no ... a shroud...

Emily screamed in horror, bubbles bursting around her face. She kicked for the surface, her lungs burning for air, never taking her eyes from her sailor. His chestnut hair floated loose, streaming around his face, growing in length, tendrils that circled his head like a halo.

No longer the sailor. Not a man after all, but a beautiful woman, vaguely familiar, blonde and as pale as a ghost, her lips a cold blue. Buffeted by an unseen current, rocking this way and that, she gazed up at Emily through haunted eyes, lifting her arms, beseeching her. Snarled in the seaweed she could only mutely plead for help.

I can't leave her here.

Emily reached for the woman's outstretched arm, but a good twelve or so feet separated them. The woman wriggled and strained against the slippery green fastening that held her so tightly, her arm reaching further and further ... even further ... impossibly long ...

Emily recoiled from the limb, snaking its way eel-like towards her. She kicked for the surface, suddenly acutely aware of the most salient of facts.

"I can't swim!" she screamed; her voice frantic, unaware in her dream of the absurdity of this statement. "I can't help you."

The woman's eyes widened, smouldering with a savage contempt, blackening with hatred as Emily struggled towards the surface. "I can't save you," Emily cried over and over. "I'm so sorry."

The woman opened her mouth. She might have intended to scream in fury, but instead spewed forth a jet of black ink, polluting the water with its stinking briny foulness. Emily burst through the surface, screeching and gasping for air, swallowing mouthfuls of rancid salt-water, coughing and choking and shivering with fear. She smacked at the surface of the sea, desperate to get away from the woman's clutches, but the sudden recollection within the dream of her inability to swim appeared to have sealed her fate. Helpless, she began to sink again. Below her, the woman waited, her twisted face a mask of obscene glee, arms straining upwards, eager to receive Emily.

Emily held her breath, battling against the pull of a vicious riptide, but the lure of the deep was stronger than she was. She struggled to see as the water became increasingly clouded, and in her panic began to lose sense of up and down and left and right. The more she twisted and flayed, the more disturbed the water became. Once crystal clear, it had churned itself up into a murky soup-like consistency, and the other woman had disappeared from her view, leaving Emily disoriented. Fingers splayed, Emily fought against the brine that held her in its grasp, desperate for air. She kicked wildly. She must find the surface or die. Her movements became increasingly violent. Desperate. But to no avail. The dream held Emily powerless. She could do nothing. The woman would catch her and hold her against her will. Forever.

Finally, with no other option available to her, Emily inhaled.

Instead of water she sucked in a lungful of air and screamed into the dark. She sat up in bed, flailing around, tangled in the bedclothes until, coming to her senses, she realised where she was.

Gasping, shaking, retching, she scratched at her throat, panting and sobbing, desperately trying to calm herself in case someone should hear. Drawing shuddering breaths, she focused on the dimming light of the fire that smouldered in the grate. It cast dim shadows over all that was familiar, and she scanned the room, the sight of her belongings offered some consolation. Eventually she began to quieten, and in time found she could breathe normally again. Her panic subsided.

The rain spattered against the window. She drew strength from the commonplace sound because she knew well that the house would otherwise be too quiet. Marmaduke was in his own room. The servants would be asleep too.

But at least at Hollydene she could never be completely alone.

She wondered what time it was. Difficult to tell in the darkness. Flinging back her bedclothes, she slipped from her bed and, wrapping a shawl around her shoulders, she moved to the window and gazed out into the darkness. There was no sign of the moon, the clouds too low and heavy, the rain falling relentlessly. She watched it awhile, lulled by its rhythm.

The fire had died down to the point of no return. Shivering, Emily realised sleep would elude her this night. Instead she dragged the bedcover from her bed and draped herself in it, before curling up in her armchair intending to keep watch out of the window.

Searching for those who sought her.

The lost sailors are out there.

It wasn't until the cold grey dawn stole over the horizon and she could hear the faint sounds of servants beginning their daily routines that she finally felt secure enough to sleep.

9
THE FINAL VOYAGE OF THE ELIZA MAY

First light at last.

Sally Parrett, washerwoman at The Blue Bell Inn and cousin to Agatha and Emily, rocked on her heels as a bitter breeze, gusting inland, buffeted her. Fronds of fading blonde hair worked loose by the wind, tangled in her lashes and stuck to her lips.

She barely noticed.

She'd spent the night at home, anxiety swamping her weariness, huddled by the fireplace, awaiting the dawn, listening to the wind and the rain as it penetrated every crack between the floorboards of her cottage. She hadn't slept a wink. It had been the longest of nights—and she'd known a few in her time—but now that the first grimy promise of daylight had arrived at long last, she had come to take her place at the quayside to see her man home, like many a worried wife before her.

Thomas.

She sometimes thought she had loved him all her life. From the sweet gentle boy she had known at church as a child, playing together in the narrow lanes in the old town or frolicking on the sandy beach, to the weathered and whiskered fisherman he had grown into. In many ways he was a rough man, coarse language and coarser hands, but when he reached for Sally he was a lamb. A loving puppy of a man, a true reflection of the gentle children they had been.

As the rain died away and the dawn took hold, the sky turned from black to grey to watery blue, with hints of pink and orange. The wind, in the last throes of temper, forced the clouds to skitter across the sky like frightened sheep. Sally would stand on this spot all day if necessary; she would stare straight out for miles, past the harbour to her left, past the spit-head, past the beach and the rocks to her right. Her never-wearying gaze would rake across the whole of Lyme Bay. She would note every vessel that came and went, the rowing boats and yachts, trawlers, and yes, further out, perhaps she would even spy a tall ship.

But fear had lodged deep in her soul.

And why not? Sally Parrett was Tansy Wick's granddaughter after all. She could watch those boats and ships arrive into the harbour from now until the end of time. She could watch them take their moorings, watch the fishermen haul the night's catch ashore. But her heart understood what her head did not. Her watch would be long and her husband's boat would not be one of them. Not this day. Not ever. Thomas wasn't coming home. He had ventured out on some mysterious mission yesterday afternoon, and he hadn't returned. His small boat had not been found.

Sally knew he had sailed for the *Eliza May* and she was certain somebody else had asked him to do so, because he would never have ventured there under any normal circumstances. Not by himself. Not when it was so dangerous.

He had a home. He had a hearth. He had a family. Admittedly his family consisted only of Sally and their one child, Stanley, but their son was a good boy and he made up in large part for the babies that Sally hadn't carried full term. She had been lucky to survive four miscarriages and a still birth, but she was strong. She'd always been a robust woman, like her mother and her grandmother afore her. Sally's love for her menfolk had kept her alive. In times of poor health, she had grasped a hold of this love she harboured and clung on for all it was worth. Her Thomas would do the same. Because he loved her too.

Broken fingernails tangled in the wool, Sally gripped her shawl tightly, refusing to acknowledge her increasing unease. Why in God's name had Thomas agreed to go out there when there was absolutely no need? No-one had been left on the ship to rescue. It had been a week since the *Eliza May* had run onto the rocks and there had been no survivors. The bodies were no longer washing up on the beach. If someone had asked Thomas to go out there, what had been the purpose? The ship was dangerous. He shouldn't have gone. He shouldn't have left her.

What had he been thinking?

Meg Powell, Sally's young neighbour, came to stand beside her, followed by Maisie Parrett, Thomas's sister-in-law. Maisie slipped her arm through Sally's and held her tightly. Gradually the news spread, and other women from The Lanes came to join them. They huddled together, pale-faced, eyes watering from the cold wind, locked in solidarity, woman for woman, wife for wife, mother for mother.

The tide had come in and several fishermen, avoiding eye contact with the womenfolk, ventured out to begin their business for the day. Of Thomas and his boat there was no sign. A gentle swell rocked what was left of the *Eliza May* and Sally observed several other little boats, drifting gently in and out of the rocks, navigated by men she had known all her life, engaged in the search for her husband.

But they couldn't find him. She knew in her heart of hearts they never would.

Neighbours brought her hearty soup and freshly mashed tea, but she turned all sustenance away. Giles, the landlord of The Blue Bell Inn, offered her ale but she had no interest. She merely waited, swaying backwards and forwards in her clogs. The cold settled deeply into the very marrow of her bones, her pale-green eyes locked on the fragile wreck and the men who searched every nook and cranny among the rocks, and who ventured into hidden inlets under the cliffs or scoured the harbour walls, hunting for Thomas or any sign of his boat.

At some time after midday when the tide was at its highest, there came a warning shout from a fisherman in one of the rowing boats. A harsh grinding sound caused the air above Durscombe to vibrate. Sally and her entourage rushed to the spit, gazing in helpless horror as the remainder of the *Eliza May*, lodged hard against the rocks for the past eight days or so, finally lifted herself free, her back broken. She drifted a short distance, a grotesque parody of the graceful ship she'd once been. Then, twisting violently onto her starboard side she sank beneath the surface of the sea. The sudden displacement of the water caused a tidal surge against the rocks and cliff face. A wave rushed outwards in a fan shape, eventually washing up on the beach with a roar.

Sally's anguished scream ripped through the afternoon. She clawed at the air in front of her, fingers hooked, as though she could lift the wreck from the seabed, and somehow extricate her husband from his watery grave. The other women rushed to encircle her, to enclose her grief. They held their friend tightly as her knees gave way.

"Not my Thomas. Not my Thomas," she begged, her voice muffled against Maisie Parrott's shoulder.

"Come Sally, come away," pleaded Meg, "don't watch no more."

Maisie, tears streaming down her own face for the loss of her husband's brother, knelt alongside Sally, her knees digging painfully into the cobbles as she gripped Sally tightly. "Meg's right. Let's go, my darling. We'll go home. We'll send word to Stanley. He needs to know." She turned her head and raised her eyebrows at another neighbour who nodded brusquely and sped away to search out the boy and bring him to his mother.

"Fetch her in here," Giles instructed the women, holding the door of the inn open. "Let's get a brandy inside of her and get her warm. That's all we can do now."

All we can do now.

Sally processed the words. Her second scream tore at the bowels of the town. Fishermen dipped their heads at the sound, while their hardened wives dashed away their own tears. Durscombe was a town that fully comprehended pain such as this. Sally's heart had surely broken for the loss of the man who had been her whole world, and as a community they grieved with her.

10
A CHARITABLE ACT

The gathering in the municipal chambers later that day was a solemn affair. After the buoyancy of the meeting in the club the previous evening, the change of mood was noticeably marked. Every one of the municipal officers had turned out, and now they gathered around the huge walnut table in the conference room.

Phineas stared around at everyone, his face doleful.

"What on earth possessed the man to go out there yesterday afternoon?" he asked his neighbours. "At this time of year the light would have failed quickly, and last night's storm had been forecast. He couldn't have hoped to navigate around the wreck and the rocks in the dark."

"By all accounts he climbed aboard." Pyle shrugged and swilled the brandy around in his glass. He'd heard this information second-hand at the quay this morning. He couldn't understand the fuss the other aldermen were making.

"But he was alone. Why would he have been so foolish?" Phineas asked.

"Who knows what gets into men's heads when they have a yearning to do something," Bumble cut in. "He was a seasoned fisherman. He knew the sea. And he would surely have understood that the *Eliza May's* hull wouldn't hold out much longer."

"It's folly, is what it is. This is symptomatic of the greed that devours the working men these days, gentlemen. Their need to line their own pockets," Endicott grumbled. Some of his colleagues nodded, frowning in agreement. "Trying to loot the last of the cargo aboard the ship, no doubt."

"It goes against God." Endicott's be-whiskered and ancient father-in-law, Colonel Haringey, piped up. Phineas had not been party to the discussions in the club the previous evening, but Alderman Gibbs had and now he blinked at the old man. Had they forgotten Bumble's well-stocked warehouse. Did Bumble fly in the face of God too?

Phineas cleared his throat, but Bumble jumped in neatly before he could say anything. "In light of this terrible tragedy and given that Thomas Parrett was a fine upstanding member of this community, I think it is beholden on us to help his widow at this time. No doubt she has debts to pay, her class always do, and rent to find for her landlord—"

"Would that be yourself?" Pyle asked, and a number of men snorted.

"If it isn't you Pyle, it must surely be the mayor," Endicott sniggered. Pyle and Bumble were among the two most prominent landlords in the town.

Bumble ignored the interruption. "We really ought to offer a ... tribute of some description. A few guineas to help her through the next few months until she can find her feet. What say you all?"

"Oh that's a splendid idea, Bumble," murmured Endicott. "Very generous." Croker and the other aldermen, with the exception of Pyle, nodded in agreement.

"Do we need a formal proposal?" Endicott asked, nodding at John Jeremy the clerk, busily taking notes in the corner of the room.

"Oh do move it on, man," Pyle grimaced, wanting to get the official business over so he could attend to matters of the stomach. "I'll second it anyhow."

Jeremy busily scribbled the instructions down on a sheet of vellum in his tiny handwriting.

"Who will pay a visit to the widow?" asked Bumble. "I feel the obligation falls to my office as mayor ..." he trailed off. Nobody took umbrage at the idea. He hurried on, "And yet unfortunately I have a great deal of business to attend to over the next few days."

An uncomfortable silence followed his words as each of the aldermen considered how such a meeting with the grieving widow might play out. One by one they baulked at the opportunity Bumble offered to deputise for him.

Except for Phineas.

He gazed about him in consternation. Were these gentlemen not blessed with wives who might accompany them? Phineas had no soothing presence to accompany him. No gentle female to offer the consolation that would be needed. Phineas puffed his cheeks out. He considered himself as far from an expert on women as it was possible for a man to be. In the eighteen months that Phineas and Lucy Rose Poynton had suffered through their marriage, Phineas had discovered very little of use as regards the fairer sex. He had grown up without a mother or siblings, he had no aunts. Women were a complete mystery to him, and he considered himself ill-equipped to deal with them at the best of times, let alone when they began wailing and caterwauling.

"I'll attend Mrs Parrett," he offered, surprising even himself. More than anything he abhorred a lack of decorum, and he considered it ill-mannered in the extreme for a member of the council not to present themselves to the grieving widow in her time of greatest need. To that end, he elected to take it upon himself to offer comfort. Perhaps, in lieu of a wife, he would ask Reverend Tidwell to accompany him.

And perhaps he would ask Matthew Salter to drive him.

The thought of seeing Matthew again improved the prospect of visiting the new widow, immensely.

As it turned out, Reverend Tidwell had been summoned to an urgent matter elsewhere, so it was left to Phineas to pay the municipality's courtesy call on Sally Parrett by himself. Fortunately, Matthew had not been otherwise engaged. Mrs Gwynne had located him in the garden, and he had been instructed to oversee the preparation of the carriage and horses and deliver Phineas into town for his meeting.

Phineas elected to sit up front with Matthew and they drove in silence, an amiable silence on Phineas's part, more respectful on Matthew's. Phineas observed Matthew's straight back, the proud angle of his head and his strong tanned hands, dirt under his fingernails as he held the reins with a confident ease. At times he clucked at the horses, or spoke to urge them on, and Phineas warmed to the man's soft words. Eventually—too soon for Phineas's liking—they came to a stop outside The Blue Bell Inn.

Phineas had it on good authority that Sally Parrett lived along Thimble Lane, one of the narrow and winding streets behind the pub. The higgledy-piggledy houses on the lane backed onto a river that fed directly into the sea. Thimble Lane, like several others in the vicinity, consisted of dozens of terraced painted cottages, tiny and claustrophobic, standing face-to-face and back-to-back. The lane itself was a maximum of eight feet from one side to the other, just wide enough for a mule and cart to pass through. This was where the majority of the fishermen and their families resided. Despite their size and pitifully cramped location, many of the tiny cottages were cosy enough. However, the further away from the sea you ventured, the deeper into The Lanes and the dark shadows you crept, the more pitiful the dwellings became, and the more likely you were to stumble upon Durscombe's poor and impoverished families.

"Do you wish me to accompany you, sir?" asked Matthew, evidently concerned for Phineas's wellbeing.

Phineas toyed with the idea. He would enjoy the young man's company but perhaps it couldn't be expected of him. On occasion The Lanes had something of a reputation, indeed they did, and

Matthew would make a wonderful bodyguard, but Phineas couldn't imagine anything untoward occurring in broad daylight.

"No thank you, Matthew. I believe I had better attend Mrs Parrett by myself. I will remain with her but a short time."

"As you wish, Sir. I'll water the horses at the inn." Matthew took up the reins to lead them away. Phineas nodded and took his leave, slipping reluctantly down Thimble Lane, alone.

The houses pushed in on Phineas the further along the lane he ventured. Gloom descended rapidly. The light of the day struggled to breach the shadows, leading to the false impression of permanent night. Phineas glanced around, unsure exactly which of the cottages belonged to the Parretts, until he encountered a gaggle of women wearing aprons and sombre expressions, chatting quietly among themselves. He imagined this was an indication that he must be close.

One of the women broke off from the small group. Recognising him, she bobbed a curtsey. "Good afternoon to you, Lord Tolleson. What brings you down here, Sir?"

Outnumbered by the curious women, Phineas pulled himself up to his full height and puffed his chest out in an effort to appear official. "I come on municipality business, madam. I am seeking the residence of Mrs Parrett."

The woman pulled a glum face and indicated the next door along. The outside of this cottage had been freshly whitewashed, and the windows were clean. "That's Sally's house. Her sister-in-law is sitting with her. I'll announce you if you wish, Sir."

Phineas nodded gratefully. "I'd be obliged to you, madam."

The woman knocked once and entered the premises without waiting for a response. It appeared this was acceptable down here, where everyone knew everyone else, and the intimate goings-on of your neighbours were fodder for all. Phineas, straining to hear, caught some quiet conversation from within before the helpful woman returned and beckoned to him.

"This way, Sir."

Phineas stepped up into the cottage. It was tiny, little more than one room downstairs serving as both kitchen and living area, but comfortable enough, and as clean inside as out. Sally obviously took pride in her home. A fire had been stoked high in the grate, and two well-polished rocking chairs had been placed close to it. Now a woman sat in each, a bright rag rug on the floor between them. Besides the chairs there was little other furniture, save a rough wooden table, well-scrubbed, with matching rough-hewn benches on either side. An older boy of approximately sixteen years of age was sitting at the table, his eyes red-rimmed. The boy stood as Phineas entered.

Phineas nodded at him and the lad slumped back to the bench. Phineas turned his attention to the women by the fire.

It was obvious which of them was Sally Parrett. Phineas would have known just by looking at her even if he hadn't recognised her from her cleaning and occasional serving duties at The Blue Bell Inn. She had sunk into herself, her eyes hollow with grief. She twisted her hands in her lap as Phineas removed his hat.

"Mrs Parrett," Phineas began. The mere utterance of his words —or perhaps it was gentle tone of his voice—caused a flood of tears to cascade down the woman's face. "Sally, if I may?"

Sally waved her hand at the other women present, dismissing them. The neighbour, who had introduced Phineas, squeezed Sally's arm. "Give me a holler if you need anything, my love," she said, heading for the door.

The other woman in the room, the sister-in-law, vacated her chair. Phineas began to protest but she indicated her seat. "Please," she said. "I need to stretch my legs a little, anyhow. I'll be back soon, Sally." She followed her neighbour, quietly closing the front door behind her.

Phineas, feeling awkward at the idea of sitting in Sally's presence, strolled over to the fireplace and leant against the mantle instead, his hat clutched tightly in one hand.

"I've come on behalf of the municipality, Sally. To offer you our deepest condolences. Thomas was a decent man, widely respected in the town."

Sally nodded, catching her breath. Her mouth worked for a while, and she swallowed hard a few times, before finally choking out her thanks.

"You can be proud of him, Sally. I know Reverend Tidwell will pay him a good tribute."

"But there's no body," Sally whispered, clamping a hand to her mouth. "How can he have a Christian burial with no body?"

Phineas grimaced. Of course. The fact that the body had not yet been recovered—or even sighted—did present something of a problem. It might turn up, but then again, it might not. "Well," Phineas replied, carefully considering his words, "we've seen these circumstances before." Durscombe had lost fishermen in the past, most of them well out to sea. "Reverend Tidwell will still deliver a sermon for Thomas, and we can all remember him."

Sally hiccoughed for a moment before nodding reluctantly. "That's the best we can do for him, I know that."

"Reverend Tidwell will—"

"Yes." Sally cut him off. "The Reverend visited earlier, Sir. He's attending to Mrs Scorch just now. She's dying I believe."

"Oh, I'm dreadfully sorry to hear that." Phineas genuinely was. Mrs Scorch was a woman in her forties, well known at St Michael's for her stunning flower arrangements. Her husband played the organ. They had a horde of children. How on earth would Mr Scorch cope?

Media vita in morte sumus.

The tiny cottage, the heat of the fire, pushed in on Phineas. He struggled for air for a second. In the midst of so much sorrow, with death and dying on all sides, he suddenly longed for fresh air and freedom. He pulled at his tight collar and cleared his throat.

Oh for a brisk ride across his estate on his best horse, Crab. The feel of the sea breeze in his hair.

Later.

He blinked, resuming his duty, turning his attention back to the widow. "The municipality have extended a financial tribute to you, Sally, in recognition of the high regard we all had for Thomas.

I have it here." Phineas produced a small velvet purse, heavy with the coins tied within. The purse clinked as Phineas held it out. Sally regarded the purse through empty eyes, and Phineas recognised the blankness of that look. Money could never be a substitute for the loss of her husband.

"It is intended to keep you going for a few months. Help you with the rent."

"Yes? From the municipality? That is most kind, Sir." Tears glistened on her cheeks, her voice little more than an anguished whisper that Phineas had to strain to hear. "And what then? How will we survive without a man's wage?"

Phineas glanced uncomfortably around the room, wondering how much the rent could be on a cottage as tiny as this. His gaze settled on the lad who hadn't moved at all since Phineas arrived. He'd simply been sitting quietly, listening to the exchange between his mother and the municipal officer.

"This is ...?"

The boy stood, slim, all thin limbs, and yet taller than Phineas already, with the promise of more height to come. "I beg your pardon, Sir," Sally said. "This is Stanley. My son."

Phineas studied the lad. He could see an obvious likeness to Thomas with the sandy coloured hair and brilliant blue eyes. "Do you work, Stanley?"

Stanley moved out from behind the bench to take his place beside his mother.

"I run errands, Sir, for the landlord at The Blue Bell, and for the harbour master, and anyone else who will pay."

It wasn't a livelihood, that much was obvious.

"You don't intend to work on the trawlers like your father?"

"No, he doesn't," Sally said sharply. "Thomas said it was too hard a life. He wanted something else for Stanley."

But he hadn't found the lad an apprenticeship somewhere? "Is he a good boy, Sally?" Phineas asked kindly, knowing full well what the answer would be.

"Oh he is, Sir. He is! He works hard and he's been taught to be polite and he has done some schooling. We're proud of him, Sir." Her voice broke once more. "Thomas and I. We're proud of him." Sally clutched a sodden handkerchief to her forehead and shook with emotion.

Phineas found himself overwhelmed by her obvious sorrow, and at a loss for words that might offer consolation. He had no experience of such a depth of grief, given he had never lost anyone who meant as much to him as Thomas obviously had to Sally. Not his wife, nor his father. Losing his mother was a long distant memory. His father had been a decent enough man, although distant and aloof, and sometimes Phineas wished he could be a little cooler where his own emotions were concerned. Unfortunately, the highly sensitive Phineas found his feelings ran away with him constantly.

Therefore Sally's distress struck a chord with Phineas, and he welled up in sympathy. He cleared his throat abruptly, searching for some way to fix the problem. "Ha! Perhaps Sally," he ventured, "when you can spare Stanley, you would send him to me at Hawkerne Hall? I mean, if you're both agreeable. We can take him on in the house. I'm sure Wiggy ... Mr Wiggins ... when he's better ... can find useful work for him somewhere." The poor old man still languished in bed in his attic room. "We always need more servants in the house or garden or stables." That much was true at any rate. Phineas could never understand why, but Mrs Gwynne always required extra assistance somewhere.

Sally mopped at her eyes. "That's too kind, Sir. A regular wage would be a true blessing, wouldn't it Stanley? And a chance to learn new skills too. He likes animals, does Stanley. Don't you, son?"

Stanley stared at Phineas, wide-eyed, his face bleak. He nodded.

Phineas smiled, attempting to reassure the lad. "Good. That's sorted then. Come whenever you can Stanley and we'll get you started in the stables. I have dogs too. You'll like them."

Stanley nodded and offered a watery grimace in return.

"Good," Phineas repeated with relief. It satisfied him to have offered practical support. "Settled." He assumed his official voice once more and lifted the purse. "If it pleases you, I will leave this on the table here, Sally. The municipality will help in any way we can, but ..." his voice softened, "if you need anything else, do please approach me personally."

"Thank you, sir. We are much obliged to you. And to the municipality too." Sally sank into her chair wearily, as though her spine had given up.

Phineas, understanding his welcome had come to an end, nodded at the widow, shook Stanley's hand, and took his leave. He stooped as he exited the cottage through the low door, although he didn't need to, and placed his hat firmly on his head. The crowd of women gathered in the gloomy alleyway outside appeared to have swelled in number. They gazed at him curiously. Phineas, feeling vulnerable at the sight of so many of them, recoiled. However, they were all good natured, respectful and solemn, and parted the way easily enough. He tipped his hat and several of them bid him a good day.

He hurried back along the narrow passage, the sound of the sea growing louder with every step. It was a relief to stumble out of the cramped confines of Thimble Lane onto the cobbles in front of The Blue Bell Inn, although it wasn't much lighter out there either. The sky had turned an ominous grey, and rain had begun to fall from the sky in thick ropes. Phineas spotted Matthew, standing alone, talking with the horses, his soft hat plastered against his head and his coat soaked through. Phineas had expected him to have taken shelter in the comfort of The Blue Bell Inn and avail himself of their hospitality, certainly most of the men who usually drove him around would have, given half the opportunity.

Matthew bobbed his head when he recognised Phineas and stood to attention, before hurrying to open the carriage door as Phineas drew level with him. Phineas was pleased they had opted for the covered carriage rather than an open one.

"I'm afraid you're rather wet, Matthew," Phineas murmured as Matthew arranged the foot plate. "I'm sorry I was so long."

"Don't mention it, Sir." The rain dripped down Matthew's nose, running onto his top lip. Phineas paused long enough to observe the full curve of the younger man's mouth and his strong jaw. "It was kind of you to visit Mrs Parrett."

"The least I can do, poor woman."

Phineas's gaze lingered longer than necessary. Matthew met his eyes and Phineas blushed pink. Remembering himself, he nodded sharply, and climbed into the carriage. Matthew, his face blank, carefully closed the door and disappeared from view. The carriage rocked as he climbed up to take his place behind the horses. Phineas settled back. The carriage lurched, and Matthew pulled at the horses to turn them about.

The going became harder for the horses once they had left the quay and the cobbles behind them. The road up the hill to Hawkerne Hall and onwards to the moor was quite often a river of mud at this time of year. They hadn't journeyed far out of town when the carriage passed a woman holding her skirts up to ankle height and trying desperately to navigate up the bank to a dryer place and away from the spray of passing traffic.

Phineas banged on the roof of the carriage to attract Matthew's attention, then opened the window and ordered him to rein the horses in.

He didn't recognise the woman. Pleasantly rounded, with a rich mane of reddy-brown hair and remarkably green eyes, she looked to be his own age, mid-to-late thirties. Not that Phineas was much of a judge of a woman's age. She studied the carriage with surprise rather than suspicion, as Matthew jumped down beside her.

"Excuse me, Madam?" Phineas called. "Where are you travelling? Could we offer you shelter in the comfort of the carriage?"

The woman examined Phineas and then turned to regard Matthew with open interest. If she was distrustful of their intentions, she didn't show it.

"Are you new to the area, Madam?" Phineas asked courteously, indicating to Matthew that he should open the door. The woman obviously had no idea who he was.

"I am ... newly returned, Sir," she replied in a surprisingly rich voice. Deep. Calm. Authoritative. Phineas warmed to the timbre of it immediately. "I had forgotten how changeable the weather can be by the coast. One moment fine, the next hailstones."

"Pray, please let us assist you. I am Phineas Tolleson, and this is my trusty servant, Matthew Salter. We would be happy to transport you wherever you wish. I'm inclined to assume you cannot be venturing far, not on foot at any rate."

"Lord Tolleson? From Hawkerne Hall, of course." The woman smiled and bobbed a curtsey, albeit with some difficulty in the mud. "I am Agatha Wick, of Myrtle Lodge."

"Agatha Wick?" Phineas wracked his memory. He imagined he had heard her name before, and of course nobody could have lived in Durscombe without knowing of Tansy Wick. "Tansy—"

"Was my grandmother. I have inherited the lodge."

Phineas nodded. "We are neighbours, after a fashion. I am pleased to make your acquaintance, Miss Wick. But won't you step inside out of the rain?"

Matthew helped Agatha into the carriage. She sat directly opposite Phineas and shivered dramatically. Up close, her face appeared fashionably pale beneath her dark sodden bonnet. Phineas judged her not unattractive, although others might suggest she had passed her prime.

"I know of Myrtle Lodge, of course, but I can't say I've ever had the pleasure of visiting," Phineas said.

"You know of the Lodge?" Agatha asked, and there was something instinctive about her reaction to his words, something almost defensive. She caught herself immediately, and softened her response with a smile, but even so this did not reach her eyes.

"Well, yes ..." Phineas didn't understand the sudden tension.

"You know of its reputation, I presume." Agatha scrutinized Phineas's face. "I'm sure you've heard the rumours."

"Of—?"

"Of witchcraft."

Phineas jerked in surprise to hear her state it so bluntly. Of course he had heard such things. "Yes. Rumours. Supposition. One really never believes everything one hears ..." His voice drifted away.

"Although, in the case of Tansy Wick, it is more than likely to be true," Agatha responded crisply, holding his gaze.

Phineas grimaced inwardly. *True? What was she saying? What did she mean? Tansy* had *been a witch?*

This conversation hadn't started well. Tales abounded about the mysterious goings-on at Myrtle Lodge over the centuries. Locally it had garnered a certain historical notoriety. Yet here was Tansy's granddaughter and she did not present as a three-horned demon.

As if she could read his mind, Agatha snorted and turned her head to stare at the passing scenery.

Phineas, grateful for the reprieve from her piercing examination, decided to change tack slightly. "How long have you been back at Myrtle Lodge?"

"Not quite a fortnight as yet. I arrived on the evening the *Eliza May* ran onto the rocks."

Phineas raised his eyebrows. "A dramatic arrival indeed. How are you enjoying your return to Durscombe?"

"It is certainly sleepy after Lincoln."

"Ah, you were in Lincoln? I muddled around with a chap at Christ Church College who hailed from up that way."

"Did you ever visit Lincolnshire?"

"Alas, no. But now you have returned home, Lincoln's loss is surely Durscombe's gain."

Agatha made a small noise in her throat that might have been a laugh. "That remains to be seen."

Phineas found himself scrabbling around again for some way to change the subject. Women were an unknown country indeed, and this one especially so. While not entirely devoid of social manners, she was cool in a way that intimidated poor Phineas.

"Have you no carriage for transportation, Miss Wick?"

"I do have one, Sir. I simply have no man to drive for me. I have a stable but no horse and no-one to take care of a horse. Not at this time at any rate."

"Oh I see." Phineas sighed with relief for surely here was a problem he could solve. "Madam, if you'll allow me? I have just this hour come from town where I have been with Sally Parrett whose husband was unfortunately lost the evening before last."

Agatha sat upright, then leaned forwards, her forehead creasing in shock. "Sally's husband is lost? I had not heard. I am truly sorry."

"You are acquainted with Mrs Parrett, then?" Phineas sounded surprised. Agatha nodded but didn't explain their relationship. He continued, "Her husband is missing at sea, and the presumption is that he drowned, most likely at the site of the *Eliza May*. Mrs Parrett has a son aged sixteen or so and I have agreed to apprentice him to my stables. I would happily loan you this lad, Stanley Parrett, if you are ever in need. Would that be of any use to you, at all? He is a handy boy, I am told." The horses had come to a standstill and Phineas indicated Myrtle Lodge. "And you and I *are* neighbours after all."

This time Agatha's smile seemed genuine. It set light to her eyes. A curious warmth emanated from her, and once again Phineas became aware of the sensation that this strange woman soothed him. He welcomed the odd notion. It had been a trying day and he was in need of some comforting.

"That is most kind of you, Lord Tolleson. If you are sure it is of no inconvenience to you, I would be most obliged. I have my ward at home to think of too, and the season is turning. It is a major inconvenience to be without a carriage in this poor weather."

"It most certainly is." Phineas beamed happily. "Well, it is settled. Just send word to me personally any time you have need of

Stanley. I will ensure that Mr Redman in the stables will make the lad's services available to you."

"Thank you, sir. You are kind." The carriage door opened and there was Matthew waiting to hand Agatha down. Once safely on the ground, she turned back to Phineas. "And by the same token, Lord Tolleson, you must call in and have tea with us. We will always be at home to you. No need to make a fuss. We are not *that* kind of household. Good day to you, sir." She laughed lightly and scurried into the house, attempting to further avoid the rain.

Phineas watched her go, noting the peeling paint around the window frames and the overgrown ivy that clogged the brickwork. Myrtle Lodge, having been run down over a few years, was in dire need of some serious care and attention. He was touched by Agatha's invitation to tea. His lack of a spouse meant he was continually asked to social occasions, but only by matrons trying to avail themselves of a wealthy husband for their daughters. This was quite the direst of situations to find oneself in. Phineas hated the duplicity of these occasions. No-one was ever what they seemed, least of all him.

Agatha Wick, however, interested him. No fuss, no frills. At once aloof, and yet wearing her heart openly on her sleeve. Phineas had a feeling he would always know where he stood with her.

He liked that.

11
A VISITATION

Sally lay in the marital bed, little more than a wooden framed box that took up most of her tiny bedroom, staring at the ceiling. She had extinguished her candle and the scent of tallow hung in the air. Besides the bed and a small cupboard where she and Thomas hung their clothes on hooks, the room only had the space to accommodate a hand-carved rocking chair. Once upon a time, when Stanley had still been on the breast, she had rocked him to sleep there. One tall window, overlooking the house facing them across Thimble Lane, was set into the thick wall, and a heavy curtain hung against the bottom half. It afforded her a little privacy. Lying on the bed, it was possible to see the night sky above her neighbour's roof.

She shivered with exhaustion. Grief had done that to her. Her head ached and her joints were stiff with the bone deep weariness that comes with the worst of losses. The bed seemed cold and impossibly huge without Thomas sprawled beside her. She missed the familiar weight of him and his soft snore. Soft, unless he'd had a few, for then he would make noise enough to wake the neighbours. She'd had to try to roll him onto his side so that she could get some sleep too.

Not tonight.

Not ever again.

Needing time alone, Sally had sent everyone away. She knew they would return at first light, making tea, offering to cook, fussing over her. They meant well, of course they did. But could anything ever fill the huge void that a lover's death leaves in your life.

The window was closed, as it always was, but Sally imagined she could hear the sea. This close to the seafront, the roar of the waves was a constant. Day in and day out, night in and night out. The smell of the sea pervaded her whole house too. Thomas always carried the scent of brine and fish on his skin, not quite masking his unique musky fragrance. She had grown to love the blend of those perfumes over the years. Not so his clothes when he returned from the sea, for they infused the house until she drowned them in her copper. She fought a losing battle in any case, simply opening the front door brought the outside in, both the acrid stench of smoke from her neighbours' fires, and the rich salty aroma of the ocean beyond.

What would become of her now? Without Thomas? She would surely have been lost. Except ...

It was kind of Phineas to offer to help her. He had gone above and beyond what the aldermen from the municipality would have normally offered, she was certain of that. They were not all good men, those aldermen, far from it. They feathered their own nests, took advantage of poorer folk in the town.

Exploitation, Thomas had called it. He liked to read, and he knew about these things. Knew there were men unhappy with their lot in different parts of the country. He told her that some of them had been fighting for their rights. They'd been involved in clashes, he'd said. There'd been hangings in reprisal, and this had made Thomas angry. Sally couldn't imagine such things. She didn't like to think of men being hurt, but she had to respect Thomas and his strong belief in truth and justice. He'd often spoken of such ideas, and of his desire for Stanley to have something more in life than Thomas had. He desperately wished for

Stanley to find decent work and be respected by other men. To leave Durscombe and make more of himself than his father.

What would Thomas make of Stanley being apprenticed to Lord Tolleson? She had a feeling he would not have approved, but in his absence—Damn him! Damn him!—she had to make the decision to safeguard her future and the future of her son. Lord Tolleson was a good man, everyone said so, and Stanley would have an opportunity to learn new skills. That could be all that mattered.

At least for the time being.

Sally closed her eyes. Tomorrow was another day; she would need her strength. If only she could sleep. If only ...

Maybe she dozed.

The smell of seawater grew stronger, the stagnant scent of rock pools around the harbour under a hot sun, and too much seaweed. Perhaps she had left the window open after all. She shifted slightly, drowsily making an attempt to sit up. She would have to close the window, it would be cold towards dawn, but her limbs were heavy, like lead weights. She could barely move.

From the corner of the room came the familiar creak of her rocking chair. Her eyes fluttered open. "Stanley?" she asked. The room was lighter than before. The sky had cleared, and a huge moon had risen above the rooftops. Its rays banished the shadows.

It wasn't Stanley.

Her husband slouched in the rocking chair by the window. He was dressed in the thick woollen jumper she had knitted for him over the summer. She could remember the weight of the wool in her lap and how it had made her unbearably warm during the sultry June evenings. He wore his heavy leather boots too. She never allowed him to wear them upstairs.

"Thomas?" She sat up in happy surprise, woozy with tiredness and lack of food, but delirious with joy. It had all been a ghastly mistake, then? He had not been on board the *Eliza May* when she sank beneath the waves? Had he been out on his boat somewhere else? Maybe he had drifted out into Lyme Bay, perhaps further away. "Thomas?" she asked again.

He isn't lost. He is here.

Except there was something very much amiss.

Thomas rocked forwards in the chair, his head dropping to his chest.

Perturbed, Sally swung herself out of the warmth of her bed. The bedroom was chilly, the windows wide open. She stepped towards him; her bare feet quiet on the floor. But within two steps she found herself standing in a pool of water. She looked down in surprise. It was a substantial puddle. Thomas had been sitting here a while and dripping onto the floor while she slept. Why had he not removed his clothes? Dried himself off?

"You must be cold, love," she said and reached out to him. Her hand brushed his cheek and she recoiled in shock. He wasn't just cold, he was freezing.

He didn't move. "Thomas?" she repeated, this time in a whisper. "Are you hurt?"

She knelt in front of him, her nightdress draped in the water, and leaned in to take a better look at him.

His skin was bleached and dried out, thanks to the salt from the sea. Thin blue veins threaded through his cheeks, and were apparent on the backs of his hands too. Grains of sand were evident around his hairline. Small pieces of seaweed had become tangled in his hair and attached to his jumper.

Sally ducked her head to gaze into the face of the husband she adored. "Thomas?" she coaxed. "Are you alright?"

Finally he lifted his face, swivelling to meet her searching look. She threw herself backwards in a panic, skittering across the floor like a crab in her urgent need to get away from him.

Dear God! Where are his eyes?

Pressing her back to the door, she regarded him with absolute horror, her heart thumping hard in her chest, her hand to her mouth, unable to wrench her gaze away. At first she imagined he had no eyes at all, but now she realised the whites had shrivelled, leaving him with the kind of eyes she'd see on a fish when her husband brought them home; inky and black and bottomless.

And dead.

Thomas stood and lurched towards her. Strands of seaweed, grains of sand and small pieces of wood dropped from him, lightly scattering around the floor as he moved. His movements, once so measured, were ungainly. He stumbled forwards, progressing slowly, like someone deeply asleep.

Sally opened her mouth to scream but caught herself. Stanley slept in the tiny room next to hers. She must protect him at all costs. Jamming her fist into her mouth, she bit down on it, tasting the salt of her own slick blood between her teeth, whimpering as what had been her husband reached out to her.

He grasped her hair, yanking her to her feet.

And leaned in to kiss her.

12
A RELUCTANT PROMENADE

Emily, lost in thought, stared absently into the distance and stirred her tea. The fire crackled, but apart from that, the ringing of her silver spoon as it circled the fine china of her cup, and the rustle of Marmaduke's newspaper, the room was silent. Marmaduke had feasted well, as he always did at breakfast. Emily, as usual, had settled for a single soft-boiled egg. She'd barely touched it. She sipped at her tea however, enjoying its delicate aroma.

From out in the hallway came the deep chime of the antique grandfather clock, a Fliss family heirloom. Marmaduke set down his newspaper and regarded his wife, pondering the pensive expression on her pale face, her eyes ringed with shadows.

He made an attempt at conversation. "You look very pretty today, dearest," he began. "That dress is most becoming on you."

Emily crinkled her eyes and turned up her mouth in some semblance of a smile. "Thank you." She held his gaze long enough for him to look away, disconcerted. He picked up his newspaper once more.

They lapsed into silence. Emily finished her tea and poured herself another. The tinkling of the spoon resumed. Marmaduke replaced the paper on the table, and he tried once more to assert himself. "What are your plans today?"

Emily shrugged. "I do not have any plans, Mr Fliss. I shall probably pass the day quietly here."

"You do not walk in The Victoria Gardens anymore? I had thought you enjoyed them most days."

She shrugged; her eyebrows drawn together, irritated by his line of questioning. "It is tiresome. At this time of year there is nothing pretty to view, and no-one of interest to observe."

"I suppose you are right, my dear." Marmaduke faltered. "I fear you will be very bored here alone all day, however. I have to be at the municipal offices this morning, but what about later? Why not accompany me on a walk in Durscombe? Come down to the harbour with me and let us watch the activity there."

Emily grimaced. "I cannot imagine for one moment why you think that might be of interest to me. Watching the people work is vulgar, Marmaduke."

"I find there is always something interesting to observe at the harbour. The men fishing or unloading the boats. The women repairing the nets and hunting for shellfish. People buying, people selling. It's a ... a veritable microcosm of life, my dear. Fascinating."

Emily stirred her tea once more. The spoon sounded angry this time, grinding against the delicate china.

Marmaduke hesitated to voice his concern. "You look pale, my dearest. I am worried about you."

"I'm not sleeping, that is all." Emily brushed his worry aside.

"Would you like me to arrange for the doctor to call? Perhaps he could prescribe a sleeping draught for you."

"I have no need of potions, Marmaduke." Emily's cold fury could scarcely be concealed. She bit her tongue and brought herself under control. He regarded her for a moment longer, then nodded and reached for his newspaper once more. The room softened into stillness. Marmaduke stared determinedly at the small print.

The silence between husband and wife lengthened.

Finally, Emily lay her teaspoon on her saucer, groaning inwardly.

It was unfair of her; she could see that. It wasn't as if she hadn't already considered talking to the doctor about her sleeping issue and the night terrors she had been experiencing. Perhaps a walk would do her good. The *Eliza May* had completely submerged and there was no longer anything to see, nothing that would play upon her fears. It seemed unlikely that the strange hallucination she had experienced in The Victoria Gardens would trouble her again.

"I beg your pardon, husband," Emily roused Marmaduke, her tone more accommodating. "I am perhaps overtired. I will be happy to join you for a promenade, this afternoon. You are correct of course. The sea air will do me good. It may help me to sleep."

Marmaduke sighed, audibly relieved. "I will arrange the carriage, my dear."

A clear, cold day greeted Mr and Mrs Fliss as they alighted from their carriage. What little warmth still existed in the sun failed to heat the air. The startling blue of the sea presented a stark contrast to the brick red of the cliffs. The tiniest of waves lapped gently against the sand. After the ferocity of the recent storms, it was pleasant to enjoy this late autumn afternoon.

Emily knew it pleased Marmaduke that she had made an effort. She had dressed carefully in a rich wine-coloured dress and jacket in the latest design, with a matching velvet hat made by the best milliner in Exeter. Thanks to Mary's skill with a hairbrush and pins, her thick hair had been coiled in a complicated and fashionable style. She looked prettily seasonal and she knew her husband enjoyed the fact that she turned heads wherever she went.

For that matter, so did she. Social modesty would never allow her to admit it, of course, but she did enjoy the attention lavished her way. She recognized the vanity of it, but she was too like her mother in that regard, seeking approval and appreciation—even adoration—where she could find it.

Now, strolling beside her husband she tried her best to relax, scolding herself for not making more of an effort to get out after the episode at The Victoria Gardens. No wonder she had been unable to sleep, cooped up in the house day after day with nothing to do, and dying of boredom. What had she been thinking that day? They had brought her home in a near hysterical state and poor Mary had been beside herself too.

Emily was an intelligent woman. She could only assume she had experienced some weird hallucination. That had to be the rational explanation. Irrationally, her shifting of unease, and the pounding of blood in her veins whenever she thought of the hands appearing above the edge of the cliff, coupled with the knowledge she had since discovered that Agatha Wick had returned to Durscombe, suggested that the reality of what had happened might lie elsewhere.

Breathing deeply of the tangy salt air, Emily stared around herself at the familiar sights. Durscombe was a small town but the harbour had long been the hub of industry here. At key points of the day, it became a hive of activity. Fishing of course, is a tidal affair, and boats crewed by rugged fishermen continued to come and go as long as they could access the slipways. Other men and women worked on the quay, hauling in the catch and efficiently packing everything up in wooden crates to be loaded onto drays for rapid dispatch inland.

Emily paused to watch the women, always mesmerised by their strength and capacity for hard work. They grafted alongside their menfolk, packing fish and fixing nets, but she was especially captivated by those women fishing for shellfish, cockles, winkles and the like. Even in this chilly weather, they had their sleeves and skirts rolled up, exposing the skin of their brown arms and their calves and ankles to the elements.

Promenading in her tight corset, her pantaloons and petticoats and button up boots, Emily could barely remember the sensation of paddling at the shoreline, the tiny pebbles beneath her toes, the shock of the cold water ... the freedom to splash her cousins. She could hardly call to mind her grandmother, Tansy, gathering seaweed, her long silver and black hair loose in the wind, her smile knowing ...

She and Marmaduke sauntered the length of the quay, all the way along the promenade to the cliffs before starting back. Marmaduke bowed to people they recognised, hailing those he knew well, but Emily, although always acutely aware when anyone looked her way, largely avoided meeting anyone's eye. If she perceived some absolute social requirement, or she sensed her husband's disapproval, Emily bowed her head and offered a small absent smile, praying all the while that her husband would walk on and not engage them in conversation.

She did not feel inclined to make small talk with anyone.

Including her husband.

"It is a beautiful afternoon, Mrs Fliss. I think we shall see a spectacular sunset in an hour or so." Marmaduke appeared oblivious to his wife's mood.

"It is," Emily agreed, hiding her irritation. Why could they not walk in silence?

"The days grow ever shorter," Marmaduke continued.

Emily stood patiently beside her husband as he paused, staring out across the harbour and the rocks to the vast sea beyond, obviously intent on enjoying the view. Despite her intention not to dwell on what had happened in the bay previously, her eye was inexorably drawn to the spot where the *Eliza May* had lain for so many nights. Of the wreck there appeared to be no trace, and yet she could plainly see something on the rocks. A small shape, moving.

Emily stepped forward, frowning. Perhaps a seal or something similar? But no, whatever it was had pushed itself to a standing position. She squinted into the distance. A man! His back to the shore. Too far away to make out his features, she could tell only that his hair was light and he wore a heavy knitted jumper in the style so favoured by the fishermen here. The rocks were treacherous out there, but the man balanced confidently, seemingly unconcerned about his predicament. She couldn't see his boat.

Is he marooned? Does he need rescuing? Why does no-one else see him?

Emily lifted her hand to point him out to her husband. Before she could say a word, the fisherman turned about and stared directly at her.

She squeaked in fear. Marmaduke, who had walked on a little, turned back. "Emily? What is it?"

Emily gestured at the rocks. "That man. Do you see him?"

Marmaduke followed the direction of her finger. Did she mean the rocks close to the cliffs where the *Eliza May* had lain? There was nobody out there.

"There! Do you not see him?" Emily's voice rose as she jabbed at the air. "How do you not?" Marmaduke scanned the harbour and then the cliffs. There were people on the beach but that lay away from the position Emily indicated. "On the rocks!" Emily pointed. "Over there."

The man on the rocks lifted his arm, saluting Emily. She shrieked again, louder this time, skipping backwards. "Marmaduke, you must be able to see him. A fisherman. He's right there I tell you! On those rocks where the ship grounded!"

Marmaduke frowned. "I can see no fisherman. In fact, I see no-one at all."

Emily caught her breath and wrenched her eyes from the man on the rocks. She studied her husband's puzzled face. Could he be playing games with her? Marmaduke stared back at her, his brow creasing in concern.

Emily flicked her eyes at the fisherman on the rocks and back again to Marmaduke, her heart beating rapidly, sweat prickling on her brow. Marmaduke reached for her arm. She recoiled from him, unsure of his intentions.

"Mrs Fliss?" Marmaduke wrapped his fingers around her upper arm.

She lifted her hands and tried to pull away, her body rigid with tension. For one awkward moment he thought she would scream and cause a scene. She twisted in his grasp, stared at the rocks, then her head rolled on her shoulders and she became limp, collapsing into a half-swoon. Marmaduke caught her before she could fall. Supporting her weight, he glanced quickly around, seeking assistance.

"Are you faint?" Marmaduke's voice reached her, but from far away. "Can you make it to the inn?"

Emily stirred herself, fighting the grey fog that encroached on her vision, her face pale. She stared up at him, her eyes wide with fear. "No. No. Call the carriage. Take me home. I will recover there."

Holding her tightly, an arm around her waist, Marmaduke lurched along the prom in the direction of his carriage and driver. Emily, thankfully, could just about walk. They made slow but steady progress until his way was barred by a woman in dark clothing. She stood in front of them, clasping a sizeable wicker basket and staring at the sea, oblivious to his urgent trajectory.

"Excuse me, Madam?" Marmaduke interrupted the woman's contemplation. "Would you allow us to come past, please?" Emily lolled against him, her hand to her head, eyes closed.

The woman whirled about. "I do apologise." She stood back, but then held an arm out in surprise. "Why, it is Mr and Mrs Fliss, is it not? I most humbly beg your pardons. I did not see you. That was most remiss of me." She frowned at Emily—whose head lolled against Marmaduke's shoulder, her skin grey—appraising the situation. "Is Mrs Fliss ill? Good heavens. Please allow me to assist you."

Before Marmaduke Fliss could protest, the woman had switched her basket to her opposite hand and taken a firm grip of Emily's other arm. Slowly, the odd threesome walked the last dozen or so yards towards the carriage where their driver waited. Marmaduke and the driver handed Emily up into the carriage, and Agatha tucked a blanket around her and made her comfortable, before stepping down and standing back to allow Marmaduke entry.

She smiled up at him as he settled onto his seat. Marmaduke had the sense that he recognised her, although he could not place her directly.

"Thank you," he said. "However, you have the better of me Madam, for I confess I do not believe I have had the pleasure of your acquaintance."

"Neither has your good wife for many a year, Mr Fliss. My name is ..."

"Agatha?" Emily, coming back to full consciousness, blinked to clear her vision. She hauled herself into an upright sitting position, leaning towards the door, urgently trying to clear her greyed-out, fuzzy sight. "Agatha?" She reached for the other woman, her thin white fingers woozily scratching at the air between them. "Agatha! You saw him, didn't you? The fisherman? I know you did. You must have."

"Yes, I did." Agatha Wick reached forward and clasped her cousin's hand. "I saw him."

13

A SON'S CONCERN

Agatha wiped her hands on her apron and quietly considered the young lad in front of her. Stanley Parrott, always unsure of his welcome, had inched cautiously into the kitchen, having been ushered through the back door by Hannah. He hovered in front of the blazing fire, twisting a worn cap in his thin hands and sniffing the air as if he could fill his belly up by dint of inhaling the housekeeper's baking. Not that the boy was starving, by any means. The food at Hawkerne Hall must have been suiting him for he had grown taller and wider in the weeks since Lord Tolleson had hired him, and now his trousers were too short and his jacket frayed around the edges. Agatha made a mental note to find the boy new clothes.

Phineas had been as good as his word. Initially Agatha had only requested assistance from Stanley on the few occasions she needed to get to and from town when the weather was inclement, or when she had parcels to carry. Now Stanley popped by from time to time to ask if she had any jobs around the house that required a helping hand. He had been, as Phineas had said he would be, a good keen lad and a credit to his parents.

"Why Stanley?" Agatha said. "This is early for you to call. I have no need of you today."

"Miss Agatha," he replied, dipping his head. "Lord Tolleson sent me, Miss. He said I was to help you with your garden work."

Agatha raised her eyebrows. "Did he indeed? I never asked him to." Agatha was perfectly happy to look after the herb garden, and Hannah kept her eye on the kitchen garden, but the truth was neither of them had the time nor the strength to hack back the rest of the overgrown grounds. Agatha had considered hiring a gardener, but she wasn't keen on having too many servants around. They tended to gossip.

"Pardon me, Miss. I think he said your front outlook was a little wild."

Agatha hid her smile. Hannah, meanwhile, listening to the exchange with her back to them, snorted in amusement.

"I see. Well, I must agree with Lord Tolleson in this instance. We are in need of assistance with our 'front outlook'. It is most thoughtful of him. You must be sure to pass on my thanks, Stanley."

"I will, Miss." Stanley hesitated, glancing first at Hannah at the stove and then towards the window and the perceived wilds beyond. "Where would you like me to start?"

"Have you eaten breakfast, Stanley?" Agatha asked.

"Yes Miss." Stanley watched Hannah as she sawed though a fresh loaf with her large bread knife.

"Well I have no doubt you could do with some more to keep you going as you work. Sit down with us, then we'll all venture out into the garden and create a plan of attack, shall we?"

From that day forth, Stanley turned up at Myrtle Lodge several times a week. He worked hard in the garden for hours without ever complaining. Agatha appreciated his help, and the grounds were much improved. She sought his compliance by ensuring Hannah provided him with regular and enormous meals. Agatha had no experience of boys, and Flora only ever picked at her food like a sparrow, so she enjoyed watching Stanley's attempts to satisfy his voracious appetite.

Today however, something clearly seemed amiss with the lad. Stanley didn't venture into the kitchen with his usual cheerful greeting. He didn't hang on to Hannah's apron strings, watching anxiously until she presented him with his now customary second breakfast of the day. Instead he walked quietly into the garden and aimed straight for a patch of brambles at the side of the house. He attacked them with a ferocity Agatha had never witnessed in the boy before.

Agatha could sense his troubled mood and it worried her. She remained in the library in order to observe him from the window, allowing him the space she felt he needed in order to take out his frustration and anger on the worst of the brambles. This seemed an appropriate solution, after all, what possible harm could he do to them? At midday when she suspected he had exhausted himself with over-exertion, she slipped out to check on him.

As she approached, he stood upright and dashed his hand at his face. Could he be crying? Agatha paused and cleared her throat, pretending not to have seen the movement. He ducked his head, but not before she had spotted his red eyes.

"It's looking so much better out here, Stanley," she praised him. "Hannah has some bacon frying in the kitchen. Why not take a break and have something to eat with us?"

Stanley avoided looking directly at her but forced a smile. "I'm not hungry, Miss Agatha."

"Not hungry, Stanley? Then something must be seriously amiss." She kept her voice quiet and calm.

Stanley shook his head but remained mute. Agatha stepped a little closer to him. They were of a height. She ducked her head to peer up into his face, forcing him to look at her. "Is it Lord Tolleson? Has something happened at Hawkerne House that is troubling you?"

"Oh no, Miss! Lord Tolleson is a good man."

"And the other servants are good to you?"

"They are, Miss."

"Then the only thing that could trouble you so, is your Mother." Agatha waited. Stanley fidgeted. "Sally? She is not well?"

Stanley exhaled, releasing a juddering rush of air. The weight of the world was encapsulated in that one sound. All the pain he had kept inside, his inability to do anything for his mother, all of it so eloquently expressed in one single breath.

"What is the problem? She grieves for your father. That is natural. Grief causes us to behave in strange ways at times." Agatha recalled rumours about the memorial held in Thomas's honour. According to gossip, relayed to Agatha's ears through Hannah, Sally had been inconsolable, shouting gibberish during the service. Many had thought her drunk.

Stanley rushed to explain. "Dr Giddens has declared her mad. He says he can't help her. She hasn't worked for weeks, Miss Agatha. Not at The Blue Bell. Not anywhere. She brings in no money. I give her all of mine. But she isn't caring for herself either, Miss. And I can't do that for her. I don't know how to. And she is shouting and crying and the neighbours are quite vexed. They will take her away, Miss."

"Who will take her away—?" Agatha interjected. "Who might 'they' be?"

"The doctor said they'll take her away to the Lunatic Asylum in Exeter. And they will, I know they will. She's—" Stanley choked back a sob and lashed out at the bramble bush. His hand caught on a thorn and ripped a jagged and deep gash down the length of his palm.

He cried out, clasping his good hand around the injured one.

Agatha sucked in her breath, experiencing his pain as though it were her own. The physical sharp scratch from the wayward bramble, the mental anguish for his mother. Momentarily, she clutched at her own hand, but quickly dropped it when she realised what she was doing. Instead she reached into her sleeve for her handkerchief and passed it to the boy.

"We must get that seen to, Stanley. Let's go into the kitchen and Hannah will clean and bind it for you."

"It's alright, Miss. I don't want to be any trouble."

Agatha lay her palm on his shoulder. "It is no trouble at all. I am ordering you to have it attended to. And then, after you have had something to eat and drink and you feel better refreshed, you can come and work on this bramble again. Maybe be a little kinder to it next time and it will not take its vengeance so."

Stanley's brow furrowed as he considered her, fully aware of the stories that surrounded the Wicks and Myrtle Lodge. However, the curl of her mouth told him she jested.

"I mean what I say," she said, her voice firm. "Come inside."

"Yes Miss. But my mother—"

"I will visit your mother this afternoon," Agatha soothed him. "We can ask Hannah to pack some food for her. You mustn't worry." She regarded the boy solemnly. "What will be, will be. You understand that?"

Stanley sniffed, his face downcast, seeming far older than his sixteen years. As he walked with a heavy tread towards the back door, clutching his hand, Agatha sighed. He was so young to face so much heartbreak, a boy on the cusp of manhood.

But hadn't they all been there once? And survived?

Stanley would too.

After all, he was a Wick like the rest of them.

Agatha navigated her way through Thimble Lane with some difficulty. Numerous groups of women gathered together, huddled close to front doors. They, in combination with the hordes of children running, skipping and hollering through the narrow lane, made the going difficult. Agatha swung a large basket of goodies in each hand and manoeuvred around the obstacles carefully, nodding at any of the friendlier women who made eye-contact. Others stared at her curiously, their eyes drawn to the baskets brimming with wrapped parcels, each partially covered with a cloth. Hannah had helped her put together a variety of provisions for Sally, and Agatha wanted to deliver everything to her cottage intact.

Agatha tried her best not to breathe through her nose as she walked. She found the stink of fish and brine overpowering down here. She guessed that the majority of the families hereabouts survived on seafood and some vegetables but rarely saw meat. It made economic sense, given that most families living at this end of the town were involved in fishing, or made a living from the sea, one way or another.

Agatha knocked on the door of Sally's cottage. She waited. There was no answer. Stanley had said she probably wouldn't come to the door or call out in greeting. She remained cocooned in her chair by the fire all day, he said, and slept there most nights too.

If she managed to sleep at all.

Agatha had waited long enough. Ignoring the eyes of numerous onlookers as they drilled into her back, she set one basket on the ground and pushed the door of the cottage open. She stepped through into the silence, met only by stale air and shadows. No lamps had been lit and the prevailing gloom was only mitigated by a dull glow from the fire, as the dying embers burned to ash.

She could just about discern a bump on the chair. An object covered in blankets.

Agatha paused a moment to allow her eyes to adjust to the darkness and then placed her baskets on the table. She found a lamp there, and quickly rooted through her packages to extract a jar of oil. Deftly she filled the lamp, trimmed the wick and lit it. The light warmed the room and allowed Agatha to focus.

Sally, swaddled in a blanket, stared at her from the very depths of despair, through bleak eyes set in deep hollows. Scattered around the floor, Agatha could now see broken pottery and torn clothing. The pages of a book, probably her Bible, were shredded and strewn everywhere. How could anyone stumble upon this scene and not conclude that Sally had indeed gone insane?

And the final straw? The place stank of human waste. How had the widow been reduced to this? Where were her friends? Her neighbours? How long since any of them had visited Sally here?

Agatha, moving quietly, knelt next to the rocking chair. "Sally?" she whispered. "Do you know me?"

Sally stared at her, her expression dull. Agatha thought she would remain mute, or deny her, but eventually she shifted position. Her mouth opened and closed. Finally her eyes cleared. She blinked and answered in little more than a croak.

"Agatha."

"That's right. It's Agatha."

"Yes." Sally lifted a wan hand, reaching to cup Agatha's face. "Why have you come now? No-one comes anymore."

"Stanley visits, doesn't he?"

"Stanley is a good boy." Sally slouched over and began to keen. Agatha blinked into this new pain, the great racking sobs that fought to erupt from Sally's tiny rib cage. It pained her. This poor widow, her cousin, was entirely lost. She needed urgent help.

"He loves you, Sally." Agatha told her, stroking her arm, but Sally only cried harder. Agatha frowned, perplexed at the woman's despair. "Sally? Hush now. What is it? Can you tell me?"

Sally hiccoughed and shuddered, before gripping Agatha's hands so tightly that Agatha winced in pain. Sally pulled herself straighter, staring deeply into her cousin's troubled eyes, her own wild with the heat of a sudden fever. "He will be an orphan, Agatha," she hissed, and Agatha recoiled. "Yes!" Sally hissed. "You must look out for him. Say you will? Make sure he stays good and true?"

"But Sally ..." Agatha tried to reason.

Sally flinched and tore her gaze away, shrieking loudly as she curled up and hid her face once more.

"Sally?" Agatha repeated, stroking her hair.

"Can you hear him?" Sally mumbled.

"Hear who?" Agatha glanced around. "Stanley? He's not here. There's no-one here but me, my darling."

Whimpering, Sally slowly lifted her face. She squinted beyond Agatha, studying the wall behind her cousin in abject horror, almost as though she could see someone there.

"What did you mean?" Agatha asked, shivering with cold despite her warm shawl. The fire was virtually out and the air in the room had turned frigid. "Why will Stanley be an orphan, Sally? Where do you think you're going?" She shook Sally's hands gently, trying to distract her and bring her attention back to the moment. Sally stared up at her, lost and dejected and unable to reply. "You cannot go anywhere," Agatha reiterated. "Stanley needs you."

Sally's chin drooped to her chest again, tears rolling down her cheeks. Agatha smoothed the woman's hair before standing, determined to do something useful. She began by rolling up her sleeves. "The first thing we are going to do is get some food inside you, and then we'll clean this cottage ... and you too. A clean house will help you feel better, Sally. More positive."

Agatha trimmed and lit another lamp, before finding a clean pot to heat the soup that Hannah had sent. She laid a fresh fire and fuelled it with the paper she collected from the floor. In order to pump the water she would need, Agatha had to take a bucket out to the communal well at the end of Thimble Lane, but she quickly returned and set to cleaning the dining table and laying out bread and cheese, a freshly baked pie and some apples and pears.

One of the young neighbours had followed Agatha back into the cottage and now she stood looking in wonder at the spread and then at Sally.

"How do you do?" Agatha asked, mildly amused by the young woman's cheek. Perhaps she'd been sent in by the other women waiting outside for news.

"She's tapped, Miss." The woman indicated Sally with a shrug. "The grief has got her bad."

"She just needs some help, that's all." Agatha replied tartly. "Perhaps you would care to assist me rather than stand there and ogle?" The woman eyed the food on the table again, and that gave Agatha an idea. "I tell you what. What's your name?"

"Meg, Miss." Meg made a small curtsey, unsure as to Agatha's station.

"Well, look here, Meg. If you help me, I will let you have some of this food, and I'll send some more for you to share with Sally tomorrow."

"You will?" Meg narrowed her eyes.

"Yes. I'll send Stanley down from my kitchen with a feast, and you may share in it."

Meg considered the offer for a second, before deciding it had to be in her best interests. She nodded. "Of course. It's the neighbourly thing to do, isn't it, Miss?"

Agatha bit her tongue and set Meg to sweeping and mopping the floor. Like all of the women down here in The Lanes, she was fast and efficient when it came to chores, and within thirty minutes the room had been tidied and scrubbed. It smelt a great deal fresher, too. Meanwhile, Agatha helped Sally to strip, wash and change her dress, and led her to the table to partake of the soup.

When Sally didn't have much appetite, Agatha sent most of the food away with Meg, but only after demanding the younger woman reiterate her promise to help. Agatha kept back the milk and a jug of apple juice.

Agatha couldn't persuade Sally to eat anymore, no matter how she tried. She poured a beaker of freshly squeezed apple juice for her and took a seat across the table, taking her hand, and holding out the vessel.

"So tell me what is happening to you, Sally. You're a strong woman, I can't imagine why you have fallen to pieces in this way."

"Is losing my husband not enough for you?" Sally asked, closing her eyes and rubbing her face.

"It's more than that," Agatha responded gently and nudged the juice Sally's way. Reluctantly, Sally took a sip. Agatha leaned back. "There is more to it. I feel there is." Sally shrugged and the women regarded each other, their shared history hanging in the space between them. "Don't lie to me, Sally. I want to get to the bottom of this."

Sally moaned softly. Her eyelids beginning to droop, her head rolling. "He visits me at night. Every night. He comes here to the cottage."

Agatha sat bolt upright. "What are you saying? Thomas visits you?"

"Thomas, yes. My husband." Sally's words slurred, and Agatha reached out to take the apple juice from her before it slipped from her grasp. "He comes here."

"He's dead, Sally." Agatha trod carefully. "He can't come here."

Sally laughed, a bitter sound, entirely without humour. "You know better than anyone that's just not true. He comes *here*. To visit *me*. Every night. As soon as I close my eyes, he's here." Her breath caught in her throat. "And every time ... he's soaking wet ... like he ... just walked straight out of the sea."

The hairs on Agatha's neck prickled, and a chill ran down her spine. "Does he say anything?"

"Nothing. He never says ... anything." Sally's chin nodded to her shoulder and her eyelids drooped.

Agatha reached out to steady her cousin. "What does he want? Do you know?"

Sally blinked awake. "Want? I don't know. I can't be sure. But I think ... I think he wants ... me." Sally's head sagged again and her eyes closed fully, but quick as a flash she jumped as though someone had pricked her with a pin. She struggled to focus on Agatha, her face twisting with anguish. "What have you done to me, Agatha? I mustn't sleep! I mustn't!"

Agatha pursed her lips. She had asked Hannah to mix a sleeping draught in with the apple juice. She took Sally's hands once more. "You must sleep if you need to, Sally. I will stay here with you all night. If Thomas comes he'll have us both to contend with. All will be well, I promise you."

Sally shook her head, but she was too weak and weary to

protest any more. Agatha dragged Sally over to her chair by the fire, covering her with a blanket once more. She stoked the fire and lit a few more candles, intent on banishing the worst of the shadows from the small room. Then she took a seat in Thomas' chair, opposite her sleeping cousin.

And waited.

Time moved slowly on.

Agatha hadn't expected to doze herself, but she woke with a jump some time later. Her heart beat a little too fast. Instinctively she understood the women were no longer alone in the cottage. The fire had burned low, but life remained in it. The candles sputtered and protested but they too had plenty of light to give. Sally continued to sleep peacefully. Agatha glanced at the cottage door. It remained firmly closed. She hadn't bolted it after Meg had left, in fact she wasn't even sure whether the door had bolts. That had been remiss of her.

A creaking from the direction of the crooked stairs in the corner of the downstairs room alerted her to movement in the otherwise still house. She edged forwards in her seat. Someone was descending. Slowly. Heavily.

Agatha's heart thumped. She waited, hardly daring to breathe. The shadows lengthened and the candles guttered. She knew, even as the shape turned the corner and moved into the light, whom she would see.

"Thomas." Agatha greeted Sally's husband, her voice quiet and calm. She didn't want to waken Sally.

Thomas did not look good. He walked stiffly, like a man in pain, although it occurred to Agatha that wherever Thomas currently resided, surely he was beyond pain?

He responded to her voice, turning stiffly, not just his head but his neck and shoulders too. He showed no recognition and why should he? Agatha couldn't be sure his eyes would even see her, and in any case he had no idea who she was. They probably had met as children, or known each other by sight, but that was a long time ago.

"Thomas. Why do you come back here?" Agatha asked

The whites of his eyes were missing and what was left, the black viscera, burned dark as coal, but something, some part of him, bore deep into Agatha's soul. She stared right back at him, determined not to flinch, recalling the occasions Tansy had supposedly summoned spirits and conversed with them in the kitchen of Myrtle Lodge. *'Speak to them like a favoured child,'* she'd often instructed Agatha. *'As though they're simple folk.'*

She channelled that remembrance now, keeping her voice low and speaking kindly to him. "Sally loved you, Thomas. It was not her fault that you were lost. You must leave her be. Rest easy on the other side and wait for her life to run its natural course. You cannot plague her like this."

Thomas lurched towards her, his upper body juddering. Had he understood what she'd said to him? She thought so. He remained mute, though, his lip curled in disdain. His feet slapped against the bare floor, as though he waded through water. Agatha looked down, noted the seawater dripping from him.

How is that possible?

She stood hurriedly, moving quickly towards the table where her candles still burned, trying to draw him away from Sally. She lifted one of the candle holders and held it high. Thomas, ignoring her, advanced until level with his sleeping wife. He reached out an arm, the skin on his hand as pale and lifeless as the underbelly of a long dead fish. Agatha shuddered to see how his fingernails, peeled away from their beds.

"Leave her, Thomas!" Agatha lifted the candle directly in front of her face, staring through the thin flickering flame at the man, distorting his image on purpose. He rolled his head her way, his jaw slack, no sign of life in those ghastly sockets. She made a small noise in her throat to keep his attention the way she would with a dog.

But what could she say? What should she say? What would Tansy—

She conjured an image of Tansy in her mind, imagining her grandmother standing there with them. Fearless. Completely in command.

Agatha paced forward, feeling more certain of what to do. She began to intone, her voice little more than a soft whisper, but one that caught Thomas's attention. "I call upon the spirits that reside here with us to help you find your place on the other side, wherever that may be. And I ask you to forgive those who have wronged you. I wish for a time and a place for you where you are free from pain and sadness. I seek only solace and eternal, unbroken rest for you and peace for your loved ones. I ask that the spirits protect Sally and Stanley from enmity and wrongdoing. I do not request this in my own name, but in the name of the gods and goddesses who came before us, a long time ago, for blessed are the ancestors, and blessed are those they protect. So must it be."

Thomas growled in anger, stomping towards her. Agatha waited, biding her time, then as he lashed out at her, she blew out the candle. His aim was off and he connected with her arm, knocking her about with some strength. Forced to swivel away, she lost her footing, falling sideways to the floor while sending the candle and candleholder flying towards the fire. The embers in the grate exploded in anger, shooting sparks and soot and smoke into the air almost as though she had unleashed a barrel full of gunpowder. Agatha covered her face as smuts rained down on her.

When she dared to look up again, Thomas had disappeared. Agatha could sense him no more.

Quivering, adrenaline surging through her veins, Agatha picked herself up and brushed herself down. She took her time, steadying her breathing and calming herself. Then she built the fire once more, lit a fresh candle and settled in the chair across from Sally who, all this time, had remained asleep.

She remained there until dawn, watching over her cousin as she slept. Thomas didn't bother them again, but Agatha's heightened senses recognised the restless shuffling of plenty of other lost souls. They loitered well back in the shadows, stalking the living, flitting up and down The Lanes outside.

The hairs on the back of Agatha's neck prickled and her thumbs itched.

And her knees turned to jelly, when further away, from out at sea, she distinctly heard the cries of those who begged for the chance to return home.

Late the next evening, after Hannah and Flora had retired for the night, Agatha rocked in front of her own hearth. What could she do but watch the faces in the fire, soothing those who whispered to her?

A gentle tap on the door roused her from her reverie.

"Come in Stanley," she called in a low voice. The latch clunked heavily, and the door rattled opened.

"How did you know it was me, Miss Agatha?" Stanley asked, removing his cap and stepping into the kitchen. He peered about, quickly realising they were alone. Recognising the other inhabitants had gone up to bed, he closed the door more quietly than he had opened it.

Agatha smiled. "I know you, Stanley. I expect you to behave in certain ways. I can even guess why you're here." Without getting up, she indicated the chair opposite. He took it, knowing not to argue with her, grateful to be out of the cold.

He smoothed his cap into his lap. "I wanted to thank you for all you have done. I took the hamper as you asked, and I gave it to Meg Powell."

"That's good," Agatha nodded, pleased that Meg continued to assist Sally.

"Meg said to be sure to thank you and to let you know she would be looking in on my Ma a few times a day and helping her clean and making sure she eats."

"We can't ask for more than that, can we Stanley? With a little nourishment I am sure your mother will be well in no time."

Stanley hesitated.

"What is it?" asked Agatha.

"There's talk in the town." Stanley shifted, his fingers wrapped tightly around his cap.

Agatha had resumed her rocking, but now she stilled the chair. "What sort of talk?"

"Petty talk. The sort of thing Ma tells me to pay no heed to."

"And yet you chose to heed it." Agatha frowned. The fire spat. "You've come to tell me about it."

"I don't like to hear people speak ill of you."

So they speak ill of me? T'was ever thus, Agatha wanted to say. *You should have heard the lies they spread about my grandmother.* "What do they say, Stanley?"

"They say your mother was a witch. That your grandmother was a witch. And ... that you are one too." The boy looked troubled.

"You know that your mother and I are cousins, Stanley?"

He nodded, his mouth curled down at the edges.

"Our mothers were sisters, so Sally and I share the same grandmother. Your great grandmother." *Surely Sally had visited Tansy from time to time during Agatha's long absence?* "Did you never meet Tansy?"

Stanley shrugged, increasingly uncomfortable. "I did meet her," he confessed eventually. "I came up here with my Ma from time to time."

"And?"

Stanley lifted his eyes to Agatha, shamefaced. His expression told her all she needed to know. He'd thought Tansy foolish. Perhaps the rumours of witchcraft confirmed his own suspicions.

Agatha leaned forward. "What is a witch?" she asked. "Do you know?"

Stanley thought for a while before answering. "Well, you know, Miss Agatha. It is someone who can cast spells and curse folks."

"Is that what I do?" Agatha asked him, her face serious.

Stanley glanced around the kitchen, at the bottles and jars arranged on shelves and the herbs tied with twine and hanging in bunches from the ceiling. "I don't know."

"Does your mother cast spells and curse folks?"

Stanley shook his head, appalled by the very idea.

Agatha sighed. "In times past, any woman who lived by herself stood out like a sore thumb. She might work with herbs, or help babies to birth, or she might have had independent means or have been different in some vaguely indiscernible way—a birthmark, red hair—" Agatha smiled at Stanley and tugged at one of her own strange curls. "Maybe they had freckles, or a strange laugh."

Stanley finally smiled.

"The thing is, such a woman only had to upset one of her neighbours, and some officious bigwig would be calling upon her and before you could say boo to a goose, he'd be leading her towards the village pond at the end of a rope." Agatha's eyes flashed with anger as she met Stanley's startled gaze. "Tansy was different, certainly. A bit of an oddity. And *I* am different, yes. And maybe Tansy *was* a witch, or maybe she was deluded." Agatha slapped her hands down on her thighs in anger. "Let the people talk, Stanley. To be fair, I wasn't aware that witchcraft was a hanging offence anymore."

They stared at each other for the longest time, the fire sizzling in the grate between them, Agatha waiting for him to respond, Stanley pondering on the right thing to say.

He opted for a little light-hearted cheekiness. "Most everything else is."

Agatha snorted. He wasn't wrong. "Indeed, that is so."

Fearing he had upset Agatha, a woman he had come to respect, Stanley held out his hand. "I didn't mean to insult you," he ventured.

Agatha winked at him. "Ah, don't worry, Stanley. I'm not insulted. Our family—for my family is your family—is complex." She leaned back in her seat and furrowed her brow. "I know not what my mother was, although I have my suspicions. She ran away when I was very young. She left me here in my grandmother's care." Agatha held up a finger. "Now, Tansy I know all about. She was a herbalist, but that doesn't necessarily mean she was a witch. She taught me how to make tinctures and remedies and lotions and potions, things that help people. Useful things. I gave your mother a sleeping draught last night. She has one to take tonight. She needs to sleep so she can regain her strength."

Stanley nodded, watching Agatha as she relaxed.

She rocked her chair once more. "The thing to remember is that the doctor would have given her a sleeping draught and it would have been similar to the one I gave her," Agatha told him, "but mine was entirely natural, created from the herbs Tansy grew in the garden. The herbs that I grow. In the garden that *you* tend, Stanley. With your green and magical fingers."

Stanley released the cap he had been gripping, and studied his hands.

Agatha smiled in amusement. "Unlike Dr Giddens, I won't charge your mother anything, because I don't need her money. She's family. And besides, having your assistance in the gardens and house is payment enough."

"So you're not a witch then?"

"I didn't say that." Agatha crinkled her eyes. "But I do no harm, Stanley and neither did Tansy. Besides, who knows what I am? And who is to judge?" She shuffled forward in her chair. "Now. I know I am tired. How about you? Shouldn't you be getting back to Hawkerne Hall?"

Stanley nodded, recognizing this as his cue to take his leave, but even so, he remained seated a while longer. "They talk about Lord Tolleson too."

"What do they say about Lord Tolleson?" A prickle of tension ran up Agatha's spine.

Stanley flushed a bright red. "They say he is a ... a ..." his voice dropped to a whisper. "They say he is a sodomite."

Agatha pursed her lips. "Do you know what a sodomite is, Stanley?"

Stanley kept his head down and nodded. "The groom at The Blue Bell Inn told me."

That didn't surprise Agatha. She had her suspicions about the groom as well. "Is it a bad thing?" she asked, not intending to be obtuse, but genuinely curious about people's attitudes to each other. To her mind, what happened behind closed doors could be nobody else's business but their own. Unfortunately, some of the locals evidently loved a saucy rumour and enjoyed ruining lives. She wondered whether Phineas had been indiscreet. Or had someone besides the groom been talking out of turn? If so, it was unkind.

And dangerous.

Stanley had started to twist his cap once more. "The Bible tells it so."

"The Bible is only one book," Agatha retorted. "There are many books saying many different things. As many books as there are points of view." She snapped her fingers as something occurred to her. "Have you seen the books in Lord Tolleson's library?" Agatha herself never had, but she could imagine he owned a few.

Stanley shook his head.

"If you ever have the opportunity to visit Lord Tolleson's library you should go and see them altogether. Rows and rows of them, I'll wager. A library is a fine thing, Stanley." Agatha's face lit up. "If the bible—just one book remember—can teach you so much, imagine what ten books could teach you. Or a hundred. Or a thousand! There is an incredible array of knowledge out there in the world, Stanley. All written by different people with their own experiences and viewpoints. One book cannot possibly hold *all* the truth for *all* of the people *all* of the time." She considered the boy's bemused expression. Had she misspoken? "Do you understand what I'm saying?"

Stanley nodded, but his face remained downcast.

"You doubt me?" Agatha asked, disappointed that she hadn't

captured his imagination. "Do you consider Lord Tolleson to be a bad man?"

"Oh no!" Stanley flinched, and his voice rose in indignation that she would think such a thing. "Not at all, Miss Agatha. You and Lord Tolleson are two of the kindest and wisest people I have ever met, aside from my father. You've both given me so much. And looked after my Ma. I can never begin to properly thank either of you."

Agatha thought about Meg, back in Thimble Lane. "Good people give what they can, when they can. It's neighbourliness." Agatha stood and pulled her shawl about herself. "Get away with you, Stanley. I've a bed to go to."

Stanley stood to take his leave, but instead of moving towards the back door, he spontaneously rushed forward to throw his arms around Agatha. He was as tall as her and she was momentarily taken aback, but she reminded herself he was just a lad, and laughed with delight.

"Thank you, Miss Agatha."

"Don't mention it, Stanley," she pulled away and led him to the back door. "Mind how you go now." She held it open, squeezing his arm as he passed, and watched him run down the path. The darkness swallowed him up before he'd even reached the edge of her boundary.

Once he'd disappeared from sight, she looked to the skies, regarding the stars in wonder and more than a little reverence.

"Keep him safe," she whispered. "Keep them all safe."

14
FALSE LIGHTS

Mayor Bumble hunched forwards over his ale and placed a cupped palm across his mouth to muffle the sound of his voice. "False lights?" he hissed. "What in the devil's name are they?"

His companion, sitting within touching distance opposite, adopted a similar position and narrowed his eyes. "Ssh!"

Bumble dropped his head and covered his eyes with his hand. What on earth had compelled him to turn out tonight? Engaging with this meeting was sheer madness. His Durscombe contact had arranged for Bumble to meet this Pierre Songe, a French ex-sailor, at *The Honiton Arms* near Exeter, promising total discretion. Bumble had travelled through the pouring rain for nearly an hour to get here, alone and on horseback, but still he found himself worrying in case someone recognised him.

Ever since the *Eliza May* had run ashore off Durscombe, Bumble had been obsessing about how he could replicate the circumstances that had resulted in such an embarrassment of riches. Now he'd tasted forbidden fruit he wanted more of it. Much more. He'd idly mentioned his desire to a few of the men he kept in his employ, including their charismatic leader Will Greeb, and Greeb in turn had recommended Songe to him. Although

Greeb had been necessarily woolly about the details, he had insinuated that the Frenchman had been recently working alongside a gang of wreckers in Cornwall, and the partnership with them had proven to be mutually lucrative.

Greeb had high hopes of a similar experience in Durscombe. He'd spoken with enthusiasm about the financial advantages of a three-way relationship, but so far he alone had profited. Bumble had been forced to pay handsomely in return for both Greeb's and the Frenchman's complete secrecy on all counts, but in any case Bumble was nobody's fool. He would not have trusted the nefarious Greeb with his badly scarred face as far as either of them could spit.

However, Bumble was nothing if not curious, and his desire to know more had brought him out to this meeting on a miserable night. Suspicious by nature, the mayor had arranged the meeting through Greeb on the understanding his real name would never be employed. Bumble found the duplicitous nature of this clandestine undertaking oddly exciting. In fact, apart from feeling vaguely petrified at all that he was risking, Bumble had found himself having the time of his life.

Until he'd actually met the man. A rancid, stinking, leathery specimen of lank manhood if ever there was one.

In addition, the ride across the moor to the outskirts of the city had left him cold through to his very marrow. He glanced gratefully at the fire as another patron of the inn threw a log into the blaze. It roared approval then settled back, sizzling and whistling. Bumble watched the sparks fly, then turned his attention to Songe once more.

"The thing to bear in mind," Songe murmured, as sly as a fox, his gaze shooting sideways to appraise a nearby punter, "is that you need a decent band of brothers on your side. Men you can trust." He picked his ear with a filthy fingernail, inspected the orange wax, and wiped the residue on his trousers. Bumble tried not to grimace.

"I can find trustworthy men," Bumble replied, his voice as short as his patience.

Songe sniffed. "That's a start. You say that all the sailors aboard the *Eliza May* were lost?"

Now it was Bumble's turn to squint cautiously about the room. You never knew who might be listening. "They did," he admitted. "The seas were savage. The townsfolk tried to get boats out to them but they were beaten back."

This news seemed to meet with Songe's approval. "If your seas are hostile enough, you never need fear aught else. Lady luck was on your side that night."

Bumble blinked in surprise and Songe continued, "Let's hope you can pull that off again when it's required. As I say, you will need plenty of good men to help you. You cannot have *any* survivors from the ship."

"No survivors?"

"No matter whether they're man, woman or child." He leaned forwards and stabbed at Bumble's chest with his filth-encrusted finger. "And you need to ensure there are no witnesses to what you do, none at all. Otherwise you will hang for it."

Bumble quaked. *No survivors?* The sailor's suggestion was tantamount to wholesale murder, pure and simple. Bumble wasn't sure he could pull that off or even that he wanted to. The whole business with the *Eliza May* had been grim beyond belief.

But then again ... if he wanted to pursue his ambition, what was the alternative? Bumble scratched his chin, lost in thought.

Could he trust his men? He thought so. Greeb and his cronies would have no qualms about such things. In fact, it would be better if he left it all to them. For his part, he need not get his hands dirty.

And the fishermen? He would work on it. Greeb would have some ideas. Once the rougher men from The Lanes were on board, the rest would follow easily enough. They wouldn't dare cross the coarser element in town.

And if there were complaints? Well so what? They would be complaining to the aldermen. Bumble could get his colleagues on board, so to speak, most of them at least. The townsmen—on the whole—would turn a blind eye if there was something in it for them. Dozens and dozens of men and their families had profited from the loss of the *Eliza May,* not just the aldermen. With Greeb applying pressure, they would force every man onside. He could make it worth their while. The womenfolk would not present the slightest problem — they would do as they were bid.

The only fly in Bumble's ointment? Phineas. What a stuffed shirt Lord Tolleson was.

Bumble's mind reeled with the complexity of what Songe was suggesting, the challenges it threw up, and the solutions he would find, but he only reiterated what he'd said before, "I can find men."

Songe nodded slowly. "You must want this very much. Mayor..."

Bumble's eyes flashed at the slip up.

Songe smirked. "I beg your pardon. I mis-spoke. What was your name again? John Tucker or something? A common enough name in these parts."

Bumble sucked his teeth, incensed. Greeb had obviously informed Songe exactly who he was, and now the Frenchman wanted to play with him. A dangerous game. One that would cost Bumble a pretty penny, no doubt.

Songe laughed at Bumble's ill-concealed fury, genuinely amused. "You think I don't dig around? Find out who I'm dealing with? Nobody gets my neck in a rope for free."

"The name is Parrett," Bumble spat. "I would oblige you not to forget it again."

Songe winked and leaned closer to the mayor once more, lowering his tone to a conspiratorial whisper. "What was it that the *Eliza May* had on board that you liked so much? What has got your dander rising?"

Bumble stared Songe directly in the eye, his ire disappearing as rapidly as it had arrived. He shook his head. He wasn't about to confess to Songe about the chest loaded with gold and semi-precious stones the ship had been carrying. He'd already dispatched most of his haul on its way north to London and the dealers at the wharfs in the Jewish quarter. Bumble would be an extremely rich man thanks to his illicit gains from the *Eliza May*. If he could repeat the process he would never need to worry about money again.

"I'll mind my business, you mind yours," Bumble replied, his voice gruff, his good humour restored. Songe couldn't touch him. He didn't have the clout. "Let's get to the point, shall we? What is the best way to go about this little ... venture ... of ours?"

"Hmm." Songe rocked back in his seat and gestured at the nearest serving girl. Short, mousey haired and rotund, she swept over to refill their tankards. Ignoring Songe, she loitered over Bumble's glass, dipping low, showing off her ample assets. Songe leered after her as she strutted away, and Bumble hid a sneer of disdain. The women here were more than likely pox-ridden and not worth the ride. He cleared his throat and dragged Songe's attention back to the matter in hand.

Songe studied Bumble, his face growing serious. "You'll need an insider. On the ship. A captain or first mate. Someone with a dubious financial history."

"To offer a bribe you mean?"

"Someone in need of a little something to keep their boat afloat if you understand me." Songe lowered his voice, speaking so quietly now that Bumble struggled to hear. "You instruct them to navigate onto the rocks. This person is key to the whole enterprise." Songe rubbed his hands together as though he could already feel the cash.

"But surely—given our intentions—this would be certain suicide?" Hadn't Songe just told him there could be no survivors?

"You promise him safe passage, of course." Songe wiggled his hand, the universal sigh for 'maybe, maybe not'. The 'but' hung in the air between them. A shiver ran down Bumble's spine and he dropped his gaze. No. There could be no safe passage. Certainly not if Bumble and Greeb and all of their men wanted to come out of this unscathed.

"That's where the false lights come into it. You can use them to give a signal. It's not easy manoeuvring a ship that size you know, particularly in the waters round Lyme Bay. There needs to be a reason for the ship to be hugging the coastline there."

"So we build a fire or something? A beacon on the cliffs?"

"No. No. Quite the reverse. You want a small light. Something a sailor keeping watch would expect to see on another ship." Songe gestured at the tankard in his hand, moving it slowly backwards and forwards. "This little light I'm talking about ... It needs to be moving, not static. You want any lookouts to believe they're seeing another ship." He pointed at the fire, blazing in the grate nearby. "A fire lit on a cliff is just a fire on a cliff. It would be useless to you."

Bumble nodded his understanding. There would have to be a great deal of forward planning. This endeavour would be more complicated than he'd imagined.

"Very well," he said. "That is what we'll do. You can find a captain in need of ... ah ... financial lubrication?"

"I can do that," Songe grinned. "For a price of course."

"Of course." And no doubt Songe's price would be a steep one.

The men regarded each other in silence for a time. Bumble curious, his mind racing, Songe with bored insolence.

"Then do it." Bumble nodded. "I'll take care of things at my end."

"Consider it done." Songe lifted his tankard, saluting the mayor, and Bumble raised his in return.

A reflection from the fire caught the Frenchman's irises. Bumble watched himself burn in the other man's gaze.

15
NEW FRIENDS

Early the next morning, Wiggy passed away.

Phineas cancelled his appointments and remained in his library, nursing a bottle of claret and openly weeping in front of the fire. With no-one to witness his weakness, he gave free rein to his emotions. It was at times like these that his loneliness threatened to overwhelm him. He had no confidante and no-one to turn to. The other aldermen were decent enough, but given his station as a lord of the realm and a gentleman, the expectation was always that he would maintain a stiff upper lip. Sometimes being a gentleman was a bore and a trial. He longed to journey down to *The Blue Bell Inn* and drink himself under the table with whomever happened to be gathered there, but that would not be deemed appropriate.

And his darling Wiggy would certainly not have approved.

Phineas's early memories of Arthur Wiggins were hazy. He had always been an old man. Thinking back to when Phineas had been five or six, Wiggy had already had grey hair and a lined face, and yet he wouldn't have been much older than Phineas was now. Wiggy may have appeared austere to the casual observer, but to a motherless little boy with no siblings and a largely absent father, he had shared his warm heart.

Phineas had been educated by a tutor for a while, alone at

home, before being sent away to school. He had hated the experience of boarding, and longed for Hawkerne Hall. Oxford had been marginally better, and after a few years there he'd enjoyed a Grand Tour on the continent with several of his friends. Those had been good days indeed, surrounded by like-minded fellows intent on experiencing the liberal cultures that could be readily found abroad. He widened his horizons, and every time he returned home, Wiggy would give him a warm welcome and demand to hear his stories. In truth, Wiggy had lived vicariously through Phineas. Over the years, Phineas had increasingly come to rely on him. More so after his father had passed away.

Wiggy's talents knew no bounds. He understood exactly what was needed and when, and would arrive at Phineas' elbow with an item, letter or beverage, almost as soon as Phineas thought of it. He was the most discreet of servants, gently reminding Phineas of his duties in a way that suggested Phineas was well aware of what he should be doing and had only momentarily forgotten. Wiggy always had the perfect advice to offer. He knew the right things to say, or do, he knew how Phineas should behave at an event, and what he should wear. In short, Wiggy had been Phineas's second conscience, and a total stalwart of his household.

At what stage would Phineas need to find a new butler? Could anyone in his household step up? Who could replace the old man? Phineas feared that nobody could.

Of course, darling Wiggy would have known the answers to these questions.

Phineas sighed. He would have to find someone and make do.

A soft tap on the door diverted his attention from his personal misery. He hurriedly wiped his eyes and blew his nose and squared his shoulders.

"Come," he called, and Matthew Salter entered the room. His presence was larger than his stature and he carried himself with an upright almost arrogant bearing, unusual among the servants of Hawkerne Hall. He strutted with a confidence Phineas himself sometimes lacked.

Phineas rather liked watching the younger man move.

"Excuse me, Sir. Miss Agatha Wick has called upon you. She says she had no prior appointment but asks your pardon and desires an audience." The language sounded comical coming from Matthew. Either he was repeating Agatha's exact words, or Mrs Gwynne had been coaching him. Phineas held back a watery smile, then frowned in dismay. He hadn't dressed for entertaining visitors this morning, particularly women. Wiggy would have instinctively known what to say and do in this situation and would have quickly offered a workable suggestion, but Matthew only waited for further instruction.

Time to stand on my own two feet, Phineas decided. Agatha Wick was a singular type of woman. He had a feeling she would not be overly concerned with whether he was wearing the correct waistcoat for the hour, or not. Perhaps she wished to speak with him about Stanley. It was probably wise to have a swift word with her.

"Very well. I'll see her in the parlour, Matthew."

"Begging your pardon sir, she specifically asked that you remain in the library." Matthew, well aware of the gravity of the day, spoke softly, his dark eyes flicking over his master's face.

"She did?" Phineas shook his head, bemused at this. One never entertained women in the library. Not on purpose, at any rate.

"Aye sir, she did."

"Oh." Phineas, at a loss, waved his hand at the door. "In that case, show her through." As Matthew exited the room, Phineas brushed ineffectually at his shirt and trousers in an effort to rid himself of the worst of the creases. Moments later Matthew knocked and re-entered the room with Agatha in tow. She looked splendid, dressed entirely in oak-leaf green from her bonnet to her underskirt, a basket hooked over one arm.

Her brow creased when she saw him, her face a picture of concern. "Good afternoon, Lord Tolleson. I heard your sad news. Please forgive my intrusion."

"Not at all, Miss Wick. Not at all." Phineas gestured at

Matthew hovering in the background. "Matthew, perhaps you could safeguard Miss Wick's basket?"

"Oh, no need!" Agatha clutched the basket close to her chest.

"Well then, please." Phineas indicated the chairs. "Would you care for tea?"

"That would be delightful. Thank you." Agatha chose the chair that directly faced Phineas, all the better to observe him. She perched on the edge, and settled her basket on the rug to her right. Phineas nodded at Matthew who headed for the door once more to ask the kitchen for a tray of tea.

Phineas's gaze lingered on Matthew until the door closed and hid him from view.

Agatha, for her part, watched Phineas.

When they were alone, she leaned forward. "Lord Tolleson? I came to offer my most profound condolences on your loss of Mr Wiggins. When Stanley arrived at Myrtle Lodge this morning, he brought the sad tidings."

"Thank you. You are most kind." Phineas thought he might weep again. Agatha had such a warm and open manner that one felt relaxed and completely at ease with her. Phineas rarely experienced this with anyone else.

Agatha patted his hand. "Mr Wiggins is at peace now."

Phineas blinked rapidly. "He worked so hard ... all his life. He was here with my grandfather when he was just twelve years of age. I believe his mother worked in the kitchen for some time."

"You will see to his send-off?"

"Of course. He had no other family. He never married. I'll do right by him," Phineas replied. This made him more miserable, being faced with the reality of living alone. No-one to mourn your passing.

Agatha nodded her approval, sensitive to his pensive mood. Gently she said, "I also wanted to thank you for sending Stanley to me as often as you have. I declare, I think I should probably employ the boy rather than you."

She succeeded in raising a smile. "Oh no, really. It's no bother at all. He seems to be learning a great deal very quickly. You set him a great many tasks. When you're settled and the Lodge is as you would like, he can spend more time with my stables I imagine. If that's what he wants. I wouldn't wish for him to devote his days pursuing an occupation that did not bring him happiness."

The door opened quietly behind them. Matthew had returned and, with the aid of one of the house maids, he organised the tea tray on the table between Phineas and Agatha.

"Do you consider that Stanley is happy, Matthew?" asked Phineas, as Matthew bobbed around him, fussing over the plate settings.

Matthew smiled at his employer. "How could he fail to be, Sir?"

Agatha noted the sudden flush to Phineas's cheeks and scrutinized Matthew more closely. He was astonishingly handsome with his dark curly hair, deep brown eyes and pleasant countenance. She could see Phineas appeared quite taken with him, while Matthew was perfectly polite and pleasant to his employer, if a little forward. Nonetheless, Agatha could imagine the younger man had many sides that were not immediately apparent to the casual observer.

Phineas, perhaps sensing her inspection, dismissed the servants. They departed quietly. Agatha, forgetting herself, settled back into her seat lost in thought.

Phineas's voice drifted into her period of reflection.

"Shall I?"

"Oh no. I beg your pardon." Agatha drew herself upright. "Where are my manners? Please allow me." Agatha poured a drop of milk into two delicate china cups, and then from habit checked that the tea had brewed sufficiently, before filling each cup in turn and handing one to Phineas.

"You like him." Agatha's gaze was direct and unabashed.

Phineas misunderstanding, smiled. "Who? Stanley? Of course. He's a bright lad."

Agatha glanced knowingly at the door.

Phineas discerned her meaning immediately. He blushed deeply, shocked by Agatha's forwardness.

Agatha retreated slightly. "I apologise. I know I speak out of turn, Lord Tolleson, only ... it is obvious to me."

"You disapprove?" Phineas's heart thumped heavily. "He doesn't know. No-one knows." He returned his cup and saucer to the table. "They can't know."

Agatha raised a hand to quell his rising panic. "But I know now." She shook her head. "I do not disapprove, Lord Tolleson. In fact, I rarely disapprove of much. I am certainly not easily shocked. Your secret is safe with me." She placed her tea on the table and stood, pacing across the room to the bookshelves. She wandered their length, running her fingers along the spines. Stopping every now to peer more closely at one or other that stood out.

Phineas watched her, waiting, wondering all the while whether she was planning to blackmail him in some way. He had heard of such things before.

"So many words." Her voice drifted quietly towards him from the corner of the room, wistful. Had she already forgotten Matthew?

"Do you read?" asked Phineas, an avid reader. He'd inherited a sizeable number of the books in the library from his father's collection, but he had added more. Many more.

"As much as I can, yes. My mother taught me to read and write before she ran away, and Tansy encouraged me to continue. I was very lucky. Not all girls have the opportunity." She sighed. "Have *you* read all of these books?"

"Oh no, not *every* one, by any means. But I have plenty of time. I'll read them all, and more besides."

"Which is your favourite?"

"Oooh," Phineas groaned at the complexity of the question, pleased to be on firmer footing now, sharing something he loved. He jumped up from his seat. "Well the one book I love the most and have read numerous times is this *La Tulipe Noire* by Alexandre Dumas, but this is the collection I am the proudest of. It is an original translation of *Les Mille et Une Nuits* by Antoine Galland. There are twelve volumes here, all incredibly precious. And look," Phineas plucked a book from its place, and flicked through it. "See the plates?"

"Exquisite!" Agatha positively purred with excitement. "But the book is in French? You can read in French?"

"Bien sur Mademoiselle. J'ai appris à parler plusieurs langues quand j'étais petit. J'ai eu un tuteur." Taking pity on Agatha, Phineas continued, "I can also read books in Greek and Latin."

Agatha laughed delightedly. "I have no idea what you said before, but I do adore to hear other languages. It is so exotic and exciting!"

She reminded Phineas of Wiggy in that moment and his heart glowed with warmth. "You must borrow any books you would like to read. I'll tell Mrs Gwynne, and Matthew, that they are to allow you access whenever you wish. And then you can return the books via young Stanley."

Agatha clapped her hands in exhilaration. "You are more than generous, Lord Tolleson. Are you quite sure? Only—"

"I insist. It would bring me happiness to know they are being utilised by someone other than myself. After all, as you said, 'so many words'!"

Agatha smiled and returned to her seat.

"I have a few gifts for you too, Lord Tolleson. To thank you for welcoming me as warmly as you have done. It can't have escaped your notice that people in the town gossip about me, perhaps even your servants."

Phineas began to protest but Agatha lifted her hand to wave his protestations gently away.

"You will have heard the rumours, and yet you have shown me nothing but neighbourliness." She reached into her basket and lifted out a cake wrapped in a clean muslin cloth. "I should be honest. Hannah, my housekeeper, baked this, not me. But you must have some. It is delicious." She set the cake down on the table. "And my ward, Flora, sent you some late season jam that she and I made together." With a flourish, she drew out a bottle. "And I have some cordial for you. This is medicinal, Lord Tolleson. You should mix it with brandy before you retire. It will ensure the sweetest of dreams and a good night's sleep. I insist you try it."

Agatha arranged everything neatly on the table as Phineas exclaimed over them.

Behind them, the fire crackled and spat and Agatha spun around, cocking her head and listening. She moved close to it, added another log, and soothed it with gentle words that Phineas couldn't catch.

Satisfied, she resumed her seat and supped at her tea. Together, they made a little more small talk about literature and Phineas felt his mood slowly begin to improve. He enjoyed choosing a number of lighter novels he thought she might enjoy. He offered her his selections and she carefully wrapped them in a cloth and placed them reverently in her basket.

While she flicked through one of his larger illustrated books, he took the time to return her appraisal. She presented as an odd woman in many ways, strong and yet gentle, upright and honest. Not a lady by any means, yet her manners were far better. He understood that she knew her place in society but eschewed such a notion of hierarchy. He found he enjoyed her company very much.

Sensing his inspection, she peered up at him, smiling warmly. "You should not fear, Lord Tomlinson. Wiggy loved you very much." When his eyes moistened, she continued, "He thought of you as the son he never had and was immensely proud of you. Especially because—" she paused and glanced at the fire. "Because you are so unlike many of Durscombe's other aldermen."

Phineas caught his breath. "How can you know that?"

"I don't know how I know some things. I just do."

"It is—" Phineas hesitated.

"Witchcraft? That is what they say." Agatha shrugged. "If it has to have a label, so be it. It is a gift. My gift. Often a blessing, sometimes a curse." Agatha closed his book carefully. "Where is the harm? I know you feel lonely, Lord Tolleson. I understand your loneliness. For years I lived in exile away from those who cared about me. But now I am returned and happy. And while you will grieve for some time for your Wiggy, remember you have us as neighbours. Hannah, Flora and I. You are welcome in our company at *any* time." Agatha gazed at Phineas from under her eyelashes, almost mischievous. "And ... there is young Matthew Salter."

Phineas jerked back in shock, pondering her meaning. She laughed in delight.

"I am not one to throw stones, Lord Tolleson. I mean you no harm. Sincerely. Far from it."

They locked eyes and he recognised the sincerity there. A kindred spirit.

Rising from his seat, he moved towards Agatha and took her hand. Lifting her knuckles to his mouth he kissed her fingers. "Indeed Madam. We are a pair of strange neighbours, but as you say, where is the harm?"

16
THINGS REMEMBERED

Phineas alighted from his carriage outside Applecombe, Mayor Bumble's impressive manor house, and inhaled a lungful of bitter air. Stars shone brilliantly in the dark sky above, in fact the world might have been carved from crystal, so cold and sharp was the night. A thick frost had already formed on the lawn and decorative hedges in front of Applecombe, and the ornamental path to the entrance glittered with sparkling ice. Traditionally on New Year's Eve, Bumble threw the biggest party in the area, and anyone who was anyone in Durscombe and the surrounding villages, attended. For many years Phineas had come alone, happy enough to mingle with the other bachelors and widowers. This year, for a change, he had invited Agatha to be his guest.

Agatha had initially appeared reluctant to accompany him. Phineas hadn't probed too deeply, although he'd rather hoped she would have thrilled at the idea of attending the event of the year with him. Her lack of excitement puzzled him. He couldn't imagine any other woman behaving so coolly.

But that was Agatha all over.

She had eventually accepted his invitation, for reasons she hadn't confessed, and she appeared amiable enough this evening. She had dressed for the occasion in a new satin evening gown of dark green over a large fashionable crinoline and starched underskirts. Phineas offered his arm, and gallantly escorted her the short distance over the slippery path to the grand entrance. Bumble's smart footmen, resplendent in their impeccable livery, waited there to take hats, coats and shawls. *New livery*, Phineas mused. Bumble was pushing the boat out, perhaps cashing in his rewards from the wrecking of the *Eliza May*.

Phineas and Agatha made their way inside and stood, waiting patiently in a short line, at the entrance to the ballroom. Agatha was tall for a woman, at least four inches taller than he, but Phineas didn't mind. He found Agatha's company pleasing, especially at an event such as this. Her reassuring presence this evening ensured he would not be forced to fight off the attentions of various dull dowagers and their grasping female offspring.

The spectacular ballroom had been decorated with great care. Lit by several large chandeliers, the crystals sparkled brightly, reflecting the light of hundreds of candles and the huge blaze burning brightly in the massive fireplace. Several of the older men had huddled gratefully around its warmth, pointedly ignoring their womenfolk who tittered together on the edges of the room, wafting themselves with hand-painted oriental silk fans and bitching blithely about other guests.

"Lord Phineas Tolleson and Miss Agatha Wick," the rotund doorman trumpeted. Phineas gracefully swept Agatha through the doors and bowed more deeply than was necessary to the room.

Agatha chuckled quietly, her eyes shining with mischief. "Really, Lord Tolleson. You have a sense of theatre, I think."

Phineas chuckled. "Not often remarked upon, Miss Wick. Perhaps I should have taken to the stage? Would you care for a glass of punch?"

Agatha smiled. "That would be delightful, thank you."

Phineas nodded and took his leave, disappearing to the far side of the room in search of refreshments. Agatha retreated against the wall, smiling at several women in her vicinity while simultaneously half-turning away from them, anxious to avoid having to exchange meaningless pleasantries. From the corner of her eye, she watched them cast knowing looks at each other. The gossip mill would be at full flow tonight. Not only was there a Wick in residence at a society event, something unheard of in her grandmother's time, but she had shown up in the company of one of the most eligible bachelors in Durscombe, if not Devon itself. Of course, observers would conclude that at thirty-six she was far too old for Phineas. An old maid in fact. She lifted her own fan to hide her amusement, enjoying the acidic glances from some of the younger women, knowing that many of them were intent on searching for a potential husband and would see her as an annoying obstacle.

She found herself sympathising with Phineas. As an outsider and somebody considered odd, society placed relatively little pressure on her. Rather she was seen as a figure to avoid. Someone to castigate privately. Unfortunately, Phineas, by virtue of his social situation, was lauded and in constant demand. There wasn't a person in the room who didn't believe Hawkerne Hall was in desperate need of an heir, and to that end, the matrons were readying their charges to wage an onslaught of flirtation against him. And of course while Agatha was perceived as over the hill at thirty-six, as a man of forty-two Phineas was the perfect marriageable age for a much younger woman.

The matrons were particularly indomitable this evening. Agatha smiled wryly as she observed one woman tug her daughter toward poor Phineas just as he reached to take two cups of punch. They appeared at his elbow giving him such a start that he splashed a little of the liquid on the unfortunate daughter. A pretty young woman aged eighteen or so, she'd dressed immaculately in a white ballgown with a pink sash. Unfortunately for her, the punch was red, and the splash bloomed angrily.

Phineas blushed a red as deep as the punch stain and began to apologize profusely. Agatha raised her eyebrows in exasperation. The mother seemed impossibly aggrieved; the daughter grief-stricken. Phineas fussed over them for a minute longer, then gestured at one of Bumble's servants, before offering his fervent apologies once more and rapidly excusing himself. He hurried back to Agatha clasping two sparkling glasses of punch.

"I'm afraid I have been terribly clumsy!" Phineas was obviously mortified.

Agatha soothed his nerves. "I witnessed the whole thing, Lord Tolleson. I would not fret, overly. The servants will sponge out the poor girl's dress." She pointed as a maid led the mother and daughter up the stairs to the gallery and the bedrooms beyond. "See. There they go."

Agatha followed the line of the magnificent staircase. A number of people were gathered on the gallery above chattering or leaning over the bannister and waving at those below. Gentlemen in smartly tailored suits, women in luscious silk dresses in every colour combination imaginable. Agatha's admiring smile froze on her lips. She blinked. Behind those revellers milling around up there, formless grey shadows flitted about.

A trick of the eye?

Agatha stepped sideways, unsure of what she was seeing, striving to get a better view. Nothing of substance. Surely only guests? Or their servants? Nothing untoward.

The shadows deepened, lengthened, grew limbs ... pushed their way through the animated partygoers, gathered at the balustrade. Dark heads turned her way, opaque eyes glinted.

Whispers ... like dried leaves rustling along a pavement. Unintelligible mutterings of discontent.

Agatha gasped and stepped away.

"Is everything alright, Miss Wick?" Phineas asked and Agatha jerked her attention back to him, straightening her back.

"Yes!" She breathed sharply in. What could she tell him? *Sometimes I see things?* She dared to glance back at the gallery, at the flickering translucent shapes up there, the light of their gazes somehow waxy and putrescent. She groaned and dropped her chin to her chest.

"Miss Wick?"

"A twinge in my stomach, is all." She forced a smile,

consciously avoiding the pull of the figures on the balcony by turning away from them, intent on banishing the shadows to the back of her mind.

"You are not well?" Phineas looked alarmed.

"I am quite well, do not fear, my dear Lord Tolleson." Agatha held up her glass. "I'm sure this will help."

She focused on dispelling the spectres from her consciousness. She would process what she had seen later.

"Alderman Fliss and Mrs Emily Fliss." The doorman's voice boomed across the room, drowning out general chit-chat. Agatha, thankful for the distraction, pivoted in place to observe her cousin as she entered the room.

Light on her feet, her head perfectly poised on her pale neck, Emily presented as every inch a lady. No-one would have known she and Agatha shared a humble background unless their memories stretched back a long, long way. Dignified, elegant, pretty as a flower, Emily wore a silk dress in midnight blue, embellished with complicated silver embroidery on the bodice and around a scalloped hem. Her dark hair had been piled high on her crown, but with ringlets falling fashionably around her neck. There was a ripple of approval around the room, and Agatha noted Mayor Bumble came forward to greet them, shepherding his wife, Norah. He bowed deeply, a flamboyant gesture, before rising and sweeping Emily's hand to his lips to lightly kiss her gloved fingers.

Emily had a smile fixed in place but Agatha surmised all was not well with her. Her cousin's face seemed tightly drawn, her eyes watchful. To any impartial observer she would undoubtedly have appeared at ease, enjoying the attention lavished her way, gracefully acknowledging those who gathered around her. But Agatha was no disinterested spectator. She knew Emily, understood her innermost thoughts, and recognised the rigidity in her step, the tautness around her eyes.

Emily must have sensed her cousin's gaze, for she frowned and swivelled her head to stare straight at her. The women regarded each other across the room, fewer than ten yards separating them.

Emily cocked her head and opened her lips a little way, as though to mouth a message, certain that no matter how quietly she spoke, Agatha would hear her. Marmaduke, noting his wife's inattention, placed a hand on the small of her back, an intimate gesture that—judging by the tic beneath Emily's right eye—she hated.

Emily shot Agatha a final haunted look before turning her attention to her husband once more, the bogus smile back in place.

Phineas had watched the exchange with interest. "You know Mrs Fliss?"

"I certainly knew her before she became Mrs Fliss," Agatha replied thoughtfully. "Now, not so much."

"You've not visited her since you returned to Durscombe?"

"To be honest Lord Tolleson, I am not sure I would be welcomed."

"Well it the good lady's loss. She could make use of your skills. The cordial you sent me for a nightcap works wonders. I haven't slept so well in years. I feel like a young man again."

Agatha laughed, genuinely delighted at his praise. "I shall brew another batch and send more over with Stanley on the morrow."

"You are too kind." The odd couple smiled together and chinked their cups of punch.

The evening progressed pleasantly enough. Bumble and his wife had organised a merry gathering with much dancing and jollity. Besides the punch, sparkling wine had been shipped from abroad, and a dozen servants walked around between the guests with shining silver platters laden with delightful canapés. Agatha, keeping her eyes averted from the gallery above her head, enjoyed wandering around and observing the other guests, straining her ears to eavesdrop on interesting conversations, while catching the eye of those who stared a little too long and altogether too presumptuously her way.

No-one asked her to dance.

Phineas because he abhorred dancing anyway, and the other gentleman present, presumably because she was too old, and too much the outsider. Agatha didn't mind. Quite the contrary. She had never learned to dance formally, had never had the opportunity, unlike Emily. However, she did enjoy watching the young women float around the ballroom in their gorgeous ballgowns, like colourful dandelions in a breeze.

Once, momentarily, she wished herself twenty years younger, filled with a melancholy that she rarely experienced, but twenty years ago her grandmother would not have countenanced the idea of Agatha attending a ball such as this. Tansy had despised and distrusted the Bumble family with a passion and had despaired when Lily had chosen to court them on Emily's behalf.

But for her part, Tansy had loved to dance. Agatha could clearly remember those bright starry nights when Tansy had built a small fire on the beach and set loose her long silver hair. Moon clad, she would dance beneath the heavens, to a song only she could hear, the waves lapping close to her ankles, the breeze wafting the smoke into Agatha's eyes. Eventually, when the fire burned back, Tansy would squat and read what remained in the flames.

Once ... long ago ... at least seventeen years ... what Tansy had seen in the ruins of the blaze had caused her to throw back her head and howl. Agatha could recall how frightened she had been, sitting in the shadows, watching Tansy rage. Her grandmother had taken up an athame and drawn it down her own thumb, slicing deeply into the flesh. The bright blood had begun to flow thick and fast and she had dashed her hand at the smouldering wood, the blood flying, the fire spitting and hissing in furious response. That night, Tansy had cursed the Bumbles with a vehemence that Agatha had never previously witnessed.

At the time she hadn't understood why.

And Tansy wouldn't enlighten her.

But here in Applecombe's ballroom, with Bumble's enormous fire blazing away on her right-hand side, she recalled Tansy's fury, and observed Emily smiling blankly at her husband, and she thought perhaps at last, pieces of the Wick family's mystery were gradually revealing themselves to her.

17

OVERHEARD

Emily's head ached.

As a young girl she had longed for the sparkle and the glamour of a proper grown-up ball, but the novelty had rapidly worn off once she'd come of age. As an adult, she increasingly found herself desiring the peaceful solitude of her salon or bedroom instead. Spending time among so many people—constantly smiling and laughing, murmuring appreciation for the most ridiculous of compliments, pretending to be interested in the minutiae of their boring, insular lives—often drained her for days.

She had no genuine interest in anyone at this party. They merely reinforced how dull and meaningless her own life had become.

She allowed Marmaduke to pass her around like a tray of sweet treats or sparkling drinks, alderman to alderman, local dignitary to local dignitary. Yes, she played the game—constantly chirruping and pouting and smiling on demand—until at last she thought her head would crack open with the pent-up pain and anguish she had to conceal from everyone.

Everyone except for Agatha.

Emily stole a glance at her cousin, standing in front of the fire, lost in thought. No doubt *she* would have something that could ease Emily's headache, but Emily couldn't bring herself to go and talk to her.

She simply couldn't. What would people say if she was seen with Agatha of all people? Seeking her out on purpose would mean risking her own impeccable reputation and social standing. And what on earth was Lord Tolleson thinking of, bringing the woman here? Marmaduke was right. Phineas was a law unto himself.

Why had Agatha bothered returning to Durscombe? Surely she'd have been better off staying where she'd been hiding out for years, in that godforsaken backwater up north.

Emily broke free of Marmaduke, murmuring gentle excuses about the throbbing in her temples. She ambled around the edge of the ballroom, musing on Agatha's return, still anxious to avoid her for now. The dancers were keeping up a brisk pace in the centre of the floor, the musicians teasing them with a fast gallop, and in order to escape the noise, and the draught caused by several dozen women in their voluminous skirts, Emily sought refuge in one of the side rooms.

She closed the door and peered around at her surroundings with interest. Mayor Bumble's study, she presumed, although it didn't look as though much studying went on in here. The books were lined up on shelves, pristine behind sparkling glass doors. A large leather-topped walnut desk, devoid of everything except a blotting pad and an ink pot, was dwarfed into insignificance by the two huge sofas set in front of it at right angles, and a number of high wingback armchairs upholstered in deep red brocade. Several expensive Persian rugs had been casually thrown on the floor. The overall look was divine, although entirely ostentatious. Bumble and his wife Norah, or someone they paid, evidently had sumptuous taste.

Emily meandered over to the French doors. They opened onto a private balcony overlooking the grounds at the back of the house. A huge moon lit up a world in white, the grass and the branches of the trees petrified with frost, a scene of such intense beauty that it quite spirited her away. She hesitated, but only for a second, before twisting the handle and pushing open the door. She stepped outside—the sharp icy coldness providing an instant salve for her hot head—and walked forwards to lean against the low stone wall, admiring the view. The slight breeze disturbed the branches of a nearby tree and she listened, entranced, to the musical chink of the ice encrusted branches, puffing out her breath as a child would, delighted by the plumes of steam she expelled. Quite the she-dragon.

Too cold.

She turned to re-enter the study but hadn't made it as far as the doors when, to her annoyance, she noticed several men had followed her into the room. She should have simply walked back inside and excused herself, these were *gentlemen* after all, but something, some sixth sense, gave her pause. She recognised Pyle and Endicott and several of the other aldermen, frequent visitors to her own house where they would be entertained by Marmaduke. She considered them tiresome, wanting in both intelligence and warmth, and all of them pompous beyond belief. Her mother Lily would have loved them.

She lay one hand on the door handle and paused.

"What do you think of Bumble's plan?" asked Alderman Endicott.

"I'm not averse to it, at all. Are you?" returned Pyle.

"I feel a little cautious, if I'm honest. But these ship-owners are insured after all, are they not? I mean, one supposes Lloyds takes care of them? What?"

"Oh absolutely, my dear Mr Endicott. And the loss of one ship simply means more ships are needed. That keeps men in work and off the streets. It's a winning situation, I would say. Philanthropic almost." Pyle's cajoling voice travelled through the door.

Outside, the icy air had begun to seep through Emily's thin dress. She rubbed her arms, and shivered. What could they be discussing?

"There are *some* losers, however. We should surely, as Christian men, be mindful of that," rebuked Alderman Goodwin. Emily would recognise his gruff voice anywhere. He regularly volunteered to read on a Sunday at St Michael's.

"The sailors you mean?" Pyle returned, sounding oddly cheery. "Every man knows what he signs up for when he takes to a ship, surely? That's a risk you take."

"Agreed. Most sailors are cutthroats and vagabonds given half the chance," Endicott responded. "They are no great loss to general humanity. The townsfolk will be safe, and they will all benefit from Bumble's plan. I have to say, gentlemen, I'm beginning to come around to the idea."

"I hope what you say proves to be the case this time, Pyle. Thomas Parrett was a sad loss to this parish." The gruff voice of Alderman Goodwin came again. Emily began to warm to the man more.

"Yes he was," said Endicott, obviously prevaricating between two opposing points of view.

"He knew what he was doing," Pyle said. "The *Eliza May* still had cargo in her hold and the mayor asked him to offload it. We couldn't have foreseen that the ship would disintegrate on that particular afternoon. It was just one of those things, Goodwin. Parrett needed the money. We persuaded him this one job would see him right. It was an honest job for honest wages. That's what all men want, isn't it?"

Emily caught the sound of metal scraping against flint. A moment later the perfumed scent of a cigar drifted through the open door.

"Thomas Parrett was a decent man. Neither a gambler, nor a drinker. I wasn't aware he had gotten himself into debt." Endicott again.

"I'm not certain of the details. Regrettably, I was forced to increase the rent on some of the properties I own down The Lanes. Demand outstrips supply." Pyle spoke matter-of-factly.

"Ah, unfortunate for Parrett. I can well understand why the man needed the extra work," Endicott said.

Goodwin, the voice of reason, chipped in, "It's his wife I feel sorry for. How is she managing now?"

Pyle laughed. "Good gracious, Joseph! How is it you are turning into such a Whig? I believe my clerk instructed her to vacate the cottage this very afternoon. If she has nowhere to go, there is space at the workhouse."

Emily gasped in horror. Then, realising she might have been heard, clamped a hand to her mouth. She drew back from the door.

A brief moment of silence.

She heard the sound of footsteps as boots stepped off the rug and onto the polished wooden floorboards and walked briskly towards her. Emily quickly shrank to the side, disappearing into the shadows, pressing her back into the brickwork, holding her breath all the while.

Pyle. She could make out his side silhouette clearly. He paused, standing on the door jamb, his breath puffing out in front of him, as he stared up at the dark sky. "Tremendous moon tonight fellows," he remarked, and pulled the door closed.

Emily released a shuddering breath. She would hear no more.

She remained in place for some time, too long, but she didn't dare make a move. Her shoulders were bare and the silk of her dress thin. The chill night bit through her inadequate clothing, and her fingers quickly became numb in spite of the lacy gloves she wore. She began to shiver uncontrollably, longing for her shawl, her mind racing.

Poor Sally.

She hadn't seen much of her youngest cousin for years, although they lived within a few miles of each other. Emily had simply outgrown Sally once she had been catapulted into an entirely more glamorous social circle, although looking back she fondly remembered their time spent together as children at Myrtle Lodge.

Emily experienced a pang of remorse. Sally had been through so much, losing Thomas and her health, and none of it had been the woman's fault. Emily should have taken it upon herself to do more to help her. Hadn't she heard through the grapevine that Sally had been struggling and that both Agatha and Lord Tolleson had been offering assistance? And Sally's son too. Stanley, wasn't it?

But how would Sally cope with this latest blow? Losing her cottage this way?

Still hugging the wall, and quivering with the cold, Emily could only imagine her cousin's vulnerability. She regretted keeping her distance, recognising her own weakness for the vanity it surely was. She'd always been far too concerned about her social status, worrying about being seen consorting with the lower classes and how that would look to all those elderly dowagers who knew exactly what Emily was and from where she originated.

Her blood stirred, and an image of Tansy popped into her mind.

"I made a mistake," she whispered, her breath steaming. "I'll make it up to Sally."

She would talk to Agatha, tell her what had happened.

Had Pyle and Bumble really paid Thomas to go out to the wreck? This didn't sound so much like honest work as coercion by the sound of it. Emily thought better of Bumble. She often compared Marmaduke unfavourably to the mayor. No doubt Bumble had been led astray by Pyle and the other aldermen. Why could these ridiculous men never understand that their pursuit of power and glory and wealth had untold consequences for all of the ordinary folk they used and abused as they swallowed them up in their path.

If Sally ever found out the truth about Thomas it would break her heart.

Emily would spare her that.

She shifted, cramp setting in. She needed to make a move. Inching sideways until she was level with the door, she craned her neck to peer through the glass. The men had disappeared. She turned the handle with difficulty—her fingers clumsy with the cold—and re-entered the warmth of the study, sighing with relief.

But she wasn't alone after all.

Pyle lounged in one of the wingback chairs, obviously waiting for her. She froze. He smiled at her, his eyes cold.

"I wondered when you'd venture inside, Emily, my dear." He sucked on his cigar and studied her face.

Emily, recovering her senses, lifted her chin. "Mrs Fliss, if you please. I most certainly am not 'your dear'." She turned for the exit. Pyle jumped up and in a few easy steps outpaced her.

He blocked her way. She cringed and backed away, but he grabbed her forearm with one hand, his palm hot against her cold skin. He ducked his head and leaned into her, intimately close, to inhale her scent. She gagged at the smell of brandy on his breath as he pulled her nearer, the hand holding his cigar just inches from her face. The smoke made her eyes sting.

"I'm sure that anything you imagine you heard in here this evening will remain secret. Something you take to the grave, will it not, Mrs Fliss?" hissed Pyle. His malevolence hung in the small space between them, weighted and cruel.

Emily blinked rapidly. She had half a mind to scream. That would bring people running, surely? She opened her mouth and sucked in a breath.

"I wouldn't." Pyle calmly turned the lit end of the cigar towards her. She could feel its heat drying the moisture of her left eye.

"Now what do you say?" he murmured, flicking his tongue out and running it along her chin. She tried to pull away and he held her arm tighter. "You have always been my weakness, Mrs Fliss."

"I—" Emily began, when a sudden noise startled them both. Pyle hurriedly dropped Emily's arm. The door handle turned with a clunk, and Phineas entered, intent solely on locating a cigar for himself.

"I do beg your pardon," he exclaimed when he saw them standing together.

"No, indeed!" Pyle attempted to disarm the situation. "Mrs Fliss is faint."

Phineas frowned, studying Emily with obvious concern. "Mrs Fliss, are you quite well?" he asked.

"I confess I do feel a little overcome, Lord Tolleson," Emily muttered, holding a hand to her face where the cigar had been just moments before.

"Oh! Let me help you to a chair."

"No! Not in here. No need. Some air. Perhaps you would assist me?"

"I'm quite sure you've had enough air for one night, Mrs Fliss." Pyle sounded almost amused.

Phineas shot him a sharp look. What the devil had gotten into the man? "Of course. Please." Phineas took Emily's arm. "If you're quite sure you're strong enough to walk Mrs Fliss, please allow me." He led her from the room, Emily sensing the heat of Pyle's glare burning into the back of her head.

When they were safely out of Pyle's hearing, Emily collapsed against Phineas. He bent his head to her in alarm. "I must speak with Agatha, Lord Tolleson. It is imperative," she whispered.

"Should I summon Mr Fliss?" he asked.

"On no account. No. I *must* speak to Agatha." She clasped a hand to her forehead, making a great show of feeling faint.

Phineas blinked at her. "Outside?"

"I do not wish to be alone, Lord Tolleson. You mustn't leave me yet. You must escort me to her. Please."

"Of course. And then might I locate Mr Fliss for you?"

"No!" Emily had no desire to have Marmaduke fussing over her, but when Phineas grimaced in alarm, she lightened her tone. "At least perhaps not yet, kind Sir."

Phineas patted her arm as he guided her to the far end of the ballroom seeking Agatha, alarmed by Emily's increasing agitation.

Agatha stood alone, much as he'd left her, enjoying the musicians and surreptitiously tapping her feet beneath her ballgown. But sensing the advancement of Phineas and Emily, she glanced their way, unable to hide her surprise. Catching the desperate look on her cousin's face, she allowed her eyes to drift in the direction the pair had come from. She caught sight of Pyle, leaning against the wall, staring straight at them, his face thundered with ill-concealed fury.

Instantly alert to danger, Agatha thought on her feet. "Why Mrs Fliss," she exclaimed loudly, unsure how much Pyle would be able to hear, "how beautiful you look this evening." She curtseyed and clasped Emily's hands in her own, leaning forward to kiss her cheek. "Take a deep breath," she instructed, keeping her voice low. "Act out some ordinary charade with me." She pulled away. Emily fixed a smile to her flushed face and pretended to draw Agatha's attention to the embroidery on her dress.

One eye fixed on Pyle, Agatha exclaimed over the stitching, nodding and smiling. "Keep going," she murmured in a low voice until at last Pyle relaxed his shoulders, and took his eyes from Emily. Quickly, Agatha linked arms with the woman and drew her towards the drinks table. Phineas, followed at a distance, utterly confused by the proceedings.

"What is it?" Agatha asked, her tone now serious.

"I think Sally is in trouble."

"Sally?" repeated Agatha. "How so?"

"She has been evicted from her cottage this afternoon. She will probably have gone to her sister-in-law, but ..." Emily's voice was urgent, shaking with pent up emotion.

Agatha could feel the years falling away, to a time when she and Emily and Sally had been girls. As thick as thieves. "But what if she hasn't?"

"Yes."

A memory, long buried. The fire whispering ...

Agatha exhaled as though someone had punched her in the gut. "Tansy—"

"You recall?" Emily whispered. "In the kitchen. Over the fire?"

"I do." Agatha could recall her grandmother, a ritual, a prophecy—but not the words. Not exactly. The music weaved through the air around them, but Agatha had forgotten where she was, so lost in remembrance was she. She could smell the smoke of the fire. The herbs Tansy had used. Sage. The dried flowers. She could hear Tansy's rhythmic intonation—

A dancer knocked against Agatha, bringing her back from her reverie. "I beg your pardon, Madam," the dashing young man called.

Agatha lifted a hand to her forehead. "I need to go to Sally."

"I shall come with you."

Agatha shook her head, sharply. "You're forgetting yourself, Emily. People will talk. Ask Mr Fliss to take you home."

"I will not," Emily glared. They were girls again. Agatha had always been the bossy one. Emily, the obstinate. "He will refuse to leave this party before midnight. And you cannot abandon me here by myself." Emily grabbed for Agatha's hands. Agatha looked down at the long pale fingers that entwined her stubbier ones and noticed a mark above Emily's left wrist, the red grip of a larger male hand, the fingers clearly imprinted in the white skin above her slender wrist.

She gently stroked Emily's arm. "Did Alderman Pyle do this?"

"Yes."

A red veil of fury pulsed through Agatha. How *dare* this man lay a hand on her cousin? On any woman. "Why?"

"Because of what I overheard," Emily told her. "He was engaged in conversation with some of the other aldermen." Emily's eyes flicked around the room, searching out the aldermen and their wives.

"What about?"

"Much of it made little if any sense." Agatha's brow creased in frustration, as Emily continued, "But what I did understand was the aldermen manipulated Thomas Parrett in some way. They were the ones that sent him out to that wreck—the *Eliza May*—to enter the hold, and he didn't come back. Now Sally has been evicted. We must find her, Agatha."

Agatha nodded. They had to act now. Turning briskly, she sought out Phineas. He hovered at a polite distance a few feet away, pretending not to listen to their conversation. When their eyes met, he drew himself to his full height and puffed out his chest. "At your service, Madam."

"We require your carriage, Lord Tolleson," Agatha informed him.

Phineas nodded. Agatha's determined expression told him it would be futile to argue. "Of course."

"And I need you to locate Mr Fliss and tell him we are escorting Mrs Fliss home because she feels unwell."

Phineas opened his mouth to make a suggestion, but Agatha held up a hand. "Please?"

Caught up in the urgency of her tone, Phineas snapped his heels together. He gave a smart little bow before shooting off to locate Marmaduke Fliss. On the way, he passed a footman and, pausing briefly, asked him to arrange for his own carriage to be brought round to the front door.

Phineas found Marmaduke in the salon playing cards with Norah Bumble and a few of her friends. Phineas bent discreetly to his side and whispered in his ear. Marmaduke excused himself from the game.

"Emily's ill, you say? I thought she was looking a little peaky earlier on." Marmaduke slurred his words, his eyes glassy. He'd obviously been enjoying all of the available hospitality.

"If it is no inconvenience to you, my dear Alderman Fliss, Miss Agatha Wick and I will escort Mrs Fliss home. I have to leave imminently in any case."

"Are you quite sure, Lord Tolleson? That is most sporting of you. It saves me a journey on this cold night." The ladies at Marmaduke's table tittered behind their fans, observing the exchange with avid curiosity.

"Quite," said Phineas. "I am more than happy to—" but Marmaduke was already returning to his game.

Phineas bowed to thin air and took his leave.

Agatha and Emily, bundled in their wraps, stood together in the elegant marble hallway, Emily shivering and Agatha rubbing her arms. He joined them. "The carriage should be outside by now," Phineas said, stepping ahead of them to alert the doormen.

"Lord Tolleson," Agatha reached for his arm. "There is no need for you to accompany us. This is a family matter and it doesn't concern you."

"Do you honestly believe I would allow you two ladies out alone on an evening such as this? I will not hear of it. There appears to be much at stake." Phineas nodded at the doorman who rushed to open the doors, exposing the freezing nightscape beyond. "Besides, this is an adventure. I am determined to join you."

The carriage stood waiting for them, directly in front of the steps, the horses blowing steam, and the coachman wrapped in numerous layers.

"To The Blue Bell Inn," Agatha instructed the driver as the footman helped her into the carriage. The driver glanced at Phineas who took a moment to nod his approval and the door slammed behind them, trapping them inside the carriage along with the wintry night air.

Emily shivered, and Agatha wrapped her arms around her. The driver cracked his whip, the carriage lurched and they were off.

18
ONE WILL FLY

"Can you explain what is happening?" Phineas leaned across the carriage to peer at Agatha. "Why are we heading to The Blue Bell Inn?"

Agatha and Emily exchanged glances. When Emily didn't protest, Agatha filled in some of the details. "We have to find Sally Parrett, Lord Tolleson. We believe she is in danger. I can't tell you all, but Emily — Mrs Fliss, — overheard a conversation in the study this evening that leads her to believe that this is the case. We understand that Sally has been evicted from her cottage."

This came as news to Phineas. "Surely Stanley would have heard something?"

"By all accounts this regrettable event occurred late this afternoon." Emily, buried beneath her fur wrap, sounded thoroughly miserable. "Oh! Is this coach unable to drive any faster?"

Phineas perturbed, reached to tap on the ceiling with his cane, but Agatha caught his arm. "No. It's pitch black and icy on the roads. Your coachman knows what he is doing. We'll get there as destiny decrees." She patted Emily's arm. "Have faith," she said gently. "Isn't that what Tansy would have said?"

Emily nodded and slumped back against the seat, staring out of the glass into the darkness, her eyes wild and watchful.

The coach rumbled on, and within five minutes they came upon the outskirts of the town, another two, and the lights of The Blue Bell Inn appeared on their left. Numerous pockets of men and the odd woman milled around outside, rowdy and carousing and generally having a good time. Emily baulked at descending from the carriage among the throng, but Agatha was quick to alight on Phineas's coat tails.

"Will you enquire at the Inn for Sally's whereabouts, Lord Tolleson? I'll run down The Lanes and see if I can locate her sister-in-law." Agatha whirled about. "Emily? Stay here with the driver."

Phineas caught Agatha's arm. "Wait, Miss Wick. If everyone is out and about, perhaps Sally is too. Let me check inside first."

Agatha, impatient to begin the hunt for her cousin, reluctantly agreed. She stood her ground, her arms crossed at her chest, stamping her feet to keep warm, ignoring the catcalls of the drunker men.

Phineas ducked into the inn and battled his way through to the bar where the landlord was busily serving customers. Phineas tried to attract his attention above the raucous noise of the partying crowd, but to no avail. Beginning to despair, Phineas looked around for someone he might recognise.

"How're you doing, Sir?" Maddie, the landlord's daughter, tending to a barrel of ale, squinted across at him.

"I'm looking for Sally Parrett, Maddie. Have you seen her? Do you know whether—"

"Such a sad state of affairs, Lord Tolleson, Sir." Maddie straightened up and dried her hands on her badly stained pinafore. "She was turned out of her cottage this evening on someone's say so —I don't know who, Sir—but that's cruel, on a night like tonight. All her belongings and everything in the street, and her now homeless."

Phineas flinched at the news. "Do you have any idea where she is?"

Maddie hesitated, scanning Phineas's face, perhaps questioning his motives.

"I'd dearly like to find her, Maddie. Take news to her son," Phineas explained. "Did she go to her sister-in-law's?"

Maddie shook her head. "I believe they took her things there, what there was of it, Sir. She came in here. Dad gave her a drink. All upset she was, as you can imagine. She was asking for a ride from one of the grooms."

"A ride?" Phineas repeated. "Where did she wish to go?"

"The Victoria Gardens, Sir. I don't think she managed to cadge one, so mayhap she walked up there in the end."

Disturbed, Phineas thanked Maddie. He forced his way through the crowds and back out into the chilly night once more. Agatha rushed towards him as soon as he appeared. "Anything?" she asked.

"I think perhaps we should try The Victoria Gardens. The landlord's daughter thinks Sally might have been heading that way." Phineas helped Agatha into the carriage, and the coachmen turned them about. The carriage travelled quickly along the promenade and in no time at all the horses were struggling up the steep hill out of Durscombe, before trotting along the lane that led to the moor. They turned off, towards the headland, and the driver eventually drew the horses to a stop at the ornamental garden gates.

"Why would she come here?" Agatha asked, panic pricking at her insides. Agatha reached for Emily's hand and a look passed between the cousins.

"Why don't you stay here Emily? Where it's warmer? Lord Tolleson and I will bring her back," Agatha promised, her heart beating far too quickly.

"Hurry!" Emily begged.

Phineas jumped from the carriage, and turned to assist Agatha, but she was right behind him.

"Sir?" the coachman asked.

"Stay with Mrs Fliss," Phineas called back, grabbing a lantern from the side of the carriage, before he hurried after Agatha who had set off at pace. They slipped along the beautifully laid ornamental path in their impractical evening shoes, until Agatha caught hold of Phineas' arm and hurriedly pulled him onto the grass instead. The neatly trimmed lawn lay hard and crisp beneath their feet, crunching as they scuttled across it, individual blades of grass sparkling like diamonds. They rushed through the gardens, breathing noisily as the biting air burned in their lungs.

They slowed as they approached the cliffs. The moon hung in the sky, an enormous bright globe just above the horizon, similarly reflected in the dark sea below.

Agatha gasped and yanked at Phineas's arm. They slid to a stop.

The tiny silhouette of one lonely figure stood starkly illuminated in front of the moon.

For there she was. Sally. Balanced at the cliff's edge, overlooking the rocks that had claimed the *Eliza May*. She braced herself against the bitterness of the sea breeze, hatless and shawlless, but wearing her best Sunday dress and boots.

Phineas set the lantern on the grass at his feet and held his arms up, in a silent plea. He would have cried out, but Agatha placed a warning hand on his arm.

She stepped forwards, instead. "Sally?" she called in a voice full of love. "Little Sally?" Sally turned about and studied her cousin, her face pinched and ghastly white. "Do you know who is here?"

Sally shifted her weight, regarding them both for a long moment. "Agatha," she replied, and her voice was broken, her eyes haunted. "And ... Lord Tolleson?" She clasped her hands together in front of her chest. "Oh! You shouldn't have come here. You shouldn't have come."

"We had to come Sally. We had to find you," Agatha soothed her. "We have the carriage at the gate, Sally. It's warm there. And Emily is waiting for you also. She's so worried about you, Sally. Emily is—"

"I'm here." Emily's voice drifted out of the darkness behind them. She stepped into the circle of light thrown off by the lantern. Agatha frowned, but reached to pull Emily close to her. They huddled together, arm in arm. Emily held her free hand out to Sally. "I'm here, Sally. We'll go back to Myrtle Lodge, all three of us, and—"

"No," Sally said, her voice certain.

"No?" Emily repeated. "You—?"

"Not Myrtle Lodge. Not tonight, nor any night." Sally's voice had taken on an oddly childish cast. "Tonight is the night I will fly," she said, and lifted her arms above her head. Phineas made a startled noise in his throat. "I always knew I would be the one to fly!"

"No, Mrs Parrett!" Phineas cried in horror. *In God's name, what did she mean to do?*

Agatha held a hand in front of Phineas to shush him. "You must be cold, darling," she said to Sally. "We have a fire. You can warm yourself. Step away from the edge now and come with me. I'll take you home to Myrtle Lodge where it is warm. Stanley will come and visit you."

Sally's shoulders dropped and she shook her head, a weary movement. "Not tonight," she repeated. When she looked up again, she took a deep breath and stared directly at Agatha. "You take good care of my boy, Agatha. You promise?" She turned about to face to the water.

Now Agatha felt the strength in her own knees ebbing away. She stumbled forward, reaching out, helplessly beseeching her cousin. "Sally?"

Sally laughed, a sound that chilled Agatha's bone marrow. "He's here!" she sang, pointing out and over the cliff. "Thomas is here. Do you see him?"

As one, Agatha, Emily and Phineas followed the line of Sally's finger.

"I'm coming, Thomas," Sally called out. "I'm coming!"

One large wave broke against the rocks in the near distance, and later Phineas could never be sure whether he saw a man standing there or not. But what he did remember, what he would never forget, was the fraction of an instant when Sally jumped, because momentarily she remained beautifully silhouetted against the moon, her arms up, her legs kicking her skirts out, flying.

Flying.

And then she was gone. Tumbling through the air, heading for the jagged rocks and a broken death below.

Emily shrieked and sank into a swoon. Phineas gasped and clutched at his heart. Agatha rushed to the cliff edge and fell to her knees, her hands scrabbling among the frozen pebbles scattered in the long grass there. The sea below was inky, the surf foaming against the rocks. Of Sally there was no sign.

The littlest bird had flown home.

19
A PREMONITION

The three little girls squatted in the dirt, huddling around the circle Agatha had drawn with a long stick. Heads together, one blonde, one dark, one red, they giggled in nervous anticipation. Agatha took up her stick again, this time to create a slightly lopsided pentagram. She infilled some of the points with swirly symbols just as she had seen her grandmother do on many an occasion.

Agatha, at twelve, was the oldest of the cousins, tall and intelligent and the most serious, with copper coloured hair and freckles. Emily, only eight months younger, was pretty and cheerful but ultimately always striving to be sophisticated. Sally, the youngest at nearly ten years old, was the chatterbox, the mischief maker. Her strawberry blonde hair, always as unruly as she was, had started to unravel from her plaits, and she pushed the stray locks away from her flushed face as she bent to examine Agatha's handiwork.

The girls had contrived to escape the stifling atmosphere of Myrtle Lodge where Tansy had been holding forth among the adults gathered there, including Agatha's mother, Violet and Emily's mother, Lily, both of whom were no doubt fidgeting with impatience. Sally's mother, Daisy, could only ever be present in spirit, for she had passed away when Sally was a baby.

Sally pulled at Agatha's skirt, bubbling over with excitement. "What shall we ask the spirits?"

"We could ask them who we're going to marry?" suggested Emily. This thorny question had begun to occupy her thoughts of late.

Sally groaned in disgust. "No, don't!" She didn't think much of boys.

Agatha tutted and put a calming hand on Sally's arm. "Hush, Sally. They'll hear us and come looking." She jerked her head towards the house, reminding her cousins to keep the noise down, before directing a pointed look at Emily. "Why on earth would you want to get married? You'll just live a life of servitude and never be able to do what you like."

Emily screwed up her nose. "You sound like Tansy when you say that."

"Do I?" Agatha frowned, but when Sally giggled, Agatha was quick to see the funny side and join in. She supposed she did. Tansy, like Sally, had little time for men. Emily laughed with them. "Maybe I do sound like her, but really Emily, I have no desire to marry and have my freedom taken away from me. I've seen the ladies in the big houses. They always look so *bored*!"

Tansy never looked bored. She spent all day every day being busy, busy, busy.

Emily gazed longingly towards the town. Durscombe, what little they could see of it from the grounds of Myrtle Lodge, lay below them. Every time they made the trip from the town to the Lodge they had to pass several large houses and Emily loved to study them. "Oh I don't think so. I would love to live in one of those grand houses and be a lady. I'd wear such finery that I would make the other girls gasp with jealousy. And I'd have such splendid horses. And think of the balls and the parties! I *do* want to be a lady one day, Aggie."

To Agatha's mind, Emily already lived a charmed life, residing as she did in a huge townhouse with several servants. Her father had plenty of money. Meanwhile Agatha had spent her entire childhood at Myrtle Lodge with Tansy. Violet came and went at will, gloriously unencumbered by her young daughter.

Agatha shuddered. "No grand parties for me, thank you. And I have no wish to marry at all." She wouldn't mind a horse of her own, however.

"What if you meet someone and love him?" Emily asked, curious as to her cousin's future intentions.

"Then I should just love him, I imagine," Agatha replied, tartly. "As they did in the old times. I'll have no need to marry him."

Emily pressed the palms of her hands against her ears. "That would be quite the scandal, Agatha Wick."

Sally looked from one cousin to the other, unsure what to say and not sure of their meaning in any case. Agatha regarded her littlest cousin solemnly, before starting to rock with silent mirth. She'd had them for a moment. After a beat, Emily and Sally joined in.

"I'm going to marry the boy on the quay, anyway," announced Sally, her pale green eyes shining. "When I decide I like boys."

"Which boy on the quay?" Emily pricked up her ears.

"Sally has seen a boy on the quay when we've been down to buy fish from time to time," explained Agatha. Sally nodded with enthusiasm.

"What's his name?" Emily made it her business to know everyone in Durscombe. She took after her mother in that way.

Agatha shrugged. "Well, that we don't know. She'll have to point him out to you the next time you're both in church together and you can tell us." Agatha never attended church. Tansy didn't believe in a Christian God and neither did Violet. Sally went along with her father and stepmother and half siblings from time to time. Emily, begrudgingly, was obliged to go along with her mother and father at least once a week and sometimes more.

"I shall." She rubbed her palms together, eager to uncover further details. "I trust he comes from a good family. How do you know that you'll marry him, anyway, Sally?"

"I just know." Sally stuck her chin in the air, a note of tremulous defiance in her voice.

Agatha smiled, amused both by Sally's stated abhorrence of boys and by her certainty she would marry that particular one. It wouldn't surprise her in the slightest if Sally did 'just know'. The girls were descendants of a strange family after all, coming as they did from a long line of foremothers with an array of intriguing gifts.

And right here, right now, they were attempting to emulate Tansy by divining their futures using a drawing in the dusty soil.

Agatha tapped her stick on the ground in the centre of the pentagram. "So is that all we're going to ask? Who we're going to marry? If Sally is marrying a fisherman's boy and I'm not marrying anyone, then it will be all about you, Emily."

Emily sniffed and shrugged. "Well *I'd* find that interesting and I'd like to know." She folded her arms. "If not that, then what is it you wish to ask, Agatha? Ooh!" She widened her eyes. "You could ask how old you'll be when you die. That's always a good thing to know!"

"No!" Agatha jerked away from the circle. She'd been around Tansy to know the darkness that came with divination. Some things should remain permanently hidden from view.

"*How* you'll die?" cackled Sally.

"What games do you girls play out here?" Their grandmother's voice from the back step startled them. All three jumped to attention, instantly contrite. Tansy glared down at them, balancing her slight weight on a gnarled old stick. She'd recently begun to complain of problems in her hip. She regarded the faces in front of her, each averting their gaze. But while Emily and Sally stood respectfully enough, Agatha, behind them, tried to erase the dirt drawing with her foot. She needn't have bothered. Tansy had already seen it.

"You shouldn't mess with things you don't properly understand, girls," Tansy frowned.

Emily flushed a bright guilty red. She prided herself on being a good girl and hated any kind of admonishment about her behaviour.

"Sorry, grandmother," Agatha replied, her voice smooth. She wasn't afraid of Tansy, not like her cousins were. In fact, it puzzled her that even Lily and Violet were wary of the old woman.

Lily had tried to distance herself from her mother as far as humanly possible. She lived a pleasant and relatively easy life in town, with Emily, trying her best to forget her origins. It was unfortunate, in Lily's mind at least, that every now and then they were required to attend family functions. On those occasions she would turn up at Myrtle Lodge, Emily in tow, both of them dressed in expensive fashionable gowns, and perform her duties as a daughter.

Agatha, in many ways, was more awestruck when in Lily's company. Pretty Aunt Lily was the antithesis of Tansy. Lily was delicate and genteel and gave herself many airs and graces, all of which seemed to be entirely lacking in the rest of the family.

Particularly in Violet.

Agatha's mother was tempestuous and impulsive and colourful. As far as Agatha was aware her mother had never married, and Violet had never spoken of Agatha's father. They lived with Tansy at Myrtle Lodge and Agatha had known no other home. Violet spoke of faraway places—lands full of exotic animals, where people wore silk and had jewels in their navels—but how she knew these things, Agatha didn't understand.

Violet was an enigma, whereas Tansy was a known quantity. Agatha had grown close to her grandmother over the years and held her in high regard. While she might not have defined their relationship as loving, Tansy didn't scare Agatha for the simple reason that they were so alike. Agatha understood her grandmother in a way she never would her whimsical mother. Tansy was open and honest and surrounded herself with nature. Her garden was a joy to behold, and when Agatha brought stricken animals to her, Tansy would nurse them to the best of her ability. If she somehow failed to save the unfortunate creature, she would instruct Agatha to burn it in the garden. They would stand together, solemnly observing the shapes in the flames. Her grandmother would read what she saw there and describe the animal's life to her granddaughter in absorbing detail. Eventually they would scatter the ashes, returning the dust to the earth where all life began.

Tansy observed the changing of the seasons and celebrated each equinox. She lay pots of water out in the garden every full moon and charged them with the moon's energy. She haunted the shoreline at dawn and dusk, and danced naked in the moonlight and in the rain whenever she felt like it. She offered blessings for nature's abundance several times a day and, as far as Agatha was aware, she only ever did good.

Many a time Agatha would sit quietly on a bench in the darkest shadow of the kitchen, and listen as Tansy administered advice to women who ventured up from town or out of the nearby villages. Sometimes the women would cry and rage in desperation, and Tansy would soothe them and offer some form of communion with herself and other women, before sending them home laden with tinctures and potions, and instructions on how to ease their pain and make themselves well again.

But now Tansy stood in front of them, her lined face stern. Agatha dropped her chin to her chest to avoid looking at her grandmother and dug her fingernails into the palms of her hands.

"We were playing," she tried to explain, but her words lacked conviction.

Tansy scrutinized each girl in turn, pondering over their motivation. Her hard stare lingered longest on Agatha, before she lifted a hand to chew on a black thumbnail. The silence stretched out interminably, broken only by the cries of gulls circling overhead. Sally fidgeted with the back of her skirt, until eventually Tansy spoke. "Do you girls truly want to know your futures?" she asked.

Agatha eyed her grandmother, wary of the catch.

"Oh I do!" Emily blurted out, hopping in excitement.

Sally glanced uncertainly at Agatha and shrugged, happy to let her older cousins take the lead.

Agatha lifted her chin and held her grandmother's knowing gaze, unease stroking her spine with its tickly fingers? What might they all discover? On the many occasions she had observed Tansy scattering her bag of bones on the hearth in order to read a woman's fortune, it had seemed like idle fun. But now she had no wish for Tansy to use that insight on her.

"Come," said Tansy sharply. The girls followed in her wake, up the steps and through the back door into the kitchen. The fire always burned brightly here, regardless of the season, and the room was filled with the familiar scents of herbs and preserves and baking.

To Agatha's surprise, Tansy didn't reach for the small bag that contained the blanched divination bones. Instead she plucked a jar of dried herbs from a high shelf, well out of the reach of young hands, and pulled up a stool next to the fireplace. She gestured to the girls and they sat before her, cross-legged on the floor, tucking their skirts around them.

When they had settled, Tansy pointed at the fire. "The greatest truths are often found in the flames. Look into them, tell the flames your thoughts, and they will tell me your future."

Agatha focused on the flames as she'd been instructed. The fire burned with a good energy, the flames flicking up the chimney, too quickly for Agatha to make anything out. The licks and curls flashed and spat, and any image Agatha thought she could see was immediately replaced by another.

Or so she imagined.

Tansy's eyes bore into her and Agatha had to concentrate hard in order to ignore the distraction. The more she did so, the greater her realisation that the flames were not so fleeting. Each one lived for a much longer time than she'd supposed. They twisted and shaped themselves from one base root, in countless different ways. Hands that beckoned and waved. Little spats of soot shot away from the burning fingers, and the smoke rolled and curled up into the chimney. By narrowing her eyes and staring hard, Agatha could make out figures and objects, but she couldn't tell how much her imagination was responsible and how much was not.

That could be a woman ... no ... *women* ... dancing. Women entwined in each other's arms. And there ... the sea ... and boats and ships bobbing on calm waters ... and then a man and a huge house and a garden ... and for one brief moment she thought she saw Tansy as an older woman staring out of the flames at her. She beckoned to Agatha. The flames hissed. "Fffffffffollow me," they whispered, and Agatha reared back in surprise, breaking contact.

Tansy laughed in delight. "I do believe you have the gift, Agatha," she said, her voice low. "But that's no real surprise."

Emily frowned, screwing her eyes in frustration.

Tansy opened the jar of dried herbs and shook a handful of the contents into the palm of her hand. "Dried flowers," she murmured. "Violet, lily and daisy ... and rose and buttercup for the babies I lost. She threw the herbs gently into the blaze. The fire reared up, hissed angrily, and spat as the herbs crackled.

"Tsk tsk," Tansy hissed right back at it. "Be calm." She held her hands out. "Be calm." The flames died back, and the girls watched as Tansy inched closer, her eyes bright, the flames reflected there. She stared deeply into the heart of the blaze. "Show me," she intoned, "show me what you have lying in wait for my three little girls."

She sighed and rocked and poked at the wood, threw in more herbs, and rocked a little more. The glow of the flames became brighter and Tansy moaned. "There," she said. "There you are. My little girls. My three little girls ..."

Sharing your young lives and your innermost desires
Growing and learning, happy and free
Until you are not,
'Til you are riven apart by one bloody act of violence
A wealthy man's greed.
My three little birds, two will share a secret, but not the third.
One will toil and love
One will bide her time

One will spend her life in a gilded cage.
One bird is mute, and another one is rage
But each will stretch their wings
And one will fly and one will try to fly
But each will see the darkness and hear the shadows moving
And know when death is close by—

"Mother!" A shriek of outrage from the door.

Agatha, lulled by the flames and Tansy's smooth voice had lapsed into a trance, but now she shot to a standing position.

Lily loomed in the kitchen doorway, mouth wide in shock, brows knitted with rage. "What are you doing?" She marched to the hearth and grabbed Emily's hand, yanking her up and away from the dancing flames.

Tansy hadn't moved from her position on the stool in front of the fire. She peered up through her lashes at her middle daughter, her eyes glinting.

"It's absolute nonsense, mother!" Lily raged. "You're filling these girls' heads with hogwash. What if they chose to believe any of it? They're at an impressionable age."

Agatha gawped at Lily, taken aback by her vehemence. Fresh memories of Tansy's words drifted through her mind. What had it meant? Had Tansy made it all up as Lily suggested?

Violet had drifted into the room behind her sister, curious as to what all the fuss was about. Always laissez-faire about such things, she tittered in amusement at her sister's faux outrage. "Lily—" she said, reaching for her younger sister, "Don't take on so—"

Lily shook Violet off. "They can do without these lies."

Tansy raised her eyebrows, her face stony. "Not lies, Lily. Most definitely not lies, my maid. You know better than that," she said. "For all your false airs and graces."

"I'm trying to secure a better future for my daughter, mother." Lily's voice shook with emotion. "Really ... I bring Emily to see you because I need your help to quell her night terrors, and yet here you are, intent on filling her head with fanciful notions of magic and witchcraft that only serve to make matters worse."

Tansy glared at Lily who had pulled Emily to the back door. "You're so blinded by where you think you're going that you've forgotten where you come from," she growled. "That's convenient for you, but it serves no purpose for Emily. She needs to understand the power she has inside herself. She must learn how to harness it and more importantly how to protect herself."

Lily flushed. "We're leaving now, and I will never bring Emily back here. Not ever. You are insufferable, mother."

"You would deny your heritage, would you?" Tansy pushed herself up from the stool and wagged her finger at her daughters.

"Heritage? What heritage?" Lily waved balled fists at the old woman.

"Lily—" Violet tried again.

Lily rounded on Violet. "I for one cannot bear this behaviour any longer, dear sister. Our mother makes us a laughing stock in the town. She always has."

"She is what she is," Violet shrugged. "I think everyone knows that."

Lily wheeled about, pushing Emily ahead of herself so quickly that the girl had no time to say goodbye. "I refuse to subject my daughter to her bizarre pretences any longer."

"You need my help, Lily," Tansy protested. "You know how destructive Emily—"

"Enough!" Lily hissed.

Emily's head swivelled, ducking around the side of her mother's voluminous skirts, so that she and Agatha could lock gazes for a brief moment, before Lily dragged her daughter away.

Agatha watched her aunt and cousin leave with some regret. Emily brought such light into the world, with her laughter and optimism and dreams. Now that she'd been banished, surely darkness threatened to fill the void. This had all happened so suddenly, it had to be the continuation of an argument that had been going on for some time.

Tansy sucked her teeth, evidently disapproving of Lily's behaviour.

Agatha regarded her in wonder. Had her grandmother really insinuated that something dreadful would happen to each of her granddaughters?

Which of the three little birds was Agatha?

And was there any way to change her premonition?

20
A FRESH START

Stanley ground his fingers into the earth, gently covering the shoots, before sitting back on his haunches to admire his handiwork. Agatha had requested that he separate out the daffodil bulbs from the tulips and create two distinct areas for them. So far this morning he had transplanted a hundred or so bulbs into a new, sunnier position.

Durscombe had finally shaken off the sharp grip of a long winter. Never in living memory had the snow settled so deeply and for so long. The town had even been cut off for several weeks, preventing supplies getting through from Exeter or neighbouring farms, and this had caused some hardship in The Lanes and elsewhere. Little fresh produce had been available, certainly not much in the way of vegetables, and what did make it to market had been poor quality. Even the fish were less plentiful than usual.

A grief-stricken Stanley, conversely, had been fine. He had two kitchens to choose from and he was well fed in both. He couldn't complain on that front. Following the death of his mother, he'd wallowed for a time, but both Lord Tolleson and Miss Wick had offered him plenty of support. Miss Wick had even paid for the memorial stone for his mother. She'd said it was the least she could do, given that she hadn't been able to save Sally.

Tears pricked at Stanley's eyes. He was a grown man nearly, and he didn't want to cry, but thinking of his Ma was always liable to set him off, he'd found.

"I am so looking forward to the spring bulbs, aren't you Stanley?" The quiet voice startled him. He blinked the tears quickly from his eyes.

"Miss Flora!" he said, and jumped up, wiping his hands on his trousers.

Flora smiled at him, and he thought how pretty she looked. She'd recently taken to wearing her sleek dark hair swept up in a proper fashionable style, and he admired how it accentuated her slim neck and made her look both taller and more mature.

And incredibly beautiful.

Stanley blushed at his own thoughts.

"You make a grand gardener, Stanley. Agatha says you are green-fingered." Flora didn't mention his red face, but her eyes shone in amusement.

"Thank you, Miss Flora." He held out his hands, palms down, showed her how his fingers had been stained dark orange from the red of the clay soil. Dirt was caked in the arch of his cuticles. His mother would have said he could grow potatoes in the beds of his fingernails. He swallowed, deciding he found it comforting he could think of her that way.

As if reading his mind, Flora donned a more serious expression. "How are you, Stanley?"

Stanley shrugged. "I believe I am well, Miss Flora, thank you."

"My aunt says that grief must have its way. It cannot be rushed."

"Does she?" asked Stanley, his face masking fresh pain. "What else does she say?"

"That it can catch you unawares when you least expect it."

Stanley nodded. He recognised that. It still seemed incredible that he could lose both his mother and his father within the space of a few months, and in such tragic circumstances. He regarded Flora, remembering that she, too, had neither parent living.

"What about you, Miss Flora? I mean ... do you grieve for your mother?"

Flora blinked, slightly surprised at the turn of the conversation. "I don't know," she replied honestly. "I don't think about her very much. She has never been a part of my life."

"You don't know what she was like?"

"Well, when I was younger I asked Aunt Agatha to tell me all about her. She said my mother was remarkably pretty, with a terrific sense of fun. And she was kind. Extremely kind."

"You take after her then," Stanley complimented her.

Now it was Flora's turn to blush. She laughed, and Stanley joined in, pleased that she hadn't taken offence.

"Did she have hair like yours? The same colour?" he asked.

"Yes, apparently so. Long, dark hair, Aunt Agatha says. Hair that she could sit on. And that she was very proud of."

"I love the colour of your hair."

"Thank you." Flora dipped her head and avoided Stanley's eyes.

Stanley gestured at the flower bed in front of him. "I'd better get back to work before your Aunt catches me neglecting my duties."

Flora took a step back. "Oh, of course. I'm sorry. I shouldn't have interrupted you. They'll look so pretty when they grow."

Stanley squatted once more, pushing his fingers into the earth, creating a deep enough hole in which to drop his next bulb.

Flora hovered. "Do you ever have any time free, Stanley?"

Stanley paused. "Two half days a week and a full day every other week."

"I see." Flora hesitated, then caught her breath. "Perhaps we could go walking on your next afternoon? I don't get out as much as I'd like, except with my Aunt or Hannah, and I'm sure they wouldn't mind if we just walked into the woods, or along the lanes, perhaps? We could admire the bluebells." Her words tumbled out in a rush.

Stanley held his surprise in check. Come his next half day, he'd be sick to the back teeth of flowers. "I would be honoured," he beamed at her. "That will give me something to look forward to, Miss Flora."

Flora lowered her voice. "I think I would prefer it if you called me Flora when it's only you and I, Stanley. Aunt Agatha always says everyone is born just the same, and dies just the same, and we shouldn't have to stand on ceremony."

Stanley nodded, taken aback at the suggestion, but pleased. "Your Aunt is a wise woman. Very well ... Flora."

They grinned at each other, partners in conspiracy.

21
THE SMALL MATTER OF EMILY

"She's been a stone around my neck for years now, Bumble. She is deceitful and conniving." Pyle's dander was well and truly up.

Bumble puffed on a cigar and regarded Pyle through cold eyes. He had no time for this melodrama. How had they ended up here, discussing Mrs Fliss yet again? His proposals were taking shape. He wanted to concentrate all his effort on forging strategies for the next wrecking. Now that the snows were finally clearing from the moor above Durscombe, he needed to arrange a final meeting with Greeb. His partner in crime was proving more difficult to get hold of than the slipperiest of eels, and Bumble found himself increasingly anxious about the delay in setting his plan in motion.

"You have been reminding me of this for months, Pyle. I never know what to say to you. I have nothing that will offer solace. You misspoke. She overheard some snippets of your conversation that will not have made any sense to her."

"I told you at New Year, she was deliberately hiding out on the balcony in order to eavesdrop on our conversation." Pyle locked eyes with Bumble, his lips pursed. "She should be dealt with."

"How would you have me *deal* with her?" Bumble asked, exasperated at the notion. He brushed the air in front of him as though he were being bothered by an irritating wasp. "Quite clearly, given that it was a dance party, Mrs Fliss had become warm and had ventured out in search of fresh air. Pyle, you are being far too dramatic."

"Even if her motives were innocent, Bumble, she overheard a great deal of our conversation. Sensitive topics that she should not have been party to."

The truth of this gave Bumble pause. The fact that Emily had overheard the business about Thomas Parrett was unfortunate. However, given that Parrett's wretched wife had jumped off the cliff that very night, Emily couldn't possibly gain from telling anyone what she knew, or even what she thought she knew.

"If she had any concerns after that night, I am confident she would have articulated them with Mr Fliss. He has approached neither you nor me." Bumble settled back and puffed on his cigar. "I am certain we are in the clear, my dear fellow." Surely, the matter was all water under the bridge now?

Bumble might have thought so, but unfortunately Pyle did not. The issue had been causing the younger alderman disquiet for weeks. When Pyle had become party to Bumble's wrecking plans, the mayor had made it explicit that nobody—who wasn't already directly involved in the matter—must learn about it. Bumble demanded that the participating aldermen never discuss the plan out of his earshot. Pyle had promised that Emily Fliss could not have comprehended Bumble's plans, from the conversation she had overheard.

Bumble had been reassured by this.

But Pyle had been lying. He had not confessed the whole truth to Bumble. The guilt of that, and the fear that the mayor's wrecking plans would be discovered, had been weighing heavily on him for many weeks. Pyle had become progressively more agitated by the fact that nothing had been done about Emily.

Quite frankly, the whole situation was a mess.

Bumble, lacking an awareness of all the facts, couldn't understand Pyle's continuing consternation. Bumble wanted to ignore the situation with Emily. He had a soft spot for her and, if nothing else, it paid to recognise that both she and her husband were not without influence in certain circles.

The mayor sighed, pondering on Pyle's strange manner, and staring absently through the perfect smoke ring he had blown. Pyle's harrumph brought him back to the present. "Really Pyle, why not sit down and relax? Or ring the bell for more whisky. Make yourself useful, man."

Pyle rang the bell. More whisky sounded good to him.

"I'm inclined to think that if Emily was going to repeat what she had heard to anyone else, she would have done so by now and we would know about it. Her silence speaks volumes."

Pyle's brow remained creased. He paced in front of the fire. "Perhaps I should have a word with her?"

"No. I would consider that totally unnecessary." Bumble's response was sharp. "What on earth could that achieve? If she has no suspicions, why stoke the flames of her fire?"

"We would find out exactly what she thinks she knows."

"Is there something you're not telling me, man?" Bumble dropped his cigar in the ashtray to the side of him and glared at his companion.

"Not at all." Pyle rolled his shoulders, placed a hand on the mantelpiece and pretended to study the clock. Eventually he cleared his throat. "Only—"

"Only?" Bumble's eyes glittered. *What in the devil's name was the problem with Pyle, today?*

"Given what the blasted woman overheard, what if she pieces things together? What if she jumps to conclusions?"

Bumble leaned forward in his chair and scrutinized Pyle's bearing. He'd never seen him this nervous before.

"Is that a possibility?" Bumble asked, irritated at Pyle's sudden insinuation that Emily might know more than he'd previously been alerted to.

Pyle took a moment, then nodded abruptly.

Bumble groaned and rolled his eyes, sinking deeper into his chair.

"I'm sure, as you say, if anything were going to come of it, it would have done so already," Pyle panicked. "It's just ... I thought in the interests of transparency ... as we move forward with our new plans ..."

Bumble steepled his fingers. "Forewarned is forearmed?"

"Exactly that, Mayor Bumble."

Bumble puffed his cheeks out. "So ... it would have been better for me to know the whole truth at the time."

"I apologise unreservedly, Sir." Pyle swallowed. "You'll understand why I was so keen to perhaps have a word with Mrs Fliss."

Bumble glowered. He certainly understood what all the fuss was about now. Perhaps he should allow Pyle to open communications with Emily. The problem was, he'd be far too heavy handed about it and they didn't want to alert Marmaduke to their wrecking intentions. The less Alderman Fliss knew of the matter, the better.

Bumble decided the best course of action would be to proceed with caution.

Whatever he and Pyle did, they would need to take Marmaduke out of the equation somehow. If they could somehow alienate the Fliss's from each other ...

Pyle grimaced, impatient for Bumble's response. "What say you, Mayor? Should I approach her?"

Bumble reached for his cigar. "Pyle, Pyle, my dear man. Have you never heard of the saying, *softly softly catchee monkey*? If you are so set on uncovering what the supposedly demonic Mrs Fliss is intent on doing about something that she may—" he raised his eyebrows, "—or may not have overheard, especially given that she has not actually repeated that to anyone in over three months, I would suggest you leave it to me. I'll ..."

"Talk to her?"

Bumble shook his head slowly and smiled. "No. I have another plan."

22
A NEW BUTLER

"Ah Matthew, my good man." Phineas hurriedly pushed himself into a sitting position as Matthew answered his summoning bell. Sprawled on the chaise in the library, he'd been engrossed in the *Cornhill Magazine* which had arrived by the morning post.

Matthew gave his characteristic shallow bow, never as obsequious as some of Lord Tolleson's other servants. Phineas secretly enjoyed the man's display of confidence.

Phineas swung his legs to the floor and stood, keeping his face straight despite the excitement building inside. "I have some news I think you may appreciate. I have given the matter some consideration and after a successful trial, I would like to offer you the position of," he paused for effect, "butler" he said carefully, "on a permanent basis."

Matthew started in surprise and met his master's eye.

"Only if that meets with your satisfaction?" Phineas added.

"Well ... yes, Sir. It does, Sir!" replied Matthew, his face lighting up.

"Now I understand that we haven't really discussed financial remuneration or any such matters. We'll attend to that. For now, you are welcome to take Wiggy's old rooms in the East Wing. And, ah ... if they need refurbishing, just let me know and we'll have that taken care of." Phineas wafted his hand as though this was of no consequence. He hurried the few steps to his desk and reached for the envelope lying neatly on the blotting pad. "This is the contract of employment I have had drawn up for you."

Matthew took the letter, then gazed at it in wonder.

"If you could let me know whether it is suitable, I would be most obliged to you." Phineas returned to the chaise and made a great show of disinterest. He plucked up his magazine once more and flicked through to find the correct page.

Matthew held the envelope in his hand and turned it over several times, before slitting the seal on the reverse, and pulling out the vellum within. He admired Phineas's meticulous handwriting, and slowly read through the contents, guessing at some of the words. The one thing he did understand? The salary promised was substantial.

"Sir, this is most generous of you," began Matthew, his voice humble. "I am most grateful for this opportunity."

"Oh think nothing of it. Nothing at all," smiled Phineas, and went back to his magazine, thrilled with Matthew's reaction.

"Thank you, Sir. I will never let you down." Matthew bowed, and this time from the waist.

"I should hope not," said Phineas, his eyes sparkling. Matthew retreated for the door, envelope in hand, imagining he'd been dismissed for now.

Phineas stopped him, pointing to a large box on a side table by the door. "Before you leave, I hope you don't mind, but Mrs Gwynne and I saw fit to order you a new uniform. I do hope we have your sizes correct. It was a bit of guesswork on our parts."

Matthew regarded the box warily. "Sir, you really—"

"Honestly Matthew?" Phineas shook his head at the protestation. "I'm sure you'll repay me tenfold over the years through your loyal and thoughtful service. Wiggy certainly did."

"I most certainly will, Sir. Thank you, Sir." Matthew bowed

and took up the box. He paused, unsure what else to say, before bowing again. "I'll return to my duties, Sir."

Phineas nodded his approval and buried his head in his magazine once more, but the second Matthew had closed the door behind himself, Phineas was on his feet. He scurried across the room and rotated the doorknob quietly, opening it, just a crack. Holding his breath, he peeped through the gap.

As he'd hoped, Matthew had paused in the corridor to set the box down, all the better to examine the contents within. He pulled off the lid and parted several layers of tissue paper. Inside, he found a dark three-piece suit, most becoming of a butler, and a blue frock coat. Matthew appeared to particularly approve of this item because he pulled it out and pressed it against himself, swirling this way and that, smiling all the while, like a young girl in front of a mirror in a ballgown.

Phineas almost laughed aloud with delight, but when Matthew glanced towards the study door he hurriedly backed away.

Matthew grinned, carefully refolded the frock coat and replaced it among the tissue paper. Then, lifting the box, he carried it down the corridor, whistling as he headed towards the East Wing.

23
A CHANCE ENCOUNTER

"Mrs Fliss! How perfectly lovely to see you here!"

Startled, and with a certain amount of trepidation, Emily turned to see Mayor Bumble pacing towards her across the foyer of The London Hotel. "Mayor Bumble," she greeted him coolly, wondering what he could be doing in Exeter.

"What a coincidence to see you here," Bumble exclaimed. "Are you staying overnight?"

Emily nodded. "Yes. We have tickets to the Theatre Royal." She emphasised the 'we', although she hardly needed to. There could be no possibility of a woman of her class attending the theatre alone, even here in the provinces.

"Indeed! What a lucky coincidence." Mayor Bumble glanced about, evidently seeking her husband.

Marmaduke had returned to his room to fetch his cane, but Emily didn't volunteer that information. She smiled at the mayor instead, and turned her attention to the interaction between the concierge and an elderly woman near the entrance struggling with her small dog.

"I must say, Mrs Fliss, that it is wonderful to see you looking so well. Word reached me that you had been taken ill soon after seeing in the New Year. Most unfortunate." He dipped his brow. "I heard you spent some time in the ..." he paused before continuing delicately, "sanatorium?"

Emily's spine straightened. How did Bumble have so much information about her? Marmaduke had promised not to speak to anyone of her temporary residence at the Exeter hospital. Had her husband been indiscreet? She dared to meet Bumble's gaze, suspecting him of sneering at her, but his eyes were soft, his brow creased with concern. "Are you quite well now?" he asked, lowering his voice further.

"I am, Mayor. Thank you for enquiring."

"Good, good. I should imagine that getting out and about in the fresh air will assist with your continuing convalescence."

"Undoubtedly." Emily could not help but be confused by Bumble's evident concern for her wellbeing.

How much did he know? He wouldn't have seen her on her daily promenades for she had forsaken those. Initially, following her low-key homecoming, she had much preferred to remain indoors. The memories of the incident at The Victoria Gardens on New Year's Eve would haunt her until the day she died.

However, Marmaduke had frowned on her inactivity and had encouraged her to take small walks. She had acquiesced, strolling around the grounds of the Fliss house with a concerned Mary in tow, and very occasionally she would take the carriage and allow herself to be dragged into the shops in Durscombe. Now here she was in the city, at Marmaduke's insistence. She was not a great fan of any theatre, but her husband enjoyed it. If nothing else, it would give her something fresh to discuss when she began to accept invitations to tea parties once again.

"I am pleased to hear it. I do so love to see a little colour in your cheeks, Mrs Fliss. It was such a shame to hear you were indisposed. Really, Durscombe society is not the same without you." He leaned closer. "Positively dull, in fact."

Emily regarded Bumble in surprise. He'd always been a terrible flirt, but this, when her husband could return at any moment, was audacious, even for the mayor.

"If I may say so," Bumble's breath caressed Emily's cheek, "You have always been one of the most admirably beautiful women in Durscombe, if not the whole of Devon, Mrs Fliss."

Emily swallowed hard. She could not allow this. "Mayor Bumble—"

Bumble caught up her hand and pressed it to his lips. "Ever since those halcyon days of our youth, Emily, you should know I have always dreamt of you."

Emily had often fantasised about those days too; although in her right mind she knew she should forget them. The picnics on the lawn at Applecombe. The gay carriage rides—

"May I be blunt?" Bumble murmured.

Emily attempted to pull herself from his grasp. "I would rather you were not, Mayor Bumble. Mr Fliss is sure to return at any moment."

Bumble caught her hand before it had fully retreated and clamped it in his own. She could feel the warmth of his grasp through her thin gloves. An idle thought flashed through her imagination, wondering about him, his touch, imagining the sensation of his naked flesh pressed against hers. Her heartbeat quickened. It disconcerted her, this sudden thrill that pulsed through her. Belatedly, she flushed. His eyes sparkled when he caught sight of the reddening of her cheeks.

"The fact is you are the *only* woman I have ever held in high regard."

Emily tried to pull her hand away once more. "Mayor Bumble!" she hissed. "I implore you. You are married, as am I."

"My marriage is meaningless, Emily. I harbour feelings for you."

She gasped. Could this be true? After all these years? Could this man read her innermost thoughts and desires? They had been at loggerheads for the best part of two decades, but beneath the tension and the spite lurked a shared past. Happier times.

A small part of Emily yearned to tell him the same, that she had feelings for him too, buried so deeply she had never expected the sun to warm them through again. But she couldn't bring herself to brutally betray Marmaduke in such a way. *Where is my husband?*

"Really Mayor, you cannot say these things."

"Call me Theo as you used to, I beg you, Emily."

"Mayor—Theo—that was a long time ago. Please stop."

Bumble dropped her hand with a great show of despair. Emily caught his look of yearning and lifted her hand to his face. They locked eyes, something hot and knowing passed between them and Emily's breath caught in her throat, her insides melting with a sharp pang of desire.

The elevator pinged and the moment was lost. Without looking at it, Bumble straightened up, bowed smartly, and retreated swiftly, heading for the front doors, neatly side-stepping the little dog that rushed to cut off his escape.

Emily watched him go, her mind a tangle of badly connected thoughts. Bumble was the man she had almost married, but circumstances had intervened, and he'd chosen Norah de Courcy while Emily had opted for Marmaduke.

All she had wanted back then had been status and security, and the Fliss family were far wealthier than Bumble could ever have hoped to be.

"You look flushed, my dear. Are you too warm?" Marmaduke had returned to her side.

"Yes, a little warm perhaps," Emily replied, retrieving her fan and flapping at her face to divert attention from her fluster and high colour. Had her husband caught sight of Bumble? If so, he didn't question the mayor's sudden departure.

"Are you certain you're feeling well enough to attend the theatre, this evening? I'd hate for you to be taken ill while we are out?"

"I'm absolutely fine, Marmaduke. Really. Please don't fuss!"

Marmaduke frowned at his wife's sharp response and opened his mouth to respond.

"Your carriage has arrived, Mr Fliss," interjected the concierge, coming discreetly upon them. Emily breathed a little easier.

"Thank you." Marmaduke bowed to Emily and offered his arm. Reluctantly she took it, and they walked out of the hotel together.

The Theatre Royal was packed to the rafters, but Marmaduke had reserved their usual box. Emily, her colour and temperature returning to normal levels, took her place, perching on a green velvet seat, grateful to be at a safe distance from the bustling masses in the stalls below and the circle to her right.

Marmaduke organised some refreshments for himself, but Emily only accepted the opera glasses the attendant offered. She entertained herself while waiting for the house to go up by observing other members in the audience, particularly the more animated members of the lower class seated in the front rows. She laughed inwardly when she spotted one woman in the second row sporting a marvellous hat. A stuffed hummingbird had been attached to a magnificent flower — which in itself was as big as the woman's head. Emily could only imagine that the gentlemen sitting directly behind the woman was less than enthralled with his view—or non-view—of the stage.

Lifting her gaze, Emily scanned the boxes directly opposite. Someone there evidently had the same idea. They peered through their own opera glasses in her direction. Emily squinted, unable to discern who it might be, dropped the glasses in her lap, before lifting them again.

The mayor.

Emily darted a quick look at Marmaduke. Pressing her lips together, she sat a little taller in her chair. Her husband had engaged the Earl of Romsey, who was sharing the box with them, in earnest conversation about horse racing. Emily peered through her glasses once more. Bumble had dropped his and was studying her openly, his wife Norah, sitting next to him, apparently oblivious. Emily cocked her head.

Bumble touched his heart and smiled.

Emily shook her head. What was she thinking? If Marmaduke—

She abruptly refocussed her attention on the orchestra pit. The musicians began to tune up; all fingers and fiddles and serious concentration. She made every attempt to concentrate on them, but the lure of Bumble seemed somehow irresistible. Eventually she couldn't help herself. She looked back at him. He appeared to be fawning over his wife. Emily felt a stab of irritation. He said one thing, and then behaved in a different way.

How infuriating.

It had always been so, she decided. Her thoughts returned to the young man she'd known. She had imagined herself in love with Bumble. She remembered him as a sweet boy with floppy hair. Strong and charming, forever quoting poetry and extracts from novels he had enjoyed. He had admired the way she played piano, although she was only passingly fair at best. Together they had made a lovely couple, everyone had said so, and she had assumed they would be married.

Except—

No. She didn't want to remember.

She dragged her attention to the stage as the show began. The Master of Ceremonies was introducing a song and dance act, and for a time she watched it with avid concentration. Afterwards, one man performed a comic sketch which she did not find so amusing. Bored, she picked up her glasses and aimed them at Bumble's box. The mayor had vacated his place, only Norah remained, and she held her fan to her mouth, laughing fit to burst.

Emily swept the glasses around the theatre but could find no sign of Bumble. She noted her own evident disappointment, her heart heavy in her chest. Marmaduke leaned over to ask her a question, just as the door behind them clicked open. She half-turned to look, and there was

Bumble. He bowed to Marmaduke and to the Earl of Romsey who had stood to greet him, and then turned his attention to Emily who had remained seated. Taking her hand, just as he had in the hotel foyer, not an hour since, he brushed her gloved fingers with his lips, staring directly into her décolletage before raising his eyes to hers. Emily winced at his insolence, praying her husband had failed to notice the mayor's indiscretion. Bumble held onto her hand a little longer than he should have as she subtly attempted to extract it from his grasp.

"Won't you join us?" Marmaduke asked.

"Unfortunately, Mr Fliss, my beloved Mrs Bumble awaits me on yonder side of the theatre," Bumble indicated his box. "I really should not leave her alone for too long. One never knows what mischief one's wife might find in one's absence, eh?" His eyes sparked in Emily's direction.

"Indeed," Marmaduke laughed politely. "But that is a disappointment, my dear Mayor. Is it not Mrs Fliss?"

Emily nodded, hoping her cheeks appeared less warm than they felt. "Indeed," she muttered, wishing Bumble as far away from her as humanly possible.

"You see, Bumble? You even disappoint my darling wife," Marmaduke said.

"I would never willingly disappoint the adorable Mrs Fliss," replied Bumble, his eyes flaming in the semi-darkness.

Emily lifted her fan to waft at her face and dropped her eyes, her skin tingling. Nervousness ... and something else. Desire? As she lifted her free hand to her constricted throat, she sensed Bumble following the movement. She arched her back slightly, forcing an air of nonchalance she did not feel, trying with all her will to focus on the act performing on the stage.

"I must return to my box," Bumble announced. "Perhaps we could meet for a drink at the hotel?"

"The hotel? Are you staying at The London too?"

"Ah yes," Bumble realised his mistake. He hadn't spoken to Marmaduke in the foyer, only Emily. "I assumed you were there.

The London is the only hotel in town that anyone who is anyone wants to be seen at."

The Earl of Romsey guffawed heartily. Several members of the audience glanced up at the box. Emily cringed, keeping her eyes firmly on the stage, where two men dressed entirely in white were performing acrobatics.

"Well, that would be splendid," agreed Marmaduke. "What do you say, Romsey? As soon as the ladies have retired, we'll meet Bumble in the bar." Bumble bowed to the men, ignored Emily, and took his leave.

Emily gave him the time to walk back to his box before she lifted her glasses to peer his way again. He stared right back at her, a knowing smile playing at the corners of his mouth. Emily shook her head and turned away, staring resolutely at a woman draped in a sheet and carrying a pretend Roman urn. She warbled pleasantly enough.

She spent the rest of the show thinking about Bumble and daydreaming about how different life would have been if she had only been able to accept his proposal when it had been offered.

24
SPINNING THE WEB

Greeb scratched at his scar and belched. He'd been drinking since early this afternoon. All he wanted now was a good hot meal and to fall into bed. Tomorrow was another day and he would be hard at it, probably hauling fish, if nothing better showed up.

But instead of that, he was sitting in the Crown and Anchor waiting for Bumble to arrive. The major had insisted on the meeting and yet couldn't be bothered to turn up on time. Greeb, increasingly bad-tempered, had almost decided to give it up as a bad job and head home when Bumble stomped through the door, his hat pulled low, his collar turned up.

Greeb sneered. "Not much of a disguise."

"Maybe not. Perhaps we would be better meeting in some shady doorway down The Lanes," Bumble sniped.

"We could have travelled inland, somewhere you're not so well recognised."

"Not this evening. I have a rather pressing dinner engagement." Bumble called the serving girl over and gestured for a drink. She was quick to oblige, and he sat and nursed his ale, scowling while Greeb glugged his. "Thirsty?" Bumble asked. "By the state you're in I'd say you've already had a skin full."

"That I have. But I'll still be walking a straighter line than *you* when I leave here." Greeb spat on the floor. He knew how to handle his beer. There weren't many men that could hold a candle to him when the devil had him in his sights.

He stretched, tall and languid, before settling again and regarding the mayor through half-closed eyes. "So what can I do for you, this fine evening, Bumble?"

Bumble glared, shifting uncomfortably on his stool.

"Sorry, sorry! My mistake. John Tucker, wasn't it?" Greeb said, his lip curling in contempt. "Got ya."

"I don't pay you to make mistakes," Bumble hissed.

"You haven't paid me much at all, so far," Greeb growled. "You'd do well to remember that."

Bumble opened his mouth to respond, but Greeb waved his words away. "Settle yerself down there. I'm only joshing with you."

Bumble clenched his teeth momentarily and took a breath. "Where are we up to with ... things?" he asked.

Greeb leaned across the table, within kissing distance of his companion. "I've been asking around. I've got a contact who knows of a captain that's been hired for a ship in London. She's a large one. Bound for America, in a few weeks."

"Cargo?"

"Carrying a mix of textiles, rum, silver and gold, I'm thinking. She may have a few passengers on board."

"Passengers?" Bumble pursed his lips. He didn't like the idea of spectators.

"That a problem for you, *Tucker*?"

"It may be. It may well be." Bumble gave the matter some consideration. *What were the alternatives?* "There's no-one else except this captain?"

"Look, this ain't like finding a thatcher, you know? This is a specialised business, and you need a captain who's desperate for coin. Like I said, I got the contacts, but it's risky. Very risky."

Bumble sat back and rubbed his forehead. "I understand."

"I hope you do. You need to let me know, because plans will

have to be put in place pretty quickly if she's the ship you're gunning for."

Bumble nodded, his guts churning. The reality of what he intended was beginning to hit home.

"Passengers is a good thing," Greeb shrugged. "It means more belongings. Often valuable stuff they don't want to part with. Chests. Heirlooms. Jewellery. Bonds."

"But, they're not sailors. They're—"

Greeb dismissed Bumble's misgivings with a wave of his hand. "They accept the risk when they buy their tickets."

Bumble grimaced, stared at the floor, then nodded without meeting Greeb's gaze.

Greeb rubbed his hands together. "Mark me, though. I need more money. You promised me more. I got to sweeten a few deals, grease a few palms. You know how it is."

Bumble nodded and stood up. "Next time we meet."

"When will that be?"

"I'll send word." Bumble jammed his hat back on his head. "Soon."

"Make sure it is soon," Greeb scowled, his eyes hard. "'Till then, *Mister* Tucker".

25
EXERCISE

Weak sunlight broke through the clouds, illuminating raindrops on the leaves of the ivy growing up the outside of the stable. Phineas had decided to ride out for a while and blow away some cobwebs. He'd been cooped up in his study for hours, attending to various financial matters and now his back ached and his head seemed to have been stuffed full of lint. Why the hell did he bother paying his accountant, when he ended up doing most of the work himself?

Phineas had sent word to the stables to have his favourite horse saddled, and there she was, standing in the yard with one of his grooms. "Ah Jolie," he said reaching for the bridle and stroking her nose. The sound of laughter drifted out from within the stables. Matthew Salter? Phineas pricked up his ears and nodded at the groom who dutifully assumed charge of Jolie once more as his master went in search of the cause of such hilarity.

Matthew was inside helping Ted Redman, the stablemaster, with Crab, Phineas' prize stallion. They were inspecting Crab's shoes and Redman was looking a little red in the face. Matthew, on the contrary, appeared amused.

At the sound of Phineas's spurs on the stone floor, the men straightened. Matthew's smile faded and he appeared slightly ill at ease. Phineas supposed this was because he had given Matthew a coveted job indoors, yet here he was in his good uniform, out in the stables and covered in horse muck.

"Good afternoon, Sir," Ted ducked his head and tugged a forelock. He was old school in that regard, having worked in the stables for as long as Phineas could remember. He loved his work and had a warm easy manner that the horses responded well to.

"Good afternoon, gentlemen. Is there a problem with Crab?" Phineas directed the question at Ted but looked pointedly at Matthew.

"Oh you know how flighty Crab is, Sir. I just needed a hand. He caught me a good one in the chest," Ted smiled ruefully. "Salter found that most amusing."

Matthew smiled bashfully, the weak sunshine catching the life in his eyes and the radiance of his skin. Phineas caught his breath, his heart skipping a little. He found the young man so beguiling. Just the sight of that grin made his day altogether brighter. "I see," said Phineas, keeping his own face straight. He failed to understand why he kept a full cohort of stable lads and grooms if his butler was going to be called upon every time a horse threw a shoe, but perhaps, in the grand scheme of things, it really didn't matter. Matthew appeared happy and that, in turn, made Phineas happy.

"Salter is very good with Crab, Sir, that's why I called on him. I miss him out here with me in the stables."

Phineas nodded. Perhaps Matthew preferred the stables too, but given that Phineas favoured Matthew's presence in the house where he could see him, he had no intention of returning the younger man to the stables.

Unless ... perhaps ... he would be more content in the stables. Phineas fretted about this for a moment. He didn't want Matthew to be unhappy.

Matthew mistook the look on Phineas's face for disapproval so he hurriedly patted Ted's arm and led the way out of the stable. "I apologise, Sir. I should not have come out to the stables."

"Oh no, Matthew, it's perfectly alright," Phineas waved off his apology. "But, perhaps you are not content in the house? Would you prefer to work in the stables?"

"No, no, Sir. I was only doing Ted a favour. When I was working out here, Crab was my favourite horse. I believe he and I have an affinity Sir, that's all, and he was spooked this morning, so I came to help. That's all it was." Matthew's gentle voice stroked Phineas, calmed his troubled thoughts, much as they did for Crab, he imagined.

"I see." Phineas glanced back inside the stable, where Ted had busied himself with the stallion. "He is quite the handful, Crab. Don't you find?"

"He can be spirited, Sir, that's probably why you like him, I imagine." Matthew smiled, his eyes alight with knowing amusement.

Phineas swallowed. If Matthew could only read his mind.

"Listen, I ..." Phineas thought quickly. "I can't exercise all of my horses myself. On your days off, why don't you ride out on Crab for me?"

"No, Sir, I couldn't do that." Matthew was quick to protest but Phineas stopped him.

"I'm serious, Matthew. Crab will go to waste otherwise. He's too much for me. I prefer my sweet-tempered Jolie." Phineas took the reins from the waiting stable lad and clucked gently at Jolie who whinnied and swished her tail. The stable lad remained in place, eyes agog as he listened to the conversation.

Phineas observed Matthew throwing a hard stare at the lad, forcing him to retreat inside the stables. *So commanding.*

"You would be doing me a favour," Phineas repeated. "It would please me."

Phineas studied Matthew's eyes, fearful he would remain stubborn in the face of the generosity of the gift. Matthew held his gaze for a moment, his face stony, his mouth opening to repeat his refusal. From inside the stables came the sound of Crab neighing. Matthew's eyes flickered with longing, and his glare softened.

He nodded abruptly. "Very well, Sir. If it is your wish. I thank you for your generosity."

Phineas beamed. "Wonderful!"

Matthew averted his gaze, and indicated Jolie instead. "Allow me, Sir?" He held his cupped hands out and Phineas lifted his foot, accepting the boost he needed to climb atop Jolie. He settled himself, acutely aware of Matthew's hand lingering on his thigh.

"You know I would do anything for you, Sir," Matthew said without looking at Phineas.

Phineas started in surprise. *What had the man said? Indeed, what had he meant?*

Matthew patted Jolie's rump and she trotted across the stable yard towards the gate. Phineas glanced back. Matthew, standing in the shade, watched him, his eyes smouldering.

Phineas imagined his heart might burst. He allowed a small happy moan to escape, and then he turned Jolie out into the damp countryside and let her have her head.

26
A TANGLED WEB

Emily turned her face up to the sky to enjoy what little warmth the sun offered. The afternoon was bright, albeit a little fresher than was usual for the time of year. She had resumed her walks in public but had completely forsaken The Victoria Gardens and instead she now chose to walk along the seafront most days. She kept the ever-loyal Mary in tow, but the women rarely conversed. Ambling towards the harbour, Emily would observe the sea, marvelling at its power. Once close to her destination, if the tide was right, she would watch the men and women hauling in the day's catch, but on the return leg of the journey, as she walked towards the cliffs, she would stare resolutely ahead. She could never rid herself of the image of Sally silhouetted against an enormous glowing moon on that fateful cold and frosty night a few months previously.

So here she was again, gazing out across the rocks and into the bay, trying not to think of anything that would disturb her fragile state of mind. She paid no attention to the men and women that walked towards her, as discourteous as that was, until one particular figure strolled into her periphery vision.

A familiar voice boomed out her name. "Mrs Fliss?"

"Mayor Bumble," she said, surprised by his presence, this being a weekday. She assumed he should more properly be engaged in municipality work. A frisson of excitement fluttered in her chest, and she turned her face towards him.

"My dear, Mrs Fliss!" smiled Bumble, reaching for her hand as was his custom. Emily allowed him to take it. "How delightful to see you again, and so soon after our last meeting. Your city excursion was a brief one, I take it?"

"Why of course, Mayor Bumble. We only remained one night. It is always a relief to return home," Emily replied agreeably. That was only a half truth. She had spent the days since her ridiculous encounter with Bumble in a state of turmoil, lapsing in and out of daydreams, embellishing her memories of the past. She found her home dreary at the best of times, and more so lately, even as she enjoyed the feeling of security it afforded her. Giving rein to her fantasies, albeit in her head, afforded a modicum of freedom. Otherwise, what was she? Little more than a bird in a gilded cage.

A bird in a gilded cage.

Three little birds.

Unprompted, memories of her grandmother flitted into her mind. Tansy and her poetic prophecy ...

Bumble interrupted her thoughts. "May I walk a little way with you, Mrs Fliss? I have a slight ache in my temples and am intent on escaping the claustrophobia of my offices for a short while."

"Of course, Mayor Bumble. I would be honoured." Emily gestured at Mary—who had been hanging back and pretending to mind her own business—to fall even further back. Mary bowed her head and waited for her mistress to move way.

Bumble fell into step beside Emily. They sauntered along the promenade together, to onlookers nothing but a smart, well-matched couple, but Emily had to fight to quell a surge of nervous energy.

"I did not know it was your habit to walk here in the afternoons, Mrs Fliss."

"Oh I do occasionally. Increasingly so of late." Emily glanced out at the rolling sea. "Usually with Mr Fliss, of course. It was my custom to take the air in The Victoria Gardens as you may recall, but since ... I mean ... now ... I prefer to walk elsewhere."

"Of course," Mayor Bumble said, his voice sympathetic and reassuring. "I understand." Bumble turned and eyed Mary who continued to follow them at a discreet distance.

Emily quickly interpreted his look. "Mary?" she called, and the young woman scampered forward, ever the eager puppy.

"Yes, Ma'am?"

"It looks as though it may rain, but I would like to walk back to the harbour with Mayor Bumble. Would you ask John to take the carriage and meet me there?"

Mary glanced at Bumble then quickly looked away. She bobbed a curtsey, struggling to hide the mixed emotions that crossed her face, before shuffling rapidly away, seeking John and the carriage.

Bumble snorted his approval as he watched her go, then placed a hand on Emily's arm. He tugged gently and they did an about-turn to head in the direction of the harbour.

"Emily, may I be frank?" Bumble angled his head more closely to Emily's and lowered his tone. "I have been unable to stop thinking of you, and I am having the devil's own problem concentrating on anything at all." He gestured in the direction of the town. "Municipality business be damned."

Emily started at the violence of his words, but Bumble took her arm and gently caressed the sleeve of her jacket. His touch caused her skin to tingle, as though she had been doused in warm water after an ice bath. "Seeing you here has made my day, nay my very week. I think I will go mad if you do not allow me to see you again soon."

"Bumble—Theo—you understand the situation." Emily made every attempt to sound both reasonable and responsible, but her voice trembled.

The memory of how she had once thrilled to Bumble's every touch resurfaced. In the history of her acquaintance with her husband, had he ever aroused a rush of emotions in her such as Theo had? She could not remember. Now, whenever she was obliged to dance with Marmaduke, or even sit close to him, she found herself, not repulsed exactly, but irritated. Exasperated by his mere presence.

Theo had once made her soul sing.

But that was before. Before the bad thing. The thing she chose not to remember. The thing that Tansy had put out of her mind.

"I thought we had left the past behind us. That we were destined to live our lives separately," Emily whispered. "It would be best for everyone if we did that, Theo. Why complicate matters? If other people discovered us—"

"Other people be damned, Emily!" Bumble exploded, his eyes alight with passion. Emily winced at the vitriol in his voice and glanced quickly round to make sure no-one could overhear. "Society represses us! Imagine living in a place where one could love whomever they wanted and in any way they wanted to, without ties or boundaries, without commentary or fear of judgement. What would such a society look like? We could say what we wanted, *feel* what we wanted." Bumble grasped her by the upper arms. "Why, we could wear what we wanted or nothing at all! Imagine that, Emily."

Emily giggled at the notion, and Bumble looked down at her, his eyes soft. "You are the most beautiful woman in Durscombe, Emily. You always have been. Especially when you laugh that way. You captured my heart a long time ago. Do not deny it."

"Theo—" Emily rearranged her face and stepped backwards, freeing herself from his grip. "My carriage is here."

Bumble acknowledged the carriage that had rolled to a stop behind them, Emily's manservant concentrating on making the horses wait.

Bumble stood off. "So it is."

Emily observed his frown. "What is it?"

"Will you walk this way again tomorrow?" Bumble asked

quietly, his gaze steady. Emily's insides began to burn like molten lava.

"Yes," she replied, struggling to catch her breath. "Yes, I will."

"Ma'am?" Mary opened the door of the carriage.

"Just a moment, please," Emily barked, but Bumble took the interruption as his cue to leave. He bowed stiffly and walked away, heading into town and the municipal offices. He did not look back.

Emily lingered, observing his departure, her heart beating hard against the wall of her chest.

"Ma'am" Mary repeated.

Emily blinked and turned her attention to the waiting carriage. Mary stood beside the door; her face carefully arranged to camouflage her thoughts; her pale blue eyes completely artless. How much had the servant surmised from the encounter with Bumble, Emily wondered. Would she disapprove? Probably. Was it her place to do so? Definitely not.

But what Theo had been saying about a society without limits, its inhabitants free to do whatever they chose? It reminded Emily of the ideas that Tansy had always espoused, much to Lily's disapproval. Agatha's mother Violet, however, had acted on all her desires, travelling abroad and out of the clutches of contemporary norms, taking lovers as she wished.

It could be done.

Emily smiled at Mary and with a spring in her step and a sparkle in her eye, climbed into the carriage without any assistance.

Pyle had enjoyed a long liquid lunch at The Blue Bell Inn, but once he'd headed outside and the air had hit him, he found himself feeling slightly the worse for wear. He leaned against the wall, waiting for the wooziness to pass, picking his teeth and staring into the distance.

That's when he'd spotted Bumble with Emily.

Of course he hadn't been able to hear anything that was said, not above the noise of the harbour, the cries of seagulls, the chatter of the fishwives, and the shouting as men unloaded their catch, but he could tell from the body language employed by the participants in this particular dance, that Bumble had put his plan into action.

Pyle scowled in the wake of the Fliss's receding carriage.

This was the way that Bumble intended to play it?

Fair enough, Pyle supposed. What was that saying about keeping your friends close, and your enemies closer? It evidently paid to do so.

But Pyle didn't trust Emily. He wasn't entirely sure he trusted Bumble either. He vowed to keep a close eye on them both. Pushing himself away from the wall, he followed Bumble into town, staggering as he headed for his own chambers.

27
RECRUITING

Greeb darted through the shadows as silent as a cat. He knew The Lanes intimately, the twisting alleyways and nooks and crannies. The higgledy-piggledy cottages with their thick lace curtains, the cavernous warehouses, hidden behind worn facias and chained up gates. His dark clothing enabled him to blend into the darkness, allowed him to perform the simple tasks he had set himself, without fear of observation. Of course there were always eyes in the dark, always those who would look, those who would see. But they were rarely the ones who would tell.

No-one who valued their teeth would risk saying a word against Greeb.

Not down here.

The Lanes were quieter by night. Not silent though, never silent. Greeb could hear the sound of children crying, and dogs barking. Somewhere a woman was giving birth, her exhausted shrieks fading to dull guttural groans. Closer, a man shouted in anger and a woman screamed in response. Dark deeds, habitual and commonplace, occurring everywhere the light failed to penetrate.

Greeb continued along his route, venturing further into The Lanes, where the warehouses were built on stilts over the river that flowed into the sea. He snorted and hawked a throatful of phlegm into the air. It stank here. Decaying fish, the great unwashed, poverty—thick and tangible—the whole sad and sorry place reeking of corruption.

This was home for Greeb. This was where people knew his name.

A skittering ahead told him that the man he wanted to meet had arrived before him. He pursed his lips and whistled long and low. The whistle was returned. To his right, the sound was repeated. And again, from somewhere behind him.

Good.

He unlocked the entrance to his own warehouse with the rusting key he kept on a leather thong and wore under his shirt. He slunk through the door, ahead of the others; nothing inside apart from a few dozen hessian sacks, and numerous empty barrels and wooden boxes. He rummaged around on a shelf near the door, found an oil lamp and lit it, setting it on the floor beneath the shelf so that it didn't throw too much light around. Within moments he was followed in by several men; acquaintances from The Lanes, fishermen and warehouse workers, haulers and tanners.

"What's this about, Greeb?" A bearded fisherman with startling blue eyes got straight to the point.

"Keep your voice down, William." Greeb spoke low, gesturing at the men to draw closer to him. They shuffled forward and leaned in. The limited light threw their tall shadows across the roof of the warehouse, and Greeb flicked his eyes at each of them, scanning their faces. "I've a job on," he cut straight to the chase. "I want you to be part of it. There's ample reward for everyone."

"Sounds good." James Lammas, only five-foot-high and with a face full of smallpox scars, nodded his assent although his eyes revealed a certain wariness.

Greeb shrugged. Lammas would be up for anything. He'd been absent the day God gave out wit. "Aye. It carries a degree of risk, mind."

"When aren't your jobs risky?" Henry Fitzroy, a slight man

who made his living as a tanner, asked. A couple of the other men tittered nervously. Fitzroy sneered, nudging the man next to him and winking.

Greeb grinned and stroked the side of his face, his fingers tracing the scar that ran down his cheek.

"What is it then? This new job of yours?" William asked.

"Wrecking," Greeb replied, and quickly swivelled his head to survey the assembled men, attempting to gauge their reactions. There was an instant of fear in one or two cases, disbelief in others. Greeb mentally recorded each man's response. He only wanted the strongest of these men on his team. The most fearless.

William hissed in disbelief. "Purposeful?" he asked.

"Aye." Greeb pulled himself up to his full height and stepped closer to William. He glared down at the fisherman, daring the man to back away.

But William wouldn't. He'd been born a man of the sea and had only the utmost respect for sailors and men of his ilk. "Why would you do that?" he asked. "We just had a wreck in the bay. Men from Durscombe risked their lives attempting to row out there and save the crew."

"There'll be no saving anyone this time." Greeb didn't care to waste his time on ambivalence. He wanted the men gathered here tonight to fully understand the implications of their actions should they agree to join with him.

"'Tis a cargo ship, off to America. Full of money and rum ... or stuff we can turn into money and rum."

"Passengers?" asked William. He knew there were always passengers heading to the New World. Entrepreneurs, dreamers, people hoping to make a better life for themselves far beyond the overcrowded and over-industrialised British Isles.

Greeb shrugged and rolled his eyes, but the set of his face told the gathered men all they needed to know.

William spat into the dust at Greeb's feet. "Not for me," he said.

Greeb smiled, entirely without mirth. "You've done your share of misdeeds in your time. Plenty of them, William. We've all kept your secrets. No need to be high and mighty now."

"I've done a lot I'm not proud of, yes. Misdeeds is right, but none so black as this, I swear. It's bad enough to put a sailor's life at risk, but to purposefully wreck a ship and take the lives of passengers? That's real evil there, Greeb, and I wouldn't countenance it. Not for any amount of money."

William stepped out of the circle of light and glanced around at the faces of his neighbours. Men he'd known his whole life for the most part. They averted their gazes, or dropped their chins to their chests. "What of the rest of you?" he demanded. "You're all going along with this?"

His question was met with a wall of silence. Lammas shuffled in place, as though his feet ached. He did not respond.

William furrowed his brow, his bright eyes bleak. "I'm surprised at you all, frankly."

A couple of the men muttered. Losing patience, William swore and turned about, pushing his way past Lammas, slamming into the door and disappearing into the dark lane beyond. The door swung closed with a noisy clang that echoed through The Lanes.

Greeb held his hands up to encourage everyone to stay silent. They each listened as William's footsteps faded softly away, remaining quiet and motionless for some time. Once Greeb was fully satisfied that they had not drawn any unwanted attention to themselves, he resumed the discussion as though William had never been part of it.

"At this stage I can't tell you exactly what the cargo is or how great your reward will be, but trust me, I have it on good authority that we will all do very well out of this."

"When will it happen?" Fitzroy asked, steepling his permanently orange-stained fingers together and waggling his thumbs.

"We don't have a sailing date set in stone, but it looks like sometime next month." There were general nods of understanding. It made sense to sail on the spring tides. "The thing is gentlemen; I need more hands working on this than just you who are gathered here. The more help we have, the more likely it is that this will be a success. I need powerful men who aren't afraid to get into the water. Do you understand what I'm asking?"

Greeb stared at each man in turn. "You'll be getting wet. You'll need to get stuck in, if you know what I mean?" He pretended to swing a club and Lammas jolted in shock. Greeb leaned into the man's face. "Mark my words. There's no room here for tattletales and lightweights." His words hung in the air, heavy and full of foreboding. Someone swallowed, the dry click audible in the silent warehouse.

"Ask around. Get people involved. Hell," Greeb curled a lip, "pressgang them if you have to." There were a few titters at that.

"But the more people involved ... won't that mean we have to share the spoils? We'll end up with less. It makes no financial sense," someone was whining.

Greeb sucked his teeth. He liked the sound of the man's greed. "I understand your concern there, Robbie, I do. But the way I look at it is this." He jabbed a filthy finger over his own shoulder. "I'm working on behalf of someone. Someone who lives in a big house on the hill. You know what hill I mean, right?"

A couple of the men nodded.

"Well, don't forget that the man on the hill has a tribe of servants and dozens of horses. He eats meat every night. He has bedrooms aplenty and most of them are standing empty except when he has one of his fancy parties. And when he has his fancy parties, other people who live in even bigger houses with even more horses and more servants and more bedrooms, they come and they eat his food and they drink his drink."

Greeb swivelled in place, warming to his theme. "There are fireplaces in his house that never have to keep a man warm. He has *all that* and he can still afford to gamble his inheritance away when he goes to London. He's never done a proper day's work in his life. Now—" Greeb lowered his voice and pushed a finger into Willie's chest, "—you think about what you have to do to earn a crust.

Think of the hours you put in and how you have to slave for practically nothing. A bit of a contrast that, isn't it?"

Greeb scrutinised the faces of the men in front of him, noting how their eyes hollowed out at the mention of the wealthy folk of Durscombe. He grinned, pleased with the reaction. "My point is, if *you* don't take this job *and* find other people to help us out, the man on the hill just gets to pocket more of the cash. Because I'll do the job for him, and my team will do it for me, therefore it will get done. You know it."

There were murmurs of agreement. There could be no denying how hard Greeb and his men worked when they wanted something badly enough.

"Look how fast the *Eliza May* was picked clean. There were plenty of men for hire after the event. Good men. Decent men. They all wanted a piece of it. You remember, right? If you want to be involved in this, *if* you want to be paid well, then you need to get involved now, at the start. We want to do this fast and we need to do it clean."

Greed nodded at each man in turn. A motley crew they were. Tanned by excessive exposure to all weathers and scarred by rough lives, they were a wily bunch who lived hand to mouth and fought to survive. Without exception they all nodded right back at him. "Tell me, who's in, then? And who wants to follow William out the door?"

"I'm in," came the first voice, assured and confident.

"And me," came the second, never wavering.

One by one the men swore allegiance to Greeb and his plans until every last one of the dozen or so assembled in the dingy warehouse had committed to the job in hand.

Satisfied, Greeb shook their hands. "Go now," he said. "I'll send word to each of you when I have news."

The men drifted away quietly, knowing The Lanes well enough to get about in the pitch dark, and part ways without so much as a whisper.

Fitzroy paused before he followed them out. He looked back at

Greeb, his eyes black in the dim light, his forehead creased. "What will happen about William, boss?" he asked, his voice fretful.

"He won't give the game away, Fitz. Forget about him. He knows better than to do that. There's too much hanging on this and he understands the game. We all know where he lives."

Fitzroy wasn't convinced. "I'm not so sure. He weren't happy."

Greeb shrugged. "I can't take responsibility for what he goes on to do, or what he chooses to say. But put it this way, if he says anything untoward, anything we'd rather he didn't, I'll sort it."

"Yeah." Fitzroy laughed, a wheezing rasping noise. "Yeah. You're good at that. And what about Edgar?"

He meant Edgar Ruddle, the harbour master. This was one of Greeb's biggest concerns too. He knew Ruddle, and there wasn't the remotest possibility that he would agree to be part of this plan, or even to turn a blind eye. He was made of stern stuff, had a deeply ingrained moral compass, and if he received even the slightest whiff of something untoward, he would find a way to put a stop to it. He had contacts outside the town and wouldn't hesitate to bring the full weight of the law down on their heads.

Greeb wanted to avoid that at all costs.

Greeb scratched at his scar, impatiently gesturing for Fitzroy to leave. He needed a drink and he wanted to get a few hours' sleep before heading back out to sea on his boat. The future was one thing, but he still had a living to make right now. "I'll take care of it, Fitz. Leave it to me. No-one gets the better of Greeb." He drew a dirty finger across his throat, the meaning perfectly clear.

Fitz grinned with delight, huddled deeper into his jacket, and slunk out into the dark.

28
TEA FOR TWO

Emily knew Mrs Dainty's Tea Emporium well. Housed in a glorious Georgian building on the main road to the seafront, the steps up to the shop were finished with marble, the glass in the windows and doors was always sparkling clean and the shop well lit. The tables were spaced evenly on two levels, each covered with a pristine white tablecloth and matching napkins, and laid with a gloriously delicate bone china tea service. The smell of fresh baking tantalised one's senses as soon as you entered the premises and promised a range of sweet treats and moist delights. Civilized and serene, the overall ambience ensured a temporary escape from the dust and noise of a workday Durscombe.

Emily had occasionally met her women friends here for an afternoon treat and to catch up on gossip. Behind the counter, as you would expect, there were a variety of teas specially imported from India and China and stored in beautifully embellished tins each neatly engraved with its contents. Mrs Dainty always kept a marvellous array of tiny sugary cakes and neatly trimmed sandwiches on offer, too.

Mrs Dainty, a woman in her late fifties and by all accounts a widow, was as immaculately turned out as her business. She reminded Emily of a taller, slimmer Queen Victoria. She had a tendency to wear dresses that were dark grey, charcoal or black in colour, with bright white starched lacy collars and cuffs. Her hair was habitually pulled back from her face and fastened without fuss or fancy at the nape of her neck. She ruled her waitresses with a rod of iron—one sharp glance was enough to make the staunchest of young women quiver—and ensured that a delicate air of extravagance prevailed throughout the establishment.

Emily, having given Mary a range of sewing jobs that would take up the rest of her afternoon, arrived alone. In addition, she'd organised her driver to drop her on the promenade and instructed him to return an hour later. She knew that her actions posed an element of risk—if word should get back to Marmaduke—but Theo had pleaded with her to come alone, and so she had made a particular effort to do so.

Stepping through the heavy doors, Emily ran her eyes around the room. No-one she knew, although she assumed that a few would recognise her. She waited, hardly daring to breathe, as Mrs Dainty made her way across the room to greet her.

"Good afternoon, Mrs Fliss," Mrs Dainty's lips curved in the semblance of an almost-smile. "Are you meeting anyone today?"

Emily stared at Mrs Dainty. She hadn't thought this through. How should she respond? She couldn't possibly admit her genuine intention. Fortunately, the Mayor had already seated himself at a table on the second level. He made a great show of spotting her. "Mrs Fliss!" he stood and waved. Heads turned. Emily flushed, then smiled and nodded coolly in his direction.

He rushed down the half a dozen steps to meet her. "Surely you cannot be here alone today?"

"Why yes, I am, Mayor Bumble," she answered, dropping her eyes. "Mr Fliss is otherwise engaged."

"Well, please. Why don't you join me?" Bumble held his hand up to ward off protestations that weren't actually forthcoming. "I had intended to meet Lord Tolleson here this afternoon, but it transpires he is indisposed. I would enjoy your company. Mrs Dainty? Would you mind?"

"Of course, Mayor," Mrs Dainty simpered. "I'll have my girls set another place." Emily lifted her head, all the better to show off the elegance of her pale neck, then slowly followed the mayor to his table and allowed herself to be seated. A young waitress busily re-set the table as Mrs Dainty hovered, watching over proceedings and ensuring everything was to her personal satisfaction. Emily kept her eyes on her hands, calmly looped together in her lap. Only looking up to request a pot of Assam tea.

"Accompanied by a selection of my dainty treats, Mayor Bumble?" Mrs Dainty asked and Bumble nodded his enthusiasm. Twittering happily, the proprietress shuffled away to the counter and began to issue instructions to her girls in a soft voice.

Emily dared to look up at Theo. Finally, they were alone, although Emily could sense the curious stares of several other women scrutinizing her from behind their delicate cups and saucers.

"Thank you for agreeing to come today, Emily," the Mayor began, *sotto voce*. "It is a treat indeed to have you mostly to myself."

"I only have an hour, Theo," Emily warned. "Any longer and it could hardly be explained away."

"No, indeed. And I am grateful for what we have."

Emily felt the push of his knee against hers under cover of the floor length tablecloth. She sucked her breath in, taken aback by his forwardness, and startling the waitress who had arrived with her tray. Emily held herself very still, waiting while the girl lay everything out prettily.

Alone once more, Emily relaxed. Keeping her voice low and light, knowing that their neighbours would pick up on the tone even if they couldn't hear what she was saying, she chastised the Mayor. "Theo, really. Please modify your behaviour. We have reputations to protect, after all."

"So tiresome, Emily," said Theo. "I have heard tell that in the

United States there are communities where men and women live freely, doing as they wish."

"Live freely? How so?" asked Emily, her attention piqued.

"Men, women and their children, they live together in a large commune. They share their wealth with each other, and apportion the work that needs to be undertaken among themselves. There is no marriage, only free will and free choice."

Share their wealth? Emily regarded the Mayor in confusion. She could not imagine Theo sharing his wealth with anyone. Or her husband for that matter. Most men of their class desired more, not less, and she didn't entirely blame them. Money had its advantages, and she appreciated Mr Fliss's wealth. Declining to articulate those thoughts however, she moved on. "Share the work?" she enquired.

"Cleaning and cooking and farming and raising the children."

Emily, fiddling with the folded napkin on the table, raised her eyebrows. "It sounds very much like the sort of place where my grandmother would have thrived," she said. "She would undoubtedly have been in her element. But I can't really envision you doing any cooking, cleaning or farming, Theo." Emily, struck by the absurdity of the mayor doing any of those things, emitted a gay tinkling laugh.

Theo smiled. "I love to see your face light up, Emily. Far too often you seem to have all the cares of the world on your shoulders." He reached across the table to touch her hand. She hurriedly withdrew it. "Is Mr Fliss not good to you?"

Emily hesitated. She didn't like to share information about her relationship with Marmaduke. Some things should remain private between man and wife. "He is a good man," she settled for saying. "His heart is in the right place. He loves me."

"But you do not love him, do you Emily?" Bumble pressed.

Emily parted her lips to reply in the negative. But no. She couldn't bring herself to be so disloyal. She glanced away, scanning the room. After a moment Theo gently brushed her hand. He smiled, his eyes kind when she looked his way again. "Let me pour the tea," he said.

They sipped from their delicate cups. The tiny cakes were sweet and delicious, some with jam, others filled with cream or covered in fondant. After a stilted start, the conversation began to run more smoothly. He disarmed her by talking fondly of their shared past, and he amused her by repeating stories about the aldermen, asking her to guess who had done what and who had said what about whom.

She laughed along with him and the hour passed far too quickly. She hadn't enjoyed herself so much in a long time. "I've had a wonderful afternoon, Theo." She folded her napkin and placed it on the table. "But we can't do this again."

Bumble's face fell. "My darling—"

Emily drew in a sharp breath. "Mayor—"

"I will surely die if I do not see you again." Bumble covered his heart with the palm of his right hand.

Could he be serious? Emily's own emotions churned around her chest, a maelstrom of desire and guilt, longing and curiosity. *If only...*

But it was too late for 'if only'. If only was a summer a long time distant.

Desire won the day. "But not for a while. People will talk." The tearoom was quieter now, most of the tables empty, but it wouldn't have gone unnoticed that she had been laughing with a man who was not her husband. The most recognizable man in Durscombe.

"I have a solution," Theo said boldly. "Now hear me out." He lifted a hand, to shut down her protestations before she had a chance to utter any. Leaning closer, he murmured, "Mrs Dainty has a back room."

A back room? Emily's forehead crinkled.

Ignoring her confusion, Theo went on, "You can enter these premises from the narrow lane that runs out the back here. There's a large letter D on the iron gate, and a courtyard garden. Just walk through and you'll see a white door. Come straight in. Someone will be around to greet you."

"Theo!" Emily's hand flew to her throat.

The Mayor widened his eyes in innocence. "Everyone here is perfectly discreet, Emily. Come tomorrow. I'll be waiting for you at two."

Emily stood, moving so abruptly that she knocked her chair backwards. It tottered but did not fall. "You know I cannot do that, Theo," she told him, her whisper fierce. He moved closer to grip her chair as she rearranged her skirts, his breath warm on her neck.

"I know you can. I know you want to, Emily."

Her skin prickled in response. *God, she did want to, and it was wrong. She wanted to kiss him, drink deeply of him, wanted to feel his warm hands on her cooler skin, rub herself against him, find her own heat, melt around his core ...*

The feeling was at once both repulsive and exciting. It had been so long ...

He stepped back, further than he needed to, lifting his chin. "Good afternoon to you Mrs Fliss. Please pass on my best wishes to your husband," he said in dismissal, his voice its normal volume, his tone at once pompous and blustering. Mayor Bumble once more.

Emily pressed a hand against her chest, swallowed and turned on her heel. Walking away, she didn't dare to catch anyone's eye, afraid that people would see her for what she feared she really was.

What was she?

Emily slumped on her seat in the carriage thinking first of Theo and then of Marmaduke. Two very different men, two very different approaches to life.

What she was contemplating with Theo would destroy her marriage and her reputation should Marmaduke find out. There would be no coming back from it. And yet, why was it so wrong to act on pure instinct? Her grandmother would have done, and perhaps there was more of Tansy in Emily than she had realised.

Tansy had never believed in marriage and had often spoken to her granddaughters of a different way of existing, the 'old' ways when it had been enough to swear your commitment three times and choose your partner. If it all went wrong, it wasn't the end of the world, you simply unswore it and both parties were free once more.

Tansy had believed in freedom of choice in all matters. Emily, as a child, had often wondered whether her mother Lily, and her aunts Violet and Daisy had different fathers. Certainly Daisy, who was petite and red haired and covered in freckles, looked so little like Lily and Violet—both dark haired and darker skinned—that it was hard to believe she had the same mother, let alone the same father as the older two girls.

I should be scandalised by my grandmother and her outlandish ideas, Emily thought. *My mother always wanted me to be.*

But she wasn't. She knew Agatha wasn't either. Emily wondered if Agatha had ever known the love of a man. Had she ever wanted to? Fiercely independent, she had taken after Violet.

And Lily? Emily couldn't imagine her uptight mother ever being with a man at all. Nobody except her father, at any rate, and looking back she couldn't see evidence of much passion between the two of them. A marriage of convenience, that's all it had been. Lily would never have looked anywhere else even if the opportunity had presented itself. Emily remembered how her mother considered herself a proprietor of virtue. She had set standards for her daughter and led by example until her dying day.

It had rubbed off. How could it have failed to? Emily had inherited her rigidity and brittle morality, but here, sheltered in the safety of her carriage, she saw clearly that she had inherited elements of Tansy she had never considered before. Her grandmother had a zest for life and for living, a natural curiosity about the wild and the cultivated world, a voracious appetite for experience. She threw herself into everything.

Emily had no doubt Tansy would have taken what she wanted where men were concerned.

Emily burned with desire for Theo, more than she had in her younger days. Her life could have been so different. They would have been the perfect coupling.

If only ...

29
BLOSSOMS

Stanley, chuckling, sauntered through the meadow, lazily swiping at the tall grass with a switch. He had finished recounting a funny story he had heard in the kitchen at Hawkerne Hall the previous evening and Flora's giggles were infectious. The sun was warm for the first time in months, although beginning to drop in the sky. Flora had been picking daisies and buttercups, and both of them were feeling good.

"It sounds like a lot of fun, Stanley," Flora said, falling in behind him as he created a trail through wilder terrain.

"It can be."

"There are so many servants at Hawkerne Hall. So many people to know. It's markedly different from life here at Myrtle Lodge." She stopped. "Why, I don't think I've met as many people in my entire life as you eat with in the servant's hall."

Stanley, noticing her voice had fallen behind him, halted and turned about. "A place like Hawkerne Hall needs all those workers. Just sweeping the corridors is a full-time job."

"Imagine all the dusting." Flora occasionally helped Hannah out with the domestic work at Myrtle Lodge. She was not a fan of dusting Tansy's odd collections of animal skulls and shells and carved items.

Stanley had never considered the dusting before. He shrugged. "There's lots of people, yes, but there's not a great deal of excitement. When Lord Tolleson is at home the place runs like clockwork."

"And when he's not?" Flora covered the distance between them, curious to find out more about Phineas.

"Oh, it still runs like clockwork. That's why he has staff."

Flora laughed. "Of course."

"It's a big house for one man though.

"His wife died, didn't she?" Flora asked.

"Yes. Some time ago now, I think."

"Was it in childbirth?" Phineas didn't have any children and Flora often thought that a shame.

"I don't believe so. An illness of some kind. I've heard Mrs Gwynne saying she 'faded', whatever that means. They weren't married for long, a couple of years, I think. It's a shame Lord Tolleson never had any children though. He would have made a great father." Stanley spoke with genuine affection about his employer.

"He seems a pleasant, smiling-sort of man," Flora agreed. She raised her eyebrows. "Aunt Agatha likes him."

"He likes Miss Wick too, but not in that way."

"What way?" asked Flora, lifting her bouquet of wildflowers to her face to inhale their scent.

Stanley bit his lip. Was this a genuine question? It seemed to be. He turned to her, his face pink. "Well, you know."

Flora screwed her forehead up. "Do I? What do I know?"

"When a man and a woman like each other."

"Lord Tolleson and my Aunt do like each other though," Flora argued.

"Yes, they do, but maybe not in a marrying way."

Flora's eyes remained blank. Stanley grimaced in agonised frustration.

"I don't understand." Flora held back her giggle and pouted playfully. "Tell me."

Stanley shook his head, about to turn away, but the light in her eyes stopped him. With her gently sculpted face, and sweet lips that were constantly turned up, she had to be one of the prettiest girls he had ever known. Mostly he adored her eyes. They were a soft green, always dancing and merry, and above all, kind. When he looked at her now, her blemish free skin shining in the sun, her cheeks the colour of the first blush of a rose, he could hardly bear her beauty.

He stepped forwards and cupped her smooth face with his rough hands, the dirt embedded in his nails. Leaning down, his mouth found hers. He kissed her gently, little more than the slightest brush of his lips. Startled she stepped back. He would have let her go, but she caught herself, paused and stared at him for the longest moment, before placing a tentative hand on his waist. Her other hand snaked around his back and they fell into a kiss that was light and sweet and yearning.

When they parted, Flora laughed, softly, playfully. Stanley dropped his hands from her flushed face and wrapped his arms tight around her slender frame, pulling her close so he could bury his face in her long, dark hair. She smelled fresh, of homemade lavender soap and apples. Flora relaxed in his grip, hugging him back. They remained that way for a while until they were disturbed by a group of swifts swooping through the air directly above them.

Stanley drew back and held Flora at arm's length. He needed to know she was alright. That he hadn't hurt her or crushed her. Flora saw the concern on his weatherworn face and smiled, squeezing his hands.

She shook her head as though she knew what he was thinking.

"I—" Stanley started to apologise but Flora lifted a finger and lay it gently on his lips.

"It was lovely."

Stanley laughed loudly, joy swelling his heart. He caught Flora's hand, and they started walking again, together this time. The going was easier; Stanley might have been floating on air.

They strolled in a contented and companionable silence, before Flora, who had been busily considering their earlier conversation, pulled at him. He turned to her. "You don't think Aunt Agatha and Lord Tolleson would enjoy that?"

Stanley shook his head. "No."

"Well, why?" Flora could only wonder why anyone would fail to be enraptured by such delicious feelings.

Stanley sighed. "I don't think Lord Tolleson ... or rather I think Lord Tolleson would prefer a husband to a wife."

Flora sucked her breath in.

Stanley regarded her through serious eyes. "That's what I've heard. It may not be true. But if it is true, it's obviously not ... well ..."

"Natural?"

"I was going to say, something that should be gossiped about."

Flora nodded and stared hard at the ground, her face screwed up in concentration. Stanley, an infinitely patient young man, waited. When Flora looked up next, her brow was smooth again and her eyes were clear. "Aunt Agatha has always told me that we should never wish harm on others, as that can only come back to hurt us."

"It's good advice," Stanley agreed.

"She says we should treat everyone the same. If you want love and respect for yourself, you must first offer it to others. What we give to the universe comes back to us a thousandfold."

"And what do you think?"

Flora snickered in delight, her head tipped back, the fading rays of the sun casting a bright and warm tinge across her face. "I think that if a kiss can light up your world, and fill your heart full to brimming, you should kiss long and often, whomever your partner may be!"

Stanley guffawed and caught her wrist. They came together once more, intent on testing out Flora's theory.

30
PROMISES

Bumble sidled into the Crown and Anchor, his neckerchief pulled up over his nose. These lighter, warmer evenings didn't suit his need to travel incognito. He gestured for the serving girl and plumped himself down on a bench next to Greeb.

"Evening Mister Tucker," Greeb greeted the mayor. "I thought perhaps you had cold feet."

Bumble glowered. "I can't afford to have cold feet anymore, can I? I've given away a small fortune to you and your men."

"You'll get it back, don't you worry. You reap what you sow, after all. Isn't that what they say?"

"I'd better see a return, Greeb. The sooner the better." Bumble ran a hand through his hair.

"Or what?" Greeb challenged, the Mayor's stinking mood affecting his own equilibrium. "Who else have you got that will do your dirty work for you? There's no-one in Durscombe you can hire who isn't already working for me."

"I might have to look further afield, but don't imagine for a moment that I couldn't or wouldn't or—," Bumble glared at Greeb, his eyes cold and his lips pulled into a thin cruel sneer, "—that I don't have the contacts I need, if I choose to do so."

Greeb lolled back in his seat, hawked and spat at the fire. Slapping his thighs, he pulled at his forelock. "No Sir. Yes Sir."

Bumble sniffed, unsure whether Greeb was intimidated or not. On balance, he decided probably not. But he didn't have time to make small talk. He wanted to get out of the Crown and Anchor before anyone recognised him. "What news?" Bumble lifted his tankard, took a mouthful and grimaced. The ale here wasn't a patch on that at The Blue Bell Inn.

"Good news you'll be pleased to hear. I've plenty of men in Durscombe waiting on my word."

"What of the ship?"

"One more trip to London should do it. I need more coin to pay the captain—his initial share is what I've told him—and then the deal is done."

Bumble shook his head in frustration. More money? Did this man think his finances were stored in a bottomless well?

Greeb intercepted Bumble's thought process. "Come on, Mayor," he wheedled. "This is the last of it. After this you'll be coining it in. I need this little sweetener, then we're good."

What choice did Bumble have? "Send your boy to my office first thing tomorrow. I'll let you have it then. But mark my words Greeb, that's the last of my advance. The next time I see you, I want to know the name of the ship, the name of the captain, and the date she sails. Do you understand me?"

"Aye, I do. I do, Sir." Greeb nodded and smiled in triumph, the smile crinkling the scar near his eye. He'd never looked more unwholesome.

Bumble knocked back his drink, winced, slammed the tankard down on the table and stood. He barely nodded at Greeb, just hastened from the inn as quickly as he'd arrived. A gale of laughter followed him out as he yanked the door closed.

People laughing at him?

He shrugged off his neuroticism. So what? He'd have the last laugh. He was weeks away from the biggest dividend of his life, and he had the most desirable woman in Durscombe keen to fall at his feet. The thought of the things he could do to Emily had him stirring in his trousers. He swallowed the juices flowing in his mouth. *Get a grip, man.*

That was for tomorrow.

Emily sat alone, gazing into the flames of the fire in her parlour. She had been pretending to read, but the light had grown dim and her eyes heavy, and in any case the whispers were loud this evening. Thoughts of Theo had filled her mind, and she focussed on them instead, drowning out the pitiful cries of despair that haunted her.

Now she stirred, restless, hating the loneliness that weighed her down. Marmaduke chose to leave her night after night. He'd either be at his club or in the municipal offices.

Damn him. If he had only been more of a husband. More of a man ...

She considered calling Mary. The girl would organise her, help her move to the bedroom. The handbell lay on the occasional table, next to her elbow, but Emily's hands remained where they were in her lap.

The fire spat violently. Just once. Emily nodded and Agatha's face appeared. Her cousin held her hands up, cupped, as though offering something, her eyes filled with love.

Yes, she offered love. Confidence. Friendship. Family.

But Emily didn't feel she could reciprocate.

It was unfair on Agatha, Emily understood that. Agatha had never wronged Emily. Far from it. She had always kept Emily's best interests at heart. She had written from Lincolnshire many, many times and Emily had never responded. Even after marrying Marmaduke, Emily hadn't informed Agatha of the news or notified her of her new address. Her missives went to Lily, who passed them on until she died. Perhaps Agatha had then stopped writing to Emily. She had no way of knowing.

Agatha's return to Durscombe had been a complete surprise to Emily.

Why *had* Agatha ventured back? What did she want? It pained Emily to see her unless she had to. Yes, there was a connection between them. There could be no denying that. When they were together she felt the strength of it. Agatha knew everything, and yet never passed judgement. She kept her own counsel. Just watched and waited.

Emily had chosen to steadfastly avoid both her cousin and Myrtle Lodge, since Sally ...

Sally.

Emily winced. She would choose not to remember. Tansy had always told them they could block out the worst of their memories, and Emily had become a mistress of that particular art. She preferred not to remember the past. She locked it away. Didn't think of it and didn't feel it.

"Not now," she snapped into the flames.

She banished traces of Agatha from the fire, searching instead for another face. Theo perhaps ... or something or someone who could tell her about her future with Theo. Images swam as she watched. She could not discern Theo. There were many faces there. Many spirits. She didn't want them all seeking to communicate with her.

I must close the box, as Tansy taught me.

A flicker of blue.

Who is that?

One man, persistent, swimming into her vision. The sailor from her dream. Floating in warm seas. Extending his hand, he smiled tenderly, beckoning Emily to come forth. Emily, still in her chair, stretched out her own fingers, recalling the way the sailor had made her feel and how she had longed for his touch.

Much as she longed for Theo now.

Emily's mind raced, tripping over the tumble of her thoughts and memories. Her breathing became shallow, her chest started to hitch, her breasts ached for release from her tightly laced corset.

What is happening to me?

Her womb pulsed with longing, desire coursing through her body. She stretched in her seat, arching her back, groaning.

Hot, hot. So hot.

She dropped her hands to her pelvic bone above her skirts and petticoats. The heat emanated from there. She had a sudden urge to touch herself in a way she hadn't done for so long.

She rang the bell for Mary. She would escape to the privacy of her own bedroom.

31
A SECRET LIAISON

Greeb, at home among riffraff who haunted London's docklands, shook off the whore he'd been entertaining and staggered out of The Royal Caroline, pausing just long enough to allow time for his eyes to adjust to the light. The sound of drunken singing and rabble-rousing followed him out of the tavern and into the dark night as he headed the short distance to the docks. He stumbled a little, having had his fill of ale and more, but a skin-full would never hamper his ability to think straight. He skilfully navigated the narrow gangways, bouncing along the rotting planks, steering clear of the edges, and the precipitous drop onto the sludgy riverbed below.

The tide was on the turn. Soon all the ships hereabouts would be bobbing in the water, and new ones would be coming in with their wares, seeking space to dock. The gangways would teem with life, as sailors and hauliers, suppliers and carpenters took to their employment. Left behind in the Royal Caroline, Greeb had no doubt that his whore would find herself a new companion to end the night with.

Greeb was on a mission. Tonight, he finally intended to have a face-to-face with the Captain of the *Mary Pomeroy*. They'd arranged to meet in a dubious public house known as the George and Dipper. In contrast to the Royal Caroline, the Dipper was a dive. Situated right on the waterfront, the cracks in the floorboards in the saloon bar were wide enough to show the river running below.

Walter John Hanley waited patiently for him. A family man in his mid-fifties with a good head of hair—brown, speckled with salt and pepper—and a bulbous red nose, he looked like a man who liked to smile. He stood a little over five feet, seemingly insignificant in contrast to many of the other rough characters occupying the limited space available in the Dipper. But Greeb was never one to underestimate the strength or wiliness of a seaman. He shook hands with Hanley, and they squeezed into a dark corner, balancing their drinks on a filthy barrel as they sized each other up.

Finally Greeb broke the silence. "You understand what we're asking of you?"

"I do," Hanley responded, fiddling with the rim of his tankard. He seemed anxious. His sentences curt. "It's been explained."

"That's good." Greeb scrutinized Hanley's face, noting every flick of the man's eyes, every crease of his frown. "I've got to ask," Greeb couldn't contain his curiosity, "why this? Why now?"

Hanley gulped a deep mouthful, searching for courage in his beer. "A man can grow tired of the sea," he said eventually. "The sea can grow weary of a man."

Greeb nodded. That was his experience too. Sometimes it paid to give up on the sea before it took what it thought it was owed.

"I have a wife. A family. I want to see more of them."

There the similarity ended. Greeb had no wife, and if he had children, he didn't know about them and didn't want to know about them. God help them. The world was a miserable place unless you were born wealthy.

"It's the *Mary Pomeroy*?" Greeb knew this but wanted to double check. He'd visited the dock specifically to look at her earlier in the day. She was a grand dame, fully dressed with three masts and miles of rigging and a wooden hull. There had been a flurry of activity around her, men loading cargo, trunks and barrels and huge canvas-wrapped packages. The quay had reverberated with the sound of hammers and saws from below decks.

"Aye. I sailed her back from the Caribbean. She's had a little work. All done now. She's ready to sail again."

"When?"

"Weather permitting, the 20th of April."

Greeb caught his breath. Sooner than he'd dared to hope. "And you know what to do?"

"Aye." Hanley met his eyes above the rim of his tankard. "Lyme Bay."

Greeb inclined his head sharply. No need to say more. Reaching into his jacket, he pulled out a cloth bag, tied with cord and set it carefully on the barrel in front of them. Hanley's eyes widened. Licking his lips, he looked expectantly at Greeb. When Greeb didn't say anything, Hanley's arm shot out and plucked the money from the sodden surface of the barrel. He stowed it away, his hands fumbling in their haste, before glancing over his shoulder to check they weren't being observed.

"I have one question," Hanley said.

"Fire away."

"You guarantee you can get me to shore safely?"

Greeb looked the man in the eye. "You have my word."

Hanley tapped his teeth rapidly, his fingernails making an anxious clicking noise.

"We have plenty of fishermen and small boats," Greeb reassured him. "We'll get to you."

That seemed to satisfy Hanley.

Greeb hid his sneer. The man was a naïve fool. "There's a lot riding on this, Captain. You won't weasel out of it, will you?"

Hanley shook his head.

Greeb lowered his voice so that Hanley could hardly hear him. "Only, you could go right on sailing, couldn't you? Past the Isle of Wight and out into the Atlantic, right? And you'd be gone for months." Greeb leaned closer. "Months and months. Well out of my reach."

Hanley bit his lip.

"If that were to happen, we would struggle to catch up with you, it's true." Greeb furrowed his brow, as if the thought saddened him. "But of course, what you have to remember, Captain, is that we know exactly where to find your wife and children."

Hanley's eyes widened and he swallowed audibly.

"Four of them," Greeb continued. "Chalk Terrace, Gravesend." He smiled at Hanley's evident alarm. "You could try and move them, yes. But you haven't got time between now and the *Mary Pomeroy* setting sail, have you? And even if you did, we're having them watched."

Hanley's eyes were as round as saucers.

"Do we understand each other, Hanley?"

The Captain swallowed. His face had turned a pale shade of green. "Yes."

It was all he needed to say. Greeb smiled and offered his hand. After a pause, Hanley took it, his own hand shaking and damp. He stood and watched as Greeb took his leave.

Greeb strolled out of the Dipper and contemplated his next move. He would journey back to Devon in the morning, and seek out Bumble to share the good news, but for now he needed a bed, and someone to warm it.

He whistled as he strolled back in the direction of the Royal Caroline, Hanley forgotten. Life was shaping up well, and soon he'd be a rich man.

32
A LATE NIGHT ENCOUNTER

Phineas had fallen asleep in his study, having taken a little too much brandy with his dinner. He'd been lulled into a deep state of relaxation by the fire and a good book, and only awoken when the book had fallen from his chest and tumbled to the floor. His eyes fluttered open and he groaned, his throat dry and tongue gummy.

He drained the rest of the brandy in the glass on the side table and examined his pocket watch. Just after one in the morning. No-one had bothered to wake him, but he hadn't expected them to. The fire had started to die down and it was likely that all of his servants would be abed by now. Today was Matthew's half day in any case, and Phineas felt it would be mean to disturb any of the other servants when they were taking their well-earned rest. He picked up his book and placed it on his desk, straightening the few items cluttering the surface. He liked to ensure his study was neat when he left for the day.

He wondered whether his bedroom had been prepared. He wouldn't need a fire in there overnight as the weather had turned mild, but he did like to have his bed freshened and turned down and his clothes brushed and tidied away.

Cracking open the study door, he peered out. Given the size of Hawkerne Hall, one could generally hear sounds originating from somewhere: the numerous clocks keeping time; the servants scurrying around or chatting; the scratching or whining of dogs; the rattling of loose windowpanes in the massive front windows. But tonight? Nothing. Silence pressed down on him like a heavy blanket.

"Hmm," Phineas snuffled, and yawned. "No matter, no matter," he muttered, and pulled the study door closed. He started towards the main staircase but halted at the foot of them when his pressing thirst convinced him to change direction. Turning about, he made his way to the back stairs instead, heading down to the kitchen.

Phineas didn't often visit the downstairs section of Hawkerne Hall. He considered it Mrs Gwynne's domain, and largely left her to get on with it. However, he had never felt that he *couldn't* enter any of the rooms. He was Lord of the manor, after all.

The door to the large kitchen stood ajar. He went directly in, his shoes tapping on the stone floor. A huge range dominated the long wall, still giving off plenty of heat. It probably never went out, the cook would see to that.

In the centre of the room was a solid pine table, about twelve foot in length and evidently scrubbed clean over and over again. A plate of buns, an un-iced cake and a couple of loaves of bread had been left out, covered in clean cloths. Phineas flipped the cloths and regarded the food with curiosity, reaching out and breaking off a piece of the plain sponge and nibbling on it. Tasty. Presumably the servants who started work earliest in the morning were able to sample a few things before breakfast proper. There was a large jug of small beer on the table, too. Phineas decided this would do to wash his mouth out, and was about to pour himself a vessel full when he heard a noise in the scullery beyond.

Not thinking twice, perhaps only intent on extending a late-night greeting, Phineas descended the two steps into the room. The door was open, although pushed to, so he poked his head around it to say good evening before reeling back in dismay.

Matthew. His trousers around his ankles. One of the serving maids was bent over the sink, her back arched, her skirts pulled high. Her arse shone bright white in the light of the lamps dotted around the room.

Matthew had a tight hold of her hips, pumping against her, back and forth, back and forth. He grunted loudly, and the maid moaned in response.

Phineas dropped his pewter beaker. It fell to the floor with a clang as his hands fluttered ineffectually at the air in front of him. Electing to make a quick, quiet getaway, he stumbled backwards, missed the step and fell. The maid turned her head, caught sight of her master and sucked in a breath.

"Matt," she said sharply as she tried to extricate herself from his grip.

Matthew followed the direction of her gaze. Seeing Phineas there, sprawled against the steps, he froze in horror.

"Sir!" he said, and hurriedly pushed the maid away, grabbing at his trousers. The maid dropped her skirts and tried to straighten herself up, her face red, her eyes cast down.

Phineas held a hand up in front of his face as though trying to block what he was seeing. His fantasies about Matthew had turned out to be idle after all, and the realisation that he was a foolish little man was a bitter pill to swallow. He struggled to his feet, his ankle paining him. Shaking his head, unsure under the circumstances how he should behave or what he should say, he limped up the stairs, almost tripping again, and compounding his ankle injury when he stubbed his toe.

Disregarding his need for a drink, he hopped through the kitchen as quickly as he was able, then leaning heavily on the whitewashed wall for support he wound his way up the narrow staircase and fell into the entrance hall. His throat had closed, his breath escaped in strangled gasps. Phineas was a sensitive man, easily moved and quick to tears, and the sight of Matthew—the young man he so adored—with a woman, with *anyone* else, was more than he could bear. He dashed at a tear that had rolled down his cheek and sucked in a lungful of air.

Good God man!

Feeling slightly more in control, he took a grip of the bannister and hauled himself up the stairs to the mezzanine. Almost at the top, a sudden thudding on the stairs behind him, heavy footsteps running towards him, told him that Matthew had given chase and wasn't far behind.

Phineas hobbled more quickly. His bedroom on the first floor, wasn't far away. But he hadn't ascended more than half a dozen stairs further when Matthew caught him up.

"Sir, please?" Matthew called.

Phineas gestured wildly at him. "No." He pivoted away, wobbling on his turned ankle, a jolt of pain running up his calf.

Matthew caught his arm.

Time stood still.

Hawkerne Hall remained deathly quiet. Somewhere the housemaid might be scuttling for her bedroom, or she might be hiding in the shadows observing Matthew and her master. It mattered not. She'd be a fool to risk her job twice over.

Phineas caught his breath, the blood pounding in his temples. *A servant was restraining him? Preventing him from seeking the sanctuary of his own bedroom? Had the man lost his mind?* He surely understood that Phineas exercised ultimate control over his employment.

But the servant in question was Matthew. Matthew was touching him, without his leave, and Phineas was both startled and ecstatic. Every nerve ending, every fibre, every cell in his body bloomed into life and shrieked for sustenance.

He faced Matthew, trying to rearrange his features, to hide his tears and appear suitably stern.

Matthew paused on the step below him, still slightly taller than his master. He studied Phineas' face, his own handsome features creased in concern. How could he fail to notice his employer's eyes sparkling softly with tears, the red rims of his eyes?

"Sir," he said again. His voice softer, plaintive.

Phineas waited, needing to hear what Matthew had to say. He assumed the man would beg to keep his job, promise that nothing like this would ever happen again. Phineas considered the best way to respond. Could he ever banish the image of Matthew buried balls deep in the housemaid from his mind? It was so far from his own fantasies that he despaired he could ever meet his servant's eye again. The thought filled him with sadness, the perceived absence of this man from his life created a longing for what could never have been in any case. But Matthew's lack of discretion had dashed Phineas's dreams, as hopeless as they'd been.

Matthew's hand remained on Phineas's arm. When Phineas didn't shake it loose, Matthew stared down at it, a flush spreading slowly across his cheeks as realisation set in. He loosened his grip but didn't let go. Phineas couldn't see Matthew's eyes now, but he recognised the lurch of panic in his chest.

Matthew lifted his face and met Phineas's gaze. He spoke, and his voice was quiet, firm, not at all subservient. "I beg your pardon, Sir. I know that ... what happened ... was not what you wanted to bear witness to. The thing is, I have needs, and I ... wanted them met this evening. I was weak. I had a drink this afternoon, Sir. And I declare ... it has made me bold." And with that he lent forwards and bent his head to kiss Phineas full on the lips.

Phineas's knees threatened to buckle. He would have drawn away, but the kiss was everything he had imagined. Matthew's lips, soft and warm, the faint scent of beer on his breath, the beginnings of his morning moustache scratchy against Phineas's top lip. He fought the urge to turn and run, hide himself in his bedroom, maybe lock the door, because the other part of him—the one he tried to bury—the part that desired the loving touch of another human, couldn't help but respond. Phineas met Matthew's mouth with his own, relishing the slight rasp of his own early beard as it grated against Matthew's chin, inhaling his musky working man's scent and cleaving to the solid strength of a chest held close to his own.

When the kiss ended, Phineas lowered his head and sighed, the moment of bliss dissipating. He would go back to his room now, lie in his bed, alone, and wonder what had happened and what he should do about this servant.

Matthew had other ideas, however.

He climbed the stairs until they were on the same level, reached down and pulled Phineas tightly against himself. They kissed again, this time hungrily, mouths open, greedy tongues probing. Phineas exhaled, a soft gasp of desire and clung to Matthew on the stairs until Matthew pulled away. The limited light from the lamp in an alcove caught the warmth of his expression.

"Is this what you want, Sir?" Matthew asked, his husky voice sending a thrill of pleasure that pulsed through Phineas's core.

Phineas peered into Matthew's eyes. "Yes. Oh yes," he breathed, hardly daring to hope.

"Then let's go, Sir." Matthew gathered up the lamp from the alcove, wrapped an arm around Phineas and helped him up the next flight of stairs to the first-floor landing. Phineas leaned into Matthew, thrilled by the man's strength and vitality. They stopped in front of the door of his bedroom and Matthew held the lamp up so that they could see each other clearly.

"Sir? Matthew looked at Phineas. There was no artifice on his face, no cunning in his eyes, just a straightforward question.

For a brief moment Phineas considered pulling away, ordering Matthew back to his own room. He was a peer of the realm, he could take full control of the situation, demonstrate his power in a million ways by destroying Matthew's life. But that wasn't what he wanted. Phineas had been living a lie for far too long and he yearned for something others took for granted. A little love. The sensation of someone reaching for him in the dark.

And yes, he wanted to feel the caress of Matthew's lips on his stomach. And more than that, he wanted to reciprocate. He wanted to stroke his servant's smooth skin and inhale his secret musk.

Wanted.

Needed.

So Phineas didn't pull away. Didn't banish his servant. Instead, he opened the door and he opened his heart and he allowed Matthew to step directly inside.

33
DOUBLE CROSS

Emily crept through the wrought iron gates into a small but pretty courtyard. Her heart hammered loudly as she scanned her surroundings. A bench, half hidden beneath an arbour, awaited the summer when the bushes, winding chaotically around the trellis, would bloom. She skirted a small water feature tinkling merrily away by itself in the centre of the confined space and found a lavishly tiled pathway that led directly to the door. The bushes and ornamental trees had been neatly trimmed. Someone had lavished a great deal of attention on the rear of Mrs Dainty's Tea Emporium.

Bumble had instructed her to go straight in, but Emily found herself hesitating at the door, frightened to lift her hand and push. What would greet her beyond? She almost turned away, the fear of discovery causing her knees to tremble.

But she had come this far. Curiosity won out over caution. She *wanted* to know what would happen next.

So she pressed her gloved hand against the freshly painted wooden door and pushed against it. It opened into a neat hallway, clean and sparsely furnished, little more than a pair of French dressers and a number of plants. At the end of the hall was a glass door, a dark curtain drawn across the glass, hiding whatever was beyond. Emily regarded the door with a mix of dread and curiosity. Where did it go? Should she walk through that one as well? What had Bumble said?

It opened towards her and a young woman popped her head out. Spotting Emily, she smiled and came out to greet her. She was dressed like one of Mrs Dainty's waitresses, in a traditional black and white uniform, starched collar and cuffs, but minus the pinafore apron.

"Good afternoon, Ma'am. Mayor Bumble is waiting for you in the private parlour. If you would care to follow me, I'll show you the way."

Emily hesitated. Did the woman recognise her? Would she tell anyone else?

Perhaps the servant recognised Emily's misgivings because she appeared to understand. She smiled gently, almost warily. Her eyes flicked to the back door. "You don't have to if you don't want to Ma'am," she said, so quietly it was difficult to hear her.

Emily rolled her shoulders back and clasped her hands together to prevent them from shaking. "Lead the way," she said, and followed the maid as she turned and walked back down the hall.

The glass door opened onto a corridor lined with other doors. The maid led Emily down to the far end, tapped lightly on the door there and opened it. She stepped back and allowed Emily to go through.

Emily supposed it was a parlour and a fair size one at that. There was a fire burning in a beautifully tiled fireplace and two wing chairs on either side, with a number of occasional tables and a large elaborately upholstered couch with a coffee table set in front of it. Theo was sprawled on the couch, reading a newspaper.

"My darling Emily!" He jumped up as the door opened. In three strides he had taken her hand. "I'm so glad you decided to join me. I feared you would lose your nerve. Would you care for refreshments? Tea?"

Emily nodded and the maid left to fetch a tray of tea.

"Will you sit with me?" Theo indicated the couch.

Emily perched on the edge at one end and smoothed down her skirts, averting her gaze. A pulse beat at her throat and she suddenly found it impossible to swallow.

The fire hissed loudly and she glanced at it, screwing her face in annoyance.

Be quiet. Leave me be.

Theo took a seat as far away as possible from her, lounging a little, far more relaxed than she. His eyes shone with amusement.

"Darling Emily," he said, his voice soft. "There is nothing to be afraid of. We shall drink our tea and chat, much as we did yesterday."

"Yesterday we did not do that in private." Emily arched her eyebrows.

He cocked his head, a smile playing on his lips. "So why come, then?"

Emily shrugged, shooting another look at the fire. "I don't know," she whispered. "I don't know."

They sat in silence. Each considering the situation. The waitress returned with a tray of tea and set it on the table. She looked to Bumble for further instructions. He dismissed her with a curt nod and she silently left the room. When the door had closed on her, the Mayor slid across the couch closer to Emily.

His voice was light. "If there is nothing between us, if we feel nothing, surely you can leave this room now? No-one will ever know. We can put this behind us and never speak of it. We can continue as ..." he searched for the right phrase, "... familiar strangers. But think what cold territory is there, Emily. How will we weather it, if it is not our hearts' innermost desire?"

Emily turned her head to study Theo. His eyes were soft on hers. She caught her breath, tears close to the surface, torn between rising and walking away from him forever, or falling into his arms. The part of her that was her mother observed her behaviour in horror, aghast at the shame that could befall her. Emily understood well that her place in society—the respect that the community of

Durscombe afforded her—was entirely due to her marriage to Marmaduke. She could lose it all in a stroke. With just one ill-judged kiss.

And yet, the part of her that belonged to her grandmother—the part that longed to dance naked in the rain, to ride a horse bare-back, to loosen her hair and stomp on the ground breathlessly every time she heard the sound of drums, to dive into the sea and swim like a mermaid—that part of her was an engorged stream, held back by the shallow dam of societal expectations. She wanted to feel pleasure at the hands of a man, someone, anyone but Marmaduke.

To be in the now with this man.

But not just this moment. There was their shared history of course; how she had been drawn to him as a young woman. He'd been so handsome, so daring and dashing and devil-may-care. He still had those airs about him.

She and he, they had unfinished business, surely?

Emily lifted her face and Bumble placed his hand on her cheek. He smoothed away a loose strand of hair before leaning in for a kiss ... and it was just as Emily remembered from her youth. Sweet and warm, a faint scent of tobacco. His lips moved over hers, light, careful ... and when he opened her mouth with his tongue she experienced a buzz of energy that ran the length of her spine and settled in her hips and pelvis. She moaned and stretched, suddenly uncomfortable in her clothes. He stroked the edge of her jaw and her senses hummed, alive with desire. She clung to him, pliable to his touch.

He weaved his fingers into her hair, plucked at pins and threw them to the floor. He loosened her long curls and let them fall around her shoulders, long and shining, the light picking out strands of red among the black. He inhaled the fresh scent of her, peppermint, ran the tip of his tongue down her neck. She shivered, curled against him.

He pressed his face against her décolletage, breathed warm against her, dipped his tongue into the gap between her breasts. She responded by pulling him tightly to her and he nipped at the sensitive skin along her jaw line, his breath hot and heavy. Her head began to spin as she lost herself in the moment, her blood pounding, and when he lifted her skirts, she didn't protest, only eased his way. He parted the petticoats and his fingers slid up her thigh, seeking her flaming, needy core.

The fire hissed. Her vision faded to red, her insides melting as she surrendered to him ...

The door opened and Emily blinked in confusion. The maid was showing someone else in. Who? Not Marmaduke, surely? Alarmed, Emily attempted to push Bumble away, and restore her skirts and petticoats, but he seemed intent on continuing what he had started, and he pushed her down again.

"No! Theo!" she cried, and he raised his head, his mouth slick with her lust.

Emily finding a sudden clarity of mind and strength of body she didn't know she possessed, pushed him away with all of her might and twisted on the couch, yanking her skirt and petticoats down to cover her modesty. Only then she did dare to look up and face the person who had entered the room.

Pyle?

It *was* Pyle.

"What are you doing here?" Emily yelped. She turned to Theo who had slowly rolled to the other end of the couch and was now slouched there, staring at her as though she were a tasty morsel he intended to continue to devour shortly. "What is happening?" she asked, her voice unnaturally high.

He didn't answer her, simply smiled and looked away.

Emily pushed herself up off the couch, grasping at her hair as it fell around her shoulders. She moaned as she realised the extent of her dishevelment.

"Oh Mrs Fliss," crooned Pyle. "How beautiful you are."

He advanced towards her. Truly frightened now, Emily screamed and stepped away from him, but with limited room she only succeeding in falling back onto the couch. Pyle reached for her. Emily held up her hands to ward him off.

Bumble stepped in.

"Enough," he snapped in irritation.

Pyle shot him a look that spoke plainly. He wanted some of what Bumble had enjoyed.

"I said enough," Bumble said again, his tone low, his eyes flashing a warning.

Emily, shaking in distress, gazed helplessly at Bumble. "What is happening?" she asked again. "Why is he here?"

"You should leave now, Emily," Theo told her, and his voice was not unkind.

"I don't understand."

Pyle jeered at her. "Didn't I tell you that your eavesdropping would get you into trouble, Mrs Fliss?"

Emily shook her confusion away, recalling their previous meeting. "This is about what happened at New Year?"

"What's that expression? People in glass houses?" Pyle licked his lips, reaching out to touch her hair, twirling the long locks around his fingers. "We wanted to make sure that anything you overheard stayed strictly between the people in this room."

Emily whimpered. "You staged all this just to keep me quiet?" The full extent of Bumble's betrayal hit her like a ton of bricks. Tears began to roll down her face. "But I haven't said anything to anybody."

"And that's the way we want it to stay," Pyle replied. Emily jolted her head away from him, but he had captured a length of her hair and now wrapped it around his fist. "This pays for your silence." He yanked his fist back, bringing her face close to his and she cried out in pain.

"Do we understand each other, Mrs Fliss?" he asked, tightening his hand. "Do we?"

She flinched. "Yes! Yes! I won't say a word."

"Very good." Pyle studied the line of her loosened bodice. He parted his mouth and licked his lips, meeting her frightened eyes with a knowing smile. "I'm sure Marmaduke will never need to hear about what happened in this room, even though there are witnesses."

Emily cast a wary glance at Bumble, but he concentrated on buttoning his jacket, preparing to leave. He refused to look her way.

"We'll send Penny through." Pyle grinned. "She'll help you ... dress." He loosened his grip on Emily's hair. "Unless you feel more comfortable this way."

With one final salacious smirk on Pyle's part, the two men left the room.

Emily collapsed onto the sofa, her chest heaving. For one awful moment she imagined she would vomit. She dry heaved before sinking forward over her quaking knees, pressing her hands to her mouth to stop herself screaming.

The fire hissed and she jolted upright, staring into the flames. She'd ignored the warnings. There'd been enough of them.

"I didn't know," she whispered with bleak longing. "I dared to think he loved me."

You should have listened.

"I didn't know. I didn't understand." But that was a lie, surely.

Could it be that all of this had been a plot forged by two men? A ploy to prevent her from speaking out about something she had overheard ten weeks ago? They'd put her reputation on the line for something she didn't even understand.

A tap at the door made Emily start. Penny entered the room. "Ma'am," she said and knelt next to Emily. "I've brought you a brandy Ma'am. The Mayor said you were feeling overcome."

"How thoughtful of him." Emily's voice trembled with fury as she took the glass from Penny. "How thoughtful of you all." Besides Pyle and Bumble, who else knew what had gone on here this afternoon? Mrs Dainty. Penny. How much was the girl being paid?

Penny kept her eyes cast down. Emily drained the drink and handed back the glass. "Help me," she ordered, getting to her feet. Her voice sounded imperious, haughty. Unlike her usual self. She corrected her posture, lifted her chin. She wouldn't let any of them see her beaten. But as Penny fastened the buttons on her bodice, she couldn't help quivering violently with pent up distress.

"There, there, Ma'am," Penny soothed quietly. "It will all be well. I'll help restore you the best I can."

Emily flushed at the kindness in her voice, when all she'd offered the girl had been sharp reproof. Together, they searched for Emily's hairpins on the floor, then Penny tidied Emily's thick hair—with some difficulty. She did the best she could and stepped back to evaluate Emily's appearance.

At Penny's nod of satisfaction, Emily hurried from the room. The maid followed her into the hallway and handed over the shawl Emily had been wearing when she arrived. Emily threw it over her shoulders and Penny made a move to adjust the way she'd placed it.

Emily pulled away from her.

"Ma'am," Penny indicated a mirror. Emily stepped in front of it. Her neck was blotchy. Angry pink marks where Bumble had bitten her or sucked her skin too hard.

"Oh! Damn him to hell," Emily's voice shook. He'd done it on purpose. She would have to hide these from Marmaduke, and that wouldn't be easy. She allowed Penny to adjust the shawl, and escort her to the back door. Unable to think of anything to say to the younger woman, she kept walking, down the steps, following the pathway to the iron gate.

She let herself out, holding her breath. No-one in the alley, not that she could see anyway, although there might have been a thousand people watching her every move from the windows of the properties behind. She rushed to the end of the alley without looking back, hurrying to mingle with the other pedestrians, clasping her shawl tightly and moving towards the seafront. She prayed that she would find her carriage waiting for her.

She was in luck. Her driver was already there. *What time was it? Had she been too long? Was it her imagination? Did he look at her knowingly?* She keened in dismay. Marmaduke would find out. He would put her on the street. He—

Stop that.

Tansy's voice? In her head?

Emily sucked in a lungful of sea air and glanced around. No-one else in her general vicinity except the carriage driver. And he couldn't possibly know anything. She was overreacting.

Hang on. That's all you have to do. Hang on.

"Home, Ma'am?" the driver asked her.

"Where else?" she snapped. But what would she find at home except her own loneliness and fear? She needed a sensible confidante, an ally, someone who could never be shocked or perturbed by anything Emily threw at her.

Someone who knew all of her dark secrets.

"Wait!" she stopped the driver. "No. Take me to Myrtle Lodge."

Take me to Agatha.

34
DARK MEMORIES

Agatha spotted the Fliss carriage from the window and, shaking flour from her hands, waited at the back door as it pulled up outside Myrtle Lodge. The driver handed Emily down, and Agatha came forward to take her from him. "You may return to Hollydene. I'll have Mrs Fliss delivered home safely. If Mr Fliss enquires, you may tell him she is here."

The driver nodded, jumped up behind the horses and made a clicking sound. The horses jolted and pulled slowly away. The women remained where they were, listening to the rumble of the wheels as the carriage lumbered away.

Agatha squeezed Emily's arm. "You may breathe," she said.

Emily exploded in a howl of agony, a high-pitched hysterical wailing that pierced Agatha's heart. A cloud of crows exploded from a nearby tree and took to the wing, circling over their heads, omens of darkness in the pale blue sky.

"Come inside. Hannah will make tea and you can tell me all about it."

Agatha led the way through to the kitchen, the fire burning cheerfully as it always did. Emily shot a fearful glance its way, but Agatha waved a hand and the flames sank a little. "There's nothing to fear here, Emily," Agatha said, and settled her distraught cousin into one of the rocking chairs before the fire. She gestured at Hannah, who came forward to take the steaming kettle.

Emily leaned back in the chair, her eyes hollow with exhaustion and fear.

"What can have happened?" Agatha asked, kneeling in front of her cousin and wrapping her warm hands around Emily's freezing fingers.

"It's too terrible," Emily choked.

"That cannot be true" Agatha glanced at Hannah who had filled the teapot and set a pair of cups and saucers on the kitchen table. She nodded at Agatha, and without further ado, tiptoed quietly from the room.

Agatha allowed Emily to cry as she poured tea, then she pulled up Tansy's old stool and sat beside her once more. "Tell me all," she instructed, and listened as Emily began her story, her face calm and composed, keeping her thoughts hidden. Emily confided everything; the meeting in the hotel, the walks on the promenade, ending up with what had occurred in the back room at Mrs Dainty's not an hour before.

"I've been a fool, Agatha. A real fool. I fell for ... a man's sweet talking."

Agatha handed Emily her tea. "Drink," she ordered, mulling over everything Emily had confessed to her. She nursed her own cup, lost in thought. Eventually she said, "I had no idea Mrs Dainty had that sort of operation. It is an affront to decency that she would conspire against you in this way. But perhaps I should not be surprised. I had heard rumours that she and the mayor have a dalliance."

Emily recoiled, her own humiliation temporarily forgotten. "He's having a ... a clandestine relationship with Mrs Dainty? How do I not know this, but you do? She's an old woman."

Agatha couldn't help but laugh at that. "She's barely older than us," she chided gently. "Are we so very old?" She shook her head and Emily attempted a smile, her eyes glistening, tears drying on her cheeks.

"Is there anyone else I should know about?" Emily searched for a handkerchief, and accepted one from Agatha when she could not locate her own.

"Who knows, my darling." Agatha shrugged as though it were of no consequence. "Probably. That man is a law unto himself."

"How have I ended up in this mess?" Emily batted her hands against her knees, fresh tears threatening to spill.

Agatha put one hand on top of Emily's to calm them. "Perhaps because you wanted to feel young and desirable again. Life has dealt you a few blows. You chose to marry Marmaduke, when your heart lay elsewhere. Perhaps you felt you missed out on something ... better ... or different ... or exciting."

Beside them, the coals shifted in the grate. Both women turned as one. "Ssssh," Agatha scolded it, but Emily stared into its burning centre, memories she'd thought to bury flooding back, like waves after a storm, threatening to overwhelm her defences.

Emily shivered, unsure she wanted to recall the past. "I couldn't be certain that I would have another chance to marry a decent man. I had thought that Theo would—"

"Wait for you?"

"Yes."

"Does he know?"

Emily swallowed and shook her head. "I never told him."

"Does anyone else know?" Agatha asked. "Besides us?"

"I've confided in no-one." Emily gazed down a long dark tunnel to her past. *I haven't even thought of it. Tansy made sure of that.*

"No-one else is left now," Agatha reminded her.

"That's true," said Emily.

The fire spat and hissed. Both women gazed deeply into the flames, lost in memories of the past.

The soft clunk of the croquet mallet reverberated through the grounds of Applecombe House and a second later there was a wild cheer as Emily's ball found its hoop.

"Oh, well played. Emily! Well played."

Emily threw her head back and laughed, her eyes shining in delight. This rounded off the perfect afternoon. A glorious summer day in the sumptuous grounds of her would-be lover's family home in the company of the most entertaining and eligible crowd of young people drawn from Durscombe's elite.

Theo rushed forwards to embrace her. "I believe we win!" he shouted back at their friends and there was some general twittering, moaning and laughing.

"I demand a rematch, old boy." Edward Pyle joined them, throwing an arm around Theo. "Very soon," he said, hanging off his friend to lean closer to Emily.

"It was a good game," she responded and drew away. Jonathan had a tendency to unnerve her, she always felt slightly on edge in his company. To be sure, he was as charming and pleasant as his friends, but sometimes his smiles were not sincere enough. Emily sensed something cold hidden in his depths. She was good at reading people, just like her grandmother, Tansy.

Emily squeezed Theo's arm and pouted. "The ladies are going inside," she told him.

Theo raised his eyebrows. "What do you all get up to in there?"

"I think we're supposed to take a nap before this evening."

"Oh really?" Theo laughed. "And will you? Nap?"

"Possibly not. I am far too excited." Emily hopped in place and swung her skirts about, swaying like a bell, imagining the fun she would have at the dance in just a few more hours.

Pyle snorted. "I'm sure Theo will join you if you have trouble sleeping ... if you ask him nicely."

Emily flashed Pyle a hard look. "Excuse me for now, gentlemen," she said. She hurried away; her cheeks a little pink at Pyle's insinuation. Behind her she could hear him laughing. She did not hear Theo's response.

Emily had enjoyed the time she had spent with Theo and his

friends this summer. It had been a wonderfully long hot summer and they had spent many happy afternoons walking and playing games in the grounds of Applecombe House. She'd been surprised to be invited but Lily had hardly been able to hide both her excitement and her triumph. Her daughter had been received into polite society, and for Lily, that meant she had finally made it. Emily had secretly imagined she was making up numbers, there was a shortage of young women of the right age in Durscombe after all, but she and Theo had somehow found a rapport, and their friends now recognised them as a potential couple.

This weekend, Theo had invited a range of friends from College as well as one or two local chums to spend time at Applecombe. He'd organised a variety of activities, culminating in a grand summer ball this evening. Anyone who was anyone, locally and regionally, had been invited. Emily, beside herself with excitement, suspected that Theo intended to propose to her.

And why not? She was an accomplished young lady. Over the years, Lily had played her part, making sure that Emily was inveigled into the best 'at-homes' and more recently she'd ensured Emily had been invited to parties and dinners to meet eligible bachelors. She'd travelled to Bath, Bristol and to London with her mother, while continuing a range of lessons with tutors, improving her talents in music, dancing and art.

And then of course, there was the small matter of her inheritance. Emily would never want for anything again and any man who won her hand would find himself the beneficiary, for she had no siblings with whom to share her wealth.

The icing on the cake for a would-be suitor was her striking attractiveness. As a fresh-faced beauty who turned heads wherever she went, her glowing complexion and neat figure brought her all the attention Emily could ever have asked for. And she loved it. She adored being the one that people gossiped about, the one everyone needed at their party or gathering. She was a magnificent success.

Her mother constantly reminded her she could choose from

many men. Heaven knows, Lily screened dozens—including some extremely wealthy and often elderly aristocratic widowers, with lengthy titles and estates that covered half a county—but in the end, the man Emily loved, was Theodore Edward Bumble. He captivated her as much as she did him, with his foppish hair, beautiful manners and his playfulness. No man of the world, Theo, for he had not distinguished himself at Oxford, but he would take over his father's seat in Durscombe and Emily hoped against hope that she would live at Applecombe with him, mother his children and be the hostess everyone talked about for days after each event she organised or attended.

Such were Emily's dreams.

She had grown distant from her cousins and her grandmother. Agatha had matured into a quiet and serious woman, too much so for the more flippant Emily. Agatha, plain of face and uncompromising in her attitudes, loathed the falseness of Durscombe society and increasingly withdrew from it, declining any invitations Lily and Emily charitably sent her way. She much preferred to live quietly with Tansy at Myrtle Lodge, Violet having disappeared on her travels four years before never to be heard from again. Perhaps Agatha missed her mother, but Tansy liked to keep her busy. They tended the herb garden together and brewed odd concoctions which they sold on to the local women who came calling.

Women like Sally's stepmother. Sally lived with her father and his third wife in town, but she didn't see eye to eye with her, and Sally had recently announced her impending betrothal to Thomas Parrett in any case, fulfilling her own childish prophecy that she would marry the young fishing lad she had admired from afar only a few years previously.

Emily's situation could not have been more different. She had been blessed, she understood this, yet a nagging fear at the back of her mind whispered its doubts, insisting that she wasn't good enough for the fashionable set she moved in. Many of Theo's friends would inherit titles, all she had was her fortune. Only this morning Emily had overheard one young woman, a Norah de

Courcy, describe her as vulgar to her simpering companion, on the grounds that Emily's wealth was 'too-too ostentatious'.

She knew exactly what Lily would say. She would scold her for her weakness and tell her daughter, "You are not just *as good* as those girls. Far from it. You are *better* than them. Your father worked hard to acquire his wealth. He did not receive it as a favour, quite the contrary. Your inheritance hasn't been handed down from father to son without thought for a thousand years." She would clasp Emily's hand and remind her, "Many of these families build their lives on an illusion. A title is *all* that they have. Another hundred years or so and their wealth will be ashes on the wind."

Remembering her words, Emily would toss her head and stick her nose in the air, seeking to charm everyone who came within range, including any and all of Norah de Courcy's suitors, particularly the lanky Marmaduke Fliss. Emily considered Norah—her main rival for Bumble's affections—and Fliss would make a good match. Norah with her spiteful countenance, her lack of curves, the sharp beak of her nose, and Marmaduke, who stood over a foot taller than Norah, and was a vision of gangliness too, his knees and arms seemingly at right angles to the rest of his body.

During that splendid shining summer, there couldn't have been a man who wasn't secretly in love with Miss Emily Cuffhulme. Her dance card remained full, her ready smile and winning ways proved magnetic, but it was to Theo she devoted her time and effort. It was Theo for whom she saved the final dance at every ball.

Alone in a guest bedroom at Applecombe House now, Emily lay down and tried to sleep, but she quickly gave up the pretence. She loved a party, enjoyed dressing up and having her hair curled, adored all the dancing and flirting. How could she fill the next few hours?

She preened in front of the vanity table's mirror until a slight scratching sound alerted her to someone at the door. She twisted on her stool, expecting a servant to enter but nobody did. A letter lay on the floorboards. Someone had pushed it beneath the door.

Emily, thrilled to receive a secret missive in such a way, bounced forward to retrieve it. A single sheet of cream vellum in a matching envelope. The message was short and to the point.

Meet me at the lake. Now.
T.

Emily turned the note over and frowned. Theo? Why would he be so circumspect? He could have just asked her outright. Along with everyone else. Unless...

She gasped in excitement. Perhaps this was to be a secret tryst. Perhaps he would propose to her there, by the lake as the sun set. It would be wildly romantic. She imagined feigning disinterest before flinging her arms around him and screaming 'Yes!' At the top of her lungs. Then they would run into the ballroom and announce it to all their friends and family.

Caught up in her fantasy, Emily threw on a dress in a frenzy of excitement. Not her ball gown, she would save that for later, but in any case a pretty one. Pink with flowers embroidered around the neckline. She hooked on her boots, her fingers fumbling as she tried to be quick, and grabbed a shawl before running from her room. She shot down the grand staircase, through the front doors and out into the grounds. There were still people milling around outside, enjoying the balmy evening, and they turned to watch her as she raced past them, her hair falling loose and streaming in her wake.

Slowing to a jog, she followed the carefully cultivated paths around the grounds as the sun began to sink lower in the sky. Tonight's sunset promised to be glorious, all mauves, pinks and oranges, but even now the light glowed with a golden intensity as it filtered through the trees. Swifts flitted through the air, their high-pitched calls the music that that accompanied the singing of her heart.

Theo would make her so happy. Her life would begin and end with him.

Reaching the lake, she paused, glancing around for any sign of her love. The path stretched as far as the boat house, and then petered out. Maybe she'd find him there. Or perhaps he'd been held up. It made sense to look before turning about and returning slowly to the house. She might meet him as he rushed to join her.

The boathouse doors stood open and she ducked inside, wrinkling her nose at the scent of slightly stagnant air, rotting weeds and decaying wood. Nothing to see but boats and oars and spiders.

Disappointed, she paused, intent on retracing her steps.

A sudden creak of a plank startled her. She began to turn, assuming it was Theo. A hand reached out and grabbed her by the back of the neck. She had time to scream, once, before another hand slapped against her mouth, crushing her lips painfully against her teeth. She could smell soap, expensive soap. Some kind of cologne. Definitely a man.

He began to drag her backwards into the boathouse and she panicked, wriggling in his grasp. Her feet slipped on the rough path as she fought to free herself and he tightened his grip. She imagined she might suffocate if she did not get free so she bit down on his fingers. He cursed at her, then bounced her against the side of the boathouse.

Hard.

She cracked her head, the noise loud in her ears. The pain in her skull rendered her temporarily immobile and she sank to the floor. Her head buzzed as her vision faded to grey. She held up a hand, flapping it weakly as someone leaned over her.

A leering face, his mouth moving, words lost in the roar of her agony.

"Theo?" she tried to ask, and then the world disappeared.

Her next memory was a harrowing one. Over the following years—

thanks to Tansy's intervention—if her mind ever alighted on it, it tripped and lightly moved away. This was a relief. It allowed for no further analysis, no emotion to sully her conscience.

Now, in front of the fire in the kitchen at Myrtle Lodge, where Tansy had painstakingly rubbed her lotions and potions into Emily's scalp, she began to recall that which Tansy had sought to hide. One by one the veils parted and she recalled ...

... the organic stink of the water ... Lying face down in the mulch of the boathouse ... Chewing on a mouthful of decaying leaves and twigs ... Her hands tied using her own shawl ... Her torn undergarments balled up next to her head ...

And someone was hurting her, his nails scraping at the insides of her thighs as he tried to force himself upon her ...

A searing pain, and he was invading her.

And she was gone.

Gone.

When he'd done, she came back to herself. He rolled away from her and sat up before standing and covering her up, pulling down her skirts, yanking the shawl free of her hands. She didn't dare to turn her head, but sensed him when he knelt in the dirt next to her. His hand found the back of her head and he forced her face back into the dirt, almost gently, but increasing the pressure until she thought she would suffocate. When she bucked, he pressed his lips to her right ear. "Thank you, Emily," he whispered, and with that he had gone.

Her breath hitching painfully in her chest, she'd rolled onto her side with difficulty and lifted her head to watch the figure go. Full dusk had fallen and the shadows had lengthened. She couldn't tell who her attacker had been. Even his clothes were dark.

He didn't walk like Theo.

He hadn't sounded like Theo.

That provided some consolation.

Terrorized and uncertain what to do, she sat up, grasping at her underclothes and reaching for her shawl. A splash from behind her and she was scrabbling to her feet, eyes wild, her breath ragged.

Just a fish. Only a fish.

Her attacker had gone, she had seen him disappear. He'd strolled off in the direction of Applecombe House. He wasn't coming back for her.

Was he?

But ... What if he was lying in wait for her?

She knelt, wrapping her arms over her pelvis. Were her insides running out of her? Had he ripped her open. She retched and sobbed, once, loudly. Then she shut herself down.

What would her mother say?

I must never tell her.

She rose slowly, painfully. Plucked up her underclothes and tucked them under one arm. She lurched out of the boathouse, followed the path—and her assailant, searching for him in every covered place, in the shadow of every tree. She paused only once, to throw her underclothes into the bushes and then she walked on, a slick sticky liquid smearing the inside of her thighs.

Blood? My blood.

The return journey to Applecombe House took an eternity. She kept her eyes on the house as she drew level with it. It glowed with subtle light, the illumination of hundreds of candles, in preparation for the ball.

She quaked inside at the thought of re-entering the building, almost veering away and running down the drive. But Tansy's face appeared to her.

Be not ashamed.

Less than ninety minutes had passed and yet the girl who had skipped down the steps of Applecombe House to meet her lover, no longer existed. Emily smoothed down her dress, brushed off the dirt as best she could, and rubbed at her face. She threw her shoulders back and lifted her head.

No-one must know.

She walked in through the main doors as though nothing was amiss. Most of the guests were in their rooms, preparing themselves for the evening ahead. Servants were flying here and there. She climbed the stairs, catching nobody's eye, and once in the sanctuary of her room, she rang the bell for her maid and demanded a bath. Sinking into the water she scrubbed herself clean. Again and again, demanding ever hotter water.

The man who had perpetrated the attack on her would be at the party tonight. He would no doubt smile at her and perhaps even ask her to dance. And he would know what he had done, even though she couldn't be sure who he was.

Nonetheless, she attended. She glistened like the fieriest of diamonds, and danced every dance with a queue of suitors, never letting on that her heart was frozen, her smile fixed and her laugh fake. Her youthful joy and abandonment had dissipated like so much dust on a boathouse floor.

Theo did not propose.

Emily hardly noticed.

Emily tutted and stirred as Agatha fed the fire.

Feed the fire to keep it onside, Tansy would have said.

It hissed and Emily closed her eyes. "The voices—"

"In the fire?"

"They never cease their whispering. I cannot sleep. The doctor gives me laudanum."

Agatha lay down the poker and caught up Emily's hand. "I can give you something better than that. You'll sleep."

Emily nodded, weary. "I'll need it tonight. I feel as violated today as I did all those years ago." Emily held her hands out, struggling to get warm, averting her eyes from the flames.

"Bumble and Pyle were working together today, you think?"

"Oh yes. Undoubtedly." Emily's laugh rang though the kitchen, as bitter as wormwood. "They fooled me good and proper. It can't have been difficult to do. I've not been thinking straight for a while. Marmaduke says—"

"Leave be. Who cares what Marmaduke says?" Agatha interrupted, but gently. She had no axe to grind with Mr Fliss.

"Pyle said my eavesdropping would get me into trouble. He was referring to what I overheard at the New Year's ball."

"And that was to do with Bumble sending Thomas Parrett out to the *Eliza May*."

"Apparently so." Emily frowned. "But it had to be more than that."

Agatha screwed up her forehead. "What else? Can you recall what was said?"

Emily widened her eyes, shaking her head. "Naught that made sense." She cast her mind back. "I do remember when they first came into the study ..." She inhaled deeply. "That's right. When they first entered the room. Somebody asked what the others thought of Bumble's plan."

"What was Bumble's plan?" Agatha asked.

Emily shrugged. "I don't know. They didn't ... Wait!" She sat a little straighter. "Someone mentioned that ship-owners are insured. By Lloyds."

Agatha grimaced and squeezed her cousin's hand. "Emily, what you overheard on New Years' Eve, do you think it sounded like the men were planning another wrecking?"

"Now that I reconsider, I suppose I do. But none of what they said made much sense to me at the time. Because—" she stopped and bit her lip, "I think as soon as I heard about Thomas Parrett being sent out to that wreck by one of the aldermen, I stopped thinking of anything else." Emily's face clouded. She scrunched up her face, trying to remember what had been said and by whom.

"Nothing we can prove, of course. But having lain such an elaborate trap for you today, this clearly suggests Pyle and Bumble are desperate to ensure your silence." Agatha stood and wandered restlessly around the kitchen, clearing the tea things to the sink, then gazing out of the window. Dusk was closing in and the sky was clear. A bright star hung low on the horizon. They might be in for a late frost.

"They are still planning something and they don't want anyone else to know about it," Emily said. "If we knew what it was—if I understood what they were plotting—we could tell someone. But if I say anything at all, they'll ruin my reputation."

"And your marriage," Agatha reminded Emily.

Emily shrugged, her eyes bleak. "I'm not sure it matters."

"Marmaduke is a good man. He loves you."

"But I don't love him, and I never have. If I did, today would never have happened. I would not have allowed myself to fall for Bumble's wiles."

"The man's a monster. I cannot comprehend what you ever saw in him."

Emily couldn't deny that. "Nevertheless Agatha, I was a fool to settle for Marmaduke. It was just ... once Theo chose Norah, what choice did I have?"

"You had plenty of choice."

"I had *no* choice. You, of all people, know the truth of that." Emily sighed, dropping her head into her hands.

Agatha picked her words carefully. "I understand you think you had no choice, because what you desired was to marry a powerful man. Bumble looked elsewhere. And that must have been disappointing. But there were alternatives."

"I could have been an old maid like you, you mean?" Emily scowled. "Or perhaps I could have run away to the Far East, like your mother, or stayed here in Myrtle Lodge and concocted miracle cures like Tansy."

"Not necessarily a terrible—"

Emily pushed herself upright in her seat, her anger flashing like a sudden squall. "No, you're right! I should have gone to hide in Lincolnshire like you did. Lived in anonymity. But that wasn't what I desired. It wouldn't have worked for me. It would have ruined my life."

"Well it made mine," said Agatha quietly, thinking of Flora.

Emily caught her breath. The two women stared at each other, their sudden hostility settling in the air, swirling around them like motes of dust. Their shared forbidden past suddenly a festering sore that neither could ignore.

Emily dropped her voice to a whisper. "I hardly ever allow him to touch me, you know. Marmaduke. Maybe back in the early days. Now he ... doesn't even try."

Agatha regarded her cousin with fresh concern. Tonight Emily appeared tired, much older than her thirty-six years. The events of the afternoon and the tide of memories that had been unleashed had naturally left her exposed and vulnerable. She had headed directly to Myrtle Lodge because of her distress. Myrtle Lodge would always be the place Emily came to when she was in trouble.

The tears were welling up in Emily's strained eyes once more. "I thought I would have so much more than this." She spoke softly, the fire sighing and catching at her words, as though she and it were one. "But I seem to have been a pawn my whole life long. First for my mother, and then my attacker, and later Marmaduke."

"Don't think that way," Agatha urged. "Remember what Tansy would say. That the words we form, even the ones we think to ourselves, are spells. You cannot cast them out so carelessly—"

Emily slapped at her skirts. "Bumble and Pyle are threatening to ruin me! What spells can I cast to prevent that?"

Agatha recoiled from her cousin's venom. "None in anger. Nor in vengeance."

"Then what?" Emily pleaded with Agatha. "What should I do?"

Agatha licked her lips, thinking quickly. "Maybe we should find someone, and tell what we know. Wrest control of your life back. Isn't that what Tansy would bid you do?"

Emily shook her head. "Who would believe us? Bumble and Pyle will make us look crazy. We are but women in a man's world, Agatha."

"Lord Tolleson! He would believe us."

Emily shook her head. "He wouldn't. Why would he?"

"He would believe *me*," Agatha said, more to herself than her cousin. She moved over to the window once more, increasingly uneasy. The moon had risen in the sky. She stared through the glass at the large shining orb, sadly reminded of Sally's absence. She studied the craters as though she had never noticed them before, imagining a face—no, a skull—staring back at her. As she stared, a flock of birds—the crows she'd seen earlier—flew across the bridge of the nose, like messengers of dark foreboding.

Tansy would have said that's what they symbolised.

Agatha shivered.

Behind her came the sound of clicking on the tiled floor. She spun about. The rocking chair opposite Emily—Tansy's empty chair—had started to rock back and forth.

Agatha frowned at Emily. "I didn't touch it," Emily whispered.

The hairs along the nape of her neck prickling, Agatha slid forwards to where Emily stood. Holding her hands out, she checked for a sudden draught of air.

Nothing.

The cousins stood together, eyes wide, Emily snaking a hand around Agatha's waist, as they often had as children. They watched the chair as it rocked forward and back, forward and back.

"I didn't touch it," Emily repeated.

Agatha, holding her breath, stretched out a tentative hand. She brushed the top of the chair, expecting resistance. There was none. The motion slowed until the chair stopped rocking altogether.

Only a breeze. An open window somewhere ...

"I was just thinking of Tansy," Agatha said, her tone low. The fire suddenly roared loudly. Flames leaping high. Racing up the chimney. Emily jumped backwards, away from its sudden ferocity.

"Maybe she's trying to tell us something," Emily frowned.

"I think so," Agatha agreed.

"The prophecy ..." moaned Emily as she gripped her cousin's hand. "She's reminding us of the prophecy."

"Our mothers claimed that was a nonsense," Agatha reminded her, but without conviction.

"My mother said so, not *yours*! And in any case, Lily would have said anything to remove me from this house."

"Even so—"

"Sally didn't think it was a nonsense either."

"Sally—"

"She flew."

As if Agatha needed reminding. She turned on Emily, upset at the mention of Sally. "She was unhinged by grief. That's all. Put an old woman's poetry out of your mind. The prophecy was nothing more than old lady's babble. She just wanted to scare us."

"Well she did a good job," Emily's pulled her shawl more tightly around herself. "She scared me then with her three little birds babbling. Do you remember?" Emily frowned, "two will share a secret, but not the third ... and one will fly and one will try to fly? You must remember that!"

Agatha nodded. *But each will see the darkness and hear the shadows moving ...*

Emily pointed at Tansy's rocker. "She's scaring me now."

Agatha wrapped an arm around Emily's thin shoulders, "Don't be scared," she soothed. "Tansy would never hurt us."

Later, after Agatha had sent Emily home with Stanley, she took her customary seat opposite Tansy's chair. The light from the fire warmed one half of the room, the glow from the moon cooled the other. Agatha watched the interplay of shadows as the fire gave and then took away.

On nights like this, when Flora was engaged elsewhere in the house, and she was the solitary inhabitant of the kitchen, she customarily experienced Tansy's presence, although never as keenly as she had earlier. Tansy had lived most of her life in this room. She'd been found here by a neighbour after she had passed away, sprawled in front of the cold ashes in the grate. She'd obviously been there a while, because Tansy would never have allowed the fire to die out.

And now Agatha didn't, either.

What had happened while Emily had been here? Agatha could only perceive the incident with the chair as a message, perhaps a warning of some kind as Emily feared. But Agatha did not know how to decipher the meaning. Tansy had been a mistress of divination—everything from tea leaves to birthmarks—and Agatha had learned some of that from her, but it was the fire to which she felt the most attuned. The grate was where she found her answers.

Now, as she skimmed her eye across the shape of the flames, she shivered. Trouble was coming to Durscombe, she could see it brewing. Emily's anxiety had rubbed off on Agatha and a sense of unease settled on her like grease on water.

The behaviour of Pyle and Bumble had been extraordinary. They had to be at the heart of all that seemed to be happening in town. Despite Emily's protestations, Agatha felt inclined to pass on what she knew to Lord Tolleson.

Unless he's in on it, too?

The coals shifted in the fire, freeing a pocket of air. A single flame shot towards Agatha and quickly died away. She cocked her head, listening to the hiss.

She found it hard to believe that Lord Tolleson would be involved in anything untoward, but what if all the aldermen *were*? How would she be able to distinguish between friend and foe? She was still mulling over her thorny doubts when Hannah drifted into the kitchen.

The housekeeper smiled to see Agatha so lost in thought. "Problem?" she asked, placing a coarse hand over Agatha's.

Agatha blinked. "I'm afraid so."

"Will some tea cure it?"

"Unlikely," Agatha smiled, "but it might help."

"Then that's a start." Hannah bustled around, lighting another lamp and casting away the shadows, settling the kettle over the fire and taking down the teapot.

"When people ask why I came back to Durscombe, I always say I had to ... to sort out Tansy's affairs."

Hannah nodded. She'd heard Agatha say exactly that on several occasions.

"But it's not true," Agatha said, so quietly Hannah had to strain to hear her. "Tansy left no will, and with all three of her daughters pre-deceasing her under the terms of probate, everything passed to me. But I could have stayed in Lincolnshire and issued instructions to have Myrtle Lodge sold off. I didn't need to come back here."

"And yet you did," Hannah said.

"Yes." Agatha's gaze raked the kitchen, taking in the cupboards and the shelves, the old table that had taken centre stage forever. "I felt compelled."

"Something called you back to Durscombe?" Hannah asked.

"Or someone," replied Agatha, thinking of Tansy. "I think my grandmother wanted me back here for some reason."

35
AGATHA ENLISTS PHINEAS

Agatha turned up at Hawkerne Hall clutching a number of books she had borrowed from Hawkerne Hall's library, along with a fresh batch of the cordial Lord Tolleson had previously enjoyed. She had crossed her fingers, hoping to catch him at home and return his books, and was relieved when Matthew had confirmed his master's presence and shown her into the study.

"Miss Wick!" Phineas positively danced towards her. "What a delightful surprise. You never do tell me when you're coming over and therefore I can never be prepared for our meetings. I adore that about you!"

Agatha laughed, wondering to what she should attribute his exuberance.

"I had promised you that I would seek out the Mrs Gaskell book you have yet to read but I haven't quite had the chance to do so," Phineas lamented.

"Really, there's plenty of time, Lord Tolleson," Agatha smiled. She held her hand out as though she would shake his, and he took it. "Lord Tolleson, given that we are as intimately acquainted as a woman such as myself and a gentleman like you can be—"

"Oh indeed." Phineas raised his eyebrows in surprise.

"And as we have no interest in each other bar that of friendship," Agatha continued, "may I make a bold request?"

"Of course, of course! Please do."

"Might I suggest we address each other on first name terms? As though we were, perhaps ... sister and brother? At least when we are alone? It would give me much pleasure."

"You are a free spirit, truly, Miss Wick." Phineas nodded happily.

"Agatha."

"Agatha, then."

"Thank you, Phineas."

Phineas grinned, childish delight lighting up his face.

"And now—" Agatha cocked her head to one side and studied him, "I do believe something has changed with you. What is it?"

"Tis nothing," Phineas replied, avoiding her close scrutiny. Agatha, however, paid close attention to the slight flush that swept across his cheeks.

"My dear Phineas, I do believe you possess the face of a man in love."

Phineas tapped his fingers together in a coquettish way and ducked his head. "Well, I don't know about that, Miss—I mean —Agatha."

"However, you and your young man ...?" Agatha indicated the door that Matthew had so recently shown her through.

Phineas grimaced, then pressed his lips together as though he would say nothing. It was not to be, though. Agatha could see he was bursting with his news. "Indeed. He makes my days, and—dare I say," Phineas's voice dropped to a whisper, "my nights—quite extraordinary."

Agatha covered her heart with her hands. "I am extremely happy for you, Phineas."

He embraced her clumsily, then quickly pulled away. "Would you care for tea?" He rang the bell and Agatha, perching on her seat, watched his interaction with Matthew—when the servant came through the door again—from under her lashes. She found it sweet to be party to Phineas's secret, although he hid it so badly. Thankfully, Matthew remained impassive enough for the both of them.

When the tea had been poured and they were alone again, Agatha decided it was time to get to the crux of her visit. "I needed to see you, Phineas, for I am sorely in need of your advice."

Phineas sat up taller in his seat, reflecting her serious demeanour.

"How may I be of assistance?"

Agatha faltered. On the walk over from Myrtle Lodge she had run this conversation several times, but now she concluded the time had arrived to be blunt. "Have you had wind of some plot afoot, among the other aldermen?"

"Plot?" Phineas looked bemused.

"Do you remember New Year's Eve, just gone, when Mrs Fliss —Emily—happened to overhear Pyle's conversation about Thomas Parrett?"

"She said that an alderman had sent Parrett out to the wreck?"

"That's correct. But she heard more than that. She has recounted to me, in private, that one of the aldermen, perhaps more than one, were suggesting that they might wreck a ship."

"Wreck a ship?" Phineas looked mystified.

"Purposefully."

"But, how?" Phineas stuttered, recoiling from the very idea. "That's a hanging offence. No-one would do that. The municipal aldermen are all fine upstanding gentlemen."

"Are they though? Truly?" Agatha pressed.

Phineas frowned and opened his mouth to issue a flat retort, but stopped himself. He owed her more than that, for had she not newly established the boundaries of their relationship? He contemplated her words.

Agatha waited; her pale green eyes soft on his.

"Are you certain of this?" he asked, eventually.

"I choose to believe what Emily has shared with me, and I decided I should bring it to your attention."

"But why now? It's been months."

Agatha shifted in her seat, looking uncomfortable. "It's a delicate matter, Phineas, that I feel I can share with you, but only in total confidence." Agatha lowered her voice and Phineas leaned forward to catch what she was about to say. "Emily was caught in a compromising position," she swallowed, "with the Mayor."

Phineas jerked upright and Agatha held her hands up, palms facing him, to quell his initial reaction. "I believe that Pyle and Bumble coerced her into that situation, in order to blackmail her into keeping quiet about their other nefarious activities."

Phineas clamped a hand over his mouth. "Mrs Fliss—?"

"She's ... well. As well as can be expected." Agatha hesitated. "However, I must be honest, Emily was a somewhat willing participant in her wooing. Totally misguided and wrong-headed perhaps, but ... She has been rather fragile since Sally—"

"Of course. That was distressing for all of us. The most horrific episode of my life."

Agatha nodded, tears in her own eyes. "Mine also."

"But what you're insinuating about the mayor ..." Phineas frowned, and Agatha snatched up his hand.

"I would never lie to you, Phineas, or misrepresent the facts. I confess I am gravely anxious."

"About Mrs Fliss?"

"About her safety and her health, yes. But I also have concerns about the town and its inhabitants, and all that is occurring. Do you not see?" She gripped his hand so tightly her nails pressed into his skin. "I feel there is a dark shadow over us all."

Phineas squeezed her hand in return, lightly. A sympathetic gesture that offered consolation. Agatha was a strange creature, and heaven knows the rumours about her grandmother were even odder. In the town they muttered witchcraft, but to Phineas, Agatha simply seemed highly attuned to the people and the world about them. Perhaps this amounted to the same thing.

Phineas paused to consider the conversations he had either overheard or participated in of late. He mingled with the aldermen at The Blue Bell Inn and Jerome's as well as at the municipal offices, but mainly they spoke of budgets and politics. "I haven't heard anything that I can recall, but I can't be entirely confident that the other aldermen would share such plans with me in any case. Regrettably, perhaps, I am not a part of the inner circle around Mayor Bumble."

Agatha couldn't help but be relieved. If Phineas had no inkling of any attempt to wreck the ship then perhaps Emily had misunderstood. Nonetheless, she pressed him. "If you suspected such a loathsome event as a purposeful wrecking might occur, who would you approach?" she asked.

"Edgar Ruddle," Phineas replied without hesitation. "He's the harbour master. A man who lives and breathes the sea, and has done his whole life, as did his father before him. He would know what to do. Then I'd certainly approach the law."

"That's what I imagined." Agatha sucked in a deep breath. "I do believe we should go and talk to Mr Ruddle, if only to hear what he might suggest as a sensible course of action - if Emily's suspicions should prove to be correct."

"We should tread carefully, Agatha. There is no evidence, after all," Phineas reminded her. "Only what Mrs Fliss told you. By your own admission, she is—"

"A little unbalanced," Agatha conceded. She rubbed a palm across her forehead and brushed a few stray hairs away from her eyes, tucking them beneath her bonnet. "Even so, we have to do something. I suggest, at this preliminary stage, we merely talk hypotheticals with the harbour master."

Phineas was struck, not for the first time, by how intelligent this woman was. His aldermen colleagues possessed far less common sense than Agatha, and yet between them they ran all the municipal affairs and were responsible for the community of Durscombe.

"When would you—"

"No time like the present." Agatha jumped to her feet.

"I'll ask Matthew to have my carriage brought round."

"No need. I asked Stanley to wait out the front with the trap." Agatha stood, eager to be going, but Phineas raised a finger.

"Give me five minutes," he said. "I need to change."

Agatha mooched about the library for a short while before stamping out to the main hall where a maid waited with her wrap.

Phineas dashed down the stairs. "Let's go!" Matthew rushed after him, confused by his master's sudden haste.

"Sir?" he asked, and Phineas turned. Matthew frowned. "Do you need any assistance, Sir?"

Phineas shook his head and smiled reassuringly, "No, no, Matthew. We're only paying a visit to the harbour. We'll return forthwith."

A seagull, hovering in the air just feet above her head, screamed loudly and Agatha regarded it with distrust. It flapped harder and floated across the harbour and out into Lyme Bay. She wrinkled her nose at the rich scent of brine and fish that had been absorbed by the stonework here over the centuries. The stink seemed as strong as ever, despite this being a Sunday — normally the only day of the week the fisherfolk rested. Yet there were men out there today, cleaning and painting their boats, fixing nets, mending sails. The tide was on the turn, the top of the waves tickled by the slightest foam crests.

Hearing a dull crunch of glass underfoot, Agatha, following in Phineas's wake, pulled up short. They had arrived at the harbour master's cottage to find the door open. She waited as Phineas knocked and entered, staring down at the wreckage of the brown beer bottle he'd walked through.

"Agatha?" Phineas called to her.

She carefully stepped over the hearthstone and into the tiny dwelling. The living area had been left in complete disarray, the kitchen ransacked, pots and pans, cutlery and even food strewn around the kitchen floor. In the room beyond where Edgar slept, actually little more than a curtained-off alcove, his bedclothes had been ripped to shreds, the straw mattress upended.

Phineas squatted and rubbed his finger over a small stain on the stone floor flags, then held the finger to his nose. "Whoever did this smashed a lamp and tried to set fire to the place." He stood, his gaze skimming their surroundings. "Lucky for Edgar the lamp was virtually out of oil."

"That's a blessing, certainly." Agatha said quietly, squeezing her gloved hands together as though they were cold. "Cleaning this up will be easy enough."

She pointed at the wooden staircase, set against the stone wall. "What's up here?"

"That's the harbour office. It can be accessed from outside too." Phineas came to join her. "Good views. You can watch the comings and goings of all the boat traffic." Phineas cocked his head and listened. "Maybe he's up there ... Edgar?" he called. "Are you home?"

Phineas began to climb the steep, narrow steps, his boots thumping on every rise.

"Edgar?" he called again. Above him, the unlatched wooden door to the office swung in the slight breeze of the afternoon. Light poured through. From outside came the forlorn cries of seagulls.

Phineas reached the top of the steps and lay his hand against the door. He could make out a heavy squeaking sound within.

A rope with a heavy load.

He pushed the door gently, took two steps inside and froze.

Agatha, unknowing and following too closely, ran into the back of him. "Oops," she said, and peered over his shoulder, her breath escaping in horror. They stood together, Agatha's hand on Phineas's back, frozen in fear. Edgar hung high from a rafter, swinging heavily, the noose digging into the flesh of his neck, his monstrous swollen face purple, his tongue black.

Time stood still.

Agatha sucked air into her lungs. Phineas waited for a scream that didn't come. "Oh my!" she exclaimed and pushed past him to try to get to Edgar. "Phineas, he may still be alive." She shouted down the stairs. "Stanley? Stanley, come and help us."

Phineas moved quickly, grabbing Agatha and locking her arms by her sides. "Agatha," he hurried to soothe her. "You cannot fix this. It's far too late. Edgar is long gone."

Agatha darted a fearful glance at the spectre of the harbour master swaying above them. Of course he was. He'd probably been dead for some time. She shuddered.

"Miss Wick?" Stanley's young voice, a man, but not quite. His footsteps clumped up the wooden stairs.

Agatha came to her senses. Nodding her head at Phineas, she freed herself from his grasp, and rushed to the head of the stairs, cutting Stanley off. "It's too late Stanley, we need to send for the police or the coastguard."

Agatha and Stanley stood well away from the cottage watching the comings and goings of those on official business. Stanley had alerted both the doctor and the police, and several fishermen had responded to Agatha's shout. Once given the go-ahead by the coroner, they had cut Edgar down. He had now been brought out, wrapped in one of his own torn blankets, and men huddled around the bier, talking over his body.

Phineas had remained at the scene, and had been joined by several aldermen including, much to Agatha's chagrin, Bumble and Pyle. She observed their interaction with Phineas, all sombre faced but overly solicitous. Agatha wouldn't have trusted them as far as she could throw them, but for his part Phineas maintained an indifferent exterior. In any case, Bumble pointedly ignored her. Once, ominously, Pyle glanced her way. He made a great show of tipping his hat. What could Agatha do except return the gesture, albeit with a curt nod? Pyle broke away from the main group and joined a number of bystanders, rough men with hard eyes, and pointed her out to them.

Agatha kept watching, ostensibly maintaining a neutral countenance even as the blood sizzled in her veins. What might they be saying? Probably nothing that reflected well on her. She decided she didn't need to know.

She turned away from their scrutiny, brushing back the lock of hair that had worked itself loose. The wind had started to pick up, the waves chasing each other to the shore, slapping against the hulls of the nearest boats. Agatha could smell the oncoming rain. Behind her, dark clouds massed on the hills, mirroring those on the horizon, out at sea. After a spell of beautifully brisk, clear weather, there was a storm coming.

Balance in everything, Agatha reminded herself. A storm would match the turmoil in her head and the churning of her insides. A good thunderstorm might release her pent-up tension.

She doubted it though.

She waited patiently until Phineas joined them. He helped her into the trap and settled himself beside her as Stanley drove away from the harbour.

"What did Dr Giddens say?" Agatha asked.

Phineas exhaled in irritation; his eyebrows knitted together. "He says Edgar took his own life. That's what the findings of the inquest will state too, no doubt."

Agatha shivered at the memory of Edgar swinging from the beam, the absence of a stool or chair close by, the devastation of his living area. "Do you believe Edgar did that himself?"

"No," Phineas replied, his voice flat, his generally ruddy complexion pale. He sagged as the enormity of what they had uncovered began to sink in. Agatha had been right in her suspicions. Emily Fliss could not be politely dismissed as mad. Something murky was afoot in Durscombe, for sure.

"Did you mention why we were there?" Agatha interrogated Phineas.

Phineas twisted his face. "I claimed I intended to charter a boat and had sought out Edgar in order to make enquiries. I can't be sure I was convincing enough, however."

"I feel certain Pyle and Bumble would not have believed such a tale. Not with me loitering in the background. I fear they will surely suspect that Emily has told us all that happened both at Mrs Dainty's and at the New Year ball."

"Indeed, and by extension, they will know that we have guessed at their plans to wreck another ship."

The first drops of rain smattered against their clothes. Agatha tipped her face to the sky, pleased they would soon be home.

Stanley urged the horses up the hill as Agatha turned back to Phineas. "What should we try now? Is there anyone else we can approach? Anyone who might not be involved?"

"Perhaps I should travel to London. I could stay for a few days. I have friends there. Lawyers. I'll talk to them; see what they recommend."

Agatha nodded, relieved. "But what of Emily? I'm worried about her. Would Pyle and Bumble dare to go after her?" She recalled the rough men gathered outside the harbour master's cottage, the way they had regarded her, and frowned.

"I'm sure Emily will be safe if she remains at home. You must ensure she does so. Can you send word to her?"

"I'll dispatch Stanley. Let us hope they choose not to make another move before then."

36
DARK DEEDS

Water cascaded down the sides of the cottages in torrents, pooling in dank puddles, flooding the narrow walkways. The first rain after a dry spell always resulted in a rising stench and, although the inhabitants of The Lanes were used to it, householders kept their doors and windows shut tight, and burned herbs and moss in their fireplaces to eliminate the pervading stink.

The night was fuzzy with damp wood smoke, the resulting haze hampering visibility. Greeb cursed as he stepped into yet another oozing pool of mud and slime. Once more he'd arrived to haunt The Lanes without the aid of a lantern, and once more an underground coterie of Durscombe's lowlife skittered along The Lanes in his wake, like flies in search of a long dead corpse. He led them to his lock-up, hauled the door open and disappeared inside.

One by one the men sneaked after him. Each offered their oath in exchange for a small bag of gold and a terse nod. Clutching their spoils they disappeared out of the door as quickly as they'd entered, fading into the shadows in hopeful search of a dry place to spend the night, thrilling with the knowledge of what was to come.

Riches. Adventure maybe. Escape. The promise of something ... different.

Finally left alone, Greeb sank onto a stool, listening to the scratching noises in the alley beyond. Rodents of the four-legged variety. He pulled out the two bags that remained, they chinked softly as he weighed them in the palm of his hand. Lammas and William. He knew where to find Lammas. The greasy little toad would be three sheets to the wind in the Crown and Anchor, no doubt.

Greeb rubbed a filthy hand across his chin, his beard rasping in the relative quiet of the warehouse. What had William said to him? *"That's real evil there, Greeb, and I wouldn't countenance it. Not for any amount of money,"* as though he personally was a good Christian crusader, a man who had never had an immoral thought in his life.

Greeb hawked and spat on the floor. He'd sworn to his other men that he would take care of any trouble. So far he'd kept his word. The harbour master was dead. It would take time for a replacement to be hired. That was one less obstacle to worry about.

William hardly counted as an impediment. A lowly fisherman of his calibre lacked the capacity to create so much as a ripple in Greeb's grand scheme. He was a poor man devoid of contacts. What were his options? If he approached the municipality to speak to the aldermen, he would be easily fobbed off by Bumble.

Greeb could imagine Bumble's fury to find a turncoat in his presence, however. No doubt William's appearance in chambers would ruffle a few feathers and blame would be apportioned in Greeb's direction.

Greeb wasn't afraid of Bumble, not in the slightest, but he preferred a less complicated life where possible. Perhaps William would understand he should let matters well alone.

Yes, perhaps. But why take the risk?

Greeb exploded to his feet. The time for thinking had passed. He danced out into the rain, flipping up the collar of his coat and pulling his hat square against his head. Chin to chest, he heaved the warehouse door to, securing it tightly against thieves and vagabonds. You never knew who you'd bump into on a night like this. He walked a little way, then paused to listen. Anyone could be snooping around. The rain drummed against the buildings and splashed in the puddles. From several directions came the sound of dogs barking. Water hurried along the river, greedily assimilating the offerings from tributaries that coursed down the hills surrounding Durscombe, everything rolling and tumbling headlong, rushing on its way to the sea.

In Durscombe, everything ended up in the sea one way or another.

He slipped into the maze of The Lanes, skirting the lakes of grim ooze where he could, sweeping his gaze this way and that, as the narrow walkways dictated, shooting a piercing glare down each narrow alley. Most of the tiny cottages were dark now, their inhabitants abed, candlelight visible in very few of the filth-encrusted windows. He crept down Thimble Lane, and turned into a side alley, little more than a rat run. William and his wife and four children resided here. Greeb halted for the briefest of moments, imagined the man inside, sleeping peacefully next to his wife, his conscience clear.

Clear conscience be damned. Greeb intended to dance with the devil and enjoy it while it lasted.

He snorted and unleashed a green gob full of phlegm at the doorstep before spinning on his heel. He whistled as he strolled back to Thimble Lane. It was time to locate Lammas.

Less than two hours later, Greeb's two bags of gold were burning a hole in Lammas's pocket, and a small jar of lamp oil sloshed around by his feet. Clenching his jaw, Lammas regarded William's front door with malice. It had been firmly latched and bolted from the inside.

Lammas had his orders. Greeb had made his desires clear. Lammas had considered setting a fire at the front door, but in The Lanes such a fire would be a risky business. Once one thatched roof went up, the flames had a tendency to skip from one dwelling to the next in no time.

Greeb would probably not have minded, but Lammas didn't feel right about that. Not with all the women and children he would put at risk. A more localised fire in the house would have been the answer, and the timely raising of a hue and cry. Plans scuppered, Lammas chewed on his thumbnail. He didn't know anyone who locked their doors in The Lanes, so William must have been expecting trouble. Lammas had been in and out of many Durscombe houses under cover of the night, had feasted like a king at numerous kitchen tables, and all while the householder snored contentedly away upstairs.

The dawn was not far away. Lammas decided to get a few hours' shut-eye. He would come up with another plan as soon as his head was clear.

For tonight at least, William could enjoy his righteous sleep.

37
A SHOCKING INCIDENT

Agatha shifted, unable to settle. The previous evening, she had remained alone in front of her fire, rocking in Tansy's old chair, observing every flicker of the flames, watching them lengthen and broaden, collapse and spark afresh. Despite her best efforts, the fire had stuttered. It had resisted taking a good hold, as though she'd built it using damp wood, although it was as seasoned as any she would have normally used.

The struggles of the fire had left her anxious and unable to sleep for longer than a few minutes at a time. Just after dawn, she'd decided to head into Durscombe to visit the market and pick up some fresh fish for supper, but she'd still had to wait impatiently for Stanley to show up. Hannah packed him a bacon sandwich to eat on the way, and Agatha wordlessly climbed up on the trap behind the young man, her face closed to discussion as she brooded.

It was a fresh morning. Agatha could feel the moisture in the air, but the torrential rain had petered out a few hours previously, and the clouds had moved eastwards. It promised to be a bright day, although too early in the season to be particularly warm. The trees shimmied with renewed energy; not long now and their buds would explode with fresh life. Agatha offered a blessing for nature's rich gifts as she swayed along the road.

They crested the hill and began the downward curve that would lead them into town. At last Agatha could catch sight of the sea, sparkling and blue, life teeming beneath its surface. The cliffs were to her right, Durscombe below, and the fields and forest surrounding the town to her left spread out like a glorious patchwork quilt of green and red.

On any other day she would have basked in the beauty of life, except the memory of the harbour master's face would haunt her days as long as she lived. She couldn't shake off a deep sense of dread.

The crowded market provided a welcome distraction, at least. Agatha co-opted Stanley into carrying her basket as she moved diligently between the crowded stalls, hovering at the vegetable stands, comparing prices, picking through potatoes and carrots and baby onions from farmers' baskets. Satisfied with her purchases, she turned in the direction of the quay. She had a fancy for some mackerel and the freshest fish was sold at the harbour as it was unloaded from the boats.

Stanley spotted one of his ex-neighbours and stopped to pass the time of day with her. Agatha, smiling, waved off his protestations as she took the basket from him and continued alone. The market opened out on to the harbour, equally busy at this time of day. The fishermen were unloading their catch, the women reeling in their pots and cages. There were boys helping where they could, learning their trade, hoping to earn a farthing for their efforts, while small children chased away the seagulls that swooped and hollered and dived for sprats and fish heads or other treasures while the attention of fisherfolk was diverted elsewhere.

Agatha belatedly side-stepped as a short man with a blue cap hurried in her direction. He caught the side of her basket, spilling a few potatoes. The momentary connection caused a shiver to pass through Agatha. He rushed past without acknowledging her. She swivelled in place, watching him, ignoring the lost vegetables. The crowds parted to allow the man to get through, but rather than close up again after him, the trail he left remained open, affording her a bird's eye view of what happened next.

A rugged ocean-going barge had docked at the side of the quay to unload its cargo of logs using a system of wheels and pulleys and sheer manpower. The logs had been stacked on the quayside, waiting to be carted off for use in one of the factories, or on one of the estates, close by. They wouldn't remain in place for very long.

Agatha observed the small man with the wiry frame as he paused beside the towering log pile. In turn he scanned the crowds of people coming and going, finally homing in on a large man with a neat beard who distractedly filled his pipe as he made his way towards the quay, towards Agatha, and crossed in front of the pile of logs.

The man with the blue cap darted a quick glance to his left and another to his right before casually reaching out with his foot to push at the logs. He applied a firm pressure. With a slight rumble, the logs began to slip, then momentum caught them and gravity did the rest. The logs shifted and rolled. Agatha lifted her free arm to shout a warning, but far too late. The first log, falling from the top of the pile, caught the bearded man a glancing blow on his shoulder. The pipe flew from his grasp as he began to fall forwards. The remainder of the logs cascaded down, a deadly avalanche that pinned him to the ground.

He had no chance.

The world paused. Silence on the quay. Silence in the market. Even the seagulls were shocked into stillness.

Then pandemonium; men shouting orders as they rushed forwards to help lift the heavy logs. Several women screamed. Agatha, aghast, stood alone, opened-mouthed. She watched as the little man with the blue hat skipped away from the scene, heading in the opposite direction to everyone else—towards her—his head down.

She reached out as he drew level with her, as though she would say something, but he shrugged her off and carried on. She wheeled about, watching him stride towards The Lanes, knowing he would disappear into the catacomb of alleys there.

Amongst all the activity, the stillness of one man also caught her attention. Standing stock still, he rested against the stable wall of The Blue Bell Inn, casually observing her even as she monitored the man in the blue cap. A weathered man with a nasty scar on the left side of his face, he sized her up, one eye covered in a patch, his jaw set hard, his expression icy.

Agatha reeled backwards. He'd seen the whole thing as it unfolded. And from the look on his face, he had been neither surprised, nor appalled.

Worse still, he *knew* she'd seen it all. *How* it had happened and *who* the perpetrator had been.

Their eyes locked. He telegraphed a threat that couldn't have been plainer. Agatha rocked backwards; certain she was in the gravest of danger. Following on so quickly after the harbour master's death, she suspected this latest episode was far from coincidental.

Catching her breath she clutched at her basket, her vision swimming, a pulse thundering at her temple. She retraced her steps back towards the market. She would locate Stanley and he could escort her home to Myrtle Lodge.

Myrtle Lodge. She'd be safe there.

She took a wrong turning, found herself in a side alley. She pivoted. The scarred man was following her. She rushed on, almost blind with panic, doubling back down a parallel side street and coming out in the now deserted market square. Everyone else had rushed to the quay.

She swung around, searching for Stanley, but found only the scarred man again. He stood on the street corner, alongside a companion, their heads locked together in murderous conspiracy. The second man nodded and broke away, trotting in the direction of the quay. The scarred man returned his attention to Agatha, his good eye glinting, his lip curled. She drew in a wavering breath as he smirked and stroked his scar. He lifted his nose.

I see you, he seemed to be saying, then strolled away towards The Lanes.

Agatha sagged, her knees trembling.

What had happened to this once peaceful community? Durscombe had evolved into something hostile and malevolent, unrecognisable as the sleepy seaside town of her youth.

Supper was a subdued affair that evening. Agatha had returned home without any fish. Hannah, seeing Agatha's pale face and shaking hands, had said nothing, simply set her down in front of the hearth and brought her some hot tea. Hannah knew that if Agatha wanted to talk about what was bothering her, she would do so.

She waved away Agatha's apologies. "I'll make a lovely spring stew with dumplings," she said, and set to peeling vegetables with a jaunty air, striving to cover the evident tension.

Agatha observed her for a while, inhaling the familiar scents of her kitchen—the freshly baked bread, the scones on the table, the dried herbs hanging from the beams—enjoying the rhythms of Hannah at work. Eventually some of her stress ebbed away, her shoulders dropped, but still her mind kept returning to the harbour master and the incident at the quay. The encounter with the scarred man had her on edge.

As the sky began to lose its colour, Agatha abruptly pushed herself up. "Where's Flora?"

Hannah glanced up, her knife poised to slice into a carrot. "I believe she went for a walk with young Stanley." The women exchanged a glance.

"They spend too much time together," Agatha frowned.

"She's very young," Hannah said.

"Seventeen. Stanley too." Agatha exhaled thoughtfully. "I should pay more attention to her."

Hannah lay her knife down. "Nothing more than a temporary infatuation. Didn't we all have them at that age?"

"Perhaps," Agatha sounded reluctant to be drawn.

"There must have been somebody," Hannah probed.

Agatha snorted. "One summer I recall we had a lovelorn fellow who hung around the Lodge constantly, no doubt hoping that Emily would choose to visit Tansy. I quite liked him. Tansy put him to good use performing various chores, I recall."

"What happened to him?"

"Do you know, I'm not certain. Perhaps he found a new object of fascination. Or Tansy performed a naked ceremony in the garden and scared him off good and proper."

Hannah's heartfelt laugh warmed Agatha's blood. "Did she do that often?"

"Oh, heavens, yes!" Agatha shook her head in recollection. "Tansy and her rituals. She possessed little or no shame. I adored that about her." Agatha might have been dismayed by her grandmother's behaviour too, from time to time, but instinctively she understood that Tansy's power came from her quiet confidence, the way she embraced the earth and all things natural. And that confidence extended to her naked physical self as well.

Agatha stared at Tansy's rocking chair, wishing for a modicum of her grandmother's strength and wisdom. "I wish she was here now," she murmured.

Hannah wiped her hands on her apron and came to stand with Agatha. "What would she do?" she asked, her tone matching Agatha's.

"She would gather her loved ones close and perform some outlandish protection ritual."

"I'll go and find Flora, then. You can do the rest."

Agatha hesitated. Was this the right thing to do? "I'm not Tansy. I don't have her powers."

"You're her kin. The most powerful of her daughter's daughters."

Agatha met Hannah's eyes, unable to dispute the veracity of her words. "I'll go. You stay here and finish dinner."

Hannah took up her chopping knife once more. "Do what needs to be done," she advised.

Agatha donned her sturdiest pair of boots and walked out into the twilight. Unsure where Flora and Stanley had gone, common sense told her they would stroll through the wood lying opposite the house, and out into the meadow beyond, heading for the cliffs where they could take in the glorious views over Durscombe and Lyme Bay.

Agatha navigated the wood easily, following a trail that had probably been laid down by Tansy and her foremothers, and made good time to the meadow. The ground beneath her feet became progressively softer, more sponge-like, thanks to the recent downpours. The early season's daisies had closed up as the light began to fail. The evening had turned gloomy again, the low sky holding a promise of yet more rain.

Agatha pressed on, until she spotted two small figures in the near distance. They ambled towards her, hand in hand. She lifted an arm to wave and alert them to her presence, and the pair separated as though scalded.

But she barely noticed. Her attention had been caught by sudden movement to her right, beyond the young lovers, out in front of the cliffs.

A tall ship, full sail. It whooshed past her, ridiculously close to the cliffs. Agatha reeled about as it passed, taking in the sailors climbing the rigging, the vibration of the thick ropes. She could hear the skipper shouting orders. The wind from the sails ruffled her hair.

Impossible! The sea will be too shallow here.

Agatha stumbled, her mouth dropping open. The ship sailed

directly for the bay. The rocks—so treacherous—lay just below the water.

"No!" she moaned, clamping her hand to her mouth, but in the blink of an eye, the ship had vanished.

Agatha lurched forwards. "What?"

Nothing there!

She scrabbled at the cliff's edge. No sign of a stricken vessel. Nothing.

A ghost ship? A mirage?

Flora ran towards her. "Aunt Agatha? What is it? What's wrong?"

The sea churned, a grubby grey, as far as the eye could see, meeting the horizon in a darker charcoal smudge. Agatha stared out at the waves, watching them race for shore on the beach beyond the cliffs, a motion as relentless as time itself.

Nothing could turn back the tide, nor the events that had been set in motion when the *Eliza May* had broken her back on the rocks in October.

She shivered, frozen to her marrow.

"Aunt Agatha?" Flora's concern finally broke through.

Agatha gave herself a mental shake. "I'm quite well." She faked a smile and caught up her ward's hand, pressing it between her own. "We should return home. Now."

Flora, catching the look in Agatha's eyes, locked her arm through her Aunt's. "Of course. We could all do with a warm through." They fell into step together, Stanley almost running to keep up with them.

Agatha cast a wary glance over her shoulder before they re-entered the wood, staring back in the direction of Lyme Bay.

Did I really see a ghost ship?

What portent is this?

38

THE MARY POMEROY SETS SAIL

Walter John Hanley, for all intents and purposes, had set the correct course. Out of the Thames, around the Kent and Sussex coastline and through the English Channel, skirting the Isle of Wight and out into the Irish Sea—with a proposed stopover at Cobh—before sailing into the Atlantic. Spring tides would be favourable. The owners expected the *Mary Pomeroy* to make America in good time.

The First Mate had questioned Walter's decision to hug the coastline, but Walter had explained this away easily enough. The *Mary Pomeroy* had enjoyed a complete refit of her rigging and sails while docked in London. Walter simply wanted to check everything was in good working order before he gave the ship her head.

The seas were high this afternoon, the tall waves capped with lacy heads. An unexpected squall had blown in from the west and he was heading into it. The *Mary Pomeroy* cut through the choppy sea easily enough, but the furious sky told Walter a heavier storm would be upon them by sunset.

He hid out in his cabin, ostensibly examining the navigation charts, knowing full well what he should be doing, where and when. He had been poring over the same information for days.

Now he checked his pocket watch for the umpteenth time. It wouldn't be long.

He would see the lights. That would be the signal.

The *Mary Pomeroy* was a fine ship. Probably the best of his long career. It was a shame to end her this way. He uttered a prayer for the safety and survival of his crew, especially himself, then headed for the top deck, rolling easily with the ship as it skipped over the waves. He turned his face into the fresh salt spray with satisfaction. This life was all he knew, and all he had ever wanted, but the time was right to make a complete change. His wife and children would be appreciative, he was certain.

Walter picked up his telescope and studied the tell-tale limestone cliffs. Lyme Bay lay ahead and to the right of them. They were about to become intimately acquainted.

"I'll take over for a while," he told the helmsman who squinted up at him in surprise, but relinquished his position willingly, before slipping below decks in search of a draught of something warming.

Walter turned the great wheel and repeated his prayer. Might God forgive him for what he was about to do.

Greeb had his head down over a tankard of ale in The Blue Bell Inn, half in his cups, but mainly in need of sleep. Barnacle Betsy whined and scratched at the door and Greeb resisted the urge to put the boot in and shut her up permanently. Damn the landlord for keeping the annoying little bitch, but Giles doted on her and Greeb didn't dare to cross him. Certainly not now, when he needed to remain visible and his men were keeping a watch for any sighting of a tall ship, ready with their lanterns.

A few days previously, Greeb had finally received word that the *Mary Pomeroy* was due to set sail imminently. He had spent the past twenty-four hours on tenterhooks. There had been no sign of her thus far. Greeb rubbed at the whiskers on his cheek, burning with an anxiety he had never before experienced. He drowned his fear in ale, weathering out his own uncomfortable internal storm.

Waiting. Waiting.

With a loud thunk, the door to the inn was pushed violently open. Greeb sat up with a jolt. Fitzroy bustled in, Lammas on his heels. Barnacle Betsy growled at them before rushing outside. Greeb glowered at those who turned to gawp, and kicked a stool out from beneath the table, nodding tersely as Fitzroy plonked himself down on it.

"Well?"

"She's here."

"You're certain?"

"Aye."

Greeb scrutinized the man's face, then glanced up at Lammas who nodded. Greeb rocked backwards, lifting up his tankard and draining it in one swallow. "About time." He threw the tankard at Lammas who caught it and gestured at Maddie.

She cast a wary eye over the threesome. "Coming right up, gents," she said and backed away.

"No ale for you, Lammas," Greeb spat. "We don't have the time for that. Don't just stand there. Set the false lights. Knock the men up! Get the word out! Get everyone down on the beach." Greeb rubbed his hands together, his eyes burning in excitement. "There's work to be done!"

Bumble gently replaced his quill in the ink well and meticulously blotted his signature. The large grandfather clock in the corner of the mayor's office tocked irrevocably, counting the seconds of his life down, one by one.

One more meeting, then he could send for his carriage and head home for dinner with Norah. He clenched his jaw. That would be every bit as stultifying as he could imagine. She would endeavour to talk his ear off about something nonsensical, until he was driven quite to distraction. He would bide his time until he could extricate himself and return to the club. Really, Jerome's was the only thing keeping him sane. On second thoughts, perhaps he would send a message to his wife, skip dinner and just eat at the club. Simpler all round.

He pulled an envelope out of the desk drawer and started to fold the sheet of vellum, but a sudden commotion outside his office door, alerted him to a visitor.

His clerk appeared to be having stern words with someone. "Come here, you little wretch! You can't go in there!"

The latch to his office jittered and the door was pushed open by a lad of no more than ten years of age. He rushed into the office and stood in front of Bumble. Bumble's clerk, Norwell—a youthful chap with a face full of pimples, red cheeked and stern of countenance—hurried in after the boy.

"What is the meaning of this?" Bumble asked perplexed. "Can't you see I'm working?"

The boy dashed the cap from his head and bowed grandly.

"If it pleases you, Sir? I've been sent here with a message."

Bumble glanced out of the window at the increasingly leaden sky. The trees were bowing away from the wind. *Was this it? At last?*

"I was told not to pass the message to anyone but you, Sir."

"Indeed?" Bumble narrowed his eyes at Norwell. "Wait outside." Norwell frowned, but accustomed to following orders, he duly nodded and departed.

"What's the message?" Bumble eyed the lad.

The boy hesitated and rubbed his hands together as though they were cold. Bumble, fairly certain that Greeb would have paid the boy to bring the message in the first place, sighed and dipped into his pocket for a coin. The boy accepted it, most humbly.

"Thank you, Sir. Most kind. Most kind. My message was from a gentleman you are acquainted with, Sir. He says to tell you that Mary's arrived and you should stand by."

"That's all he said?"

"Yes Sir. That's all." The boy looked hopeful. "Is there a return message, Sir?" Either he was enjoying his role as special envoy, or he'd figured out a quick way to make his fortune. Bumble shook his head brusquely and indicated the exit.

Time to make haste. With the dark falling, they had the jump on any nosy officials.

The boy pouted and headed for the door. Swinging it wide open, he turned to address Bumble once more. In a voice loud enough for the whole floor of the building to hear, he announced, "Oh! And there's a ship in the bay, Mayor. You should come and look. Seems like she's in distress."

Bumble grimaced at the sound of chairs being hurriedly pushed back and the general consternation beyond his office door. Someone started barking questions at the hapless messenger. Bumble cursed. The word would be out and there would be no containing it. The whole town would know in next to no time.

He stormed to the window, staring out in the direction of the seafront. Should he continue with his evening plans? Pretend nothing was afoot? No. The innocents among the townsfolk would expect him to be on site, guiding a rescue operation and supporting the fishermen. He would have to go to the quay.

Reluctantly, he reached for his overcoat. It was going to be a long night. He hoped to God that Greeb had all eventualities covered.

Agatha stood in the garden of Myrtle Lodge, her face turned upwards. Closing her eyes she stretched to ease a crick in her back. The wind was picking up. She smelt salt on the breeze, and something more. Her eyes fluttered open and she glanced seawards, wishing she could part the trees as easily as she might part her seedlings.

What lay beyond the woods, beyond the cliffs, in that stretch of infinite water?

She discarded the trowel she'd been holding and, forgetting about the earth that caked her nails and stained her skin, she started to walk, quickly crossing the garden, and trotting across the lane to the wood. Then she dropped all pretence and, lifting her skirt and petticoats, she ran as hard as she could, racing for the cliffs, fortifying herself for what she would see there, praying all the time that she'd be wrong.

As she disappeared into the trees, she heard Hannah calling her name.

She didn't slow down.

Emily replaced her cup on the tea tray and picked up her book again. The light was fading fast. Outside the grey sky had started to close in, the windows rattling in their frames. She angled herself slightly to catch a better light from the window. She would need to call Mary to have the lamp trimmed soon. The words began to melt into the page and she sighed heavily. Dropping the book to the floor, she smoothed her skirts over and over, ironing out any hint of a crease, gazing all the while through the windowpane, staring into her garden, but not actually seeing anything.

A light tap on the door startled her. She flushed as the butler entered.

"I'm sorry to disturb you, Madam. A young man is at the back door. He has a message for Mr Fliss who is currently not at home."

Emily knitted her brows together in irritation. She neither knew, nor cared, where Marmaduke was, but surely Alfred could take the message. She was about to suggest this when the fire hissed. She glanced at it, her insides squeezing together.

"Send him in," she replied, and was not at all surprised when Stanley entered the room a few moments later.

"What is it, Stanley? Is Lord Tolleson well?"

"Lord Tolleson is in London, Ma'am." Stanley ducked his head shyly. He stood in awe of Emily. She was the grandest and most beautiful person he knew.

"The folks at Myrtle Lodge, then?"

"All well, Ma'am. But I received word from them. I came to tell you that there has been sighting of a ship in the bay. It looks like she will founder, Ma'am. Miss Wick is worried for you and asks that you remain at home."

Emily jolted upright, her face pale, her breath catching in her slender throat. They had surmised correctly and now it appeared that Bumble had gone ahead with his devious plan. What could she have done differently? Might she have prevented this? She scoured Stanley's face, as though she would discover the answers there.

"Ma'am?" he asked, his voice full of concern. "Should I ring for someone?"

"Thank you, Stanley," she replied, forcing herself to relax a little. "I am quite well. Please thank Miss Wick for her message."

She nodded a dismissal and sat calmly until he had left the room. The second the door had closed, she jumped to her feet, clawing at her throat in distress. The fire spat and roared as though someone had stoked its flames.

Is there nothing else I can try? Is there no-one who can help me?

Perhaps Marmaduke could do something, warn someone, anything to prevent the ship from wrecking. But where was he? Where would she find him?

She rang the bell for Alfred. She would go in search of her husband.

He had to listen to her.

39
DISASTER IN LYME BAY

The weather had been set fair when the *Mary Pomeroy* left safe harbour in London, but the unexpected squall had caught the crew by surprise. In those conditions, and knowing that a storm was imminent, it hadn't been difficult for Walter Hanley to feign a problem with the ship's steering and guide her further inland. He hugged The Needles on the Isle of Wight before steering ever closer to the red cliffs of West Dorset and East Devon.

Between them, Greeb and Bumble had planned the demise of the *Mary Pomeroy* with admirable precision. Hanley's silence had been bought easily enough and, in turn, the captain had bribed a number of his crew, promising them financial reward and safe passage back to their families. Greeb had other ideas. His army of men now stood ready on the quay, intent on ensuring no survivors ever made land. The one thing Greeb and Bumble could not have made any provision for was the weather, but Mother Nature had played right into their hands.

Conditions had deteriorated further in the hour or so since the ship had been sighted. From a distance, to any casual observer, it appeared as though the Captain was fighting to save his ship from running aground. There were plenty on the quay, and the surrounding cliffs that overlooked the bay however, who knew better. The ship loomed larger and larger, rolling and lurching among the waves.

Once Lammas and Fitzroy had departed The Blue Bell Inn, Greeb had borrowed a horse from the landlord and made his way to The Victoria Gardens. In the failing light, he surveyed the scene with grim satisfaction. When he was certain the *Mary Pomeroy* was heading straight into Lyme Bay, he returned the horse to the inn and waited. He wanted to be close to the action and whiled away the time sinking a little more rum.

A clear head might help what was coming, but he doubted it, so he drank his fill.

Dark jagged rocks, enormous chunks of landscape that had long ago broken from the land and fallen into the ocean, loomed mercilessly in the ship's path. The sea lunged against the cliffs and fell back, foaming and hissing, only to try and try again, as though the water could dominate the land. The *Mary Pomeroy* bobbed around like a child's toy in a barrel and now, even if the Captain tried to change his mind, she'd be lost.

One ferocious wave caught her broadside. The ship lurched hard-a-starboard and her fate was sealed. Juddering and shaking, she ran against the first outcrop of rocks and wrenched sideways. From the rigging high above the captain's head, one of his men shrieked as he lost his footing. The scream, abruptly silenced as the sailor crashed on the hardwood deck below, froze the blood in the veins of every man who heard it. The sailor's head spattered open like a broken egg, his blood running into the gaps in the wooden boards. Hanley dipped his chin, bile burning in the back of his throat.

The *Mary Pomeroy* rolled to her left, temporarily freeing herself from the rocks, but the damage had been done and she'd started to take on water. The tide pushed her forwards, further into the bay, and Hanley, clinging to the wheel for all he was worth, steered for shallow waters, desperate to ensure his crew had the best chance of making it to shore. He had too little time, the water cascading in through the holes in the breached hull only added to the weight of the ship, and she began to sit lower in the water, her bottom scraping those rocks hidden beneath the surface of the roiling sea.

The *Mary Pomeroy* was breached, her timbers punctured. She *would* go down.

The great ship shuddered and righted herself, prompting a sudden flurry of activity on the decks, as sailors dashed from port to starboard and back again, peering over the sides in a desperate attempt to ascertain the damage. Hanley, adrenaline pumping, recognised the game was up. He gave the order he dreaded. "Evacuate the ship! Every man for himself!"

The cry went up. "Every man for himself!" and suddenly men were climbing over the sides, swinging from ropes, hurling barrels and anything that might float into the water — even as the *Mary Pomeroy* lurched — before throwing themselves into the sea below.

Agatha, standing alone on the high cliffs not far from Myrtle Lodge, yanked at her shawl. The wind blew fierce, the rain jabbing like needles at any area of exposed skin, but she remained oblivious to the elements, ignorant of the water that soaked through her clothes. Her coldness lay deep within.

Hannah had followed her employer through the trees and joined her at the cliff edge, clutching Agatha's wrap, as worried for Agatha's state of mind as much as the weather. Now they stood side-by-side, gazing at the unfolding scene in horror, Hannah's fingers gripping Agatha's forearm. The sky above them, thick with foreboding, was reflected in the angry, oily black of the sea. Agatha grimaced as she watched the *Mary Pomeroy* roll viciously at the mercy of the churning waves and winced as men tumbled from the decks, smashing onto the rocks below. An occasional scream drifted the women's way, but for the most part, the shrieks were drowned out by the rush of the wind and the roar of the waves. The pleas and the prayers of those men who remained on board were as lost as the men who shouted them.

Greeb, warmed by his consumption of rum stepped outside The Blue Bell Inn and stood within the light of a flaming torch, surveying the scene. His battered top hat, cocked at a jaunty angle, cast a shadow over his bad eye. From a distance he might have been just another interested bystander, entranced by the spectacle unfolding among the waters in front of him. His watchful men knew better. He shrewdly appraised the grim reality of the job in hand, pleased with the *Mary Pomeroy's* positioning in the bay. Hanley had performed his part beautifully. Alright, the ship was slightly further out than Greeb had anticipated, but this meant the crew were much less likely to make it to shore under their own steam.

Nonetheless, there is nothing so strong in the human psyche as the will to survive. Greeb spied the first sailors fighting their way to the shore despite the height of the waves. The tide was with them. He hadn't factored that in and he didn't like it. If there was a possibility some would make it, his men would have to stop them.

He'd prepared them for that, at least.

Fitz, standing on the quay with a cluster of women, turned casually about and met Greeb's eye. With an imperceptible nod of his head, Greeb gave the signal Fitz was waiting for. Fitz straightened his cap in salute, swivelled and walked rapidly towards the prom. On his way he purposefully bustled into a woman standing watching. He apologised and headed for the beach.

The woman set up a shrill plea. "Oh save them! Save the poor souls! Won't someone help them?"

That was the signal for Greeb's dark army to take to the water.

Men, some local to Durscombe, others no-one in the community recognised, rushed down from the promenade and along the sand, moving quickly and quietly, splashing through the shallows to meet the waves. A few gasped at the chill of the water, but others, hardy fishermen, simply set their teeth with grim determination and forged a path, wading thigh deep through the foamy surf, turning themselves sideways to avoid being knocked off their feet by the larger breakers.

From a distance, an innocent bystander might have been forgiven for assuming these men were heroic, risking their necks to save the souls of those swimming from the wreck to the supposed haven of the shore. However, looks can be deceptive and never more so than that night. Each man wading towards the ship, had one brutal intention and so some carried a knife or a club, others a large stone, while the rest intended to rely on their fists.

Hanley, busy trying to navigate the *Mary Pomeroy* away from the rocks to give his men a fighting chance, did not see the advance of Greeb's army. But if he had, why would he be worried? He'd had Greeb's assurances of a safe passage, after all.

Emily had been unable to contain herself.

None of the servants knew the current whereabouts of Mr Fliss and, in spite of Stanley's message from Agatha to remain at home, Emily gave in to her curiosity. She needed to see the tragedy unfolding for herself. Oblivious to any danger, Emily ordered her carriage and had one of the grooms drive her towards Durscombe along the coastal road.

Nab Hill curled through a heavily forested section of the countryside and for the most part the route into town had been cut through the trees, effectively blocking any chance of Emily catching a glimpse of the bay. Emily lay her cheek against the cold glass, not really needing the view to know exactly what was going on in the waters below. Dark shadows flitted across her vision. She closed her eyes, trying to block them out, massaging her temple with a gloved hand, but this only made the voices worse.

Men's voices.

Dozens of them.

She couldn't make out the words, but the meaning was clear.

Save me! Save us! I'm not ready to die.

Moaning, she banged on the roof of the carriage as soon as the trees thinned out and the groom pulled over at the far end of the promenade, below the Victoria Garden cliff face. Emily, her heart thumping, her head whirling, struggled to open the carriage door in the face of the buffeting wind and the groom jumped down to assist her.

"Wait for me," she told him and crossed the narrow road.

From this vantage point, twelve feet or so above the beach, the waves rolling in so close beneath her feet she could feel the spray, she could clearly make out the torches in the harbour and on the quay in the near distance. The *Mary Pomeroy*, a bigger ship than the *Eliza May*, listed badly on the rocks to her right, shuddering as she was hit by huge wave after huge wave. Emily stumbled forwards, straining to make out the scene as the light failed around her. She imagined she could see some members of the crew in the sea already.

Yes! They could make it!

She clamped her hands to her mouth, watching as men flailed in the water, some driven back against the rocks, others sucked away or down by an invisible riptide. One or two swam past her, mere feet below the place where she stood, fighting to reach the beach. All she could do was stare achingly after them.

She paid attention to the particular progress of one man, long dark hair plastered against his scalp, as he struggled to make his way towards her and to the safety of the shore. He thrashed his way through the ceaseless cresting waves, his face twisted in fear and panic, his mouth opening and closing as he gulped in a mixture of air and salty water. When he finally managed to find his footing on the sand below, his relief was obvious. He stood for a moment, his chest heaving, dropping his shoulders, but then another large wave knocked him from his feet. He struggled upright again, and this time swung his arms to help him fight his way more quickly through the recalcitrant sea, aiming for the sand, spitting and retching as he came. Survival was a mere stone's throw away; if he could just make it to shore ...

Agitated by his faltering progress, Emily clapped her hands to her face and trotted along the promenade, urging him on, her eyes wide, willing him forwards to safety. Nearly there. His face was clearer now. Something inside her shifted. A sense of dull recognition.

She pulled up, regarding him through a foggy haze. He seemed so familiar to her. A dream half-remembered.

Further along the beach, figures were running towards the sailor, would-be rescuers making their way along the sand. Dozens of them.

"Thank goodness!" Emily said. But even as the wind whipped her words away, she understood—from their purpose and speed—that the sailor below was in grave danger. She rushed to the edge of the promenade.

"Turn about!" she whispered to a man no older than she, who smiled in relief at the sight of the men who hurried towards him. "Turn about!" she shrieked, but her words were lost in the roar of the waves.

Perhaps the sailor sensed her gaze, for he looked up. He faltered, the sea swirling around his knees, water dripping from him, staring her way, then he turned to greet the men on the beach.

"No!" Emily shrieked.

One man raised his arm. A club swung through the air. The momentary confusion on the sailor's face was quickly replaced by the horror of his understanding, but before he could react the weapon had smashed into his right eye. The exhausted sailor staggered and fell, disappearing beneath the waves for a few long seconds before surfacing. Coming up for air, he choked and spluttered, the blood running freely, cloaking one side of his face. His assailant was ready. One further sharp blow to the top of the skull, a vicious crack, and the sailor sank below the waves in a mess of blood and brain and bubbles.

Emily shrieked in horror and despair, falling back towards the carriage and calling the groom. He sprinted to her and half-carried, half-dragged her back to the carriage and arranged her on the seat. She trembled and wailed, clawing at the air in front of her.

"Ma'am?" he asked, and she gestured him away, waiting for the door to close before hastily leaning forward, retching, grateful to be alone.

She righted herself, shaking, dabbing at her mouth with her handkerchief. Where was Marmaduke? Could he be somewhere close? Some kind of acquiescent spectator? This wrecking and the murder unfolding before her had been endorsed by the Mayor. How long before a signal was given, and the remaining townsfolk joined the men at the shoreline to haul in the shipwrecked goods?

She knew, sitting alone in her carriage, it would do her no good at all to demonstrate her abhorrence. Because who would care? Who would care?

Agatha.

But even she would be powerless to help anyone here tonight.

40

A LONG NIGHT

Agatha and Hannah had returned to Myrtle Lodge, chilled to the bone and soaked through. After changing out of her sodden clothes, Agatha built the fire in the kitchen grate, piling it high with hands that trembled, while Hannah attempted to distract herself by sorting through a pile of herbs heaped on top of the kitchen table. She'd begun bundling rolls of sage together, when a terrified scream reverberated through the quiet house.

Flora.

Agatha froze. Flora was not given to hysterical displays of emotion; she was a sensible young woman with a good head on her shoulders.

Agatha raced to the parlour; a strange room that she rarely used. Most of Tansy's odd collection of stuffed animals and birds were housed in glass bell jars here, along with a small library of books, two or three shelves, not impressive by Phineas's standards, but nothing to be ashamed of. The furniture, perhaps fashionable a hundred years previously, and the mirrors, once opulent, were old and far past their best. Agatha had taken it upon herself to thin the clutter the room had housed in Tansy's time, and Hannah kept the room miraculously clean and free from dust. Visitors could be entertained here when necessary, but as a rule, the fire wasn't lit and the room lay silent and still.

Tonight Flora had been searching through the books for something new to read. She 'd been seeking a distraction, given that Agatha refused to discuss the events of the evening. News about the loss of the *Mary Pomeroy*, so soon after the *Eliza May*, had unsettled her. Agatha had gently suggested she find something to read to take her mind off the disaster.

Agatha burst into the room, with Hannah close on her heels. They found Flora standing as still as a statue in the centre of the room, her eyes fixed on the pair of glass doors that opened into the garden. A number of books lay littered on the rug, pages carelessly cast around the floor.

"Flora?" Agatha took her hand. The girl was freezing.

"What happened? Are you hurt?" Hannah bustled around them both.

"No, no. I—" Flora shook herself and turned her pale face towards the women. "I'm sorry. I didn't intend to startle you." She glanced towards the doors once more.

Agatha followed her gaze. The light in the parlour made it impossible to see outside. "Did you see something there?" she asked.

Flora swallowed. "I thought for a moment I saw a man. At the door. I thought... he was trying to gain entry."

Agatha directed a sharp look Hannah's way. The housekeeper pursed her lips and nodded. She tried the doors. They were locked. "I'll have a quick look around outside, and see whether we have a prowler," she said.

Flora reached out as Hannah passed her, as though to prevent her leaving, but Agatha took the girl's hand.

"Did you recognise him? This man?"

"No," Flora frowned.

"Could he have been an itinerant? A passing journeyman?"

"I suppose he might have, Aunt." Her tone suggested otherwise.

"But you think not?"

Flora took a deep shuddering breath. "No." She tensed in alarm as a figure came into view beyond the doors, but relaxed when she realised it was the housekeeper. Hannah smiled and waved, then leaned over to examine the ground.

"I think he was dead."

Agatha choked in surprise. Flora's words hung in the air between them. Agatha waited for Flora to say more, but the girl fell silent, watching Hannah's examination of the bushes in front of the doors.

"Dead?" Agatha finally enquired, keeping her voice steady but her pulse beating a little faster than normal.

She had never discussed the gifts Tansy had passed on to her granddaughters with anyone, least of all with Flora, not wishing to scare her. In turn, Flora had never questioned Agatha's odd ability to do certain things that defied rational and scientific explanation. Perhaps there was some tacit understanding that these things were not to be discussed outside Myrtle Lodge, but they were perfectly normal within its four walls. If Flora had ever been curious about any of Agatha's rituals and practices, or any of the brews, potions and concoctions that Hannah and Agatha infused in the kitchen, she never said so.

Flora sighed, a sound that originated deep in her soul. Tears began to spill from her eyes, running quietly down her cheeks. "He was so sad, Aunt Agatha. So terribly sad," she said. "He wanted to live. He was going to the Americas." Her voice broke, and Agatha gathered the girl to her, holding her tightly, her own eyes bright with emotion.

"I'm sorry, my dear child. I am so sorry."

"He was dead, wasn't he?" Flora asked.

Agatha, mute with pain, could only nod.

Flora pulled back and stared into Agatha's face. The two were almost the same height. "I know you see them too."

"Aye." Agatha frowned. "I do." She hesitated. "But you said '*them*'? So, this isn't the first time you've encountered a spirit?"

"I've seen several."

"How long have you been able to see them?" Agatha wanted to know. "In Lincolnshire?"

Flora shrugged. She pulled her shoulders back and breathed a deep hiccoughing breath, trying to pull herself together. Agatha could sense her relief at finally being able to unburden herself, to bring the matter out into the open. "Yes. Since I was a child. For as long as I can remember."

Agatha had never known. She stroked Flora's shoulders. She should have paid more attention but there had never been an inkling ...

"Sometimes I'd catch fleeting glimpses of something I couldn't explain. Now they come and they go. None of them has ever bothered me, or threatened to hurt me." She cocked her head. "Is that what you experience?"

Agatha, recalling her hostile encounter with Thomas Parrett, remained quiet.

"But this one," Flora continued, "was so ... terribly sad. Bitter even. Angry with it." She stared at the window. "I was afraid."

"Most will do you no harm," Agatha said, breaking away from Flora and pulling the heavy drapes across the doors. There was truth in what she'd said, but there had been a malevolence about Sally's husband Thomas she'd never come across before. Perhaps in his case this had been due to the manner of his passing.

However, Agatha did not feel this was something she could discuss with Flora at this time. "There are ways to protect yourself, and as a matter of urgency I should share these with you. I will do that tomorrow. In the meantime, I think you should rest. There is no-one here now. You are quite safe."

Flora reached for her Aunt. "I don't want to be alone."

"You may sleep with me tonight," Agatha replied, her voice soft. "Hannah will keep you company until I retire."

Word had reached Emily that Marmaduke had been attending a recital until he'd been informed about the ship in the bay. Emily lay alone in her own bed, drowning beneath the weight of several extra blankets, and shivered. Her eyes flicked this way and that, scrutinizing every shadow cast by her candle as the light flickered across the walls. The windows had been bolted. The shutters locked into place. The thick curtains were drawn. She had triple checked everything before finally climbing beneath the covers.

The only refrain Emily could hear, even beyond the mansion's barrier of brocade, glass and wood, were the wails and the shrieks of dead men,

She lay on her side, gripping the edge of her counterpane with claw-like fingers, staring hollow-eyed in the direction of Durscombe. If she could banish the walls and the trees and stare down the valley towards the beach, she would be able to make out silvery shadows. She would *see* them, the lost sailors, scrabbling across the rocks, wading through the water, and stumbling through the sand, seeking a place of safety in town. She would watch as, out of desperation, they would drag themselves up the cliffs, hand over hand, until they could grasp a rocky outcrop and haul themselves over the red clay edge, to sprawl on the grass to recover.

Under cover of darkness wouldn't they attempt to cast about for some friendly face? Someone who could offer them assistance? A warm meal? Dry clothes?

You won't find it here, she whispered. *Not in Durscombe. You'll seek in vain.*

No sailor would receive a welcome in Durscombe, dead or alive. And when the spirits finally understood their plight, when they recognised the futility of the situation, when they ultimately acknowledged the one salient fact that they were dead, surely their combined fury would rain down on the town. Why wouldn't their souls demand vengeance?

Who in Durscombe can assuage the spirits' anguish? Reverend Tidwell? Would he try?

In the morning she would write to Reverend Tidwell and, God

help her, to Mayor Bumble. Perhaps if she could explain that the spirits were not at rest, something could be done.

Marmaduke would help her. He had to.

He was her last hope.

Agatha rocked in her chair, staring deep into the fire. Hannah had taken Flora a cup of valerian tea and honey to help ease the young woman's anxiety, and had remained in the bedroom to keep her company. Agatha, alone, shifted restlessly, fearing what the night would bring. There were dozens and dozens of fresh and unquiet spirits in and round Durscombe. She'd be sure to hear from some of them in the next few hours.

Agatha did not fear the spirits for she could banish them if she chose. Unlike Emily, she had worked closely with her grandmother to learn more about this particular gift and had grown skilled in interacting with the dead. She'd had ample opportunity to learn, after all. She'd lived here at Myrtle Lodge with Tansy for most of her youth, while Lily had tried everything within her power to keep Emily as far away as possible.

Agatha considered her gifts to be both a blessing and a curse. Had she been given a choice she might have wished to be born without them, to have had a more conventional upbringing, but she'd grown easy in her own skin, comfortable with the knowledge that she was different, and had accepted that, as Tansy would have said, 'what must be, will be'.

That had been one of her favourite expressions.

Tansy had known dozens of ways to kill and cure, including many that the medical men did not. Tansy would never have been caught by surprise in any situation. She could not be shocked by anything or anybody. She was a solver of life's problems. She was odd, she was astute, she was canny, and she suffered fools badly. Agatha had loved her in her own way, and now recognised what an honour it had been to be her apprentice.

Agatha glanced across at Tansy's chair. "What can be done, grandmother?" she asked. "It is not right what is happening in Durscombe. I can banish the spirits, but only one by one, and what use would that be? If they are unhappy, they will find a way to return. The spirits of these poor sailors need to find peace. And surely peace will only come when justice has been served."

As if in agreement, Tansy's chair rocked slowly back and forth.

The sun rose on a calm morning, a huge bright orange orb in a watery lilac sky. The previous day's storm might have been an ill-remembered memory, but not for Emily. She strolled briskly along the cliff edge, replaying the previous afternoon's events obsessively in her mind. Ahead of her, the sea sparkled—the slight swell catching the sun—but her attention remained riveted on the wrecked hulk of the *Mary Pomeroy*.

The tide was out. Children and young men were labouring to bring ashore chests and barrels and anything they could find that had any value. They skipped in and out of the shallows, avoiding the places where the sand had been stained red. Blood, washed out like a watercolour, running in rivulets, trickling back towards the sea. The next high tide would erase it.

A number of corpses lay where they had been washed up.

Emily turned her head away from lolling tongues, black faces, fleshy wounds. The seagulls were not so fussy. They strutted around the bodies, hard beaks pecking away, ferociously accurate, homing in on the tastiest, softest and most accessible treats.

Emily hated the corpses. Not because she was sentimental or squeamish—although she was both—but because she knew that the souls of these dead men, and those that floated out at sea, were unquiet.

She knew how deeply they desired a final resting place.

She knew ... because they had told her so.

All night long.

41

MR FLISS FAILS

"My wife is a lady, Sir. You cannot possibly expect her to wade ankle deep into the sea with the common folk." Marmaduke Fliss's shrill voice could be heard the length and breadth of Municipal Hall. Not for the first time in their conversation, Mayor Bumble winced, his head pounding.

"I can assure you, Mr Fliss, that we would never want to inconvenience Mrs Fliss," Mayor Bumble responded calmly, smoothing out the blotting paper on his desk and frowning up at his visitor. "It is simply that the aldermen are unhappy that Mrs Fliss takes such a dim view of current proceedings." Mayor Bumble snatched up a letter from a pile and waved it. Fliss recognized his wife's neat handwriting.

"Here I have yet another complaint from Mrs Fliss. She has written to myself and to the aldermen on no less than nine occasions over the past three days. Nine letters. Three days!" Mayor Bumble spat. "In fact almost every delivery seems to bring yet another missive from your wife, Mr Fliss."

"Mrs Fliss is indeed a prolific letter writer." Marmaduke found himself almost apologising for her. But not quite. Emily would make his life a misery if he didn't fulfil his errand on her behalf.

"Well really, Mr Fliss. It would perhaps be expedient on your part to ensure she is quite entertained at home. There really is no need for her to witness any event she finds distasteful. I am entirely certain we would not miss her from the promenade or The Victoria Gardens if she does not wish to observe our forays to the wreck."

Fliss did not like the direction the conversation was heading. What did Bumble mean by forays? He made it sound as though it was an excursion on behalf of a gentleman's club.

Nonetheless, Marmaduke had one task. Emily had requested Mr Fliss petition the mayor on her behalf. "I'm afraid my wife is adamant—"

"You are the head of your household, are you not, Mr Fliss? Perhaps you can convince your delicate flower of a wife that her time would be better employed inside her home being industrious, conceivably by throwing herself into more feminine and philanthropic endeavours if she has no other outlets."

Bumble's words stung, as they were intended to. "Mayor Bumble, you know as well as anyone, that my wife is charitable in the extreme."

"Given her family background, that is to be expected, I think."

Marmaduke Fliss stared at Bumble in consternation. The mayor had a tendency for frank talking, yes, but this bordered on rudeness. What, in the devil's name, was the matter with Bumble? Fliss took a deep breath and lengthened his spine. He would not stoop to the mayor's level.

Silence.

Fliss waited, but it became apparent that Bumble had no intention of apologising for the remark. As time stretched interminably, a flustered Marmaduke decided that it seemed safest to gloss over it. He considered his position. Perhaps it would be wisest to leave the mayor's company until he came to his senses. Emily's beautiful face drifted into his mind. The thought of her distress if he didn't press her case, as she had directly asked him to, steadied his resolve.

"It is the souls you see." Marmaduke sounded more confident than he felt.

Mayor Bumble frowned. "The souls?"

"Mrs Fliss," Marmaduke grimaced, "thinks the souls of the dead will haunt the town."

"Souls? As in ghosts?" Bumble started in surprise. "Good God, man. What poppycock! You know better than that. Your wife is unhinged."

"Perhaps it would be better if Mrs Fliss were to explain herself to you," Fliss wheedled.

"I would hesitate to call your wife mad, Marmaduke, as that would be to do you a discourtesy, I am sure. But if I were in your shoes, I would have Dr Giddens out to examine her."

"Grant her five minutes, Mayor, if only to allow Mrs Fliss to explain herself. I beseech you. That's all she asks."

"I can assure you that I have no desire for an audience with your wife, Mr Fliss. But please extend my courtesies to her." Bumble directed his visitor's attention to the door. "Good day, Mr Fliss."

"But—"

"Good day, Sir."

Fliss regarded Bumble for a long moment before quietly taking his leave.

Bumble sighed with relief. He had some sympathy for Marmaduke Fliss. Emily could obviously be a harridan when roused, you just had to know how to control her. Hadn't he recently proved that was possible?

He stared down at the pile of letters. Let her complain. She was playing directly into his hands. If she created too much of a fuss he would have Dr Giddens certify her as insane. It wouldn't be too difficult, given she'd recently enjoyed a short spell in the Exeter sanatorium.

He sucked his teeth. To think that once upon a time he had been her likely suitor.

She'd been incredibly beautiful at eighteen and he had loved her as best he could. In fact, he'd never loved another woman in the same way. That haunting beauty of hers had been destined to ensure she was able to marry way above her station. But after his summer party, she had disappeared without so much as a by-your-leave.

He'd heard through his aunt, who knew Emily's mother, that Emily and her cousin Agatha Wick had taken a short tour. Emily had not written to him, and perhaps the younger Bumble had been hurt by her on-going silence.

He couldn't recall.

Eventually she had returned to Durscombe, but she had not sought out his company. For years he had snubbed her at every opportunity. He had married the dull Norah, and this had pleased his parents greatly, while Emily had found solace with Fliss. Naturally she had married for money and security, and this still rankled the Mayor. Fliss was a weak-minded fool, incapable of controlling his increasingly wayward and outspoken wife.

The thing was, in spite of all that had passed between them recently, and even though Bumble would have denied it, deep inside he still carried a torch for Miss Emily Cuffhulme. He squashed such thoughts ruthlessly, taking pleasure instead on inflicting pain on her. Fortunately for the municipality, his cold, rational side had the upper hand. He would do everything possible to retain power, money and privilege. Emily Fliss was nothing but a deluded fool.

Bumble plucked Emily's most recent letter from the top of the pile and glanced over its contents one more time, before crumpling it into a ball and flinging it into the fire. It curled and twisted in the flames, blackened and turned to ash.

"I apologise profusely my dear. I—ah—" Mr Fliss stumbled over his words. The parlour was warm and he was noticeably perspiring, but not from the heat of the fire. Emily, her porcelain face as still as a pond, could be entirely formidable at times.

"You were not well received by Mayor Bumble I take it, Mr Fliss?" she asked, her voice soft and low and infinitely sad. She did not invite her husband to take a seat.

"He ... No, my love. I was not."

Emily nodded. Her eyes sparkled with tears, before her face retreated into shadow.

"He had received my most recent letter?"

"He had, my angel. And all of the others."

"You reminded him of the souls?"

"I tried, my precious. Really I did."

They fell quiet. Mr Fliss read his wife's disappointment in the void between them, keenly felt the absence of affection, and lamented his inability to please her. He had never been able to reach her, to inhabit the same space. Of course she was so much younger than he. He had showered her with gifts, had tried to elicit her smiles, had courted her love. And failed dismally each and every time. Her rejection enshrouded him. Did the other aldermen sense it? Is that why they found him lacking?

Marmaduke attempted to cross the chasm between them, as he always did. "The recital that had to be abandoned the other evening has been rescheduled for tonight, my sweet. Would you care to attend with me?"

"I would not, Mr Fliss. I have a headache. I shall retire early. With your permission, of course." But she wasn't seeking permission. She saw no need to. Mr Fliss did not control Mrs Fliss, no matter the societal norms. She had favoured him with her hand in marriage, and very little else.

"Very well, Mrs Fliss. Good night to you." Mr Fliss made his bows and retreated from his wife's presence.

He doubted she even noticed.

After her husband had retreated, Emily slumped in her chair in weary despair. What could she do if no-one would listen to her? How could she silence the whispering? Even now they were muttering away to her. The voices, initially sad and confused, were becoming increasingly fervent, demanding justice. They cajoled and threatened. If she didn't help them they would not be responsible for their actions. The hair on her neck prickled as icy lips pressed against her ear lobes, and damp mouths spewed forth obscenities at her failure to act.

She nodded. "I hear you," she soothed. "I do."

The voices had issued an ultimatum, and she was their messenger.

42
EMILY IN THE MUNICIPAL OFFICES

In weary resignation, Mayor Bumble rose from his desk. "Mrs. Fliss. What an unexpected pleasure."

"Mayor Bumble," Emily tilted her head and offered a half curtsey, gracefully dipping her knee. For appearances sake, she waited until Bumble's servant had left them, before sinking onto a chair without waiting to be invited. She was mostly pale, save for the dark rings around her eyes.

"For pity's sake," Emily snapped. "How is it you refuse to see me?"

"Mrs Fliss," Bumble responded, loading his voice with ice. "I really don't think—"

"That's quite correct, Mayor, you *don't* think. I've sent you a dozen letters this past week and still you have barred me from these offices." Her hands twisted in her lap, fingers restless.

"This is not the place for you and I to be seen. After what happened—" Bumble tried a different tack. Emily's face flamed. He'd hit his target.

But if he expected her to break down, to beg forgiveness for disturbing him, he couldn't have been more surprised. She glared at him, her eyes hollow with disgust. "Nothing happened at Mrs Dainty's that you did not intend, Mayor Bumble!"

Bumble walked around his desk, reappraising his visitor. He found himself grudgingly admiring her courage in facing him down. Any other woman would have folded in the face of his superiority. He had convinced himself that Emily Fliss would present no further trouble. He'd left her in Mrs Dainty's back room, a shivering, hysterical wreck, her spine ground out on the rocks much like the *Eliza May*, but something had changed in the intervening weeks. She looked gaunt, no less magnificent, but something in her eyes appeared harder than before, and the lines around her mouth had deepened.

"It is imperative that I speak with you about the crew of the *Mary Pomeroy*."

"You can't come here with more of your absurd propositions, Mrs Fliss." Bumble paced purposefully to the fire and stood with his back to the flames.

"Have you taken the time to read my letters?"

"Well," Bumble shrugged, turning his back to fiddle with a delicately painted statuette on the mantelpiece.

"Have you?"

"Mrs Fliss, I implore you. If you don't have anything new or pertinent to say, then we really are wasting our time here."

Emily considered Bumble's back, despairing at his haughtiness. She couldn't reach him by talking to him on a level, but she understood his arrogance, and recognised that somewhere inside he would be flattered by her attentions. Setting aside her own revulsion, she stood, rolled her shoulders and took a deep breath. She glided smoothly towards the Mayor, adjusting her expression, smiling a little.

Sounding altogether calmer and sweeter, she addressed him once more. "But surely it is our time to waste, Theo?" She yielded the pet name he favoured as a weapon in her arsenal. He turned to her and she gazed up at him from under thick black eyelashes, reaching to straighten his cravat. He caught her hands.

"Emily," he warned.

"You know about the souls, Theo. I've written to you about

them. They talk to me all the time. All night. Every night. There were some after the *Eliza May* went down, but it has been far worse since the loss of the *Mary Pomeroy*." Her breath was soft on his chin. "I can't sleep anymore. Mr Fliss insists on calling the doctor and he gives me sleeping draughts. But still I cannot sleep. It is torture. You can't know what it's like, Theo."

"This is between you and your doctor, Emily." His insinuation seemed clear. He considered her hysterical.

"But *you* can stop it," Emily's eyes filled with tears. "Don't you see? *You* have the power. You and the aldermen. Between you."

Bumble remained stone-faced. "It cannot be done."

"Then at the very least, bring the bodies ashore so that Reverend Tidwell can confer a decent Christian burial."

Bumble rolled his eyes.

"Please, Emily. Let nature take its course."

"Think of the families, Theo," Emily begged, her voice rising in consternation. Think of the souls of those poor departed sailors! They have no peace!"

"Out of the question. We cannot overburden St. Michaels's or Reverend Tidwell any more than we already have."

Emily wailed and sank to her knees. "You don't understand! I can't bear it anymore. They call to me. They demand a proper burial on the land. We cannot leave them to float around in the sea, at the mercy of the waves. They get no rest. Do you not see? They will not grant me a minute's respite until I give them what they desire!"

"Emily, please stand up." Bumble reached for her.

Desperate tears streamed down Emily's face as she clasped his legs. "If you ever loved me, Theo, and I know you did, when we were young, that summer, you did ... I know you did. I beseech you. Stop the wreckings. Have the townsmen bring the bodies ashore. Let's give those unfortunates a decent burial. Help me quieten the *undead*."

"The undead?" Bumble pulled away, alarmed by Emily's passion, the venom in her voice. He rang for his clerk in haste.

"Such fantasy! You are not yourself, Mrs Fliss. This is most inappropriate for a woman of your station."

"Theo please!" Emily shrieked.

The door opened and the servant entered, promptly sizing up the situation. He waited for instructions.

Emily cried loudly. "You condemn me to a life of torment, Theo. And to think that you once swore your love for me."

"That will be all, Mrs Fliss." The Mayor dismissed Emily with a curt nod and turned to his now overtly curious manservant. "Ensure Mrs Fliss is delivered safely to her husband forthwith, and extend my regret to him for the condition he finds her in."

Bumble bolted from the room and made haste, far away from Emily's screams.

43
A VISITOR

Mayor Bumble had eaten too much cheese and partaken of too much port. The resulting indigestion was the cause of his insomnia, he was certain. He blinked into the darkness. All the excess acid in his system had the effect of making him cranky. He reluctantly rolled over in bed, and sat up, belching loudly.

"Oh. That's better," he lied. He didn't need to worry about disturbing Norah, though. She kept to her own room on the floor above.

Now that he was properly awake he found he needed to piss quite badly, but could barely summon the energy to abandon the warmth of his covers and fish around, under the bed, for the chamber pot.

A window shutter banged in its frame. Bumble groaned. That was all he needed. Outside, the wind had started picking up again and the shutter had obviously not been secured properly. Tutting loudly, Bumble threw back his blankets and swung himself out of bed. The floor was cool beneath his feet. He shuffled across to the window and opened it, intending to catch the shutter and latch it.

The moon shone bright as a candle. Dark clouds skidded quickly across its face, obscuring it from time to time and, although a slight sea mist had crept in—hugging the land, low and flat—visibility remained fair.

Movement on the lawn.

Bumble leaned out of his window to gaze down in surprise at the figure there. Such audacity! He stood with his back to Bumble, staring out to sea. From the reverse he had the appearance of a fit young man, dressed in breeches and a white shirt rolled up above his elbows. Bumble could clearly make out marks, like tattoos, on his lower arms. His dark hair hung lank, damp, from the mist most probably.

A troublemaker, Bumble surmised.

"I say," called Bumble, acutely aware that he was dressed in his nightshirt rather than his official mayoral garb. "You, man! What do you do there?"

No response. The man didn't even turn around.

Bumble considered ringing for one of his servants. Relenting, he gave the interloper one final opportunity to explain himself. "I trust you aren't finding mischief at this hour of the night?" he called.

This time the figure began to turn. Bumble narrowed his eyes, puzzling at the man's odd gait, his stiff, unnatural manner. *Something peculiar ...*

Suddenly Bumble didn't want to see the man's face. A cold sweat broke out across his brow. "Be off with you," he shouted, backing away. He noisily slammed his shutters closed and pushed the window down. He would read the riot act to his servants in the morning. *Who the hell was encouraging riff-raff to come to the manor at this time of night?*

He mopped his brow and slunk towards his bed, muttering all the while, then fumbled for the chamber pot beneath. He moaned with delight as he relieved himself, before gratefully slipping beneath his blankets, still warm, eager for sleep to be the master of him.

He may have dropped off, he couldn't say for certain, but at some stage he became conscious of a sharp crashing noise emanating from somewhere downstairs. He lifted his head, ears straining, pulse racing. Could it have been the front door? When there was no further disturbance, Bumble breathed a little easier. A servant had dropped a vase or some such. It would come out of their wages, make no mistake.

He snuggled down into his pillow.

But wait—

Now more annoyed than alarmed, Bumble lifted his head again. Someone was climbing the main staircase. The stairs were half-carpeted, but the wood was old, and he recognized the creaks and whinges of the timber. Surely this couldn't be a servant? They were obliged to use the back stairs. If it transpired this was one of his idle domestics, he would find out and he would terminate their employment. That would educate them in the ways of better serving his paternal benevolence.

A moment of quiet—presumably the person climbing the stairs had reached the landing—that seemed to stretch out interminably. Bumble, weary to the bone, had decided he'd been imagining things when he recognised the distinct sound of feet slapping wetly against the polished wooden floor in the corridor outside his room. The footsteps were heading in the direction of his bedroom.

Why would one of his servants have wet feet? It *had* to be an intruder.

The man from the garden!

The mayor threw back his covers and leapt out of bed, intending to flee. But where could he go? The only exits to his room were the window he'd so recently secured, and the corridor from which he was being stalked.

Perhaps he could fight. He snatched up a poker from his fire side and crept to the bedroom door. The footsteps ceased. Bumble held his breath, listening for any clue as to his assailant's intention. He listened to the uneven drip of water coming from immediately behind his door; a soft plink plonk, like water dripping from clothing. There were no other sounds.

Eventually, the dripping ceased too, and the house lapsed into silence once more.

Bumble's heart beat hard against the wall of his chest. The person behind the door obviously lay in wait for him. If he abandoned his sleeping chamber, no doubt he would be set upon and robbed of his life and all belongings.

Bumble shifted, painful cramp in his right calf, uncertain how to proceed. The trespasser beyond remained as quiet as the proverbial church mouse.

Bumble's insides twisted into loops. The hand that clasped the poker shook in consternation. Fear made him weak, but he couldn't stay in the same position forever. Adrenaline built up in his blood stream and his head began to hum. When he couldn't take it any longer, Bumble extended his hand, damp with sweat, and gripped the door handle. He gently twisted the knob, and pulled the door open, peering into the dark hall beyond.

There was nothing to hear and nothing to see.

There was nobody in the hall at all.

The only evidence that there ever had been, was the puddle by the Mayor's door.

And a line of damp footprints that led to the threshold of his bedroom ...

... but not away again.

44
PHINEAS RETURNS

Phineas's return to Durscombe was delayed slightly, thanks to the inclement weather. Storms raged across the south of the country and Phineas was forced to sit it out in Bristol for longer than he had anticipated. He arrived back in East Devon as the winds died down, the sea an angry, muddy brown below a pastel turquoise sky.

Phineas jiggled his knee in impatience as the coach left the moor behind and headed directly for town. His travelling companion, the elderly Mrs Kitzkoff-Smyth, a Russian heiress who had married an Englishman—a rather minor member of the Royal family who had promptly died and left all her money to his younger brother—gazed at him in irritation. She lived in gentrified poverty in a large townhouse and had spent the past forty years complaining about her lot in a very thick accent to anyone who would listen. The coach had provided her with a captive audience and Phineas could feel the beating of a tom-tom drum in the front of his head.

He couldn't reach Durscombe quickly enough, but finally they were there, trotting along the promenade, and pulling in at The Blue Bell Inn. Peering through the window of the carriage, Phineas spotted Matthew waiting patiently for him alongside several other coachmen. His heart soared at the prospect of their joyful reunion.

Damp and travel soiled, headachey and feeling distinctly green around the gills, Phineas climbed down from the carriage outside the inn and massaged his temples. He stared in dismay at the broken hulk of the *Mary Pomeroy*. News had reached him in Exeter of the disaster, but here it was in all its gory detail. He shuddered, thinking of the crew.

Matthew joined him as he walked towards the quay. Master and servant exchanged respectful greetings, but Phineas recognised their happy reunion would have to wait. He hobbled a little, his legs stiff with sitting for so long. He couldn't tear his eyes away from the *Mary Pomeroy*'s tangled rigging, her ripped sails. What a glorious vessel she must have been.

"It's a bad business, Sir."

Phineas nodded, increasingly queasy. He nodded at a number of dark shapes bobbing in the water. "Are those corpses, Matthew?"

"I believe so, Sir."

"Why the devil have they not been brought ashore?" Phineas swallowed his nausea. He needed a stiff drink. Glancing around, he noted that the harbour seemed quieter than usual. The flurry of fishing boats and related activity more subdued than he'd expect midweek. Here and there, men and women, their faces devoid of expression, stood alone, staring out to sea, watching the bundles of flesh and clothing that floated among the waves.

Phineas turned about, his back to the sea. What could the people of Durscombe be thinking? What had happened to his community? Durscombe was ideally situated to make the most of the gentle southwest climate. The soil was good and rich, the ground fertile. There was plenty of wood for fuel in the forests nearby. The sea provided more fish than the town could consume. Life, for most, was decent. For sure, there were pockets of poverty here, as there were anywhere, particularly in the shanty town that had grown up along the river, but it wasn't endemic, and philanthropy was an area in which the municipality had tended to excel.

In short, the people of Durscombe were good citizens. Everyone knew everyone else. They worked hard and took care of each other.

So what had happened here?

Why did nobody care about the corpses floating out to sea?

But there was something else. Uneasily, Phineas pivoted to stare at the bodies once more.

It had been three days since the *Mary Pomeroy* had run aground and broken her back on the rocks. Three days since the sailors had abandoned ship. In those three days the south west had been rocked by storms.

But the bodies hadn't moved.

"Did any bodies come ashore, Matthew?" Phineas asked.

"Some, Sir. In the immediate aftermath." Matthew swallowed, wondering whether to tell Phineas about the rumours he'd heard. Of men waiting with weapons. "There appeared to be a delay in moving them to the church."

Phineas could imagine. No doubt Bumble had dragged his heels over the proper disposal of the corpses. Phineas didn't understand Bumble's reasoning. How could the man be so devoid of Christian compassion?

"And the storm was as bad as they say?"

"Yes Sir. For several days. The tides were high. The waves breached the harbour wall at one stage."

"And yet these bodies float here still?"

Matthew followed his gaze and stared thoughtfully out to sea. He finally grasped what Phineas was getting at and narrowed his eyes in confusion. "That is odd, Sir. They haven't moved at all."

The men stood in silence, Phineas's headache beating behind his eyes. Matthew was right, this *was* a bad business. It did not look good for the town. Phineas owed it to Durscombe, and to his role and responsibility as one of its aldermen, to take the matter in hand.

He would need to confront Bumble.

"Matthew, wait for me here. I must see to a few things."

Phineas couldn't find any of the aldermen in their municipal offices, although he did eventually locate a group of them enjoying a late lunch at Jerome's. So engaged in conversation were they, that they barely noticed his entrance.

"Good afternoon, gentlemen," Phineas piped up. Bumble, Pyle, Endicott, Gibbs and Croker looked up at him, their expressions ranging from guilty to cocky.

"Shall I set another place, Sir?" The waiter asked quietly, but Phineas shook his head. The thought of food made him nauseous, but not as much as dining with these men.

"Bring me a brandy, if you please," he requested and settled into a spare chair, locking eyes with Bumble. Bumble shifted uncomfortably in his seat, snorted and averted his eyes.

Phineas studied Bumble, somewhat taken aback by his appearance. Usually immaculately turned out, today his swollen eyes and dishevelled hair highlighted a pale face. Even his dress was slightly unkempt, the lapels of his frockcoat speckled with dandruff. Phineas reconsidered whether he had been doing Bumble a disservice by assuming that the mayor didn't care about the fate of the sailors, and yet here he was, holding court in the club, just before three on a working day with a table full of food in front of him.

Pyle tucked into his lunch with gusto. "Are you sure you won't join us, Phineas? This is very good."

The waiter returned with a large brandy and Phineas tipped it down in one and gestured for another. The waiter brought the decanter and, with a respectful nod, withdrew.

"So what brings you here, Lord Tolleson, if not to dine?" Pyle asked, swiping at his lips with his napkin.

"You are surely well aware what brings me here," Phineas replied, his voice calm. "I do not know the ins and outs of how the ship came to be wrecked, but I am certain I know why. What is most pressing to my mind, is why the crew have not been retrieved."

"Oh, not this again, Phineas," Bumble moaned.

"No-one is asking any of you to do it yourselves, for Heaven's sake!" Phineas poured a generous measure of brandy into his glass. "Bumble? Just send some fishermen out there!"

"We don't want the bodies brought ashore," Pyle said, his mouth full of chicken. He fixed Phineas with a glare and chewed.

Bumble nodded; his weary eyes hooded.

"Why not?" Phineas demanded, his temper rising. "That's a downright preposterous position to take. They should be given a resting place ashore, not left to rot in the sea. They'll wash up soon enough, and it will be all the worse."

Pyle grimaced and dropped his fork onto his plate. "Really Phineas," he said. "I'm eating."

"For God's sake man!" Phineas exploded. A number of other diners glanced their way.

"You're creating a scene, old chap," Pyle wagged his knife at Phineas. Phineas clenched his fists under the table and willed himself to calm down. He had never hit a man in anger. Today might be the first such occasion.

"We can't bring them ashore," Pyle said, and he sounded amused, "because we can't risk people knowing how many of them did not actually drown."

"Pyle!" Bumble shot out. Endicott gasped.

Pyle shrugged and resumed eating.

"Didn't drown?" Phineas repeated and heard the quake in his voice. "If they didn't drown ... then?" He looked at each of the men in turn. Each face remained stony, except for Endicott who had the grace turn away, a faint flush to his cheeks. Bumble's eyes were hollow and, if Phineas was not much mistaken, fearful.

Phineas frantically turned over the facts in his mind as he knew them, piecing together what Emily had overheard and combined with Agatha's fears. He remembered the stories he'd heard of false lights being used to lure ships onto the rocks in Cornwall. The tales of sailors being bludgeoned to death, because, if there were no survivors of a shipwreck, all property belonged to the landowner where the goods washed up.

"No survivors?" he asked.

"Not a single one," Pyle responded.

All the strength left Phineas's legs. "What have you done?" he whispered.

Endicott studied his plate. Bumble stared at Phineas coldly. Pyle lifted his glass and saluted him.

"You are ... fools," Phineas hissed, his voice cracking with emotion. "No. You're worse than that. You're... *murderers*." He pushed himself to his feet, scraping his chair back, and stumbling away from the table. Pyle grimaced at the sound. The waiter dashed forward to assist Phineas, but he waved him back.

"For your information, Mayor," Phineas waved a finger at Bumble, "I have spent the past few days in London. I spoke to my contacts in government and I shared a number of concerns I already had. I believe they are planning a trip to the Devon coast, forthwith."

A stunned silence followed his words. Even Pyle appeared to have had the wind knocked out of his sails.

"You did what?" Bumble asked. "Are you insane, man?"

Phineas drew himself up to his full height. "Quite the reverse, I would most humbly suggest."

"You would discredit us, by spreading nonsensical rumours in the City?" Pyle looked around at Endicott for assistance.

"Your actions discredit you, Lord Tolleson!" Gibbs nodded.

"Are we not brothers-in-arms, Phineas?" Endicott asked. "Working only for the good of the municipality?"

"You should resign," Bumble jabbed a finger at Phineas. "It is clear you do not stand with us."

Phineas glared at the men in front of him. "I cannot stand with you in this, that much is clear."

"You will resign then, Sir?" Bumble demanded.

"I will," Phineas responded. "I do."

He turned on his heel and, holding his head high, marched out of Jerome's leaving the rest of the aldermen to their lunch.

Matthew, on Phineas's instructions, had waited for Phineas inside the Blue Bell, nursing a single draught of ale. As soon as he observed his master heading towards him, he knew that something terrible had occurred. Phineas appeared grey and drawn.

"Sir?" he asked, jumping to his feet, his face etched with concern. Phineas seemed about ready to collapse.

Phineas placed a trembling hand on Matthew to steady himself, soothed by his man's strength, then darted a glance back the way he had come.

"May God have mercy on their souls, Matthew," he said, so quietly Matthew could barely make out the words. He supported Phineas as he struggled to climb into the carriage.

Matthew glanced down Curzon Street in confusion, and then back out to sea, at the dark shapes floating there. He couldn't be entirely certain Phineas was alluding to the lost sailors.

45
STALEMATE

Agatha, wrapped in a shawl, hand fed a small bonfire in the garden. As the carriage clattered into the drive, she straightened up and smoothed down her grubby outdoor apron. She hadn't been expecting visitors and had not dressed for the occasion. She relaxed when she recognised the driver as Matthew Salter. Good news! Phineas had arrived back from London.

She stuck her head inside the back door of Myrtle Lodge and called up the passage, "Hannah?" before rushing to greet the carriage.

"Phineas," she exclaimed in pleasure, standing alongside Matthew as he opened the carriage door, but her relief quickly morphed into concern. "Oh Phineas! You do not look well. Matthew help him into the kitchen."

Matthew reached out to take his master's arm, and Phineas gladly allowed him to do so, relieved to have friends around him as they supported him into the warmth.

Hannah bustled around preparing tea as Agatha helped Matthew settle Phineas into her rocking chair. Phineas shivered and held his hands towards the fire. Agatha clasped them in her own rough ones instead, her nails still filthy from the garden work she'd been doing, and briskly rubbed them together to bring life to his extremities.

"You're so cold, Phineas," she said. "What on earth has happened?"

"That wreck, Agatha."

"Yes?"

"We were too late to stop them."

Agatha nodded in mute sympathy. "We were."

"But it is worse than that. Do you know what they did?" Phineas's eyes were alight with pain. He squeezed Agatha's hands tightly.

Agatha didn't want to hear what he seemed determined to tell her, but she knew she must. She cast an eye around the room, checking that Flora was not lurking in the shadows.

"The mayor, Bumble, and the aldermen. Pyle. Gibbs. Endicott. Perhaps all of them. They didn't simply *arrange* for the wrecking. They gave the order to *kill* the survivors." Phineas's chest heaved. "The sailors didn't drown, not all of them. They were murdered, in cold blood. Bumble must have hired henchmen to do his dirty work."

Agatha stared at Phineas; her mouth open, shocked by his words. She had suspected the truth, but it was hard to hear the words spoken out loud.

Emily had been right all along.

Agatha sent Phineas home with Matthew. Hannah packed them a basket containing soup and a cordial to help Phineas sleep. It wasn't that she didn't trust the cook at Hawkerne Hall to provide sustenance to Phineas, not at all, but she wanted to ensure he was well looked after.

After joining Hannah and Flora for their evening meal, but unable to eat, Agatha took down her pestle and mortar and began to crush a handful of small seashells together with some seaweed she'd dried out in front of her bonfire earlier in the day. Keener than usual to be alone, she'd sent Hannah off to bed early. Now that the kitchen was empty, and the creaking of floorboards above her head had settled, Agatha banked the fire. She pulled up Tansy's stool and squatted in front of the flames before throwing the contents of her bowl deep into their heart.

Agatha chose not to ask a direct question, instead she let her thoughts wonder. Phineas was worried about the town, and the effect that the wreckings would have on the inhabitants. What would become of Durscombe?

The fire burned fiercely, spitting and hissing, and Agatha shrank back from the anger she could see within the flames. She jerked her head away as a puff of black smoke coughed out at her, drawn into the centre of the kitchen where it settled in a haze. It made Agatha's eyes smart and she attempted to waft it away, one eye on the fire in the grate.

She watched the flames die back until the embers prickled and glowed. Usually she would have to spend an hour or more watching the fire shrink, until she could read the symbols and meanings left behind, but tonight the fire caved in on itself and within minutes it had gone out completely. Only ash and charred wood remained.

Impossible.

The fire had been burning all day and been well banked. It should have burned by itself for another few hours at least. How had it gone out? It was a bad sign.

Agatha shivered as a chill permeated the room. The cold crept in from outside, finding its way beneath the doors, and between floorboards. It seeped into her bones. The black haze hanging in the air behind her, shifted, swirling slowly. Agatha stood, followed it around, reaching a hand to it. It had no form. Her fingers touched nothing of substance.

From the corner of her eye, Agatha spotted a flare of bright light. Startled, she spun about. One single part of the fire had erupted into life. A single orange flame burned high in the corner, leaping and dancing by itself. Agatha drifted towards it, watching in wonder.

Tansy's chair began to rock.

46

HAUNTED

Bumble lay in his bed, his limbs rigid. He'd sunk a decanter's worth of whisky this evening, much to Norah's profound disgust, but he still couldn't relax. Instead his throat was parched and his belly queasy. He'd tossed and turned for the first ninety minutes or so, but couldn't find a comfortable position. Now he sighed and lay stretched out on his back, his eyes staring at the ceiling.

He started at every noise in the house, no matter how quiet or familiar. Apart from the year of his Grand Tour, and the years he went up to Oxford, he had lived at Applecombe his entire life. He knew every noise the house made. Every creak of every door, every whinge in every floorboard. Every scrape of every shutter. Every dog's bark. He knew the sounds of the pans in the kitchen and even the click of the fireside companion sets in every room. The house breathed and sighed, and he had always felt like the largest constituent part of it.

But that was no longer the case.

Something alien had breached the sanctity of his home. It visited him in the darkness, and he shrank from it, unwilling to confront the unknown. It had visited him a few nights ago, and every night since. It remained unchallenged, because so far nobody else had seen it.

He had quizzed the servants. He had interrogated Norah. They denied the possibility that a stranger could have entered the house and remained hidden. The only person who had any knowledge of the strange presence, was he himself. He'd begun to consider the possibility that Applecombe was haunted.

Should he summon Reverend Tidwell to rid him of unhappy spirits? Did he need more evidence?

Uncertain how to proceed, he gritted his teeth and girded his loins and waited for the apparition to show itself, all the time wondering how best to deal with it when it did. He was a rational man, cool-headed under most circumstances, but the thought of a spirit slipping through his bedroom door scared him senseless.

To add to his increasing anxiety, the confrontation with Phineas had struck a chord. Bumble had no desire to be found on the wrong side of the law. If it was true that the government was sending representatives to make enquiries into the wreckings at Durscombe, the aldermen would need to take action forthwith. Pyle had over-stretched himself, and while he might be furious with Phineas, his anger was all for naught. Bumble could see clearly that they would need to take action immediately to conceal what had gone on.

A boom reverberated through the house. One of the grand front doors had slammed. Bumble stifled a shriek and sat up. How was it that none of the servants could hear this? The vibration still rumbled down the empty corridors.

With trembling knees and elbows, Bumble hauled himself out of bed and crept towards the door, needing to ensure it remained securely locked. He huddled against it, his ear pressed to the wood.

Footsteps climbed the stairs, just as they had the previous few nights. He listened to the slap, slap sound of wet feet as they strolled slowly along the corridor, heading straight for him. They stopped—as they always did—directly outside his door. He held his breath, imagining a face, glistening with saltwater, pressed against the other side of the wood.

He shuddered.

"Go away," he whispered. "If thou art a spirit, rest in peace. There is nothing for you here."

Water dripped, inches away.

Bumble wept.

47

DEATH AND TAXES

The next evening found Bumble in The Crown and Anchor awaiting Greeb. The pub buzzed with life, although Bumble felt like death warmed up, his pallor ghostly. He stifled a yawn and glanced warily around at his fellow patrons. A motley crew of ne'er do-wells and ex-convicts you were never more likely to meet. Bumble couldn't understand why Greeb favoured this particular hostelry, but given the fact that many of these men would probably have been Greeb's associates at one time or another, he supposed between them they offered strength in numbers for his nefarious friend.

Greeb had yet to make an appearance. A busy man, he evidently had fingers in many pies. Bumble tapped his empty whisky glass anxiously on the top of the barrel in front of him, then unable to bear it for another second, gestured at the barman to set him up with another.

Greeb appeared at the same time as his fresh drink. He stood back and regarded Bumble from a distance, narrowing his eyes. "You do not look like a well man, my friend."

Bumble shrugged off Greeb's opinion. "A good night's sleep will see me right."

"What is it that keeps you awake at night?" Greeb leered. "Mayhap you could introduce *her* to me."

"If only." Bumble glowered into his glass, then snapped his head back and drained the lot. Greeb raised his eyebrows. "Tell me, *friend*," Bumble slumped toward his companion, "how is it that with all that you've done in your life, *you* sleep at night?"

Greeb grimaced at the stink of Bumble's breath. He cocked his head to one side, his good eye glittered, his scar furrowed. "What makes you think I do?"

Bumble sagged; a man lost.

Greeb leaned closer, his voice so quiet that Bumble had to strain to hear. "I don't know what your problem is, Mayor, but you asked to see me, so spit it out. I've matters to attend to."

"What?" Bumble asked, his voice too loud. "What other *matters* do you have to attend to?" He swayed slightly, his eyes glassy. "What do you have to do? Who else has need of you the way I do? I reward you handsomely, don't I?"

Greeb took a breath. A slow smile of genuine amusement spread across his face. Bumble was caught off guard. He smiled back, a little uncertainly. Greeb's fist lashed out, his stubby fingers catching hold of the swaggering Bumble by his cravat, hauling him across the barrel, glasses tumbling to the floor.

Greeb aligned his mouth close to Bumble's ear. "Shut it, or I'll slice your fucking tongue out of your mouth, right here where you're standing."

Bumble whimpered and Greeb released him, steadying him when it seemed the mayor would collapse. "Now tell me what it is you want, or I'll walk out of here and you and I will never speak again."

Bumble adjusted his clothing and nodded meekly. "I have one more job for you, Greeb." Greeb rolled his eyes and laughed, shaking his head in disbelief. "Just one more," Bumble pleaded. "Please."

"I think we've concluded all of our business." Greeb stepped away.

Bumble reached out and clasped the crook's arm in desperation.

"You have to be brave or insanely stupid to manhandle me, Mayor," Greeb rasped. His black gaze settled on Bumble's face, his patience running thin. "Unhand me."

"Please," Bumble begged. "I'm in big trouble. Chances are if I don't sort this particular problem, I'll hang."

Greeb shrugged. What was it to him, after all?

Bumble maintained his grip on Greeb's arm, desperate to make him understand. "If I go to the gallows, I'll make damn sure you come too. You *have* to help me."

Greeb shook Bumble's hand away, inhaling noisily, his lips pressed together in fury. Bumble backed off, his hands palm up, then smoothed down his own frockcoat and straightened his cravat. He waved at the barman, seeking a fresh drink.

Greeb sucked his teeth. A phrase he'd often heard repeated came to mind: *Tis impossible to be sure of any thing but death and taxes*. Greeb avoided paying tax where he could, but he fully expected death to seek him out prematurely, and probably less than pleasantly. All he could hope for was a quick end. He'd had a tough existence, populated by an interesting array of dishonourable companions, whores and associates. He had never knowingly earned an honest shilling in his entire life. He had no friends he could rely on, no family that he knew of ... but plenty of enemies.

He wasn't remotely surprised that Bumble had dared to threaten him with the law. He had never trusted the man and expected nothing of him.

Greeb studied his companion, his eyes shrewd, and traced the scar on his face with a calloused finger. A desperate man is a dangerous man. What game was Bumble playing now?

"You don't scare me, Mayor," Greeb drawled. That much was true. Greeb had nothing to fear except perhaps death itself. "I have connections the length and breadth of this country and beyond. I can travel a long, long way from Durscombe. I guarantee I'll survive far longer than you."

"I don't doubt it, but you stand a much better chance of living to a ripe old age, if you help me now."

Greeb pursed his lips.

"I'll pay you," Bumble added.

Greeb pondered on Bumble's worth. He came from a wealthy family, owned a big house, but even so there were rumours he'd overstretched himself. Given that the spoils from the *Mary Pomeroy* had yet to be sold on, and Bumble had probably not received his share, his funds might be limited. This might well be make or break time for the mayor and the Bumble dynasty, such as it was.

Greeb could make this an expensive lesson. "What exactly is it you want me to do?" he asked, and clenched his fists as Bumble smiled, scenting victory.

"There's two parts to this," Bumble began, leaning forwards, eager to explain. "I'm expecting some visitors from London. They'll probably travel via Bristol and stop at Exeter and then continue over the moor. It's imperative they never get here."

"How many visitors?"

"Hmm. Difficult to say. Let's imagine three or four."

Greeb nodded. "And the second part?"

"Well, this is a slightly more delicate matter." Bumble lowered his voice. "Lord Tolleson of Hawkerne Hall. I'd like him to meet with a ... tragic accident."

The men locked eyes: Bumble's smug but full of fear, Greeb's a cold, black, bottomless void. Bumble hardly dared to breathe, waiting for Greeb's response.

"It will cost you," Greeb finally broke the silence.

"Of course—"

"It will cost you a great deal. And I'll want all of it up front."

"I can't—"

"Up front or there's no agreement." Greeb picked up Bumble's glass and drained it.

Bumble pulled his lips into a nervous smile, a rictus grin of panic. "You don't understand—"

"I understand that I'm your *only* hope for avoiding the gallows, Mayor." And while he didn't much care whether Bumble lived or died, he knew he could fleece the man for a grotesque amount of money. The kind of money that meant Greeb could disappear on a ship out of Bristol and never set foot in the British Isles again. He'd heard stories of places where maidens had dusky skins, and wore few if any clothes. A guinea would go a long way in a place like that.

Bumble swallowed. What choice did he have? "Very well."

Greeb spat into his palm and held it out for the mayor to shake. "Leave it to me," he said.

48

A TOWN BECALMED

The residents of Durscombe awoke to a strange sight the following morning. A low mist had settled in the valley beneath a sky the colour of spoiling milk. It enshrouded the town in a hazy smog and limited visibility to twenty yards or so.

Even more peculiar, the sea—a magnificent slate grey—was as still as a pond. Here and there the mist parted, and the rocks suddenly appeared, black and sinister, only to be lost again as the slight window closed.

Phineas, standing on the quay, had never known a phenomenon like it, the absence of waves lapping at the shingle on the shoreline struck him as peculiar. A line of dry seaweed at the edge of the water indicated that the tide was neither coming in nor going out. It was simply unheard of.

Over the past few days, Agatha's cordial had done him the world of good. He had slumbered particularly soundly the previous night, until Mrs Gwynne had awoken him with a breakfast tray, fearful that something untoward had happened to him when he overslept.

He had been busily asking around, trying to find fishermen who would venture out towards the vicinity of the *Mary Pomeroy* and rescue the corpses of the sailors, still bobbing in place as they had done for four or five days now. The situation was becoming desperate.

But none of the fishermen were keen to help Phineas out, and Phineas had the distinct impression that even without the unusual weather conditions, and the all-pervasive mist, he would have received the same short shrift from any man he approached.

A flat no.

Part of it was superstition. Phineas understood this, but equally he fancied that someone, on behalf of the municipality, had managed to get to the fishermen before him.

Phineas had started to wonder whether the answer lay within his own household. Of all the servants he employed at Hawkerne Hall, surely some of them could row a boat. If it came down to it perhaps he would go out himself with Matthew. But now, as he headed down to the beach, the shingle crunching underfoot, he watched the mist ebb and flow around him, and understood that realistically, setting out around the rocks in a rowing boat would be a perilous undertaking.

He arrived back at The Blue Bell Inn just as the first coach of the day arrived from Exeter. The driver, stepped down from his seat at the front to help the inn's grooms unhitch his horses. He growled in exasperation. "This damnable mist!" He'd lost the track a few times, he explained, and had been lucky to make it over the moor. "It just comes upon you. Out of Exeter the sky was blue, and the air clean. Then I was coming over Mother's Moor and the mist closed in, about three miles yonder," he gestured back the way he had come, along the promenade and up behind Nabb's Hill.

Phineas, standing among several other onlookers, nodded in sympathy, and the driver addressed him in his broad Devonshire brogue. "'Tis alright for me, see? I only do this route and the Exeter to Plymouth route. I'm used to these mists on the moors. It be the London drivers I feel sorry for. They'll stop and change horses in Exeter but they can't know what they're in for."

Giles, The Blue Bell Inn's landlord, roared with laughter. "Well, they'll soon find out, Ned."

Ned snickered in agreement. "That they will. Let's hope they don't run off into a ditch."

"What time is the Bristol coach due in today?" Phineas asked as Ned moved towards the inn, his thoughts turning to the officials who would be following him down from London.

"I'd expect it within an hour or so, Lord Tolleson," Giles replied. "Though there's no accounting for delays when the weather has taken a turn for the worse."

Phineas nodded, but he wasn't sure the weather *had* taken a turn for the worse. Ned had said that the mist was localised.

It appeared that Durscombe was a town becalmed.

Phineas took shelter inside The Blue Bell Inn to await the coach from Bristol. He remained on tenterhooks for nearly two hours, but there was a limit to the number of brandies he could nurse, and still remain sensible as time drifted slowly by.

After checking his pocket watch for the umpteenth time, and petting Barnacle Betsy, he left the hospitality of the pub and ventured outside. The mist had not yet cleared and without a breath of wind there seemed little chance it would do so. Somewhere up above his head, the sun was shining, but at this time of year, the rays would not be warm enough to burn the mist away either.

Phineas wandered down to the harbour wall. It had been well over two hours since the last carriage had arrived into Durscombe and the sea had neither receded nor advanced any further. Phineas shook his head, bemused by the peculiar phenomenon.

Unable to remain inactive any longer, he decided to head back to Hawkerne Hall. He would collect Matthew and venture up to the moor to see if what Ned had claimed was true. Phineas was curious. Did the mist only hang over the town? How far would he have to ride towards Exeter before the mist lifted?

He reclaimed Jolie from The Blue Bell Inn's stable, and headed home. He found Matthew in the yard, when he arrived, sharpening a knife for the cook. Glad of the offer of a ride out, he saddled Crab while Phineas, after checking for messages, continued on Jolie.

They climbed up Nabb's Hill at a slow pace. Tendrils of mist drifted through the trees and blocked their view of the sea to their left. Durscombe was invisible below a thick soft blanket of dirty cloud. They stuck closely to the road, taking it slowly, all the way up to Mother's Moor. Under normal circumstances they might have let the horses have their heads, but that would be foolhardy today, given that they often couldn't see any further than their horses' ears.

Phineas found the silence eerie. They encountered no other travellers as they ventured along the road, and besides the clip clop of the horse's feet and Crab's occasional uneasy whinny, there were no other sounds. No sheep, no gulls, no birds of any description.

And nothing at all to see. Until—

"Wait!" Matthew's sharp voice; alarmed.

Phineas pulled Jolie to a halt. A large dark shadow had loomed out of the mist in front of them. Cautiously they walked the horses forwards. A carriage. It had been pulled to the side of the road, as though to let someone else go past. Four horses were still attached to it, nibbling at the grass on the verge without undue concern.

Phineas dismounted and handed his reins to Matthew.

One of the carriage horses lifted its head as he approached and gently whinnied. Phineas stroked its nose, then lifted his eyeline.

"Oh," he exclaimed softly, catching sight of the liveried driver who lay sprawled across the front bench seat. Phineas edged closer. The man had been shot between the eyes. Phineas dashed a gloved hand at his own brow and sidestepped the scene, fighting a wave of nausea, then curled his upper body around to peek inside the carriage window.

"It is the London carriage, Sir," Matthew's voice behind him startled Phineas. Matthew pointed at the shield on the carriage door. Phineas swallowed and crept forwards, peering warily inside.

Empty?

"Where are the travellers?" Phineas asked. Certainly there had been some. Trunks were piled on top of the roof and belongings scattered inside the carriage itself; a cane, a hat, a shawl, several carpet bags. Phineas pulled the door open and scanned the abandoned contents searching for a further clue as to who the occupants might have been. He spotted a battered leather satchel and drew it out, his hands suddenly clumsy as he fumbled to open it. He riffled through the contents. Official government papers; stamped and dated. These belonged to the men he had been expecting. The ones he'd invited to investigate the wreckings of the *Eliza May* and the *Mary Pomeroy*.

The occupants of this carriage had been travelling with at least one woman, if the shawl was anything to go by. So where were they all now?

Phineas swivelled, staring into the thick mist, surveying what little he could see. "Ahoy! Ahoy there!" he shouted, and waited for a response. None came.

With a deepening sense of disquiet, Matthew, too, twisted about. "I think we should head back into Durscombe, Sir, and report what we've seen. Anybody could be out here."

"But what if they've simply wandered off?" Phineas asked, voice full of doubt as if inclined to agree with Matthew. "They might be lost in this mist."

"We can gather a search party, Sir," Matthew replied. "An *armed* search party."

Phineas nodded. It made sense. He reached to take Jolie's reins from Matthew when a sudden movement in the trees to the left, approximately thirty feet away, caught his eye. The mist had shifted slightly. Something wavered just above eye level. The mist closed and whatever it had been disappeared from view. Phineas stepped forward, squinting into the near distance, following the swinging movement. The mist thinned again, unveiling a foot.

Feet.

Several pairs of feet.

Legs.

Three men hung from the trees. Phineas jolted backwards in alarm, and stumbled into Crab, who reared in surprise, spilling Matthew to the earth. He lay there for a moment, winded, eyes wide as he followed his master's gaze. Phineas reached for him, to pull him to his feet, and they remained hand in hand, staring in horror as the bodies twisted this way and that, the faces mercifully hidden by the mist.

Phineas calmed his breathing. "We should check they're dead, Matthew," he said, reluctant to get any closer. Matthew nodded. They started forwards, Matthew taking the lead, moving single file through the gorse, trampled in places by those who had come before, until they were standing directly beneath the trees. The bodies twirled above them, the faces contorted and purple, arms tied behind their backs. They would find no signs of life here.

"A lynch mob," Phineas said. "And what of the woman?" He shivered, his eyes flicking around their surroundings. "Damn this mist."

One of the horses neighed softly again. Matthew pricked his ears, his heart thumping in fear. Nothing to hear, only the horses, but a sixth sense told him it was time to leave. "We need to get out of here now, Sir," he said, his voice so low it was barely audible.

Phineas didn't need telling twice.

49
FLOATING

The Crokers only used the best silver and the rarest crystal glasses—or so Mrs Croker kept telling Emily—but the constant clinking of cutlery and crockery had started to make Emily's head ache. Mr and Mrs Fliss had long ago accepted the invitation to dine with the Crokers, along with several other aldermen and their wives. The dinner marked the occasion of the Crokers' thirtieth wedding anniversary, but if Emily had been able to excuse herself, she surely would have. The Crokers had a magnificent house and had gone to extreme lengths to decorate the dining room. Candles sparkled on every available surface and a huge fire burned in the grate.

Emily shot it a doleful glance. It hissed and crackled in response.

Bumble was conspicuous by his absence, having cancelled at the last minute. While that may have been some consolation to Emily, she'd been horrified to discover that Pyle and his simpering wife Jane were in attendance. Emily sensed the loathsome Pyle's eyes on her every time she moved or spoke to her neighbours. She averted her gaze, scratching her nails on the inside of her wrist beneath her glove every time her anxiety became too much to bear.

The talk all evening had been of the murders on the moor.

Lord Tolleson and his manservant had raised the alarm in town, and the police and a few carpenters had been sent up to the moor to retrieve the bodies. A hue and cry had been set up all over town, but the perpetrators were in the wind—probably in Exeter and beyond by now—and nobody had any idea who they were in any case.

"It's a sign of the times," Mrs Croker wailed. "This would never have happened in Durscombe even a few years ago."

"The town is growing too quickly," her husband said, and his neighbours nodded vigorously. It would be bad form to disagree at his dinner table, after all.

"I remember when the town consisted of the fishermen's cottages and Curzon Street and very little else!" exclaimed Mr Croker's dowager mother, Anne. "Now I don't know half the people who live here. Really Alderman Pyle, you should restrict numbers."

Pyle smiled his charming smile. "I can assure you we do, my dear Mrs Croker. We have the poor law in place to keep a check on things after all. I fear Durscombe has suffered a population boom of its own making," and he winked.

A few of the ladies tittered, others blushed and turned away. Mrs Croker fanned herself. Emily fixed her eyes on her plate, refusing to engage with Pyle in any way.

"Alderman Pyle. Does anyone have any idea who the victims were?" asked Mrs Croker and he shrugged.

"Not at this time," he answered, deliberately vague. "I believe that enquiries are ongoing."

"But they weren't local to Durscombe, were they?"

"No," Pyle said. "They weren't known to anyone in town as far as we are aware."

He was lying.

"Perhaps they were coming on business?"

"They were on the London coach, so I'll assume this is feasible, Mrs Croker."

Beside him, Jane raised a finger. "Perhaps they travelled here to take a look at the wreck." Pyle shot her a sharp look.

"I only mean that it is quite the spectacle," Jane frowned.

Emily watched the exchange with interest from beneath her eyelashes.

"Mrs Pyle has a point, Alderman Pyle," the dowager Mrs Croker chipped in.

"How is that, Mrs Croker?" asked Pyle, his voice hard, his smile lapsed.

"Don't they have people in the capital who investigate these things? I'm sure I read that in *The Times* somewhere. Why, I remember a case in Cornwall, oh it was many years ago now—"

Emily observed Pyle's shoulders drop as he listened to the old woman prattle on. He'd thought she was on to something—something that might have incriminated him, perhaps—and then realised she didn't actually know anything.

Emily glanced around the table, nobody else appeared to be taking the elderly dowager seriously.

When Mrs Croker had finished her story and everyone had exclaimed politely and smiled, Mr Fliss spoke up. "I suppose if they were on official business from London, someone will come looking for them sooner or later."

Pyle stared at Marmaduke with such animosity that he flushed. Emily felt almost sorry for her husband. He was correct though. Three suspicious deaths in a coastal town that had suffered a number of wreckings of late, would not go unnoticed. Were these the men Phineas had travelled to London to confer with? Had he succeeded in bringing attention to the town's plight after all? The thought cheered her immensely.

She giggled. Softly, but enough to catch Pyle's attention.

This time she met his gaze and stared him down, her dark eyes black with loathing. The look he directed at her in return was thunderous.

It was a tiny victory, but Emily cherished it.

Once home, under Marmaduke's watchful eye, Emily sank the sleeping draught her doctor had prescribed for her and retired to bed. Marmaduke kissed her forehead and bade Mary tuck her in before leaving her room.

She lay still, her eyes closed, waiting for sleep to claim her. Without the distractions of the dinner party, or her husband or servants around her, the voices were more intrusive than ever tonight. The laudanum draughts the doctor mixed had become increasingly strong to counteract her night terrors and the dreams that plagued her. The household had been disturbed night after night thanks to Emily's hysterical screaming, and Marmaduke had decided enough was enough.

She welcomed the darkness when it came, snuggling deeper into her bed, drifting away on a cloud of oblivion.

A light found her ...

She floated on her back, turning closed eyes towards its warmth, the underside of her eyelids red, flashing orange. She wiggled her fingers, felt the warm sea eddy around her body, cocooned and secure, until she felt strong enough to face the world once more. The mist had lifted, and the sun burned bright above her, the sky a dazzling blue, not a cloud in sight. She curled her knees towards her chest, twisted and dropped her feet so that she could stand upright in the clear water.

Breathless with anticipation, she gazed around her. He would come.

He didn't disappoint.

A gentle splash, sparkles catching the sun, the flash as he darted by, like a long fish ... and there he was. Her sailor. His long dark hair pushed away from his face, his eyes dark, his skin brown. He reached for her and she swam to him.

"I'm sorry," she told him. "I saw you in the water again. I wanted to save you, but I couldn't."

He didn't reply, merely smiled at her. His hand reached for

hers and grasped it. They tangled their fingers together and he held her at arm's length.

"If I could have warned you, if I could have stopped it happening, I would have. You must believe me."

He pulled her to him and wrapped his muscular arms around her slight frame. She moaned, secure in his grasp, flushing hot with desire. He squeezed her gently and her head rested under his chin. The waves lapped gently against them, and they swayed together in the water. She lifted her head, met his gaze ...

I could drown in those eyes.

Something shifted beneath their feet, and the water sucked them down.

And down ... and down ...

A riptide?

Emily held her breath as her head was dragged underwater. She wouldn't panic. Her sailor didn't release his hold. *Take us up,* she thought, but he only held her gaze and secured his hold on her.

He's strong. He can propel us upwards, she thought, but the current had them tightly in its grip. It continued to drag them down. When she could bear it no longer, when she knew she must breathe or suffocate, she tried to push the sailor away. He refused to yield. She couldn't break free. She kicked. She thrashed. He tightened his hold, crushing her against his chest.

The darkness was coming for Emily. A darkness that was thicker than any she had previously encountered. With one final superhuman effort she kicked out against him ... and screamed in anger and frustration.

I summoned you. I can banish you.

She breathed in.

Salt water filled her lungs. Her vision greyed, popped ... and a welcome blackness settled over her.

She came to her senses on the shore. The sea lapped against her legs. Coughing and retching, she pushed herself to her knees, tangled in her long white nightshirt, her hair loose, clumps of seaweed hanging from her like ropes.

The sailor stood on the beach, twelve feet or so in front of her, gazing in the direction of the town.

"Why would you try to kill me?" she asked him, her voice quivering with outrage. "Why would you do that?"

He turned to regard her. His movements out of the water were oddly laboured, his forehead wrinkled with pain, his eyes bleak. They spoke of desolation.

Paler by the second, his beauty moved her. A man so handsome, he had been cruelly cut down in his prime by those who considered some human lives to be surplus to their needs.

"It's alright," she told him. "I understand. You matter to me."

A single tear tolled down his cheek. His eyes rested briefly on her face before turning away again. He faced Durscombe, transfixed by the sleepy town.

"Don't," she said.

He ignored her and with a supreme effort began to lurch up the beach.

"No. No! Don't leave me here." Emily tried to rise but slipped in the sand, her limbs tangled in her sopping nightgown. "Wait for me!" she called after him, pushing herself upright. She managed a few steps before tumbling onto her knees once more. She pressed her hands into the sand to give herself leverage but, all around, the seaweed shifted and slithered and rushed to cover her calves. She screamed and beat her hands, ripping at the gelatinous, stringy matter, pulling it off in clumps and flinging it aside. It made little difference. She was covered in an impossible amount of stinking, writhing algae.

She staggered upright, wrenching herself free and lumbered blindly forward, straight into the path of a woman. Or what remained of her. Emily stared into pale eyes covered in a grey lustre, set in a ruined face. The skin, which hadn't been eaten away, was mottled and blue. Her matted blonde hair had taken on a green sheen. The woman had evidently been in the water for some time; barnacles were embedded in her skin.

She reached for Emily who shrieked, flinging herself back,

scrambling through the sand, intent on reaching the water, intent on getting away, intent on waking up.

Wake up!

Emily threw herself forward in her bed, her heart thumping painfully, panic smudging the edges of her existence.

"Sally," she murmured, "Sally."

50

THE BUMP IN THE NIGHT

Norah Bumble was not known for slamming doors, but the exasperation she felt at her husband this evening seemed to warrant an outpouring of vitriol. Not only had he cancelled their dinner party plans with the Crokers, something Norah was definitely going to have trouble smoothing away with Mrs Croker, he had upset their own cook by demanding she produce supper having already been granted the afternoon off.

He'd then caused a scene in front of the servants when he'd called her to task for her latest spending spree. She couldn't understand his anger. As far as she could see, she had done nothing out of the ordinary. Since when did a woman of her station ever check the price of anything she bought? It simply wasn't done. Instead, as was expected, she instructed her dressmakers and milliners to charge her husband.

But at the dinner table he'd exploded. Norah had simmered quietly while he ranted, unwilling to stoop to his level when they could so obviously be overheard by all and sundry.

How was Norah supposed to feel? What would the servants think? Would word get around? Could her husband be so short of money that he begrudged her a couple of new hats? The idea that he was considering limiting what she purchased, and from where, was vulgar in the extreme.

She'd never hear the end of it.

The whole point of marrying the wretched man in the first place had been so that he could keep her in the style to which she'd grown accustomed. Norah enjoyed their extravagant lifestyle, and she had no wish to rein in her frivolous spending at this stage of her life. She had a social standing to uphold, and she fully intended to do so.

Enraged by Bumble's bad mood and lack of manners, she had taken her leave from the dinner table earlier than normal and retreated in quiet dignity. She wasn't a newly married maid of twenty after all, to be bullied by an inexperienced spouse. But by the time she had climbed to her suite on the second floor of Applecombe House, she had reflected on Bumble's behaviour and had turned coldly furious.

What could be the matter? His recent conduct had been completely out of character.

Norah stared in the mirror while her maid brushed her hair out. She lifted her fingers to her eyes as if to smooth out the wrinkles that were starting there. A small reminder of her own mortality, and her fading looks. She had never been a great beauty. Not in the way that someone like Emily Fliss was, but she had held her own. She could never understand why Theo had chosen her over Emily. He and Mrs Fliss were well matched in so many ways.

Ambitious. Unforgiving.

Norah dismissed her maid and extinguished the light. She hoped she would sleep through the night, and prayed that her ridiculous husband wouldn't wake the house with his shrieking again.

As Norah snuggled down into her bed, Fitzroy stumbled out of The Blue Bell Inn. Greeb had seen him right and now he had a pocket full of money, and a belly full of beef and ale. Home for Fitzroy was little more than a wooden shack built on poles to the side of the estuary. At low tide, the drying seaweed made the whole place reek, but as a non-skilled, non-fisherman in a fishing town, his chances of finding work were generally patchy. He tended to find seasonal employment, as and when he could pick something up.

Working with Greeb over the past few months had paid dividends. It wasn't wholesome work, to say the least, but it kept the wolf from the door, and tonight he felt rather pleased with himself. He whistled as he swaggered down Thimble Lane, bumping from wall to wall as he manoeuvred along the narrow alley, scraping his knuckles but never missing a note.

The mist had closed right in. Thick and heavy, it blurred the edges of the buildings and dulled sound. The Lanes had lapsed into dreary misery with none of the usual cacophony that accompanied human existence. Despite the relatively early hour, many people must have already taken to their beds. The stillness unnerved him.

At the end of Thimble Lane he stepped onto the wooden walkway that would take him to the shanty town. The boards buckled and jolted as he hopped over them. The resulting clanking noise seemed absurdly loud in the otherwise still night.

He paused to pat his pockets, digging around in search of his pipe.

A muffled rasp drifted his way.

"Hello?" he asked. He was not afraid; he could only imagine it would be an acquaintance. Nobody ventured this far into The Lanes unless they had something to hide. The place was a warren of undesirables.

But there was another noise. A repeated squelch.

Fitzroy cocked his head. The squelching stopped. He sniffed and moved off once more, the planks bouncing underneath him.

The squelching began again. Closer this time.

Feeling uneasy, Fitzroy halted. This time he turned around, squinting into the mist, seeking shapes. "Hello?" he asked, the tiniest tremor apparent in his voice. He cleared his throat. Nothing to see and nothing to hear. He pulled his pipe out of his pocket with shaking hands and popped it into his mouth.

A splash and the walkway bowed behind him. Half-turning, Fitzroy spotted something slithering onto it. Without hanging around, Fitzroy shrieked, his pipe tumbling from his mouth, bouncing on the wood and dropping into the water with a dull splash. He took to his heels, running into the mist, and into the darkness, thundering down successive wooden gangways until he came to his own lowly front door.

He entered and slammed the door behind him. He had no need of a lock because there was nothing worth stealing. Instead, he slumped against the wood, breathing heavily, holding it closed.

He remained that way for some time. When he was certain that he hadn't been followed, he relaxed a little, emitting an incredulous laugh. Out of habit he patted his pockets, searching for his pipe.

Damn.

He pushed himself away from the door and giggled nervously again, reaching out, searching for the table where he kept his scant belongings, including a lamp and his flint. He grunted in triumph as he located a spare pipe, gripping it in his left hand while feeling about for the lamp. *What could have made that odd sound?* he wondered. A large octopus, maybe. Or some other—

His hands made contact with something that wasn't the table. He paused. Sucked in a breath. Felt upwards.

Cold.

Wet.

The door burst open, allowing a little light into the dark room. He shrieked, face to face with something that had once been human but had wallowed in the sea for far too long. Tiny sea urchins sparkled in the dim light, speckling the hair and beard of the creature in front of Fitzroy. The bloated pale flesh had slipped from the skeleton, lending the appearance of a melted candle. A ragged wound above the left eyebrow exposed a fractured skull and some dull brain matter.

As Fitzroy opened his mouth to scream, the figure in the doorway ambled forwards and reached out. He clamped Fitzroy's head in a vice-like grip and twisted his hands.

Just once.

Fitzroy dropped to the floor, his head lolling at an unnatural angle, the broken bowl of his pipe rolling in circles on the dusty floor beside him.

Norah started from her sleep, and blinked into the darkness, uncertain what had woken her. She frowned, catching her breath, and pushed herself up on her elbows, listening. The house seemed quiet enough.

She exhaled loudly, yawned and relaxed. Could it be Bumble moving around? She had no sense of the time, but given how dark it was, she'd hazard a guess of sometime around two, no later than three.

She plumped her pillows and was about to settle back when she heard somebody climbing the main staircase.

It had to be Bumble, although given how much wine and whisky he'd consumed earlier, she would have imagined he'd have passed out in his room by now.

Norah scowled, recalling Bumble's repeated assertions that someone was entering the house in the night. She'd dismissed his ramblings, naturally, blaming an over-active imagination. He'd been working too hard.

She frowned into the darkness, following the progress of the person on the stairs through the creaks and groans of the old wood beneath their feet, then noted the ensuing silence when they reached the first floor landing. What was he waiting for? It couldn't be Bumble. An intruder, then?

Norah, held her breath and waited. If it *was* Bumble and he'd carried on drinking, he would bump into the furniture or knock over a plant on his way to his room.

Footsteps in the corridor below. Slow and sure. Absurdly it sounded as though the person had wet feet. Had Bumble taken himself outside for a walk in an effort of sober up? Had he fallen into the lake?

Irritated, and ready to give her husband a withering reprimand, Norah threw herself out of bed and grabbed her robe. Knotting the cord tightly, she threw open her door and marched down the hallway in her bare feet. She made no pretence of being quiet. It really didn't matter if she woke the servants up. This was her house.

Stamping down the stairs, she turned the corner into Bumble's hallway and paused. Dull light—it couldn't have been moonlight given the density of the mist—glinted through the window at the end furthest from her, illuminating the figure standing at Bumble's door.

Whoever it was, it was clearly not her husband.

One of the servants?

She took a few tentative steps towards the man. She would confront him. Why would he choose to wander around their private quarters at this time of night if his intentions were honourable?

She splashed through a small puddle and halted, peering down in consternation. The floor *was* wet, her robe dunked into a pool of cold water.

Furious, she started forward again. "You there," she called. "What is the meaning of this?" The man turned to her. Norah faltered, squinting to get a better look at him. His face was cast in shadow, his back to the light emanating from beyond the window. "I'm calling the servants," she said, lifting her robe and taking another few steps so that she could get a better look at the person dripping all over her floor.

His skin was grey, verging on blue, and in places had slipped from the muscles so that it sagged around the bones. His eyes were glazed, shining a dull yellow, like an animal's eyes caught in the glow of a torch. As he lifted his swollen hands towards her and opened his mouth, Norah recoiled in horror.

"Theo," she squealed, "Theo!"

The sailor shambled her way and Norah screamed. She stumbled backwards, slipping on the wet floor and crashed to the ground, her wrist twisting awkwardly beneath her. She shrieked again as the sailor staggered towards her, reaching down to clamp his cold, slippery hands around her neck.

By the time help reached her, Norah was incoherent with fear and wailing like a banshee and, for some strange reason that her servants couldn't quite fathom, covered in sand.

51
SHARED CONFIDENCES

Emily tapped on the ceiling of the carriage to ask her driver to pull over. Flora, walking along the narrow lane with Stanley, had stepped to the verge to allow the carriage to pass. Now she peered curiously inside and smiled when she spotted Emily.

"Good afternoon, Mrs Fliss," Flora said, a little flushed.

The driver handed Emily down. "May I walk a little with you?" she asked Flora. The younger woman glanced at Stanley. He bowed and doffed his cap, retreating out of sight behind the carriage.

"I was about to call on Agatha," Emily said. "Were you going that way?"

"Yes, Mrs Fliss."

Emily experienced a pulse, low in her womb. Unexpectedly, her heart yearned for something she could never have. Turning to examine Flora's earnest face, she said, "Please call me Emily. I'd like it very much."

"Emily," Flora nodded.

They fell into step together and Emily noticed they were almost the same height. Flora would be taller than her by an inch or so when she had fully grown.

"Was that your young man?" Emily enquired.

Flora blushed and shook her head. Emily lifted her hand and gently placed it on her young companion's arm. "You may speak freely. I will not repeat what you say."

Flora considered this, confused by Emily's sudden warmth towards her. The charming and fashionable Mrs Fliss seemed particularly vulnerable today. Smaller than Flora remembered, somehow brittle and transparent all at once, as though she were fading away. Eventually, when she responded, she chose her words carefully. "I like him very much."

"But?"

"Stanley works for Lord Tolleson. In his stables. And helps us in the gardens. I sense my Aunt does not approve of anything more than friendship."

Emily thought about this. "I'm not so sure," she said. "Agatha has always been rather unconventional."

"Has she?" Flora giggled at this. "Even as a girl?"

"Oh, yes, most definitely as a girl." Emily widened her eyes in merriment. "She takes after our grandmother in so many ways."

"Did Aunt Agatha ever love?" Flora asked, curious to learn more about Agatha as a young woman.

Emily shuffled through her memories. Agatha's love interests, or lack of them, were not something she had ever given much thought to. "No, I think not. Not to my knowledge. Not while we were both living here in Durscombe at any rate."

"We never had any gentleman visitors in Nettleham either." Flora spoke frankly with the sincerity of youth. "She devoted all her time to me and to needy women in the parish. And you know," Flora turned to Emily, "given that she cannot genuinely be my Aunt as she has no brothers and sisters, I have often thought I was lucky to have her."

Emily frowned. "Does she ever speak about your mother and father?"

"Never about my father. She has sometimes said that my mother loved me very much and wanted the best for me. That she was a good person, who suffered a great wrong in her life."

"Agatha said that?" Emily's eyes shone.

"She did." Flora darted another quick glance at Emily, noting how pale the older woman was. She did not look well. "But in any case, Agatha has always loved me like her own."

Emily nodded and turned her face away. The women were quiet as they strolled slowly along the lane towards Myrtle Lodge, Emily's carriage following on some distance behind.

"Would you have liked children with Mr Fliss?" asked Flora.

Emily started at the artless question. "Perhaps," she swallowed. "I imagined I would ... once. But it never happened for us." She exhaled; a slow wavering breath. "But Flora, if I could have, I would have wanted a little girl just like you."

Flora laughed in delight. "Well I shall adopt you as a second mother," she announced. "And perhaps I can share some of my more private thoughts with you if I feel Aunt Agatha would disapprove."

Emily blinked. "I would like that," she said. "You can confide in me about anything you wish."

"I hope you don't regret that promise," Flora smiled and linked her arm through Emily's. They turned into the drive of Myrtle Lodge with their heads together, engaged in discussions about young love.

Agatha was taken aback by Emily's appearance, her gaunt face, the clothes that hung from her shoulders, the dark circles that pinched her eyes. Agatha sent Flora off on an imaginary errand with Hannah and settled down with Emily in the kitchen.

"The voices?" she asked, without preliminaries.

Emily nodded. "So many. I cannot shut them down. The sailors. They reach out to me."

"What is it they desire?"

"What you would expect. Peace." Emily shivered, despite the

warmth of the spring day and the fire burning in the hearth. "But increasingly they are angry. They demand justice."

Agatha pointed at the grate. "I see them in the flames. If I choose to sit and watch, that is. *If* I choose to listen. *If* I choose to give them a voice." She nodded. "I too see their fury."

Emily leaned forward. "But they let you alone?"

"I take control," Agatha reminded her cousin. "I shut them down."

"I cannot."

Agatha frowned at Emily. From when they were children, Tansy had instructed them repeatedly to shield themselves before dabbling in any communication with those beyond the veil. How could it be that Emily had failed to learn that lesson? How had these poor souls infiltrated so far into her cousin's reality?

Emily dabbed at her forehead with a shaking hand. "Everywhere I go, people are talking as though the town is bewitched. They claim that spirits stalk The Lanes."

"Is that what they are saying?" Agatha regarded Emily in horror. She'd heard some strange rumours too, but had chosen to ignore them. Until now.

"The townsfolk speak of witchcraft."

Agatha pressed her hand to her mouth. *That mustn't be.* "It's just a few raised voices, Emily," she said, but doubt clouded her assertion. "People who don't know better."

"But that's just it," hissed Emily. "They are not mistaken."

Agatha shook her head. "They are," she replied firmly, although she didn't believe that herself. She could brook no talk of witchcraft. Those rumours had to be shut down. It would be dangerous ... for her ... for Flora.

"What can be done?" Emily wailed. "How can I control the whispering?"

"I know not. What has happened here, it is bigger than us. The town is locked in the grip of this strange unearthly mist and it affects everyone. No-one can enter or leave. The sea neither ebbs nor flows. I am at a loss, myself."

"And I've been having dreams," Emily continued, as though Agatha had not spoken.

Agatha, studying her cousin's face, nodded. It didn't surprise her. Emily had always been susceptible to the most vivid of dreams. A long-forgotten memory ... Lily turning up at Myrtle Lodge, a young Emily trailing behind her, surfaced. Lily had spoken to Tansy about Emily's nightmares.

On several occasions.

And Tansy had pursed her lips and whistled low and tunelessly, her brow wrinkling as it always did when she was disturbed by something. "There is trouble there," she had said, and Lily had snapped at her mother and stormed out of Myrtle Lodge.

Not for the first, nor the last time.

Agatha blinked at the memory. *What kind of trouble?*

"There is one sailor in particular. I do not know his name. They split his head open, the night the *Mary Pomeroy* wrecked. I wanted to warn him, to keep him safe, but I failed. He is drawn to me, and I to him and I find—oh—" Emily gasped with longing, "I want to be with him."

"Emily!" Agatha responded sharply. "Think what that would entail. Do you realise what you are saying?"

Emily slumped. "I'm going out of my mind, Agatha. And not for the first time."

Not for the first time. No.

Agatha could still recall the frantic nocturnal visits from Lily. The arguments. "You did this!" Lily would scream and Tansy would order her to hush as she shooed Agatha out of the kitchen. Little Agatha would climb up to her bedroom in the attic, far away. She could hardly make out the substance of the arguments, although the level of bitterness was crystal clear.

"I know," Agatha said.

And in the morning Lily and Emily would be gone and Tansy would perform protective rituals in the kitchen and cleanse the whole house and yard with sage, as though ...

... As though Emily was something to be frightened of.

Agatha's heart faltered. Tansy had been afraid *of* Emily, rather than *for* her. "I know," she repeated, but this time not for Emily's benefit, but because the realisation of what had been going on between Lily and Tansy was so profound.

"I take the draughts the doctor gives me, and they help me to sleep."

Lily blamed Tansy for Emily's disturbances, and Tansy, despite her best efforts, could find no way to settle the child or prevent her night visions.

"I like the stronger draughts because then I don't hear the voices."

And it hadn't been Lily who forbade Emily from visiting Myrtle Lodge. Tansy had asked her not to come, to prevent—

"But this one sailor. He breaks through—"

—Emily leading Agatha astray. Because Emily had powers that Tansy did not. She could see the dead, their souls, just as they all could. Probably even Lily. But Emily chose not to protect herself or anyone else. And unlike Tansy, she could call them into the world at will.

"And then I saw Sally."

Agatha came abruptly back to the present. "Sally? How do you mean?"

"She was in my dream. Dead."

Agatha reached out and took Emily's hands. "You have to stop this. You have to send them back."

"What do you mean?" Emily tipped her head in confusion.

"Do you not see? These are not random occurrences. Someone is drawing these souls here to Durscombe." Agatha heard the tremor in her voice. "It is you, Emily. You're calling on the dead. Bringing them here."

Emily shook her head, oblivious. "Sally scared me half to death. The sailors are not like that."

Agatha bit back a wail and dropped Emily's hands. Why could her cousin not see what she had done? "You have to send them back. The way they came."

"But how? There is no way to turn the tides!"

"Send them back!"

"You sound like Tansy," Emily pouted. "Oh my, didn't she go on? But we cannot undo what has been done. Don't you see?" Emily rose. "I am so tired. I will go home and rest.

"Perhaps you should stay here. With me. I can try and help you." Agatha caught Emily's arm but her cousin shook her free.

"I just need some sleep. Tansy would have given me something. Like she used to. If only she were here."

"Indeed. If only she was." Agatha's gaze settled on Tansy's chair. It remained still, but to Agatha's mind, it offered the faintest glimmer of hope.

52
GHOST TOWN

It was Cornelius Minchin who discovered Fitzroy's body. Fitzroy had bragged about being flush at The Blue Bell Inn and Minchin had offered to fence some wares his way. Fitzroy would never be his first drunkard of choice, given the man couldn't keep a secret. However, he wasn't overly bright either, which rendered him largely harmless.

When Fitzroy didn't arrive to their planned meeting at the scheduled time, Cornelius hadn't been particularly worried. Everyone knew that Fitzroy was a laggard and a petty criminal and couldn't be trusted with so much as a dog. Cornelius wasn't one to judge of course—he abided on the wrong side of the law most of the time, himself. However, Fitzroy had given his word, and when your word is all you have, it can be worth a great deal.

Cornelius was a young, large, ruddy-faced man. He was the fourth son of five of Albert Minchin, a pie shop proprietor, and although there wasn't enough work in the family business to keep Cornelius gainfully employed, at least he never needed to go hungry.

Cornelius arrived at Fitzroy's sometime during the middle of the afternoon. Out here in shanty town, a stinking miasma drifted upwards from the lank river, mingling unpleasantly with the dank, salty mist. The combination dulled the walls and paintwork and made every house indistinguishable from its ramshackle neighbour. However, Fitzroy's home was a particularly tiny and crooked abode, and Cornelius was quick to recognise it when he eventually stumbled upon it.

The door consisted of a number of wooden planks roughly fastened together and shoved in the hole to cover the entrance. There was a hinge but little else. For decency's sake, Cornelius knocked, but he didn't wait for a response. He placed his doughy palm against the wooden door and pushed. He was surprised when he met resistance.

"Fitzroy? Open up! Tis me, Cornelius."

There was no reply, just the faint sound of dripping water from somewhere.

Cornelius pushed against the door once more. This time it juddered on its single hinge and opened a fraction. Cornelius peered through the resulting gap but could see little. There were no windows in the tiny shack, and any fire there might have been had burned out long ago.

Cornelius leaned his shoulder to the door and put some weight behind it. He heaved, then heaved again. Finally, he started to gain some ground. He was able to curl his fingers around the door and use his knee for leverage. With one final thrust, whatever was blocking the door on the other side tumbled away, and Cornelius could step into the gloom.

He backed straight out again.

"Jesus!" he exclaimed, gagging as the stench hit him. Rotting fish and stagnant briny water, with a scent Cornelius recognised from working in the pie shop as a child during mid-summer. Over-ripened pork.

Cornelius scowled, gave it a moment more, clamped a hand over his nose and mouth and edged back into the shack.

He found Fitzroy there, his lower body obscured by seaweed. Cornelius lightly tapped Fitzroy's head with the toe of his boot. It rolled unnaturally, and Cornelius, fighting a wave of nausea, gazed in disgust upon the visage of a man whose face had been half eaten away by rats.

Or something equally as voracious.

News of Fitzroy's murder spread like wildfire through Durscombe. Coming so soon after the murders on the moor, and coupled with the prevalence of the mist, and the abnormal behaviour of the sea, it was probably understandable that many of the townsfolk were becoming nervous.

Fishermen with furrowed brows congregated on the quay, casting black looks in the direction of the wreck of the *Mary Pomeroy*, and the dead sailors bobbing on the surface of the water. By now the bodies should have sunk, or been washed ashore, and yet their situation had not altered in days.

Reverend Tidwell resided over an increasingly anxious congregation, primarily of women, who whispered that the town itself had been cursed. There were other women who believed that their husbands had been bewitched. Why else would they have risked their lives by heading out to sea to save the men from the *Eliza May*? And then gone out to the *Mary Pomeroy* with the express intention of ensuring none of the sailors made it ashore? It was all senseless.

The town was now full of men who couldn't earn a living, women with their husbands under their feet, and children at odds with their stressed and irate mothers. Everyone was hungry and frightened. The tension had to spill over somehow.

Greeb had paid his men for the work they had done. Most of those spent their cash at the London Inn, The Crown and Anchor or The Blue Bell Inn. The ready supply of spirits loosened both tongues and purse strings, and soon, angst and aggression were spilling over into the streets and punches were flying.

One fight led to another. Grudges were held. Men worked themselves up into a rage and were dragged away by friends, only for those fists to flail elsewhere. In the blink of an eye, it seemed that whole town was at loggerheads. Neighbour pitted against neighbour, brother against brother.

Bumble was desperate.

The doctor had arranged for Norah to be admitted to the Exeter sanatorium that very morning, and Bumble—thanks to yet another visitation and Norah's shrieks and lamentations—had managed little in the way of sleep. In addition, he had the worst hangover he'd ever experienced. He'd practically drunk the Applecombe cellar dry. This morning's breakfast threatened to make a reappearance, and his head thumped with every move he made. He remained in his office, with his face in his shaking hands, praying firstly that he wouldn't vomit, and secondly that the municipal officers would choose to leave him well alone.

It wasn't to be. Hearing of the disturbances in town, Pyle popped his head around the door.

"I heard your news," Pyle said. "So sad. Is there anything I can do for you, or Mrs Bumble?"

Bumble shook his head and bit back against the wave of nausea that threatened to overwhelm him. "Nothing," he muttered.

"You look sick, old friend." It might have been Bumble's imagination, but Pyle spoke with barely concealed glee. "Perhaps you should let me take care of things here."

"I would be grateful." Bumble nodded and instantly regretted the sudden movement; he could barely contain his stomach contents a moment longer. He waved Pyle towards the door, his bloodshot eyes begging the man to take his leave. There was nothing he could do now except allow Pyle to take over and make decisions on his behalf. Temporarily. He decided he would face up to his responsibilities on the morrow and put Pyle firmly back in his place when he felt better able to cope.

Pyle, taking his leave, worked quickly to capitalise on his provisional powers. Most of his fellow aldermen were at their wits' end, what with all the unrest and rioting on the streets of Durscombe. Endicott had been waxing lyrical to anyone who would listen, that the aldermen were preparing to deal with a bloody revolution of the kind the French were so damned keen on. Pyle remained unruffled and set about putting a curfew in place. He sent the few police officers he had, to clear the streets and shut down the pubs and inns.

By sunset, Durscombe was little more than a ghost town.

53

WHO WILL HELP?

On the fifth morning after the mysterious mist had descended—and the morning after the day of unrest—the people of Durscombe awoke to a world bathed in the eerie calm of milky white light. The cloud hugged the ground, so low that the sun could not penetrate it, and the townsfolk of Durscombe, free from the curfew until six p.m. began their daily routines feeling out of sorts and irritable. The sea remained completely still, barely lapping at the coastline.

Emily Fliss entered Mrs Dainty's Tea Rooms with a certain amount of trepidation. She had received an urgent message to attend the mayor as soon as she was able in this very place. With memories of the last time she had visited the establishment still fresh in her mind, she had been understandably reluctant, but the messenger had underlined the urgency.

Emily had heard from Mary that Norah Bumble had been carted off to the Sanitorium in Exeter, spitting and shrieking. *Deranged*, Mary had called her. The prospect of Bumble without a wife to hold him in check filled Emily with a variety of mixed emotions. Once upon a time it would have been welcome news, but now ... not so much.

Nonetheless, it was on sufferance that she reacquainted herself with Mrs Dainty and the faded and unappealing gentility of her establishment. She nodded curtly at the proprietress as she entered and allowed a waitress to lead her to a private table in the back parlour. Mayor Bumble hastily jumped to his feet and offered his bows.

"Mrs. Fliss?"

"Mayor Bumble." Emily, standing ramrod straight, did not extend her hand but stared coldly at the mayor instead. He'd been ignoring her letters for weeks and yet here he was, begging for an audience with her. How the world turned. She took in his wan face, his unkempt beard tinged with grey. He looked like a man who hadn't slept for a week.

Bumble cleared his throat. "Please," he indicated a seat. As she perched, he pushed the chair in a little. Mrs Dainty made herself scarce, leaving them with a tray of tea. Bumble poured prematurely, before the colour had time to deepen. Emily noted the shaking of his hand.

"Mrs. Fliss? I fear I must offer my profound apologies for our last meeting." Emily reached out to take the cup and saucer from Mayor Bumble, fearful that certain calamity would befall the faded linen covering the table if she did not immediately do so.

"You seem agitated, my dear Mayor."

"Your assumption is correct, Mrs Fliss. I am extremely agitated and that is why I asked to see you."

"Why here?" asked Emily curiously. "Why not in your chambers in the town hall? Why not in public?"

"I can assure you I am not trying to hide away, Mrs Fliss, only ..." Bumble's hands fluttered at his cravat.

"Well?"

"I have a delicate situation."

"Indeed? And what makes you think I will endeavour to be sympathetic regarding your situation?" Emily coolly appraised the Mayor. He'd had her removed from his chambers like a piece of baggage after their previous encounter.

"Emily, please help me. I think I am damned," Bumble's voice quivered with suppressed emotion. "I am hearing voices. I am seeing ghosts!"

Emily settled comfortably back in her chair and sipped her tea. "What can you mean?"

The Mayor quietened his voice, leaned forward to whisper. "Since our previous audience, every night since then, I have experienced ... a visitation."

Was that *alcohol* Emily could smell on his breath? She delicately turned her face away.

"A visitation from whom?" she asked, her tone mild, disinterested almost.

"I don't know him."

"It is a him? But not a servant?"

"It is not human; it is a spirit!" Bumble hissed violently.

Emily lengthened her spine and glanced obviously at the door.

Her intent was not lost on Bumble. He flushed. "I'm sorry. I am not myself. Forgive me, Emily please."

"Mrs Fliss," Emily reminded him. "Who is this spirit?"

"I don't know who he is." Bumble shrugged, desperately trying to recall details. "A young man in breeches and a white shirt. Dark hair. Marks on his arms."

"Tattoos?"

"Tattoos. Yes."

"The marks of a sailor." Emily recalled her handsome sailor, the way he had fought to reach the shore. He'd very nearly made it. Almost been safe, wading through the shallower waters of the bay before being cruelly cut down. And who had ordered the sailor's demise? Why, the man who had the audacity to sit before her. She opened her mouth to comment. And closed it again.

"I've seen him in the grounds of Applecombe. He hangs around for a while, and then, when I retire for the night, he lets himself in through the front door. A front door which is locked and bolted every evening—I have checked it myself—and he climbs the stairs. He dares to approach the very door of my bedchamber. Every night, Emily! Every night."

"You've challenged him?" Emily raised her eyebrows.

"He disappears."

"And you *alone* have seen him?" she asked, purposely keeping her voice delicate but with a slightly sinister edge. He paled further at the insinuation. She was suggesting he was hallucinating. That he was insane.

"Yes. No. I don't know. I think Norah may have come upon him a few nights ago. She has entirely taken leave of her senses. We have been unable to ascertain what happened to her."

Emily hid a smile. Bumble frowned.

"Perhaps this sailor is trying to tell you something," suggested Emily. "Had you thought of that?"

Bumble shook his head. "What? What could he be trying to tell me?"

Emily shrugged. "Mayor Bumble—"

"Please call me Theodore as you used to, I beg you."

"Mayor Bumble," Emily began again, her voice crisp, stern. "Did you never read the letters I sent you? Did you not hear my entreaty to you, just the other day?"

Confusion and fear crossed the mayor's face. Emily took a modicum of pity on him. "Theo," she said, more gently, "it is as I told you previously. You *must* bring the bodies of the crew and passengers of the *Mary Pomeroy* ashore, and you *must* give them a decent burial."

"Alas, alas," Bumble cried. "I am afraid that cannot happen even if I command it. The townsmen will not do it, Emily. While they might have before, they are now so chock full of superstition, they believe the wreck, and everything associated with it, is cursed."

Emily stared at him in surprise. "You are the Mayor, are you not? You must order them to bring the bodies ashore."

He shook his head. "I cannot force the people to do something against their will."

"You *must*." Emily's eyes burned; her voice full of heat. She had briefly imagined she held the cards now, that he would do her bidding. He would bring the bodies ashore. Bury them. Silence the voices.

Then she could sleep.

"You have no idea what you're suggesting, Emily."

Emily slammed her cup down, spilling her tea. "I know what those poor souls desire, Theodore. I've heard them. They cry out to me. Ever since the *Eliza May* sank I've had no choice but to listen to their ranting and wailing!"

"But why can no-one else hear them? No-one else except you and I?" Bumble raised his own voice in response. Mrs Dainty bustled into view.

"Perhaps they cry out to all of us, Theo, but no-one else is listening. After all, are *you* genuinely hearing what they ask?"

In the long silence that followed, Emily heard Mrs Dainty's front door open and the jangle of a bell. From outside came the jubilant call of seagulls. Perhaps they were feeding on the corpses that had washed up on the shingle.

Bumble had retreated into himself. The only sounds he could hear were the rattling of teacups in saucers. He experienced a sudden craving for a delicate sweet cake. Something to revive his flagging energy. He was exhausted. Perhaps he would sleep tonight.

"You must bring the sailors in," Emily repeated quietly. "You must bury them. And you must halt any wrecking in the bay from this night forward."

Mayor Bumble smiled absently, no longer seeing his companion. He had once considered her the epitome of womanhood, but now she had nothing to offer him, no solutions to any of his problems. He would get thought this crisis and he would pull himself together. He could still have a great and glorious future as Mayor of Durscombe.

"I really can't do that, Mrs Fliss," he replied eventually.

But Emily had gone and the tea in his cup was cold.

He'd been alone for some considerable time.

Had she ever really loved that man? Emily could not hide her exasperation. She swept out of Mrs Dainty's, turned right down Curzon Street and headed for the promenade where she would find her carriage waiting. It seemed to Emily that all of her options were now exhausted. Lord Tolleson had tried, and by all accounts the men sent from London were now dead, with no apparent sign of any replacements. Agatha, who in Tansy's absence could always be relied upon to find a solution, had nothing to suggest.

And Bumble?

He couldn't see the wood for the trees.

Or the corpses for the mist.

How was it that he couldn't make the connection between what had happened to the crew of the *Mary Pomeroy*, and the strange visitations he'd been experiencing. How could such irrefutable proof be denied so easily?

Emily headed home, feeling isolated and confounded. What could she do?

Who would rid her of the voices now?

Finally, the calm broke.

For the following three nights a storm raged hard across the southwest of England and Wales. The wind chased its tail, sped inland and then fled back out to the Atlantic. The sea boiled and churned, bubbled and hissed. Many a fisherman and sailor, out at sea, bucking about on the waves, spat into the palm of his hand and attempted to ward off the evil spirits. Others dug deep into their stash of alcohol and waited for the tempest to pass. Along the coast, the storm shutters were up. In Durscombe the curfew remained in place. The taverns were empty. Lanterns swung perilously from yardarms.

The storm facilitated further destruction of what had once

been the *Mary Pomeroy*. She creaked and groaned, juddered and moaned as her giant timbers splintered. More debris, and further bodies, were washed into the sea.

Emily Fliss slept less on each consecutive night. She lay on her front and jammed the bedcovers and pillows against her head. The storm at times was loud enough to cover up the whispering voices, but she knew that when the rage had quietened, they would find their way to her once more, and the lamentation and wailing would begin again in earnest.

And who would help her?

Only a few miles away, Mayor Bumble was also awake. For each of those three nights he cowered in bed, his ears straining to listen for his intruder. Every night someone climbed the main staircase of his lavish house, and every night Bumble hopped out of bed and stood by his door quivering, ready to yank it open and expose the trespasser.

But it was always the same.

When he finally summoned up the courage to do so, there was never anyone there, only a rank puddle of water. Every morning he issued instructions to his servants to clean it up, even going so far as to stand over them while they mopped it up, but nonetheless, the next morning he would fling open his door and re-discover it there; increasingly noxious, stinking of the sea and bitter decay, growing worse as the days dawdled past.

The howling winds and stinging rain, driving against the windows of Applecombe House, increasingly unnerved Bumble. There seemed to be nowhere he could escape from nature and its relentless capacity for destruction. He heartily wished for the calm and the mist to return.

But then when it did so, on the morning of the fourth day, he began to glimpse figures in the mist.

And they couldn't possibly be there.

54
A TOWN IN DISCONTENT

Agatha co-opted Stanley with the intention of visiting the market in town. She'd delayed buying supplies while the storm raged but now Hannah had presented her with a list of provisions they urgently required in the kitchen, and Agatha felt she had no choice. The mist had returned with a vengeance, thicker than ever, and there was no telling when it would lift.

Durscombe had the feel of a town under siege. Deserted boats, that should have been out at sea, filled the harbour, listing to one side. The fishermen gathered in morose clumps on the quay, smoking pipes and idling the time away, Barnacle Betsy sniffing around their feet. Warehouses, empty of fish, remained closed. Even The Blue Bell Inn, generally a hive of activity and focal point for the harbour, seemed quiet.

The marketplace was subdued too. As Agatha wandered around the few stalls that were open, she surveyed the available goods with dismay. She had heard rumours that supplies were not being brought in from the local farming communities such as Abbotts Cromleigh, because people were terrified of crossing the moor or driving through the forest. Outlying towns and villages, by all accounts, feared that Durscombe had descended into chaos.

Agatha had to forgo fish, there wasn't any, so she filled her basket with vegetables of a quality she would usually disdain, along with some butter and sugar, and arranged deliveries to Myrtle Lodge of things she required in quantity such as flour and eggs.

Female stallholders huddled in wraps and blankets behind their stalls, while men loitered aimlessly in small groups, their hats pulled down and collars turned up for extra warmth. As Agatha tended to her business she became aware—numerous times—of local women nestling in doorways and whispering about her. She attempted to ignore the feeling of eyes boring into her back as she moved around. Several times she caught people staring at her. They looked quickly away whenever she tried to meet their eyes.

Unnerved and unhappy, Agatha curtailed her shopping trip, and headed back to Stanley and the trap, intending to drive straight home to the sanctity of Myrtle Lodge. But something held her back. She placed her basket on the seat, indicated Stanley should remain where he was, and walked the short distance to the prom to stare at the beach beyond.

There was not much to see; not much that could be seen. She watched as the mist rolled across the sea, thinning out in patches and then folding back on itself. Spidery fingers and puffy clouds drifted across the beach. Darker shadows flitted in and out of focus. Agatha blinked. They could have been boats but the shadows were too small. They could have been figures ... but the idea was preposterous.

The hairs on Emily's neck stood up on end and she swung about. A small group of locals, men and women, had gathered behind her. They watched her, their faces hard with hostility.

"You! All this started when *you* came to town," one of the women challenged. Agatha vaguely recognised her as a cleaning woman at The Blue Bell Inn. Once a friend of Sally's, probably.

"That's true." Maisie Parrett, Sally's sister-in-law, huddled close to the first woman. "You came here with your young girl, the day the *Eliza May* wrecked, and Durscombe has suffered naught but trouble ever since."

Agatha shook her head. The *Eliza May* had already been on

the rocks as she and Flora had arrived in the carriage. The wrecking of the ship had nothing to do with her. She tried to side-step the group, but they moved as one to block off her escape.

"There's talk in the town of witchcraft, Agatha Wick," the cleaning woman said, and the icy grip of fear inveigled its way into Agatha's innards. This was not what she wanted to hear.

"There's folk here that well remember your grandmother."

"Aye, many of us remember Tansy and her queer ways."

There were murmurings around the group. Other people gravitated towards the gathering, sensing trouble brewing, looking on with interest. They congregated in front of her, many faces staring in accusation, curiosity or apprehension. Agatha glanced from one to another, keeping her features soft, trying to get a better sense of their intent.

Finally she found her voice. "Tansy's been gone this past year. And if you do remember her, you should remember her properly." She pointed at an older woman at the front of the group. "You'll know she did a lot of good for folk in this town. Yes, she was strange, I can't deny that, but her heart was in the right place. *Always*. Tansy loved this town and the people who lived in it."

The oldest of the women had the grace to nod, and drop their eyes. Not so the younger women. From the rear of the crowd, someone faceless hissed, "She were a witch. She were known to curse those as crossed her. Nobody dared say nothing against her whilst she were alive."

"And when she died, we all breathed in relief, because the town was free of her at last," one of the fishermen piped up. "But then *you* turned up, with your maid, and things have been going wrong ever since. These past few months, we've had nothing but bad luck. *And* death. *And* murder. And *you're* at the root of it, Agatha Wick."

"You're as much a witch as she was," spat Maisie Parrett.

"Now Maisie, you know that cannot be true!" exclaimed Agatha. "Sally was her granddaughter too, and you wouldn't have called her a witch, would you?"

"But look what happened to her! Maybe *you* brought that on her. I lost my brother and then Sally killed herself. And all of that happened after *you* came back to Durscombe! You should have stayed wherever you were! Far away from us and this town!"

"And you associate with that sodomite at Hawkerne Hall!" another woman shrieked. "It goes against nature!"

Agatha reeled backwards. Stanley had been right. There had been rumours in town about Phineas. For the most part, folk would have respected the boundaries of his privacy as something befitting his station, but now they seemed to feel emboldened enough to voice their innermost bile.

"For shame!" Several townsfolk took up the cry and echoed around the marketplace, the chorus of malcontent building.

"You should climb back into carriage and leave right now," Maisie Parrett shouted, her face red with fury.

"If she knows what's good for her, she will." A deep growl from a man at the back of the group. Tall, with a lopsided top hat, and a scar that ran from his forehead, through his eye and carved into his cheek. Agatha recognised him instantly. He sneered as their eyes locked. The man from the quay, the day the log pile had fallen.

She fought to remain calm, took a deep breath and lifted her chin. "You'd be better off taking a good look at the real evil at the heart of this community, rather than casting damning aspersions of witchcraft and ... and sodomy about, when you don't know all the facts—" she said.

"Get out of it!" Maisie Parrett shrieked, beside herself with rage.

"Begone, witch!" The scarred man called, and others took up the refrain.

"Begone, witch!"

Agatha bit down on her panic. She raised her voice. "You would do well to consider that the rotten core at the heart of this community is located in Municipal Hall. Perhaps you should speak to the aldermen, and—" she nodded at Greeb, "—their willing henchmen." She turned on her heel and hurriedly marched away from them, resolutely outstepping them.

A chorus of cries followed her, chants of 'witch' and 'witchcraft' and 'hang the sodomite'. Agatha gulped in a lungful of air, tears pricking at her eyes, battling the urge to run. She conjured up an image of Tansy in her mind—her grandmother would have shrugged off this confrontation—and smiled ruefully.

"What has become of Durscombe, Grandmother?" asked Agatha. "It truly is a municipality of lost souls."

Later than expected, Agatha returned to Myrtle Lodge. She had walked along the quay to the harbour, cut through Thimble Lane and doubled back along Curzon Street, until she arrived at the trap where Stanley had been waiting for her. Wherever she had gone, she had felt eyes upon her. The whole of Durscombe was on the lookout for someone to blame for its current sorry circumstances, but they were searching in the wrong place if they thought it had been she who had cursed the town.

Badly shaken, she attempted to smooth her features out as Flora ran from the Lodge to greet her. Agatha wrapped an arm around the young woman as they walked into the kitchen.

Hannah exclaimed at the lack of provisions, but when Agatha tried to explain about the paucity of supplies at the market, and her voice shook with emotion, Hannah held a finger up to stop her. "What we need is some tea," she proclaimed, and Agatha nodded at her gratefully.

Agatha made a great show of shivering. "Flora, be a dear, run upstairs and find me a shawl. I am surely coming down with a cold." Flora, always biddable, happily obliged.

Agatha sank into her seat. "There's trouble, Hannah," she said in a low voice. "I've sent Stanley to Lord Tolleson with a message."

"What's happened?" Hannah had never seen Agatha quite so nervy.

"People in the town are insane. They're accusing me of witchcraft." Agatha flicked her eyes to the ceiling. "I fear for Flora, too."

"How can that be so? We have surely travelled a long distance from the seventeenth century, have we not? We do not hang women for witchcraft now!"

"It is superstitious nonsense. Fear of what they don't understand. Perhaps it is being stoked by one or two individuals, I cannot know." She fought to keep calm. "They accuse me of bringing harm upon the town, because our arrival coincided with the wrecking of the *Eliza May*." Agatha clenched her hands into fists. "It is ridiculous. They seem to believe Durscombe in is the thrall of some sort of curse, when the blame lies only with the aldermen and the mayor!"

"They are seeking a scapegoat?"

Agatha drew in a shuddering breath. "Yes. And when they find one, they won't stop to consider the matter any further."

"What are we to do?"

"I reason we should lie low for now, and not make any rash decisions. But there is a threat against Lord Tolleson too. I asked Stanley to give him a message. Perhaps I was too vague. I should correspond with him, I think." Agatha rubbed her forehead. "If Stanley does not reappear soon, you will have to take it for me."

"I'll do that, don't worry." Hannah patted Agatha's shoulder. "Speaking of letters, this came for you." Hannah bustled towards the kitchen table, moved a pie dish and picked up a stiff envelope. "Brought by one of the gardeners from Hollydene."

"Emily?"

"I imagine so." Hannah handed Agatha the envelope and a letter opener, and Agatha slit it quickly to free the contents.

My dearest Agatha

Sally repeatedly appears to me in my dreams. I do not understand what this portends. The draughts the doctor prescribes for me leave me heavy with despair. I cannot think. I cannot reason. The voices are relentless. Nothing I can do will make them stop and Bumble refuses to bury the corpses.

Please help me—
Your ever-loving cousin,
Emily

Agatha frowned. "We must prepare a cordial for Emily. Something to help her rest." She jumped up and scurried across to the pantry. "I wonder whether we could impress on Marmaduke that Emily needs peace and quiet. Would he allow me to take her and Flora away somewhere quiet? Perhaps—"

From above their heads came the sound of a heavy thump and shattering glass, punctuated by a shriek.

"Flora!" Agatha dashed for the door and thundered upstairs, Hannah on her heels. They found Flora quivering on Agatha's bed, the bedroom window smashed inwards, and a large rock from the garden among the shards of glass on the rug.

Hannah soothed Flora while Agatha cautiously approached the window and peered outside. She thought she could see the figure of a man hunkered down among the bushes, but she couldn't tell whether he was alone or with friends. The drifting mist fooled her vision. There might be dozens of predators lying in wait for them out there, or none at all.

Agatha trembled. She couldn't risk sending Hannah out with her messages after all.

55
AND ONE WILL TRY TO FLY

Emily waited for hours to hear from Agatha, but to no avail. She remained in her room, still and quiet, staring out into the shifting fog, to where the sea should be. The twitch of her fingers, twisting and clenching in her lap, was the only outward sign of her mounting agitation.

Later, Mary helped her dress for dinner, in a beautiful pale blue gown with darker blue embroidery along the neck and the hem of the skirt. This had always been one of Emily's favourites. She sat on the stool in front of her vanity mirror and stared at her sallow complexion, the bleakness of her black eyes, and all the time the fire crackled in the grate and the voices whispered, mercilessly taunting her.

She smoothed a dull lock of hair away from her forehead. "Make me beautiful," she told her servant and Mary began to style her hair, decorating it in her own fashion, with beads and feathers, her soothing hands restoring a little peace to Emily's world.

For now.

Once Mary had finished, Emily adorned herself in her most ostentatious pearls, a gift from Marmaduke on their wedding day. Thus embellished, she joined her husband downstairs. He smiled at her in surprise and sang her praises. For once she returned his smile, but realising she pitied him when she saw the look of adoration in his eyes, she hated her cold-hearted self.

She took her customary seat at the huge Fliss dining table—set with the most expensive and prettiest china—with only her husband for company, while the servants offered them food from silver platters. Emily's throat had twisted into a great knot and she could not eat a morsel, but tonight, she listened when her husband spoke, nodding at the appropriate moments, going through the motions as she had several thousand times before, but actually seeking to please him for once.

Let him remember ...

The world pressed in on her. She no longer had the strength to fight it. Her thoughts were worth nothing and, in any case, she could barely make them out above the din of the voices. They were all she could hear; so numerous and speaking so loudly that her head was a cacophony of bright white pain.

Perhaps Marmaduke mentioned that she looked tired, perhaps he said he loved her. She heard nothing, smiled automatically and took her leave from him at the usual time. Mary waited for her upstairs but Emily waved her away.

The doctor's medicinal draught was set out on a tiny tray on a side table. Emily perched on the edge of the bed and stared at it for a long time, listening to the voices droning on and on, trying to decipher their words and meaning.

If she took the draught, *if* she fell asleep, there would be dreams.

She would meet the sailor again.

And Sally.

It could not be countenanced.

At some time after midnight, when Marmaduke and the servants had also retired, Emily took out a bonnet from her closet, blue to match her dress, and tied it securely beneath her chin. She left her coat behind, slipped down the stairs, and stole away from Hollydene.

The damp of the mist settled on her clothes as she walked, but she paid it no mind. She trod softly, making every effort not to disturb the gravel on the drive. She reached the gates without being seen and turned right into the lane. She followed the well-trodden road towards Durscombe, eventually meeting the iron railings that signalled the boundary of The Victoria Gardens on her right.

The whispers were louder, laced with excitement. She had come to the right place.

She pushed open the gate, just as Sally had four months previously, and followed the same pathway. Spring planting was well underway, and the flowerbeds had been freshly weeded. Emily noticed none of this. She only glanced around, peering through the shifting mist, to search for the man who was her destiny.

And there he was. He waited patiently, in the very centre of the gardens, next to an ornate timepiece donated by Mayor Bumble's grandfather in 1827.

Her sailor.

Her breath caught at the sight of his handsome face. Dressed in dark breeches and a voluminous white blouse, with his lower arms covered in tattoos, he was unmistakeable. His hair flowed loosely over his shoulders, damp from the water.

He held out his strong arms, his face patient and kind, inviting her to join him.

"I'm sorry," she said. "I did try."

She hurried forwards and caught his hands. He tugged at her gently, leading her through the gardens, towards the cliff edge. They stood together for some time, gazing out at a horizon neither of them could see, the slightest breeze brushing her face like a lover's caress.

"I summonsed you," she told him. "I was lonely. Yearning for love. For my lost youth. It was a mistake. If I could turn back time ... if I could find a way to set you free—"

She gazed into the distance but searched back through her memories, lost in an unspecified moment of time, longing for a future she could never have. Finally she came to her senses and turned to the sailor. "Can you forgive me?" she asked, but he'd disappeared.

She was all alone.

Perhaps he'd never really been with her in the first place.

The whispering had increased in ferocity.

You did this, the voices hissed. *You did this!*

She stared down, over the cliff edge, wispy clouds drifting beneath her, listening to the angry spirits of the sailors from both the *Eliza May*, and the *Mary Pomeroy*, as they spat their wrath.

How could she ever hope to silence those voices?

The answer seemed simple enough. It would be quick. She would break her bones and spill her brains on the rocks below.

And so she jumped.

A brief moment of freedom ...

But her demise was neither simple nor quick. Her bonnet caught on a tree root several feet beneath the cliff's edge, jerking her to an abrupt halt. Struggling to free herself, the heels of her boots drumming against the cliff edge, dislodging pebbles and chunks of red rock, she slowly strangled to death, hung by her own slight weight, as the voices screamed with incoherent rage at her escape.

56

THE TORRID TRUTH

The crowds parted as Agatha and Flora made their way to the front steps of Hollydene. After the grim discovery of her body this morning, Emily had been rescued and Marmaduke sent for. He had accompanied her remains, walking behind the horse drawn bier as it transported her home.

Marmaduke had the foresight to send one of his servants to Myrtle Lodge, painfully aware that Agatha was Emily's only surviving blood kin. If anyone continued to loiter in the bushes and trees surrounding Myrtle Lodge intent on doing harm, the appearance of Marmaduke Fliss's livery was enough to send them scurrying away. In turn, a grief-stricken Agatha quickly took advantage of the situation to send Hannah to Phineas with a letter about the building hostility towards him in Durscombe, along with news of Emily's tragic demise.

Word had spread through the community, and a curious crowd had gathered outside Hollydene, awaiting news. Agatha clutched Flora's arm tightly and with eyes cast down, they made their way through the throng. Agatha could hear the mutterings of discontent, and on one occasion someone hissed the word 'witch' at her, but out of respect for Marmaduke Fliss, the crowd remained ruly.

Emily had been laid out in her parlour and Agatha and Flora

were shown through. A sheet covered her face and Agatha left this in place. She knelt next to Emily and took her cousin's cold hand between her warm ones, kneading the stiff fingers as though she would work life back into the flesh. Flora knelt beside Agatha, her arm around her aunt's waist, while Agatha wept for Emily and the happiness her cousin could have enjoyed, if only one man hadn't stolen it from her on a hot summer's day eighteen years previously.

The loss of Emily's innocence was very much on Agatha's mind. Once her initial grief had been assuaged, she moved through to the drawing room with Flora beside her, ready to offer her condolences to Marmaduke. She wanted to thank him for thinking of her, and although she considered sending Flora out of the room, she found the young woman's presence a comfort.

Solemn servants wearing black armbands circulated among the guests with small glasses of spirits, despite the relative earliness of the hour. Agatha was not surprised to find the aldermen and their wives out in force. Fliss was one of theirs, after all.

Agatha held back, observing the various relationships such a tableau revealed. Mrs Endicott, Mrs Pyle and the younger Mrs Croker were gathered around Marmaduke offering sympathy. The gentlemen clasped small glasses of brandy or whisky and chatted in small groups.

Reverend Tidwell entered the room and Agatha retreated further, her back against the wall, realising as she did so that Mayor Bumble and Alderman Pyle were to her left. They contrived to speak in low voices, befitting the occasion, and although Agatha knew it was wrong to listen in on their conversation, she couldn't help it. The free-flowing availability of spirits had obviously loosened their tongues.

"It's a damned shame. What can have driven her to it?" Bumble was saying. Agatha raised her eyebrows in disbelief. Could he seriously fail to recognise his own responsibility for Emily's demise?

"Really Bumble, don't take on so. She's always been more than a little mad." Pyle snorted his derision and drained his glass.

"Of late, admittedly. But you know, I once thought to make her my wife." When Pyle remained silent, Bumble continued. "That summer after we had finished the Grand Tour? I fully intended to ask for her hand at my father's annual summer ball."

"Ah yes, I do recall." Pyle turned away, searching for a servant with a full decanter.

Bumble sighed. "That was the sweetest summer of my life. The last time I can remember being genuinely happy and care-free." He smiled. "Emily ... she was a ray of sunshine. As exquisite inside as out."

Pyle rolled his eyes. "She was not of our class, Bumble. You would have made a poor match."

"I didn't think so," Bumble's voice was wistful. "I'd even spoken to old man Bumble about it. I persuaded him that her fortune was worth the risk. I'd heard rumours that her father was probably worth more than the Tolleson family, although not very ostentatious with it. She would certainly have brought more to our union than Norah eventually did."

Pyle sneered, draining his fresh glass. "New wealth though, Theo. It is not worth the paper it is printed on. I maintain she was not a good match for you."

Bumble frowned at Pyle, evidently exasperated. Agatha shared his irritation. Could the man not respect poor Emily's memory for even one morning?

Bumble sipped at his brandy. "I wasn't aware you were that well acquainted with her, my dear fellow."

"We were intimately acquainted Bumble," Pyle winked at his companion. "Intimately."

Agatha turned her head slowly, a sudden feeling of dread settling over her.

Bumble blinked. "What are you insinuating, man?"

Pyle backtracked, and attempted to wave the question away but Bumble was insistent. "No, tell me. What can you mean?"

Emboldened by the liqueur, his face flushed, Pyle laughed. "It was nothing. It was a hot day. The day of the party. I may have gotten a little carried away, and taken what I fancied, that's all. It was meaningless. It didn't go anywhere. She never said anything."

"What are you saying?" Bumble frowned, his voice rising in agitation. One or two mourners glanced his way.

"Keep your voice down, Theo," Pyle urged, his face turning pink as he tried to contain the situation. "Her husband is across the room."

"Did Emily ... surrender herself to you?" asked Bumble, his voice quieter now, but Agatha was not the only person listening.

Pyle refused to answer. He turned his head away.

Bumble took Pyle's silence as guilt. "She left me after that day. Did you know that? She went away. I assumed she didn't love me and so I married Norah, and when Emily came back she chose Fliss. But all along ... you ... *You* did that?" His voice rose and the room fell quiet. "And then when she needed help, when she came to me and begged me for help, *you* convinced me that she was a lunatic. A monster. *You* told me she would bring the municipality to its knees."

Reverend Tidwell stepped towards the men. "Gentlemen—"

"For shame, man, for shame!" Bumble glared at Pyle.

"Mayor—" Pyle raised a hand, attempting to placate his old friend.

"And now you call me by my title?" Bumble raised his glass, laughing bitterly. "What did I do, Alderman Pyle, in the name of our *friendship*? What nefarious activities have you encouraged me to participate in? It transpires that you betrayed me in the worst way possible, all those years ago."

"Nefarious activities? Really Bumble, you're being melodramatic in the extreme. You should consider your own actions, particularly where the recent wreckings are concerned."

The room had fallen silent. Pyle nodded at his wife. She gazed at him, mute. Everyone, even the servants, waited for what would happen next. Pyle cleared his throat. "But now, will you excuse me? I think Jane requires my assistance." He stepped backwards, colliding with Flora.

Agatha reached for her ward to gently move her aside but held off when she caught the steely glint in Flora's eye.

Flora turned her shining gaze upon Pyle, deep sadness radiating from her pale face. She had never looked so lovely, so much like Emily than at this moment. She waited, issuing some kind of silent challenge. Pyle contemplated her, his eyes slightly fearful, his nose wrinkled with contempt. But then he pushed past her, dismissing her forever.

Agatha wanted to grab Flora and pull her close. For all these years she had kept Emily's secret and never breathed a word. Tansy had known, for it was Tansy who had sent the cousins away. Lily had agreed to the plan in order to save her only daughter from the shame. Agatha had been willing enough and, when Lily had insisted that Agatha remain closeted in Lincolnshire with Emily's baby, she had agreed. Lily considered the stain of illegitimacy the baby bore, as undesirable. She never asked to see her own granddaughter even after Emily had returned to Durscombe.

And so it had fallen to Agatha to bear the responsibility for Flora's upbringing, far from the grandmother and the cousin she adored. It had been a sacrifice she'd been prepared to make, for she loved the baby as her own.

Agatha faced Flora, holding her at arm's length, and suddenly it was as though the world was comprised solely of the two of them. Everyone else in the room disappeared. "When did you know?" she asked, her eyes filling with tears.

"The last time I saw Emily, we were talking. She told me that if she had ever had a little girl she would want her to be just like me, and then she took my hand ... and I just knew." Flora glanced towards the closed door, towards the parlour where Emily lay, her face ashen. "But I didn't properly know until today. And ... that awful man." She began to shake. "Oh, my poor mother."

"Darling Flora," Agatha reached for her, but Flora stepped away.

"If that man is my father," Flora struggled to say the word, "then surely today I have been doubly cursed!" Her face crumpling in despair, she stumbled backwards, wailed and took to her heels, pushing through the people standing in her way.

Agatha remained in place in the centre of the room, aware of the silence around her. Women stared at her, openly curious, while many of the gentlemen bowed their heads, unsure where to place their gaze.

With the exception of Marmaduke. Agatha locked eyes with him. He had overheard the whole thing too.

57

TWO BIRDS WITH ONE STONE

Greeb, seeking shelter under a large oak tree, shifted position as a carriage rattled past him. It slowed to a stop outside the front entrance of Hawkerne Hall. A single manservant rushed outside to help Agatha Wick step down and followed her as she raced inside, her skirts billowing. The carriage, bearing the Fliss livery, rolled smoothly away, passing Greeb once more before disappearing from view.

Greeb sucked on his teeth and pondered on this happy development. Lord Tolleson and Agatha Wick together in one place. They were the final pieces of the puzzle. Once he'd taken care of them, presumably Bumble would be clear of any threat to his status and he'd relax. Greeb could take his money and run. He had formulated an escape plan, and he was hoping to put it into practice by tomorrow at the latest.

In the meantime, Agatha had played right into his hands.

Two birds with one stone.

Greeb's luck was changing for the better.

Two birds with one stone? Ha! Greeb thought, later.

The afternoon had worn slowly on, and now he huddled miserably into his coat, moisture dripping from the branches above and running off his top hat. The damp chill seeped into his bone marrow. He'd been watching Hawkerne Hall for hours, dismayed by the amount of activity. Single horses had been sent out, ridden by the stable boys and groomsmen. They would return only to be sent out once more. The constant to-ing and fro-ing unnerved Greeb.

As dusk fell, and people were dispatched with torches, it became evident that a search was underway. Greeb sank lower into the foliage, concerned they might be looking for him. If that had been the case however, surely they would have started a little closer to home.

But in any case, none of the men appeared to be armed.

No. They weren't coming for him.

He debated making a run for it. The upside of the search meant that fewer people, specifically male servants, were hanging around the hall, but the downside was that Hawkerne Hall was lit up like a ballroom. Greeb needed to get to Lord Tolleson without being apprehended.

As he watched yet another batch of servants head out into the dismal evening, burning torches held aloft, the answer came to Greeb like a bolt from the blue. He would lure Lord Tolleson out. The definitive way to do this was to threaten his prize horses. Everyone knew how much he adored his blasted horses.

Creeping along the tree line, keeping his body low, Greeb navigated the boundary of the Hall and made his way to the rear where the large stable buildings were located. Storm lamps hung from iron brackets, but the light did little to make a dent in the mist that enshrouded everything. Greeb pressed his back against the wall, hugging the shadows as a rider trotted by him, heading off to who knew where. When the coast was clear, he cautiously edged towards the stable door. Unhooking one of the storm lamps as he passed it, he slipped silently inside. Many of the stalls were vacant but four or five horses whinnied as he strolled by in search of clean, dry straw.

He'd removed the cap from the side fill spout of the lamp, in preparation to empty out the oil onto the hay, when he was challenged.

"Hey! What are you doing there?"

Greeb remained relaxed and turned slowly. An older man, carrying a saddle, had entered the stables after him. They squinted at each other in the subdued light.

"I've been sent to help," replied Greeb, dropping his arm so that his face couldn't be seen in the illumination from his own lamp.

The man deposited the saddle on a low wall and walked towards him. "Really?" He sounded suspicious. "And you'll be wanting a horse, will you? I've had no instructions."

Greeb sighed. In one swift movement he tossed the lamp to the ground where it exploded, fire racing to catch the oil as it seeped into the hay, and drew a knife from his pocket. He leapt forwards, grabbing the older man by the shoulder and plunging the knife deep into his chest. The man reached up and caught hold of Greeb's hand, gripping him tightly. He wasn't young, but he was strong and determined to put up a fight.

To Greeb's fury, the man screamed out a warning. "Fire!"

Within seconds a younger lad had run through the door. "Mr Redman?" he shouted. "Mr Redman?"

Greeb threw the old man to the ground and ran straight at the stable boy, wielding the bloody knife. The boy swung himself out of the way and ran. He took up the cry, "Fire! Fire!"

The cry was taken up inside the house. Cursing his luck, Greeb sprinted for cover among the trees, throwing himself down in a patch of nettles. Panting, he lay there, observing as a number of figures rushed out of the house. The shorter frame of Lord Tolleson came into view, but surrounded as he was by his servants, Greeb feared that his moment had passed.

"Sir! Sir!" Matthew had burst into the library, where Phineas had been waiting with Agatha for news of Flora. So far the search Phineas had organised had yielded nothing. He'd dispatched Mrs Gwynne and one of his maids to Myrtle Lodge to wait with Hannah, and periodically he sent one of the grooms over there to check for news. There hadn't been any.

In the meantime, he sought to keep Agatha company, worried as she was about Flora, and in the early stages of grieving for Emily.

Agatha sprang to her feet as Matthew hurried into the room. "Do you have news?"

"Beg your pardon, Ma'am," he said, acknowledging Agatha's deep-rooted fear, "not of Miss Flora." He turned to Phineas. "Sir, you'd best come. The stables are on fire."

Phineas darted a quick look at Agatha.

"Go!" she urged, and without further ado he ran after Matthew.

He could hear the stable boys shouting as he stormed down the back steps. Fortunately, his staff had worked efficiently. Yes, the stables were ablaze, but the fire appeared to be contained. It had not breached the roof, although Phineas imagined it was just a matter of time. To his relief he found two of the lads were already leading the horses out.

"Sir?" one of them called. "Mr Redman is inside! He's hurt."

The other lad set his horse free and paused by the door, retching, his face covered in soot. Not wishing to send him back, Phineas ushered him out of the way. After taking a deep breath, he scooted inside. His beloved Jolie stamped nervously in the corner stall, but Redman lay on the floor, grievously injured. Phineas, uttering a quick prayer for Jolie, knelt beside Redman.

"Easy man," he said, above the sound of the flames crackling. "We'll get you out of here."

"I'm sorry, Lord Tolleson—"

"Just stay with us, Redman," Phineas urged him, stinging tears streaming from his red eyes, his lungs already full of the cloying smoke.

"There was an intruder. He—"

"Hush." Trying not to breathe too deeply, Phineas began to grapple with the man's arm, slinging it over his shoulder so he could hoist the groom to his feet. All at once Matthew was beside him, his mouth and nose covered in a handkerchief. He eased Redman to standing.

"I've got him, Sir. You get the horses," Matthew urged.

Phineas slapped Matthew's arm gratefully and hurried to the rear of the stables. The smoke was worse here, the fire climbing the walls and catching in the rafters. Bright orange sparks floated through the air. Phineas dashed them away, coughing and retching, his eyes smarting as he flailed around searching for halters. He worked quickly, releasing the horses from the stalls. Crab reared in fright and made a dash for the doors. Phineas let him go. Jolie nuzzled into Phineas and he was able to lead her calmly through the smoke, into the misty outside air, away from the stable. He handed her over to one of the stable boys.

A bucket chain was in full flow, stretching from the well in the yard to the stables. Many of his female servants had come out to help, and for once Phineas was grateful that he employed so many servants.

He found Matthew kneeling next to Redman. Blood bubbled from a single gash in Redman's chest, and a thin line of blood dribbled down his chin. Matthew, his face grim, gave his head a tiny shake. No hope, and no sense in sparing a man to fetch the doctor. Phineas clasped Redman's hand.

"Are the horses safe?" Redman managed, blood spattering his face as he breathed out.

"Thanks to you raising the alarm, Ted. We've managed to get all of them out." Phineas answered, his voice husky from the smoke. "I promise you, they're all perfectly safe."

Ted attempted a smile. "I'm glad of that."

"And you will be soon, too" Phineas added. "Stay with me, Ted."

"I'm going home," Ted whispered, and relaxed in Matthew's arms.

Phineas leaned in to check Ted's breathing. Nothing. He rubbed his own eyes in despair, then reached out to close Ted's. He sat back on his haunches and blinked at the burning stable.

"What happened? Who did this?" he asked Matthew.

Matthew shook his head.

A dull explosion startled them both. Glass showered the ground around them and they cowered over Ted's body, waiting for the shards to stop falling. One of the maids screamed. Phineas lifted his head. Several of the windows in the main house had shattered. He hurriedly dropped Redman's hand and with an anguished cry, jumped to his feet. A few of the grooms had ventured around the side of the house and now they gestured to Phineas. He ran towards them, his heart hammering, rounding the corner and staring up in horror. Hawkerne Hall, home of the Tollesons for centuries, was well ablaze and this time a chain of water buckets was not going to fix the problem.

Phineas rocked back on his heels, attempting to process what he was witnessing. His ancestral home up in flames, hundreds of years of his family's history ablaze, his remarkable collection of books and art ... and Agatha.

"Agatha?" he shouted, and wheeled about, looking around wildly. "Agatha?" Had she already come outside?

He ran to the rear door. A number of his servants, the kitchen staff, were stumbling out of the burning building, fear in their eyes. "Where is Miss Wick?" he demanded, but they only shook their heads. Why would they know?

"Dear God!" Phineas ran up the steps and shouted inside. "Agatha?"

A figure floundered towards his voice, out of the billowing

smoke. A young female servant. He caught her arm as she fought to get past him. "Have you seen, Miss Wick?" he asked.

She heard the urgency in his voice and paused. "I believe Miss Wick had been shown up to one of the bedrooms, Sir."

"Which one?" he asked, and she shrugged. "Which floor?"

"The first floor, Sir," she responded, and tore free.

That was all Phineas needed to hear. Behind him, Matthew was shouting his name, but he paid no heed. He ran into his home and into the flames.

The heat hit Phineas as soon as he propelled himself through the door. He slid to an abrupt stop, throwing his arms up to protect his face. Once the initial shock had faded, he dropped his arms and squinted through the smoke. He bolted through the back rooms, making his way to the grand entrance. Two things rapidly became apparent: the fire appeared to have started in the direction of the library, where he and Agatha had been sitting waiting for news of Flora; and somebody had been moving around the ground floor, systematically smashing all the side lamps, and spilling the oil on the floor.

Judging by how quickly the blaze had started to spread, there could be no coming back from this. Hawkerne Hall was doomed.

The fire had already reached a number of nearby rooms. No doubt his collection of books would happily feed the greedy flames, while the floor to ceiling curtains—so beloved of his mother and his late wife—were assisting the effortless spread of the blaze.

Phineas had to act quickly. He took the stairs two at a time, shouting Agatha's name with every gasp. The walls seemed to glow with the heat of the blaze, and the smoke travelled up the stairs faster than he could. He paused on the landing, leaning over his knees, struggling to catch his breath, his lungs on fire, unsure which hallway he should take.

"Agatha? Agatha?" he called.

Above the roar of the flames, he imagined he heard her shouting a response. He took off along the hallway leading into the east wing, trying the doors to every bedroom he passed. The first room was in darkness, and the second, and the third.

From the floor above came the thump and crash of objects falling to the floor. The whole of Hawkerne Hall would be alight very shortly. He heard several more windows shatter outwards, and the sound spurred him on. He *had* to find Agatha and he *had* to get them both out.

Door number four. Phineas threw it open and cried out in relief. Agatha cowered on the floor inside, huddled beneath the window. She looked up as he rushed in and motioned for him to go back. Puzzled, he ran forward a few steps. "We have to get out—"

He spotted movement from the corner of his eye and started to turn. Too late. Someone lunged at him and he fell to the floor. He twisted away. Something smacked against his skull and he pulled himself into a ball, closing his eyes tightly, wrapping his hands around his head for protection.

Agatha screamed.

Agatha opened her mouth to shriek again as the assailant raised his arm high above his head, intending to hit Phineas for a third time. She recognised him. The man with a scar. The one in the crowd of people in Durscombe who had called her a witch. The man on the quay. He had frightened her before and she was frightened now.

But what is fear in such a circumstance? Nothing but a useless emotion. As the scarred man raised his poker, intent on delivering a death blow to Phineas, Agatha bit down on her own panic. She had to save Phineas.

She clambered to her feet with some difficulty, cursing her tangle of skirts. The sudden movement was enough to give Greeb pause. She rushed at his left side and he threw out an arm to fend her off. They collided and he knocked her backwards, but the poker flew out of his hand, even as she tumbled to the floor.

He backed off, searching for his weapon as she reached deep inside her mind in search of further protection.

She pushed herself to her knees, her spine lengthening, a rod of molten iron running from her scalp, feeding her arms, her ribs, her pelvis, her thighs with a new strength. She raised her hands, and turned her thoughts inwards, envisaging the hearth in Myrtle Lodge. Her eyes rolled back in her head and she focused on Tansy's armchair. She nudged it. It rocked backwards and came to a stop. She prodded it again, harder, and this time it set up a rhythm, rocking back and forth, back and forth, back and forth until Tansy materialised, sitting in it, pushing it herself. Back and forth, back and forth, back and forth ...

Lights flashed on the periphery of Agatha's vision, on and off, on and off, in time to Tansy's rocking. Above her head an orange orb began to glow, growing and brightening with every thump of the rockers on the floor in Myrtle Lodge.

Agatha fixed on the orb and reached out for it. Afterwards, she and Phineas would discuss what happened that night, but only ever in hushed tones, and always half in disbelief.

The ceiling was ablaze, plaster and chandeliers crashing to the floor. The acrid smoke wafted about them, thick and black. Greeb was poised, standing with one arm behind his head, ready to smash the poker into Phineas's skull.

Tansy, manifested at the door of the bedroom, stepping out of the orange light. The Tansy as Agatha remembered her from eighteen years previously, clad in a simple black shift, her white hair wild and free, her eyes burning with fierce determination. She strolled forwards, her palms up, reaching towards Greeb and shoved the air ahead of herself—a sharp force—that pushed against him, sending him flying back towards the door.

He lay winded momentarily, before leaping to his feet, as agile as a cat. Snarling with fury, he launched himself directly at Tansy brandishing the poker. He struck out at her but missed his target. Tansy had form but no substance.

She danced away, as lithe on her feet as Flora, teasing him, her eyes glimmering like candles. He screamed in anger, flailing violently at her again and again, spittle flying from his mouth, but to no avail. Finally, beaten and exhausted, the smoky air hampering his ability to breathe, he dropped the poker and slumped in place, reaching out with one arm, his fingers trembling when they only met air.

"What is this?" he hissed. "What are you?"

Tansy grinned, her face shifting, a skull. Greeb gazed into her eyes and saw only death there.

He turned tail, sprinting along the hallway and the stairs. He tumbled down them in his panic and lay in a heap at the bottom of the first flight, convinced he was going to die. Burning debris fell around him, the sparks igniting his coat. He caught his breath, collected himself, and hauled himself upright. Throwing his coat aside, he ran for the huge front door, now standing ajar. He hurled himself down the grand stone steps straight into the crowd of anxious servants gathering there. Some of them pointed at him and, fearful about what they would do if they caught him, he elected to keep going. He barrelled through them, knocking them aside like skittles.

Keeping his head down, he ran for the trees and disappeared into the mist.

Tansy waited by the door. She floated a few inches above the ground, her aura calm, glowing softly – just bright enough to illuminate an escape route. Agatha crawled towards Phineas and reached for him. At her touch, he moved his head and opened his eyes. She saw the blood on his face, an indentation on his forehead. Time was of the essence, but her body seemed too heavy, too sluggish. She would not make it on her own.

Agatha lifted her head, fighting her own exhaustion. "I don't think I can," she whispered.

Tansy's strength radiated towards her and, recognising she must somehow channel Tansy's energy, Agatha nodded. Breathing deeply, she filled her lungs, envisaging her grandmother's singular strength flowing into her and spreading throughout her body. With a huge effort of will, Agatha stood. She bent over Phineas and gripped his arm. With her help, he was able to push himself from the floor. He leaned into her and together they hobbled towards the bedroom door.

The walls were ablaze. The floor and the ceiling, the whole of Hawkerne Hall, was now burning. Tansy led the way, gliding along the hallway. As if in a dream, Agatha followed her grandmother through the thick black smoke. By some miracle, she never stumbled, didn't once put a foot wrong, and all the time she breathed normally, as though the air was neither cloying nor acrid. And even as Phineas began to cough and retch and become heavy in her grip, she held him as though he were as weightless as a babe-in-arms. Down the stairs they went, smoothly, one stair after another, glass shattering around them. Sparks flew, plaster fell, and fire rained down—but all of it avoided them—until they made it to the entrance hall.

The front doors stood open. Matthew, frantic, stood at the top of the stone steps, calling for them, his hands clamped to his head in panic.

"Matthew!" Agatha cried, her voice failing her, and yet he heard her above the crackling fury of the flames. Dodging the falling debris, he scrambled towards them. As Phineas sagged into unconsciousness in Agatha's grip, Matthew scooped up his master and clasped him firmly to his chest. Agatha caught hold of his arm and together they carried Phineas through the thick smoke and outside to safety.

Agatha fell back as Matthew dropped to his knees on the lawn, gently placing Phineas on the grass and cradling his broken head. "Sir? Stay with me," he begged, his eyes bright with tears. "Stay with me, Phineas. My Phineas."

58
CONFRONTING THE PAST

Marmaduke Fliss had found the constant procession of people in and out of Hollydene exhausting. He had worked hard to maintain his stiff upper lip, but now he couldn't prevent the trembling and he needed to spend some time alone with his thoughts. Macabre as it might have appeared, he elected to revisit The Victoria Gardens, the very place where Emily had chosen to end her life. There he could be alone and indulge himself in memories of her.

At dusk as the light began to fail, Marmaduke excused himself from those who remained in his house, reassuring them he would return forthwith. He headed out into the mist and, leaving his horse stabled, recreated Emily's final journey along the lane towards Durscombe until the familiar iron railings brought him to the park. He meandered along the carefully cultivated paths to seek out her customary spot on the headland and stood there quietly, head bowed, weeping a little.

How many times had she come here to gaze at the wrecked hulls of the *Eliza May* and the *Mary Pomeroy*? He guiltily recalled her constant agitation at the loss of life. He had failed to understand just how traumatic she had found these events, how badly both had affected her. In his defence he had taken the advice of Dr

Giddens, but perhaps he should have sought an expert opinion from further afield. Exeter or Bristol, perhaps even London.

The mists were thinning out and Marmaduke could see how little of the *Mary Pomeroy* remained. The timbers of the stricken ship shifted against the rocks. The deep sound travelled inland, an eerie bass, that resonated around the quay and the poorer houses of the town on the periphery of the municipality.

A polite cough startled Marmaduke. He turned to find a young woman staring at him. His heart leapt. In the half-light he almost believed it to be Emily, but as she crept towards him he recognised her as Agatha Wick's missing ward. A young man, cap in hand, standing slightly further away, observed them both.

"Mr Fliss?" the young woman said.

"Miss Wick," Marmaduke replied, recovering himself slightly. *Except she wasn't Miss Wick, was she?*

"I beg your pardon. I don't mean to intrude. I—we—spotted you here," she gestured towards the young man. "We wanted to ensure you were quite well." She edged a little closer to him, and he realised that her eyes were red-rimmed too.

"That's most kind of you," said Marmaduke, and his voice wavered. This was Emily's daughter, the closest living person to his deceased wife. Earlier, he'd listened to Agatha's simple and calm explanation silently, fully understanding that his position in society should decree the extent of his moral outrage. Flora was Emily's illegitimate child, her guilty secret, and yet he had been moved by Agatha's love and devotion to both his wife and her daughter. How could he blame Flora for the sin of her father? It went against everything that Marmaduke understood Christian love to be. Emily had found herself in an impossible situation, but she had perhaps done the best by her daughter by gifting her to Agatha's loving care.

Flora's hands twisted in consternation as she waited for him to speak again. So like Emily.

Marmaduke swallowed, tears swimming in his eyes. Through instinct he held his arms out to Flora. She flung herself into them.

"She was my mother," she cried.

"I know. I know."

They found comfort in each other's presence.

"Agatha is worried about you, you know?" he said to her. "People have been out looking for you."

Flora nodded. "I shouldn't have run away but it was all too much. I needed to find Stanley." She indicated the young man, hovering some distance away, his face a picture of obvious love and concern.

"Pleased to meet you, Stanley" Marmaduke held out his hand . Stanley smiled shyly and moved to shake it.

"Stanley Parrett. He works for Lord Tolleson," Flora performed the introductions. "Stanley, this is Marmaduke Fliss. Mr Fliss is—" she thought for a second, "my mother's husband."

Flora spoke so warmly to Stanley that Marmaduke couldn't fail to discern there was a relationship between them. He took in the boy's work clothes. What an odd bunch the Wick women were. None of them seemed to have time for societal norms or propriety. Part of him admired them for that, albeit grudgingly. Flora appeared to have the inherited the best of both Emily and Agatha.

Behind them the *Mary Pomeroy* groaned, an almost human sound that made them all start. Cautiously, Marmaduke crept to the cliff edge. Flora and Stanley tried to follow but he bid them stay away from the edge.

As the mists parted in front of him, Marmaduke could clearly discern the rocks and the hulk of the *Mary Pomeroy* below. She shifted in place, swaying and rolling, backwards and forwards, as though trying to break free of the rocks that imprisoned her.

The creaking and moaning grew louder, travelling through the still night. In the near distance, before the harbour, Marmaduke could make out the dim glow of torches. People were coming out of their homes, defying Bumble's curfew, investigating the source of the noise.

"I should go down there—"Marmaduke said. He had a civic responsibility to Durscombe after all. He turned to Flora and Stanley, intending to send them back to Hollydene, but on the horizon, the bright orange glow lighting up the thinning mist, distracted him. Somewhere, not too far away, there was a huge blaze. "Dear Lord!" exclaimed Marmaduke.

Stanley and Flora followed the direction of his gaze.

"That has to be Hawkerne Hall," Flora clamped a hand to her mouth.

"Lord Tolleson!" cried Stanley. "I need to go!"

"If you go, I'm coming with you," Flora said, catching hold of his arm.

"Absolutely not!" Marmaduke interjected. "It's too dangerous."

"But—"

"I won't hear of it," Marmaduke told her. "Stanley, go back to Hollydene and tell my stables to give you a horse. Flora, you should wait there until Stanley comes back for you." He turned his head in the direction of the town. "I'm going into Durscombe." He pulled Flora into a brief hug. "Stay safe," he said, and took to his heels.

The *Mary Pomeroy* was agitated. The uncanny sound of the timbers, shrieking and roaring, echoed throughout Durscombe. Dozens of townsfolk had gathered on the beach, including Mayor Bumble, drunk and self-important, and wearing the full regalia of his robes of office. He stomped down the sand, taking his place next to Pyle, who cast him a sideways look but otherwise ignored him.

Growing numbers of women congregated alongside their menfolk. They huddled together, their heads swivelling as they listened.

"Can you hear that accursed whispering?" Maisie Parrett asked her neighbour, and the woman, wide-eyed, nodded in mute fear.

Nobody could understand what was being said, but they agreed there was a sense of urgency to the tone. The women strained to hear, but the whispering ebbed and flowed along with the mist.

"What are they saying?"

"Nothing that makes any sense."

"Tis just the waves shifting the shingle around," a young woman muttered, but she made the sign of the cross anyway.

A be-whiskered old gentleman clutching a bottle of rum waved in the direction of the Mary Pomeroy. "She's breaking up, that's all." Nobody seemed convinced.

Marmaduke arrived on the beach and stumbled across the sand, searching for the mayor among the gathering throng. As he crossed in front of an elderly woman, she took a firm hold of his jacket and held him back. "Do you not hear them, Alderman Fliss? 'Tis the souls of the sailors calling out to us!"

Marmaduke pressed his hands together. "I pray, Madam—"

"Do not shy from it, Alderman! Those sailors have found us wanting in neighbourliness and compassion. They come for us! What say you?"

He recalled, with dismay, his wife's pleas and her restless hands. He reached for the woman, to mollify her, perhaps offer comfort and tide the swell of her disquiet, but she jerked away from him, refusing to be placated. "They demand justice, Mr Fliss! Can you not hear them?"

The *Mary Pomeroy* moaned again. Marmaduke turned warily to listen. The unearthly groaning of the ship could be construed as voices, he supposed. He was about to say so when his attention was caught by the movement of thick curls of mist. They glided slowly away from the site of the wreck, travelling inland. Marmaduke watched as his neighbours, those closest to the shore, were swallowed up by the mist. They disappeared from view, only to reappear as the mist cleared or drifted on.

It was the oddest phenomenon.

He shook off his unease and abandoned the old woman, continuing along the beach and keeping his eyes peeled until he spotted Bumble with Pyle. The mayor had removed his hat and dropped it on the sand at his feet, where it lay trampled and forgotten. He swayed in place among a crowd of onlookers, inebriated perhaps. One of the group shouted and pointed. The others craned their heads in the direction of the *Mary Pomeroy*. Bumble pushed through them to gain a better vantage.

Marmaduke turned to study the ship once more.

Still on the rocks, and starkly illuminated by a phosphorescent green light, the skeletal remains of the *Mary Pomeroy*, so twisted and broken, had taken on a new life. The ominous light spilled forth from the holes in her stern and backlit the mist that swirled and twisted like smoke from another world.

Marmaduke narrowed his eyes. Surely his imagination was playing tricks on him? Were there *shadows* in the mist? Souls striding from the wreck to the shore? And did they walk on the surface of the sea as though the water was as solid as the very ground he stood upon?

It could not be.

One lone woman, standing closest to the water, the slightest wave lapping at her feet, suddenly shrieked and covered her face with her hands, yet all the while she continued to observe the spectacle unfolding in front of her by peeping through her fingers.

More shouting emanated from the crowd around Bumble. They were closer than Marmaduke. He frowned.

It was not his imagination after all. There *were* figures moving from the sea to the shore. They lurched forwards, eyes unseeing, fixated on making it to land.

A stomach-churning scream froze Marmaduke's blood. One of the aldermen, Endicott possibly, standing by the water's edge, dropped to the sand like a stone. The other men gathered there with him hastily backed away.

What do they see?

Marmaduke fought the urge to back away, to run home to Hollydene and bar the gates and lock the doors. That's where he should be, keeping watch over Emily, looking after Flora. But his natural instinct was to attend to his civic duty and investigate; offer help where required. Now was not the time to stand by and watch. He should speak to Bumble. Snap the mayor out of his reverie.

He darted forward, trudging along the beach, feet sinking in the wet sand, making a beeline for Bumble and Pyle. He kept a close eye on the mist. It had started to behave peculiarly. Like a living, breathing organism, it stretched and curled, wispy fingers seeking the location of its prey. It draped itself around unwary bystanders and when it moved on, only bodies lay in its wake.

As Marmaduke reached Bumble's side, an outlandish scene unfolded in front of him. The mist skated across his vision and drifted away, fading in and out, at times thick, glowing green and oddly impenetrable, and then evaporating so that one could see clearly all the way to the *Mary Pomeroy*, still shining unnaturally bright in the near distance.

Marmaduke shuddered.

It had been no trick of the light or crazy hallucination. Grey shapes, human, did indeed march determinedly inland. Their feet made no impression on the water, not a ripple nor a splash. Instead they drifted, perhaps six inches above the surface of the still sea, faces turned resolutely to the shore.

"What is this?" cried Marmaduke, gripping Pyle's arm.

Pyle thrust him away. "We're under attack! The French, perhaps!"

Marmaduke blanched. He gestured at the odd mist, the figures lurching from the *Mary Pomeroy*. "Do you not see?"

Pyle's eyes were as round as saucers. "We should send for the army."

"Send for the army?" Marmaduke couldn't believe what he

was hearing. "It's too late for that!" Never given to violence, Marmaduke had a sudden urge to punch Pyle square in the middle of his cold-hearted, interfering face.

Mayor Bumble, in contrast, appeared oddly relaxed. "The indomitable Emily, your magnificent wife, was quite correct in her assertions, Mr Fliss. The spirits have arrived. They have come for us."

"Spirits?" repeated Marmaduke. It was exactly as Emily had said, but still he didn't want to believe what he was seeing *and* hearing. "These are the spirits of those who lost their lives aboard the *Mary Pomeroy*? Just as Emily feared?"

"Oh worse, far worse, Mr Fliss. It would appear that these are the lost souls of every ship that ever sank in our bay." He cupped a hand around his ear. "They have plenty to say to us. Can you not hear them?"

Pyle gawped in horror at Bumble. "Hear them?" he stuttered.

Marmaduke listened. All around he could hear people talking, whispering, crying, jeering, the rumble of crowd noises. Odd words that sounded familiar but that he couldn't quite understand. He couldn't be entirely sure where the voices came from—perhaps the crowd gathered on the beach or perhaps the spectres floating in mid-air as they approached the shoreline.

But underlying it all, the tone of discontent. Whispering ... cursing ...

Oaths of vengeance ...

Yes. Marmaduke could clearly hear them now. Their entreaties. Their desire to be free. Their anger.

His wife's face filled his mind. A sob erupted from his chest and he turned away, looking towards the cliffs, searching for *the* spot up the hill but below The Victoria Gardens. The lonely location where his wife had chosen to end her life.

Everything she had told him had been true. All her entreaties to him ...

Pyle, his shoulders slumped, his lips pulled back in dread,

baulked at the look on Marmaduke's face. "What are they saying, Fliss?"

"What are they saying?" Bumble smiled. "I'll tell you what they're saying, my treacherous friend. They will have their vengeance! That is what they're telling us." He laughed, genuinely amused. "You should leave now. You are not safe, Alderman Pyle. Nor you, Alderman Fliss. None of us is."

Pyle stepped away. "You're right. We should leave."

Marmaduke glanced fearfully towards the *Mary Pomeroy*. An increasing number of bodies lay where people had fallen by the water's edge. Most folk were now retreating, tripping up the beach, running across the promenade, screaming and shouting. Men yelled at those who hadn't made it down to the beach, instructing them to get back. *Get away!*

"We can't leave the townsfolk here alone—" Marmaduke tried to say, but Pyle had turned and run. He struggled up the beach as best he could, without once looking back.

Fingers of green mist threaded their way inland. Sticky vines clung to the cliff face, moving stealthily upwards. The Victoria Gardens were up there, and beyond that, Hollydene House.

"Bumble, we should leave." Marmaduke pulled at the mayor's arm, but Bumble remained transfixed, staring in spellbound fascination at the *Mary Pomeroy*. Marmaduke tugged ineffectually and, when he couldn't move the man, he gave up. One look at the oncoming shadows and his innards twisted in fear.

His thoughts turned to Flora. She was all he had left of Emily. He must ensure her safety at all costs. Turning about, he abandoned the mayor and flailed through the sand until he reached the promenade, then casting one horrified glance back in the direction of Bumble, he sprinted for the road out of town.

The whispers followed him all the way home.

Mayor Bumble didn't watch Fliss leave. Indeed, he hardly noticed that everyone else had deserted him. He focused only on the spirits drifting across the sea and floating up the beach towards him. He held his arms open to greet them.

The majority of the townsfolk had decided discretion was the better part of valour, and elected to save their skins. They scurried headlong into town, diving down the narrow alleys and gunnels like rats seeking shelter, assuming they would be safe in their dwellings no matter how humble.

The mist had other ideas. All pervasive, it hunted them down, spreading inland, feeling its way into the darkest of shadows, and where it led, the lost souls followed.

Only a few brave or more foolhardy citizens—largely men who reckoned themselves either tough or invincible—remained on the beach or watched from the quay. When the spirits reached them and the foolishness of that decision became evident, they tried to ward off the grim inevitability of their impending demise by utilising makeshift weapons. Once again , the rocks and driftwood wielded by so many of them on the night the *Mary Pomeroy* was wrecked, became the weapons of choice. But this time there was one fatal flaw in the plan.

You can't kill a man twice.

Bumble, oblivious of the fate of those around him, searched for just one man.

The man who would be his destiny.

And when the sailor drifted across the water towards the mayor, Bumble recognized him immediately; his long white blouse untucked from dark breeches, his lower legs and feet bare, his dark hair falling over his eyes, and the marks—rough homemade tattoos —that decorated his arms.

At the final moment Bumble faltered, lifting his arms to fend off the sailor as he reached him, but it was an ineffectual, half-hearted gesture. This close to him, Bumble lost all sense of bravado. He whimpered in fear, recoiling from the sight of the sailor's ruined skull, the huge chunk of hair and bone missing, an open wound oozing congealed blood and brain.

Bumble's teeth rattled in his head. He tried to voice an apology, but his words were gibberish. In any case, there was no chance of forgiveness on the sailor's part, because there was no flicker of natural life to be found. Opaque, water-ruined eyes stared back at Bumble; indeed, they stared *through* him.

Bumble moaned. He'd been damned the moment he had given the go-ahead for the wrecking of the *Mary Pomeroy*. The image of his burning face, reflected in Pierre Songe's eyes, sprang unbidden to his mind.

The sailor's jaw fell open, wide, improbably wide, the jaw unlatched. He reached for Bumble, grabbing the mayor's head, squeezing it between impossibly strong palms, crushing the skull, simultaneously pulling him close.

No words passed between them, nothing was said at all.

Wider and wider gaped the hole in the sailor's face, and Bumble, clamped tightly in a death grip, could do nothing. His breath whistled through his own constricted throat as he peered fearfully at the fate that awaited him. He sobbed once and pinched his eyes tightly closed. His senses were assaulted by the roar of the sea rushing out from the sailor's mouth—a deep chasm of hell—and the briny tang of long dead fish.

Bumble had one final sensible thought—Emily smiling at him, her dark eyes alight with love and life, a croquet mallet in her hand, her long shining hair loose—and then he knew no more. With one savage twist of Bumble's head, the sailor condemned the mayor's body to the depths, to be forever abandoned to the murky water of Lyme Bay.

Just one more lost soul haunting the municipality of Durscombe, a town destined to remain eternally unquiet.

PLEASE LEAVE A REVIEW

I really hope you enjoyed *The Municipality of Lost Souls*. If you could spare a minute to leave a review, I would be most grateful.

You can leave your review at Amazon or at Goodreads or both.

Many thanks!

MORE FROM JEANNIE WYCHERLEY

Beyond the Veil

The Haunted Durscombe Novels Book 2

Upset the dead at your peril ...

Because the Keeper of Souls is not particularly forgiving.

Death is not the end. Although Detective Adam Chapple has always assumed it is.

When his ex-wife is killed, the boundaries between life and death, fantasy and reality, and truth and lies begin to dissolve. Adam's main suspect for the murder, insists that she's actually his star witness.

She claims she met the killer once before.

In an after-death experience.

Fresh out of leads, Adam seeks the help of self-proclaimed witch,

Cassia Veysie, a woman who insists she can communicate with the dead. However, the situation rapidly deteriorates when a bungled séance rips open a gateway to a sinister world beyond the veil, and unquiet spirits are unleashed.

Can Cassia and Adam find a way to shore up the breach in the veil and keep the demons at bay?

With time running out and a murderer on the loose, the nightmare is only just beginning ...

Order Beyond the Veil here

Crone

A twisted tale of murder, magic and salvation.

Heather Keynes' teenage son died in a tragic car accident.

Or so she thinks.

However, deep in the countryside, an ancient evil has awoken ... intent on hunting local residents.

No-one is safe.

When Heather takes a closer look at a series of coincidental deaths, she is drawn reluctantly into the company of an odd group of elderly Guardians. Who are they, and what is their connection to the Great Oak?

Why do they believe only Heather can put an end to centuries of horror?

Most important of all, who is the mysterious old woman in the forest and what is it that feeds her anger?

When Heather determines the true cause of her son's death, she is hell-bent on vengeance. Determined to halt the march of the Crone once and for all, hatred becomes Heather's ultimate weapon and furies collide to devastating effect.

Crone – winner of a *Chill with a Book Readers' Award* (February 2018) and an *Indie B.R.A.G Medallion* (November 2017).

Praise for *Crone*

'A real page turner, hard to put down.'

'Stunningly atmospheric! Gothic & timeless set in the beautifully described Devon landscape .... Twists and turns, nothing predictable or disappointing.' – Amazon reviewer

'Atmospheric, enthralling story-telling, and engaging characters' – Amazon Reviewer

'Full of creepy, witchy goodness' – The Grim Reader
'Wycherley has a talent for storytelling and a penchant for the macabre' – Jaci Miller

ALSO BY JEANNIE WYCHERLEY

The Complete Wonky Inn Series

The Wonkiest Witch: Wonky Inn Book 1

The Ghosts of Wonky Inn: Wonky Inn Book 2

Weird Wedding at Wonky Inn: Wonky Inn Book 3

The Witch Who Killed Christmas: Wonky Inn Christmas Special

Fearful Fortunes and Terrible Tarot: Wonky Inn Book 4

The Mystery of the Marsh Malaise: Wonky Inn Book 5

The Mysterious Mr Wylie: Wonky Inn Book 6

The Great Witchy Cake Off: Wonky Inn Book 7

Vengeful Vampire at Wonky Inn: Wonky Inn Book 8

Witching in a Winter Wonkyland: A Wonky Inn Christmas Cozy Special

A Gaggle of Ghastly Grandmamas: Wonky Inn Book 9

Magic, Murder and a Movie Star: Wonky Inn Book 10

O' Witching Town of Whittlecombe: A Wonky Inn Christmas Cozy Special (TBC)

Spellbound Hound

Ain't Nothing but a Pound Dog: Spellbound Hound Magic and Mystery Book 1

A Curse, a Coven and a Canine: Spellbound Hound Magic and Mystery Book 2

Bark Side of the Moon: Spellbound Hound Magic and Mystery Book 3

Master of Puppies: Spellbound Hound Magic and Mystery Book 4 (TBC)

Printed in Great Britain
by Amazon